PROJECT ANASAZI

MICHAEL BRIAN O'HARA

authorHOUSE®

AuthorHouse™
1663 Liberty Drive
Bloomington, IN 47403
www.authorhouse.com
Phone: 1 (800) 839-8640

Published by AuthorHouse 09/17/2019

ISBN: 978-1-7283-2770-9 (sc)
ISBN: 978-1-7283-2768-6 (hc)
ISBN: 978-1-7283-2769-3 (e)

Library of Congress Control Number: 2019914321

Print information available on the last page.

PROLOGUE

"I had been exploring a long winding valley that stretched for many miles, ending at this towering mesa. The sunlight at high noon cast eerie shadows on what looked like a wide opening more than 500 feet up the south wall. The base of this sandstone formation was surrounded by a thick forest of pinion and juniper trees. Upon reaching the mesa, I looked for a way to climb to this opening.

"After spending what seemed like an eternity searching for an entrance at the base of the mesa, I was ready to quit this place. Then I found a strange rock formation hidden behind trees and vines growing along the mesa's wall; it seemed out of the ordinary compared with the sheer sandstone wall. Placing both hands on the edge of this rock formation, which I estimated to be eight feet high and four feet wide, I was astonished to find that the rock moved easily, like a door on some invisible hinge.

"Beyond the entrance I could see a narrow passageway leading up a steep incline. Slowly, I moved beyond the doorway and made my way up the well-lit passageway. I discovered the light was coming from small window-like openings on the outside wall allowing me to see out beyond the mesa. At the end of the passageway I found an extremely large room. It appeared to be some sort of main meeting room. As I entered, it suddenly filled with light, allowing me to see quite well. "My eyes immediately went to the source of the light. Circling the room, where the wall met the ceiling, was a single, continuous tube of light that looked like a modern-day fluorescent lighting fixture. It could not be, I thought. How did this modern day lighting fixture get in this place that certainly had been abandoned for centuries? And how did the light turn on by itself? Any questions I had would not be answered by the occupants of this place, of that I was convinced. On the walls just about eye level, were drawings, hundreds of them, everywhere I looked around the entire room. I could hardly contain my excitement. In this great room I didn't need the flashlight that I had been holding.

"With slow, measured steps, I moved along the wall to get a better look. The drawings were extremely well-preserved and had an unusual quality about them. I moved toward the far wall to get a closer look at several strange drawings that caught my eye. What I saw took my breath away. Were my eyes deceiving me? I was gazing at what appeared to be a drawing of a strange looking costume, not like any Indian ceremonial costume I had ever seen before in petroglyphs or museums.

"Much higher on the wall I was able to make out a reddish brown petroglyph of a crescent moon and what looked like a star. My God, I thought! Have I found a petroglyph similar to the one at the ruined Chaco Canyon Pueblo of Penasco Blanco, more than 100 miles from this site? On another wall I spied a petroglyph of what looked like geometric designs in some form of a numerical pattern. What did it all mean? Then I looked toward the tube of light and there on the wall just under the light was a drawing of a strange looking object that seemed to be capable of flight. In fact, there were many such objects, some of enormous size and some smaller, clearly etched into the sandstone wall, all circling the room as if in a predetermined flight formation.

"My heart was beating so hard my entire body was trembling. I had to see what was beyond this great room full of surprises. Surely there must be other surprises. Making my way through several rooms, some small and one quite large, I finally found myself on the edge of a magnificently preserved cliff dwelling. It was easy to see how this settlement was overlooked. It had the appearance of a dwelling that had been inhabited until a short time ago, and definitely bore all the signs that the residents had some ties to the Anasazi Indians. Of course I knew this was impossible. The Anasazi had disappeared more than seven hundred years earlier.

"Suddenly I had this strange feeling that I was being watched. A cold chill ran down my spine and the hair on the back of my neck stood on end. It was at this moment I decided to leave this wondrous place. Retracing my steps I made my way back into the great room, taking one last look at this truly remarkable place, and then hurried down the narrow passageway to the outside world beyond the hinged doorway. The ease with which I was able to move the rock back into the original position amazed me. I gathered up some brush from the surrounding area and piled it high and wide enough to hide the stone doorway. I then made my way back to my vehicle and headed back to Socorro to pick up additional supplies and a camera that would allow me to thoroughly investigate my discovery. Upon my return the next day, the trail markers I had left from the dirt road in the valley through the sagebrush and rocky terrain to the edge of the thickly wooded forest were not there. In fact, the entire area where I was sure the stone door opening to these dwellings had been seemed to be different. There was no sign of the brush I had placed on the west wall of the mesa. How could this be? It was as if some Indian spirit-world force had swept away every trace of what I had found. I spent the next week combing every inch of that area where I was sure the doorway had been. Even the opening I had seen 500 feet up the south wall of the mesa was no longer there. Three days into my second week of searching and finding nothing I finally gave up, thinking I had imagined the entire episode except for one thing - the drawings I had seen on the cave walls were still vividly engraved in my mind."

Brad Davis, seated at the desk in his motel room, finished highlighting in yellow the last sentence of archaeologist and amateur Indian historian Steve Bryant's lengthy article about accidentally discovering new cliff dwellings hidden in the south wall of a large mesa. Bryant's depiction of these cliff dwellings and the strange drawings piqued Davis's curiosity even more about the Anasazi Indians. Davis learned that when Bryant had told the editor of the Albuquerque newspaper about his unusual find everyone considered the man to be some sort of crazy academic looking for funding to pay for his research. The refusal of the *Albuquerque Sun-Times* and other local newspapers to print his story led Bryant to write his own story which was published by *New Mexico Magazine* around the time he disappeared. Bryant, obsessed with the idea he had to prove to the world that his discovery was not his imagination, disappeared somewhere in the vicinity of the Mangas Mountain shortly after his article appeared in the *New Mexico Journal of Indian History*. To this day, two years after his journey back to the mountains, no trace has ever been found of him.

Did Bryant really discover new evidence about the Anasazi, or were his revelations merely an overactive imagination, thought Davis? At least it gave Davis a point of reference to begin his own search in the same area where supposedly one man had already found a trace of this tribe.

The one thought that stuck in Davis' mind was Bryant's saying he had found a petroglyph in his newest discovery that was the same as a petroglyph in Chaco Canyon. During a one week vacation to Chaco Canyon last summer, Brad Davis had seen the very petroglyph to which Bryant was referring. He remembered it well. It showed a hand above a crescent, a star, and three concentric circles around a dot.

According to Dr. Timothy Beal, a noted archaeoastronomer at

the University of New Mexico, the drawing depicts the astronomical circumstances of July 4, 1054 when a star exploded with such force that it remained visible in the daytime sky for three weeks throughout the world and at night for almost two years. Amazingly, a recent archeological dig in England came across an airtight chamber that contained goblets, jewelry, dishes and coins from the mid-eleventh century, and most surprisingly, a diary. Museum curators worked feverishly to document the contents of the diary before the modern-day air turned the record to dust. Unfortunately, many of the pages crumbled as they were turned, losing much history from that time period.

The diary was determined to be the personal journal of William the Conqueror during the Battle of Hastings in 1066. The museum scholars were able to determine that William had been writing a journal, detailing the Battle as well as recanting a series of occurrences 12 years earlier that he had observed on the very spot he eventually launched the historic battle. His writing mentioned observing "a bright glow in the sky that was almost as bright as the full-days sun." He viewed it at the same place in the daytime sky for a two week period over two years. William's writing referred to this strange occurrence as a sign from God that he had been chosen to lead a battle against the English. Hence the Battle of Hastings in 1066, so said the scholars in their writing of the journal's interpretation.

One thing the scholars were unable to understand was the reference to bright, rapidly moving stars across the heavens. The passage read, "I am still haunted by those visions more than 12 years past the tyme I first observed these strange signs in the heavens. If I not thought myself drunk with spirits, nor filled with demons of the mind, I would be hard pressed to explain stars that race across the heavens just above our heads, dancing about the burning light of the day tyme sky, and casting an eerie glow to the nighttyme skyes. Not once, but thrice times ten, have I seen these sights in a fortnight this year and last. And the night before I am to do battle with the English at Hastings, I have again seen these strange lights in the skye."

It was during his last term in NYU that Brad Davis became fascinated with the Anasazi, a tribe of cliff dwellers who suddenly disappeared in the thirteenth century. Having completed all of his regular course requirements for graduation Davis needed an additional six hours of electives to graduate. Feeling he had had enough of boring, heavy duty classes, he decided on two courses that he thought would guarantee easy A's, enabling him to boost his GPA. His first choice, music appreciation, did allow him to breeze through the course. However, his second choice, the history of the American Indian, was something he had not bargained for.

Had Davis done some research before signing up for this so-called "easy course" he would have discovered that Professor Hiram Jenkins was one of the most demanding academicians on campus. The professor, a balding, short, stocky man with a close-cropped grey beard, was well-known for his love of Indian folklore and for demanding the same kind of devotion from his students. Years later Davis would fondly remember the tough assignments handed out by a professor who, in the last days of his college career, changed his life forever. It was those assignments that created Davis' excitement and started him on a never-ending quest to discover everything he could about the Indians of all the Americas.

Throughout his early school years Brad Davis wanted to do nothing more than write advertising copy for one of the big agencies in New York City. He dreamed of writing a cereal jingle that everyone would whistle or sing. Perhaps he would write a commercial that would be the next "Where's the beef?" slogan. Such were his dreams until he met Professor Jenkins. The professor had a way of breathing life into a story he was telling about the Navajo or other tribes that roamed the North American continent. So fascinated was Davis with Indian history, he spent hour upon hour studying everything he could about Indians.

In addition to reading scholarly documents, he read every book Louis L'Amour and Tony Hillerman wrote. L'Amour's writings of the Anasazi filled Davis with excitement. He had to know more about this tribe and why suddenly they seemed to disappear from the face of the earth. Was there a connection between the Anasazis, Mayas, Incas and the Aztecs? Their empires all seemed to have had a high level of sophistication and intelligence. Why did these people seem to disappear without a trace? There had to be answers that historians and anthropologists would yet find. Davis became obsessed with finding those answers.

What he did learn from Professor Jenkins' class was that the Anasazi Indians mysteriously disappeared in the latter part of the thirteenth century as suddenly as they had appeared in the first century. Where did they come from? Did their disappearance have anything to do with the long drought that set in during the latter half of that century? Or had they been annihilated at the hands of the raiding Indians from the north: Navajo, Apache and Ute, who became the inhabitants of the land left behind by the Anasazi? Were the Anasazi absorbed by the Hopis and other Pueblo groups? Was there a connection between the fact that Aztecs and Mayas engaged in bloody sacrifices of thousands of people? Did the Anasazi flee from this?

There is evidence that they first lived in pit houses on top of mesas. Later they moved down into great open caves in the cliff faces and onto the floor of canyons where they built houses of indigenous stone. An interesting feature of these houses was the fact that the doorways were wider at the top than they were at the bottom. The reason for this was thought to be that animals and water were most likely carried in across the brave's shoulders allowing for easier entry into their dwellings.

As to the probable link between the Anasazi, Maya, Aztec and Inca civilizations, archaeologists in the last fifty years have unearthed treasures and relics from newly found digs throughout all the Americas. This has resulted in the governments of these countries stepping in to protect these new excavation sites from the scavengers who prey on these finds for personal gain. The archaeologists have been surprised and mystified about the treasures they have unearthed. They have found trinkets, pottery, weapons and even mummified parrots indicating, indeed, all these civilizations had some common bond. Davis found this possibility mind boggling since the barriers between these cultures were not only thousands of miles, but geographic features such as steep mountains, great rivers, and expansive forests, and the absence of major trade routes.

How did they know of each other? How did they communicate? Was there a common language, as yet undeciphered? And, always the same questions about their ability to build huge temples and cities! How did they know about mathematics, geometry of design and how to calculate so accurately the seasons and the movement of the sun, moon and stars? So many questions! Archaeologists, anthropologists, historians, even amateurs have their theories. Brad Davis was not satisfied with anyone else's hypotheses and knew he would not rest until he found his own answers.

When graduation day came Brad Davis, instead of seeking an advertising job in New York, headed for the offices of The National Geographic Society in Washington. It was there he felt he could pursue a career working for an organization dedicated to exploring the wonders of the world. To Davis, the National Geographic Society was the ideal place to work. allowing him to explore and then write about his findings.

The only problem Davis had with his job expectations was that *National Geographic Magazine* was not looking to hire aspiring explorer-writers, nor could they see any openings in the near future. Not to be deterred, Davis persistently pleaded for any type of job that would allow him exposure to the vast world of wonders that *National Geographic Magazine* covered each month. A sympathetic personnel manager reluctantly agreed to let Davis replace a woman who was leaving to have a baby. So it was as a clerk in the first floor gallery store that Davis began his career.

Several months had gone by and Davis found he was not getting anywhere quickly. He had spent those months reading every back issue on anything to do with Indians. His copious notes of research gleaned from those readings led him to write a great deal about his findings. He even prepared a title for his writing, hoping to get the attention of *Discover Magazine* or some other historical magazine. He had given up hope of ever getting a real job at *National Geographic*.

Davis carried his portfolio to work every day, adding to his writings whenever he had a spare moment. In his haste to leave work one evening, he forgot his portfolio on the top counter by the store's cash register. When he arrived home, he realized he had left his work behind and rushed back to the Society's headquarters building. All the doors were locked and not a security guard could be found anywhere. He only hoped he would find his writings exactly where he had left them when he returned the next day.

Such was not the case. He looked everywhere, checking the waste baskets, behind the counter, in the drawer. Nothing!! Somehow his weeks of research were lost forever. He would have to start all over again. The doors to the exhibit hall and store opened promptly at 9:00 a.m. A new day was beginning and Brad Davis was sick over the thought that he had lost his opportunity to deliver himself from this boring job he had only taken to get his research writing career started.

"Young man, may I have a word with you?" The voice came from a bookish-looking woman. She was on the thin side, with old-fashioned hairdo, and glasses sliding off her nose, wearing a meticulously tailored suit with a buttoned jacket over an off-white designer blouse.

"Yes ma'am!" came Davis's reply. He had been unaware of the woman's presence as he searched for his papers in the shelves under the counter.

"I was wondering if you could possibly tell me about some papers that were found here on the counter last night."

"Papers! You found my papers?" Davis straightened from his hunched position and faced the woman on the other side of the counter. Rather tall for a woman, she was just a shade shorter than the six-foot Davis.

"Are they yours, then?"

"If you're talking about the papers I left on the counter last night."

"Wait just a minute young man," the smiling middle-aged woman interrupted. "One of the security guards was making his rounds last night shortly after closing and found these papers on the counter. He felt they might be important, so he dropped them off at my office while I was working late. I took the papers home with me and read them before going to bed."

"If they are about the many Indian tribes of North America prior to the discovery of America by Columbus, they're mine!" Davis said excitedly.

"It's an extremely interesting and imaginative concept you put forth in these writings."

"Thank you. I thought my theory was worth putting on paper." The sense of relief Davis was feeling, knowing he had not lost his papers, almost made him giddy.

"Let me introduce myself. My name is Miriam Brownell and I am managing editor of *National Geographic Magazine*." She extended her hand.

Reaching out to grasp the woman's hand Davis almost shook her hand off. "Pleased to meet you Miss Brownell. My name is Brad Davis." His heart was beating like a drum! Not only had he not lost his valuable work, but he had finally gotten the attention of someone important who had read and liked his material.

"How long have you been working here, Mr. Davis and why are

you working as a clerk when you have this great talent?" Brownell handed him his file.

Davis, excitement boiling over, took the file with both hands and immediately began telling the editor his whole life story including his love for Indian history.

From that initial encounter with the editor, Brad Davis found himself working full time behind a desk as an assistant to one of the contributing editors, doing everything from getting coffee to reading manuscripts. It wasn't long before he was offered the opportunity to research and write the history of the Caribbean Indians.

Over the next twenty years Davis immersed himself in his work, leaving no time to pursue his dream of exploring the mysteries of the Anasazi or to become serious with any of his many female friends. Davis earned a reputation of being a first-class researcher and writer, his stories appearing on a regular basis in the magazine. In fact, his reputation was so good he had many offers to write and edit for other major publications during his time at *National Geographic*. As the years passed each new job offer was becoming increasingly difficult to turn down. He soon found himself bogged down in more editing and managing than he wanted. Then, one day he made the fateful decision to quit his job, begin his research in New Mexico, and write a book about the tribe that had intrigued him since his last semester of college.

Davis placed Steve Bryant's magazine article and his notebook into the folder on top of the desk, carefully looking around the motel room, making sure he hadn't forgotten anything. Satisfied that nothing was left behind he closed the door to what had been his home for the last week. The two-story Days Inn, a block from the University of New Mexico, allowed Davis to spend all his waking hours in research on the Anasazi Indians, a tribe of Indians who once lived throughout the southwest.

As Davis approached the Jeep Cherokee he had rented when first arriving at the Albuquerque airport, he noticed what looked like an advertising flyer placed between the windshield and wiper blades. In his rush to be on his way, he took the flyer and laid it on top of his research folder on the front seat, unmindful what the paper was. Starting the engine, Davis, out of curiosity, picked up the flyer to see what the paper was advertising. To his amazement he found that he was not looking at an advertisement, but a printed message. He studied the contents of the paper and read out loud... *"IT HAS BEEN DULY RECORDED IN THE TIME OF SILLIUS 45793 THAT A BAND OF EXPLORERS HAS LEFT OUR LAND TO JOURNEY THROUGH THE CONTINUUM TO SETTLE AND CREATE NEW EMPIRES. THEIR COURAGE AND RESOURCEFULNESS WILL BE REMEMBERED FOR ALL TIME."* Evidently someone had slipped a message with the strange inscription under the Jeep's windshield wiper sometime during the night. Who would put such a note on his windshield? And for what reason? Did it have anything to do with the research he was doing?

Was it a clue to the disappearance of the Anasazi Indians? As he continued to ponder the strange message, he convinced himself that no one knew about his research project except Susan. Now he had another mystery that needed solving.

Davis made up his mind at that very moment that this piece of paper with the strange message was not going to distract him from his primary goal. His research had turned up many interesting things, but none so interesting as the Steve Bryant article about his discovery of a new cliff dwelling in the Mangas Mountains halfway between the towns of Aragon and Horse Spring. Brad Davis slipped the gear shift into drive, and headed the Jeep south out of Albuquerque. Little did he realize he was about to embark upon a journey that would affect him for the rest of his life.

CHAPTER ONE

"How you doing, mister! You going to want to fill up?" a congenial old man dressed in a plaid shirt, dungarees, dusty old cowboy boots and a tattered leather jacket greeted Davis as he drove into the Speedway Gasateria.

"Yeah, I want it filled." he replied.

"I need to have you pay before pumping."

"Here's my credit card."

After traveling for over an hour down Interstate 25 to Socorro and then west on U.S. highway 60, Davis had decided to stop for gas and lunch. The town of Magdalena, population 850, was typical of all small towns in New Mexico, except that this town was located in the Cibola National Forest and was surrounded by many Indian reservations, Indian ruins, and centuries of mysterious Indian folklore.

According to local lore, the town of Magdalena was named in the early 16th century by a small group of Spanish soldiers. A rock-formation profile of Mary Magdalene, similar to one in Spain, was their inspiration. To this day, people remark how the profile seems to

1

overlook the town that bears her name. The local Indians say Mary Magdalene's image was a sacred spot for their people, protecting those seeking refuge from attacking tribes.

Magdalena got its start as a mining town and boomed after the Atchison, Topeka and Santa Fe Railway built a spur line between this town and Socorro. This allowed it to grow in importance as a depot for shipping tons of ore from the mines, cattle and other livestock. Toward the turn of the century Magdalena was the biggest livestock shipping point west of Chicago.

Today, those glory days are just a memory, hardly worth mentioning in history books or local folklore. The Magdalena of the 1990's boasts of having one lawyer, one gas station, one restaurant, a combination country food and hardware store, a small elementary and regional high school, a gem store and an Indian jewelry store. All serious food and clothing shopping, banking, medical and dental services had to be done 27 miles away in Socorro. Two blocks from the main street stands the abandoned two-story school buildings that served the children from surrounding reservations. Government cutbacks and dwindling enrollment made it a target for closure. In reality, local townspeople cared little for the school, and the elders of the surrounding Indian tribes preferred to teach their children on the reservations.

Any of the townspeople who don't work locally, as ranchers, teachers, retail merchants or government employees, commute to

Socorro. Anyone not working is probably well over 65 and retired, most likely living in the Enchanted Forest mobile home park just south of the two block-long downtown business district. The majority of trailer owners are retirees from blue-collar jobs in the Chicago and northern Indiana area. A few well-to-do retirees live in the Rancho Cibola development, a community of 20 homes. These people, for the most part, are comprised of retired doctors, lawyers, and other professionals from Denver, Houston, and Chicago. A major Albuquerque home developer attempted to build an upscale retirement community last year, but the townspeople turned it down.

Davis topped off his tank, twisted the gas cap back in place, closed the hinged gas tank door, and replaced the pump back in its holder. The elderly gas station attendant wrote down the price of the purchase and gave the receipt for Davis to sign. Upon signing his name and tearing off his copy, Davis asked, "Say, old timer, can you tell me where I can get a bite to eat in this town?"

"Reckon I'd be lying if I told you anyone in town is better," the old man said with a broad grin, showing his badly stained teeth. "Truth is," he chuckled, "there ain't but one restaurant in town, but you really can't go wrong with Mattie's food across the street there at Mama B's. Papa B used to run the place along with Mattie until he died a few years back. Mattie has been running the place all by herself ever since. It's also the town meeting place. When we need to talk business, the restaurant becomes the town hall."

"Guess I better get over there, if I don't want to starve," Davis replied.

"Enjoy your meal, Mister!"

Brad Davis slowly got back into his Jeep, waved to the old man and drove across the street and parked in the lot alongside the cafe. The restaurant was exactly what Brad Davis expected: a Formica counter top bar with red Naugahyde stools and a tin ceiling, similar to many eastern diners found in the New York area thirty years ago. Instead of booths, the cafe had about 12 tables, all neatly adorned with checkered table cloths.

Taking a seat at the bar, he was greeted by a fairly attractive bleached blond who could have been as old as his mother. Hair pulled back in a bun, eyes outlined in heavy mascara, overly rouged cheeks, black waitress uniform with a dirty white apron, all added to the typical eastern diner look.

"Need a menu or would you like to order one of our specials?" asked the woman.

What are your specials?" Davis inquired, as he looked around for a wall listing of specials.

We have the same specials every day of the year," the woman answered somewhat sarcastically. "Our establishment is known far and wide for its specials."

"Just how far and wide is it known," Davis shot back in an annoyed tone of voice.

Before the woman could reply, a tall, well-built, dark-skinned man stepped up to the counter from where he was seated and greeted Davis.

"Greetings friend, my name is Big Bird." Davis held back a smirk when he heard the man introduce himself. The man had deep-set, expressionless eyes. His angular face and high cheek bones were definitely those of an Indian, thought Davis. Under his broad brim straw hat was hair as black as ebony and tied in a pony tail reaching to his shoulders.

The Indian continued, "I would recommend the shredded barbecued beef sandwich or the barbecued beef platter, depending on how hungry you are," Big Bird continued. "Mattie, here, is one of the best barbecue beef cooks this side of Nashville."

The woman smiled and forgot how out-of-patience she had been with the stranger.

"Okay, I'll try your sandwich," Davis said politely.

"Sure thing, Mister," as she disappeared behind the doors to the kitchen.

"Don't mind her," the soft spoken Indian offered. "She's been running this place shorthanded for the last two weeks. Mattie's the owner and chief cook. Always at this time of year she has a hard time finding good help that will stay around for a while. Lot of transients passing through, working just enough to afford to move onto the next town. I've advised her to sell many times, but she refuses. Says it's a promise to her late husband that she has to keep."

"How long has her husband been dead?"

"Over two years now."

"Well, I would say that's a long enough time to grieve, especially if your promise is killing you."

"True, and I have been trying to convince her to sell for some time now."

Davis frowned. "You keep saying you've advised her. Are you her business advisor?"

"You might say that."

Davis' frown deepened. The Indian did not miss the disbelieving look in Davis' eyes. "Actually, I'm an attorney and as you might expect, you won't find many lawyers in these parts, let alone Indian lawyers."

"An attorney, you say. I'm amazed that anyone would be a lawyer in a town like this. There doesn't seem to be enough business to keep an attorney busy."

"Quite true. There's a little odds and ends type of work that requires an attorney's attention. I often assist with legal matters up at the reservation, too. When things get slow, I offer my services as a guide through the national forest and the many ruins throughout the area, including the Anasazi ruins in Chaco Canyon."

"You really are an Indian?"

"You could say that," Big Bird said, smiling mischievously. "I was born on the Alamo Navajo Indian Reservation, attended the University of New Mexico and graduated with honors from Yale Law School. So, what am I doing in Magdalena, you ask? Easy! I want to be near my tribe, but do not want to live on the reservation. Living on the reservation is not good for any Indian. The reservation has taken away our inner spirit. Too many have become lazy, fat drunkards. This is a terrible thing that has fallen upon our once free and proud Indian nation. Some day all the Indians of this land will break free of this bondage that has held us prisoners for hundreds of years."

"Sounds like you are planning an Indian uprising."

Big Bird smiled. "Do not worry, my paleface friend, we are not planning on raiding your village or scalping your white brothers." The tall Indian's face turned serious. "But, let me tell you this: the elders have foretold of a time when the white man who has stolen our land will one day answer to a higher authority who will come and make this land as it was once before. This story has been passed down from elder to elder ever since the Anasazi left this world."

"Whoa, back up just a minute, Big Bird! Are we talking superstition, wishful thinking, or some real, documented evidence?"

Big Bird's voice became somber. "There are writings cast in stone foretelling of a deliverance day."

Well, of course," Davis shot back, "every one of us knows that someday the world will come to an end and we'll all end up in front of the Almighty. Every religion teaches that."

"I'm not talking about religion or judgment day. I am talking about atonement day and it will happen soon. The signs are in the heavens."

Mattie finally returned with Brad Davis' sandwich after what seemed an extraordinarily long time. He quietly sighed, glad for the moment to change the subject. I think Big Bird has been adding something to his birdseed, thought Davis. Taking a bite of his sandwich, he looked up at the Indian and said, "Hey, you sure were right about this sandwich. It's delicious. Mattie, can I trouble you for a Pepsi?"

"Here, it's Dr. Pepper or nothing," the woman sassed as she filled Davis' glass.

"Your name is Brad Davis, is it not?" Big Bird said, half asking a question, half answering the question.

"How did you know my name?" he replied in a surprised voice. "I never mentioned my name to you!"

"There are many things of this earth and the heavens which are known to me," Big Bird responded.

Davis, while curious as to how this total stranger knew his name, was equally curious to find out if this Indian called Big Bird had a real name. "I suppose you have another name besides Big Bird?" Davis asked matter of factly.

"Harold Big Bird, but Big Bird suits me fine. Everyone calls me that. There is nothing else to know."

"How did you get that name? No disrespect intended, but was someone watching Sesame Street when you were born?"

The Indian sat down on the stool next to Davis, looked straight into his eyes and said seriously, "When I was born my mother sought the advice of the elders who instructed her to name me Big Bird. My mother thought it strange that I was not to be called Running Wolf or some other brave warrior name. She asked the elders why such a name and they said, 'It is written that your son will become one with a Big Bird and lead all the chosen tribes to a land once inhabited by our ancestors'."

"Are you serious?" Davis asked incredulously.

"It is written, Brad Davis. It has also been written why you are here. End of conversation." With that the Indian rose from the stool and left the restaurant without another word to anyone.

"Wow!" Davis exclaimed.

"And you think I've got an attitude problem?" responded Mattie. "He sends shivers down my spine. Every now and then he goes off the deep end. He goes in and out of reality at the drop of a hat. He's been that way ever since he came home from Vietnam in the mid-seventies. There's a story he was a captive for over a year, but the military supposedly has no record of it. Scuttlebutt is that he put some sort of spell on his captors and when the troops came to liberate his prisoner of war camp, all the captors were incoherent and hiding under beds, and the ten U.S. soldiers, all Indians, were in control of the camp. No one could ever explain how only Indians were in this one prisoner of war camp. Big Bird has always dismissed any questions about the war and his imprisonment."

"Sounds like he's lived many lives already," Davis said shaking his head.

"You got that right! By the way, if you're wondering how he knew your name don't bother figuring it out. Somehow or another he knows the answer to almost everything. He's sort of a strange bird, no pun intended!"

"It's sort of scary that someone you never met before knows your name. I almost had the feeling he knew everything about me. Mattie, I don't want to pry, but Big Bird said you hang onto this place because of a promise you made to your husband."

"And a stupid promise it was," she said looking away for a moment. Turning back, she looked at Davis and said, "But in my family, a promise made is a promise kept."

"Even if it's going to kill you, Mattie?"

"Right! That morning when Sam Johnson, that was my husband's name you know, left to help that weird Bryant fellow he made me promise. It was almost like he knew something was going to happen to him."

"Wait a minute! Did you say, Bryant? Like in Steve Bryant?"

"Yeah. Why, did you know him?"

"No. I've only read his research and stories on the Anasazi Indians."

"Well, I think those Anasazi Indian spirits had a hand in killing my Sam."

"Why do you say that, Mattie?"

"My old man goes off with Bryant that morning and when that Bryant fellow returns he's half loony, talking about some find he made in some caves. He never came by to say anything about where my Sam was. I only found out later when Sheriff Cooper came to the house that night and said that Bryant fellow told him there had been some sort of accident and my husband fell off a cliff and broke his neck. I asked him where my husband's body was and he said a search and rescue team went out to find him. Funny thing is they searched everywhere in the vicinity where Bryant said it should have been. There was something very suspicious about his death. No charges were ever brought against Bryant because they couldn't prove any foul play."

"What about your husband's body? Did they ever find it?"

"Oh, yeah! Very strange, though. A week later a bunch of Indians out hunting, or at least that's what they said, came across Sam's body and brought it right here into the restaurant. They said they knew Sam and brought the body straight to me. Funny thing is I had never seen any of those Indians before. They put Sam's body up on the table right there by the front door." She pointed to the only rectangular table in the restaurant. "They said they found the body at the bottom of a steep ravine, nowhere near where Bryant said he had fallen. Sheriff Cooper couldn't get any better location information from them. In fact, the sheriff didn't seem as if he really wanted to know anything in great detail and the Indians were a little evasive on the precise location. So, we still don't know exactly where it happened out there. And, the strangest part of all, the sheriff had said Bryant told him Sam had died of a broken neck from the fall. But, the body brought in one week later, showed no signs of a broken neck, nor was there any sign of decomposition. The sheriff couldn't or wouldn't give me a believable explanation."

The blue Ford Taurus pulled out of the Dunkin' Donuts onto Central Avenue and headed east for two blocks before turning into the University of New Mexico driveway. The two middle-age male passengers were dressed almost identically, dark grey pinstripe suits, white shirts, paisley ties, and black wingtips. It was obvious from their meticulous dress that they were not students nor were they businessmen.

"Okay, we'll start at the administration building and see if we can get the answers we're looking for," the driver, and taller of the two men, said.

"What's the guy's name again?" The question from the man called Jack almost sounded ridiculous in light of the fact that both men had spent the last hour going over a file containing the man's name. The driver showed his annoyance by letting out a muffled grunt that he had to tell his partner the name again.

"I'm sorry, Fred. It just doesn't make any sense why we have to include him as part of this investigation."

"Well, if you would remember the directive we have on this case you would also remember this guy is a world renowned expert in this field and might provide us with some rational answers," responded Fred.

Parking in the visitors' parking lot, both men exited the car, carefully making sure the doors were locked. As they made their way toward the administration building, Jack and Fred, out of habit, kept looking over their shoulders, as if checking to see if they were being followed. Entering the main hall they stopped a young student, arms full of books, and asked where they could find the office of the university president.

"Top of the stairs, down the hall and the last door on the right," the student answered.

Taking two steps at the time, both men climbed the spiral marble staircase to the second floor. Following the long corridor, they came upon a door marked OFFICE OF THE PRESIDENT - James Phillips. Walking in they were greeted by a young woman sitting at the secretary's desk, who looked more like a freshman than a secretary to a president of a university.

"May I help you?" The young voice from behind the desk asked.

"Are you Mr. Phillips' secretary?" asked Fred.

"Just this morning," answered the petite brunette with big blue eyes, responding with a bright smile. "I'm a graduate assistant filling in temporarily for the regular secretary who had a doctor's appointment. May I help you with something?"

"We hope so," chimed in Jack. "We're here to see Mr. Phillips."

"Do you have an appointment?"

"No, I'm afraid not."

"I'm sorry. I can't let you in to see him if you don't have an appointment. His calendar is very full today."

"Well, you better tell him that there are two gentlemen from the government who would like to speak with him," Fred said in a commanding voice.

"Are you policemen?" the temporary secretary asked in a quivering voice.

"No, ma'am!" responded Jack, as he produced a badge from his inside jacket pocket.

"FBI!" the pretty brunette exclaimed as she stood up, moving away from her desk and toward the door leading into the university president's office. "Just a minute, please." With that statement she knocked on the president's door and let herself in. In less than 15 seconds a distinguished man in his early fifties emerged and motioned the two FBI agents to enter into his office.

"You can go back to your desk now, Debbie, and thank you." The woman stood not moving at the door, seemingly transfixed at the idea of being in the presence of the FBI.

"Debbie!" the president said sharply.

"Oh, I'm sorry," as she closed the door behind her.

"Please have a seat." The university president, both arms extended, hands facing up, motioned toward the two high-back leather chairs in front of his desk. Both men took a seat with no further acknowledgment. "Now, gentlemen, what is it that brings you to the University of New Mexico, and how can I help you."

Fred responded first. "We're interested in talking with Professor Timothy Beal!"

"May I inquire why you would like to speak to Professor Beal?"

"It has to do with his field of expertise," Jack replied.

President Phillips stepped from behind his antique oak desk. A robust man with a round face and tinted glasses, James Phillips had been appointed University of New Mexico President almost twelve years ago, after having served a little over 10 years as one of the top policy makers in the EPA. The job as president was his political reward for years of service to the government, compliments of the Republican party. "Beal is an archaeoastronomer. What in the world would the government want with someone who teaches courses on ancient civilizations and their use of the sun, moon and stars in developing calendars? You know I was not in favor of hiring Dr. Beal when he applied for a position here ten years ago. The Board of Directors overruled me. They said it just made good sense in the 'Land of Enchantment' to have these courses as part of the curriculum. We're surrounded by Indians, dead and alive, in this state and I think we make too much about their place in history. In fact, it's ancient history as far as I'm concerned. The Board granted him tenure last year, again over my objections." Phillips stopped talking abruptly, suddenly embarrassed, realizing he had been rambling. Stepping back behind his desk, he sat in his high-back swivel leather chair, pulled out a cigar and lit up. "Care for a cigar?" Both agents shook their heads. "Gentlemen, please let me apologize for running on like I did. I'm afraid Dr. Beal has a knack for hitting my hot button. Don't get me wrong, I really like the man, even if he is a little weird in his teaching. He is constantly taking field trips to ruins out at Chaco Canyon and other locations throughout the state. He no sooner gets back from the Taos Pueblo and he informs me he plans a trip next week to Casas Grandes because of some new archaeological find. I wish he would spend more time in the classroom. Again, I'm sorry. He's not teaching today, but I will give you his home address. Phillips flipped through his address file until he came to Beal's name. He wrote down the professor's address on a small piece of paper and handed it to Agent Smith. I hope you find him at home. Can you give me an inkling of why you need to talk with him? Has he done anything that might jeopardize his position here at the university?"

Fred and Jack, their faces expressionless, ignored the question, both reaching the door at the same time. Opening the door, Fred turned toward the president and in a stern, ominous voice said, "President Phillips, thank you for your time and help. I would appreciate it if you told no one of our visit today. In fact, for the record, this meeting never took place. Do you understand that clearly, President Phillips?" The two FBI men did not wait for an answer as they closed the door behind them, smiled at the pretty thing staring up at them from behind the secretary's desk, and exited into the hallway.

CHAPTER TWO

Davis finished eating his meal, glancing around at the few people in the restaurant. "Mattie, may I have a cup of coffee, please? Mattie put down the knife and pushed away the cherry pie she was cutting. Without saying a word, she wiped her hands on her apron and proceeded to pour him a cup of coffee. As she was placing the cup in front of Davis, she looked up to see Sheriff Frank Cooper enter the restaurant.

"Still serving lunch, Mattie?"

"Always ready to serve you, Frank."

Sheriff Cooper was definitely no youngster. He carried his trim figure very well on his six-foot frame. It was obvious this man with a full head of white hair kept in shape through exercise. The only telltale signs of his real age were the deep wrinkles across his smiling well-tanned face. Frank Cooper at age 67 was allowed to keep his job because of his fitness and the fact it was difficult to find anyone willing to replace him out in this central New Mexico town. Following ten years service in the military police at Roswell Army Air Field, he resigned and moved to Magdalena where he immediately joined the three-man police force. In less than eight years, he took over the sheriff's job and had been at it ever since. He had made it known on his 67th birthday that he would retire at the end of the year and the town had better seriously seek his replacement.

Sitting down beside Brad Davis he introduced himself. Davis shook hands and introduced himself to the sheriff. "Just passing through?" The sheriff asked.

Davis half turned to respond to the question. "Sort of. I'm out here doing some research with the hope of writing a book on my findings."

"Well, welcome to our part of the country! Where are you from?"

"Born and raised on the East Coast."

"What are you planning to research?"

"The Anasazi."

"Really," the sheriff smiled, "I don't know why that surprises me."

Mattie returned with a turkey sandwich. "Here you are sheriff, your favorite, white meat, no mayo, on toasted whole wheat, little bit of lettuce, two slices of tomato and a pickle on the side."

"You're a marvel, woman."

"Oh, sure, I'm a marvel. You've been ordering the same sandwich for as long as I've known you."

"Thanks just the same." The sheriff turned his attention back to Brad Davis. "I don't mean to sound insensitive, but just about everybody has researched and written about the Anasazi. Why would you waste your time at something everyone else has done to death?"

Davis was not about to share his theories with the sheriff. "I have a certain passion for trying to uncover some new revelations about these Indians. I find them very interesting."

"Where do you plan on looking for these new revelations?"

"Near the town of Aragon up in the Mangas Mountains."

"I'd be careful of that area. The town has been deserted for the last twenty years and Mattie's husband Sam got killed on an expedition up there over two years ago. At least, that's where we think the accident took place. In fact, some researcher like yourself went up there and was never heard from again. Very desolate country and the way the Indians tell it, very spooky."

Davis stiffened. "What do you mean by spooky?"

"During the last two weeks strange lights have been seen at night across the whole Plains of San Agustin. Old folk around these parts say they remember seeing strange light like that way back in the late '40's and a few times in between then and now. Nobody knows what causes them or where they come from. In fact, some nights here in Magdalena you not only see the lights, but you also hear a strange humming noise, like an engine running. Even Taos, up north, hears the humming sound."

"What do these strange lights look like?"

They're not really lights, it's more like a bluish glow."

"Davis held back a chuckle. "Surely, you're not serious sheriff? Do you think they're from the Indian spirit world?"

The sheriff put down his sandwich and faced Davis. "All I know is that the Navajos living in these parts have a great respect for that area and do not travel too far beyond their homes after dark. And, let me tell you something else, if you don't already know it. Ever since the atomic testing that took place in this state during the 1940's strange occurrences have been happening throughout central New Mexico. I know for a fact some of the strange things that have happened. In July of 1947, I was an MP stationed at Roswell."

Davis was becoming increasingly interested in this conversation. "Are you talking about the supposed flying saucer that crashed near Roswell and the government denied the report, saying it was a weather balloon?"

"Weather balloon, my ass! I was there. The crash site was near Corona and I saw the gouge in the debris strewn field on the ranch." Sheriff Cooper, his face an ashen color, suddenly pushed his plate with the half-eaten sandwich away from him. Standing, he looked down at Brad Davis and said, "I've said more than I should have to you. I took an oath never to reveal what we saw back then in 1947. Please excuse me." The sheriff quickly turned and walked toward the door. "Be careful, Mr. Davis. I would recommend you forget about your expedition out to that area. You may find more than you bargain for!"

Davis watched as sheriff Frank Cooper exited the front door of the restaurant. "Hey, Mattie. What got into the sheriff?"

"I only saw him react that way once before. It was around the time shortly after that Steve Bryant fellow and my husband went up into the forest. When the Navajos brought my husband's body back into town after finding him, the sheriff was called to handle matters. When he talked to the Indians and then took the sheet off my husband he acted the same way you just saw him act now. His face looked the same then."

"What do you think caused him to react that way?"

"Don't know. But, I do remember him commenting something about the condition of my husband's body after having been dead for a week. I kept asking him why my husband's body was a strange color."

"What color was it, Mattie?"

"Sort of a greenish grey."

"Well, I've never seen a body that's been dead that long, but it sounds like a normal color for someone dead for a week."

"Not according to the coroner. The sheriff wouldn't let the coroner do an autopsy to rule out foul play and to explain the strange color of the body. The sheriff had the coroner sign the death certificate saying Sam died of a broken neck received in a fall from a great height. On his medical report the coroner insisted on listing the fact he was unable to explain the unusual color of the body."

"If your husband had fallen from a great height, wouldn't there have been bruises and other broken bones?"

"Yes, but there were none that I could see."

"Was there anyone else who saw the body besides you, the Indians, and the sheriff?"

"As a matter of fact there was. I forgot that when the sheriff looked at the body I noticed he seemed to act strange, like he had seen a ghost. He excused himself and made a phone call. It wasn't 15 minutes when old man Brantfield came in and huddled in the corner with the sheriff, pointing back to the covered body. After a few minutes Brantfield walked over, lifted the sheet and looked down on my husband. He reacted the same way as the sheriff had when he first saw the body. Brantfield, visibly shaken, had to sit down almost right away. I don't know why he reacted that way, he didn't know my husband that well. Then, I notice old man Brantfield starts getting the shakes and the sheriff escorts him out of the restaurant."

"Who is Brantfield?"

"He's over eighty years old, retired from the military and lives up in the estates. From what I gather, he and the sheriff were in the service together back in the late 40's and early 50's."

"Where?"

"Roswell."

"Was Brantfield an MP like the sheriff?"

"Oh, no! Brantfield was a big deal. Put in over 40 years. People around these parts have always called him general. I guess that's what he was. As far as I'm concerned I don't care what he was. He's just another paying customer."

"These tales of UFO's, strange lights, and green grey bodies are all really interesting tales that I might someday like to research and write about, but I came out here to research the Anasazi. Another day, perhaps."

Davis paid his bill and bid Mattie goodbye. The owner-waitress of Mamma B's merely shrugged her shoulders and turned to resume cleaning the coffee urn. Davis was intrigued with the conversations he had been part of in the restaurant. He had always been fascinated with tales of superstition and space travel. Probably, he thought to himself, it was the mystery of the Anasazi culture and the challenge to find logical answers to their disappearance that had led him here to this remote part of east central New Mexico. UFO's, space travel! It was difficult to believe without tangible evidence, but definitely in the realm of possibility. At least, with the Anasazi, there was enough proof of their existence on this earth. And, with that thought, he once again began thinking of the days and months of exploration and research ahead of him.

As the Jeep headed west on Route 60 toward the town of Datil, Davis looked out on the vastness and beauty unfolding before him as he contemplated what his research had uncovered. The Four Corners region, comprising Colorado, Utah, Arizona, and New Mexico, is, for the most part, high desert and where the Anasazi made their home. The lowlands are mostly above 5,000 feet, with temperatures ranging from 100 degrees Fahrenheit in the heat of the summer to below zero at times in winter. Floors of the steep canyon, where Davis had explored last summer, were scattered with sagebrush, cactus, and an undefined type of grass that could survive with little rainfall. Most of the areas where the Anasazi lived lacked year-round streams. In the valleys, rain has been measured at 10 inches a year, and 15 inches on the higher mesa tops. Climatologists have speculated that rainfall has changed little since the time these Indians roamed the lands here. Well-preserved burial sites revealed that the early Anasazi averaged just over five feet tall. From every indication they were very much like present day southwestern Indians - brown skinned, with straight or wavy black hair.

Approximately 25 miles beyond Magdalena, Brad Davis saw a spectacle he had never seen before. There on the south side of the road he saw 27 huge satellite dishes, each mounted on its own railroad car, all pointing toward a fixed spot in the heavens. Davis remembers having read somewhere that this is the site for the Very Large Array (VLA) radio telescope which enables astronomers to use the satellites as a large wide-angles lens or a telescope, depending how the dishes were spaced. The government had chosen this site in the Plains of San Agustin because of the immense expanse of flat land and because the air is dry and free of vapors that can distort radio signals. Also, the arid climate allows for very little manmade static electricity to interfere with the clarity of the signal.

Datil was just beyond the next ridge. Slowly driving through the town, which looked almost like the town in which he had spent the last two hours having lunch, Davis began looking carefully for the road marker for Route 12 that would take him in a southwesterly direction toward the Mangas Mountains. It wasn't difficult to spot the marker for the two lane macadam highway which led out through the Plains of San Agustin. A strange chill came across his body, causing him to shiver. Was the chill due to excitement of exploring the unknown? Or, was it fear of the unknown? His thoughts immediately returned to the conversation in the restaurant. Why, suddenly, was he thinking about strange lights and dead bodies? He didn't put much credence in what these locals said about such matters. After all, isn't New Mexico the Land of Enchantment? A public relations gimmick concocted by the New Mexico Department of Tourism, no doubt, he quietly laughed. Even so, the changing colors of the sky, sandstone buttes and mesas and the wide-open valleys made Davis think that there really may be something to the "Land of Enchantment" tourism slogan.

Horse Springs, some 28 miles southwest of Datil, loomed up on the horizon. It had taken Davis less than 25 minutes to travel the distance. During that time he passed two cars and one tractor trailer going in the opposite direction. No other vehicles were heading in the same direction he was driving. This was the time of the year when few tourists traveled through these parts. Late spring through early fall was high tourist season. The fascination of people touring Indian ruins was a boom to the economy of the many small towns and reservations throughout all of New Mexico. Everyone got into the act, selling jewelry, rugs and other trinkets made by local Indians.

Tourists would buy anything at any price to be able to say they bought something from a real live Indian.

The vastness of the landscape made Davis realize how truly desolate the countryside was. He counted maybe 10 or 12 houses, small pueblo style dwellings, all set back 100 yards to a half mile from the road. Not wanting to take a chance of running out of gas, Davis decided to top off the tank. He knew his four-wheel drive Cherokee could handle any type of terrain he may encounter. He certainly didn't want to run out of gas, miles from any gas station.

The gas station in Horse Springs consisted of three pumps, one for regular, one for premium, and one for diesel. A building that looked as old as the countryside contained a small office and a not so modern service area for repairing cars. After waiting almost two minutes for someone to come out and help him, Davis leaned on the horn. No one emerged. Again, he leaned on the horn, this time hard and long.

"Hold your horses, Sonny. Ain't you got no manners?" A woman, who looked no younger than 90, came shuffling out to the car. Her dark face was deeply etched with creases that came from years of exposure to the sun. Weighing less than 100 pounds, the woman was attired in a multicolored full-length dress with long sleeves, and a bright red scarf to shield her head from the afternoon sun. She was barely five feet tall. Clenched in the old woman's toothless mouth was a pipe. She took a deep drag, smiled, and slowly exhaled.

"Now, tell me what you want," the woman with a raspy voice asked.

"I would like some gas and directions."

"Gas will cost you. Information, if I've got it, won't!"

"Fill it with premium, please?"

"Got no premium. Delivery truck never came this week and don't expect one till next week."

"Well, I'll take regular, then."

"Would you mind pumping it yourself. The arthritis in my hands is killing me today."

Davis inserted the nozzle into the gas tank and proceeded to pump gas. "I'm glad there's some regular left," he said with a sigh of relief.

"Well, don't know how much you can get out of there, but you're welcome to whatever you can pump."

"Guess I lucked out. My tank is full. That comes to ten dollars and forty-five cents." Reaching into his pants pocket, Davis counted out the exact change and handed it to the Indian woman. "Here you are. Can you tell me where the cut-off is to get over to Mangas Mountain?"

"What do you want to go there for?"

Davis was surprised the old lady could muster any interest. Evidently, the mention of Mangas Mountain piqued her curiosity. "I'm a writer and I'm doing some research on the Anasazi Indians."

"Anasazi, Anasazi! That's all I ever hear out here. Why don't you write about my people, the Navajos and Pueblos? We're still here in the flesh. Not like those others that haven't shown their faces for all these centuries. But, they're still here, you know. They never left. You just never see them. You feel them all around you and you especially feel their spirits at night. Strange things that go on out here are not the doing of the living Navajo or Pueblo Indians. They have been unforgiving to all those who disturb their space. I would advise you to turn around and go back to where you came from."

"Thank you for your advice, but I am committed to finding answers about the spirits you speak of."

"Remember, you have been warned. Let me sell you a rattlesnake bracelet to protect you from their evil spirits."

"Are you putting me on? A rattlesnake bracelet?"

"Rattlesnakes have been empowered by our gods to protect Indian treasures and grave sites from evil spirits. If you know so much about Indians how come you don't know that rattlesnakes protect guarded Indian sites?"

"Sounds like pure superstition to me. Who says rattlesnakes protect guarded sites?"

"No superstition! All Pueblo Indians know this. Even my Navajo father knew this. You will need the bracelet to survive the evil spirit world of the Anasazi. Another guy like you wouldn't buy the bracelet. He didn't believe me and he never returned."

"What are you talking about? Who was this someone else, just like me?"

"Never knew his name. Can't even remember what he looked like. Just remember his noisy and smoky Chevy Blazer. Don't remember much, but I sure do remember cars like that."

"How long ago are we talking about?"

"A year. Maybe two. Maybe longer. When you get to be my age, your mind can't remember things as well as you did ten years ago."

"Okay, I'm sold. How does it work?"

"It works by itself. The natural movement of your hand makes the bracelet rattler make noise scaring off those spirits."

"How much?"

"Twenty five dollars."

"Twenty five dollars!! You have got to be joking!"

"No joke! You want big medicine, it costs big money!"

"Okay." Davis took out his wallet and gave her a twenty-dollar bill and five singles. She placed the bracelet in his hand. All right, now tell me how I'll know the cut off for the dirt road over to Mangas Mountain."

It's the second dirt road you'll come to. The first dirt road is in the middle of town. It's called route 36, but there ain't no signs. It goes north up to Pie Town. Don't be stupid like that other fellow I was telling you about. He just didn't listen good. He was looking to go to Pie Town and not paying attention. He took the second dirt road.

Told him not to take that road. No wonder nobody's found him. He's probably lost in Mexico and doesn't know how to get back."

"Wait a minute! Are you telling me that Steve Bryant took the second dirt road?"

"Don't know any Steve Bryant."

"I'm sure he's the one you remember from coming in here a couple of years ago and not buying a rattlesnake bracelet."

"You think so? Maybe! If this Steve Bryant was a little on the weird side and drove a noisy Blazer, I'd say it must have been him. Don't remember too many people or cars like that coming through here. Not many strangers stop here at all. I just take care of the local folks, mostly. Once in a while some tourists, or people just plain lost, stop in for gas and directions. "Just like you! Like I said before, I can't remember what this fellow looked like. I only remember this fellow with a Blazer that had chattering pistons and smoked more than me. Don't hear that problem much out here. It was powder blue and dirty as all get out. Inside of the car was a mess with books and writing paper all over the back of the vehicle. Now that I think of it I was sitting out front here in my rocking chair getting some sun when I could have sworn I heard that same valve tapping again on another day. In fact, maybe I heard that car even more than one time. Distinctive sound, you know. When I looked up, sure enough it was that dirty Blazer, except dirtier than before."

"How long was that after the first time you remember the Blazer coming in for gas?"

"A week, maybe two weeks."

"How about a month later?"

"Look, sonny, I told you before, at my age every day runs together."

"Thanks for your help. By the way, do you have a name?"

"Little River! And, don't ask me how I got my name. It's a long story."

Goodbye, Little River. I have a feeling our paths will cross again."

As Brad Davis headed out of the gas station onto Route 12 heading south, he looked in the rearview mirror to see Little River flailing her arms and shaking her head. He could almost hear her saying, "He's as stupid as that other fellow." Davis took the bracelet from his wrist and put it in the glove department. "I guess I'm a sucker for a bargain."

Davis, mistaking the dirt driveway to a house set back about a mile from the main road as the first cut off, actually turned on the road leading to Pie Town. He didn't realize the second dirt road leading to Mangas Mountain was the next cut-off.

CHAPTER THREE

"Days Inn! May I help you?"

"Room 142, please."

"Thank you."

Eight rings later the voice of the motel operator said, "I'm sorry. There doesn't seem to be any answer. Would you like to leave a message?"

"Yes, please."

"What is the name of your party?"

"Brad Davis."

"Brad Davis? No, I'm sorry there's no one listed here by that name."

"There has to be. I've been talking to him every day this past week in room 142."

"Let me double check that for you, madam."

"Ah, yes. Mr. Davis checked out this morning."

"Did he leave a message for me?"

"What is your name, miss?"

"Susan Adams."

"No, I'm afraid there is no message for you here."

"Did Mr. Davis leave a telephone number or forwarding address where he could be reached?"

"No, I'm sorry............"

Susan Adams hung up the telephone before the motel operator could finish her sentence. "Damn you, Brad Davis,!" she said out loud. "You were supposed to call and tell me when you were checking out of the motel. How am I going to find you if you disappear into the New Mexico landscape?"

This is not the first time she and Davis have lost contact with each other. She envisions him going into the mountains and not contacting her for several weeks. Just last year he was on special assignment for *National Geographic* in Honduras. Davis was supposed to call her before he checked out of his room in the Honduran Mayan in Tegucigalpa. In his excitement at having found a guide who would take him high into the mountains north of the city, he completely forgot to call. Evidently, she thought, his level of excitement was at fever pitch again. Having dated him for close to three years Susan knew what made Brad Davis tick. It was just one of many qualities she loved about him. As angry as she would get with him, it was impossible to stay angry when he started talking about his adventures. She remembered how he almost seemed childlike when he talked about his Honduran trip. He was doing a story on the village of Los Angeles and its impoverished inhabitants.

The entire village consisted of one dirt-lined street with a row of attached one-story dwellings on each side. Down the middle of the street were three or four 100 foot trees that were bordered by crudely arranged rocks. Walking down the street one could look into each dwelling and see that whole families cooked, ate and slept in one room. A woman in one or two of the dwellings could be seen sweeping the dirt floor with a crudely fashioned broom. About 200 yards from the north side of the street was the open market where everyone was able to purchase or trade for fresh fruits and vegetables brought in from the surrounding poor farms. Beyond the market stood St. Theresa's Catholic Church. The church was situated at the highest point in the village and had a commanding 100-mile view of the valley below and the distant mountain peaks.

Brad would tell of the miracle of St. Theresa to anyone who would listen, which was quite often. Mining and sheep herding were how most Los Angeleans made their living. Since mining was a dangerous occupation and cave-ins were commonplace, St. Theresa's church bells were used to announce a call for help when there was a mine disaster. The story goes that on one spring day when the children were at school and everyone was about their business, the church bells began ringing indicating there was a mine cave-in. All the townspeople rushed to the mine entrance and were able to save all the miners. The miners had said it was lucky that everyone came as quickly as they did because the gas buildup in the mine would have killed them within a short time. All the rescuers asked who knew about the cave-in and rang the church bells. No one could be found who had rung the bells. Being extremely devout and religious people, they believed it was St. Theresa herself who rang the bells. To this day, villagers pray to the saint for whatever favor they seek. Being poor people, they leave pieces of their hair, combs, bobby pins, whatever prized possession they own at the base of her statue. Davis was touched by their humility and faith, but always regarded the miracle as superstition. Brad loves the mysterious and superstitious. It's what drives him and Susan knew she might as well get used to it, he was never going to change.

A University of Massachusetts journalism graduate, Susan Adams had learned to deal with Brad Davis' love of exploration. She always felt he would follow his instincts and work on a project until completion, even if it took forever. On the other hand, she was impatient and wanted instant results. An incompatible pair, if ever there was one. "Opposites attract," he would say.

Susan was 13 years younger than her fiancé, and she would always kid him about her not wanting to marry an older man. Born in Arlington, Massachusetts, outside of Boston, Susan was the oldest of her family. Blue-eyed and blond, she was always the most attractive girl in her class. It was easy to see why Davis fell in love with her the first time he met her. From the first day she interned with him at *National Geographic,* they were inseparable. It was through his help she became an assistant editor with *Newsday* in Long Island City.

"All right, Mr. Davis. You won't tell me where you are. Fine! I'll find you myself," Susan exclaimed loudly. Almost everyone in the newsroom heard her retort and smiled. After three years at the newspaper co-workers were accustomed to her talking out loud to herself. They knew of her relationship with the well-known Brad Davis. Turning off the computer, she picked up her pocketbook and headed for the editor's office. She put her head into his office and said, "I've got two weeks' vacation and I'm taking it right now." Before the editor could react, she was down the hall and out the door.

Davis checked his watch. It was almost four o'clock and it had been half an hour since he turned onto this road heading to Pie Town. He had first realized he had taken the wrong cut-off about ten minutes into the drive. The sun was coming in the driver's side window, which meant he was driving north, not south. Figuring he had plenty of time to explore, Davis thought this would be a good opportunity to see the countryside in this direction.

The drive along the high mountain dirt road had been breathtaking. At an elevation of over 9,000 feet, Davis could see for miles in every direction. To his right were the Plains of San Agustin stretching out across the expansive landscape, reaching up to Cibola National Forest rising on the northeastern edge of the plains. What impressed Davis the most was the vastness of this area and how unspoiled it all seemed. Off to the right were the red sandstone mesa-buttes that were geologically formed millions of years ago, shaped by the forces of nature.

Brad Davis kept asking himself why he hadn't turned his Jeep around and headed back the way he should have when he knew from Bryant's writings the area he was searching for was in the Mangas Mountains. Was Bryant mistaken about the location? Or did he purposely mislead everyone so he could keep the find to himself? Instinct rather than logic had worked more times than not for Davis during his career of exploration. It was the reason he was so successful. Instinct or a gut feeling, whatever he called it, always worked for him and that's what led him to take the chance based on what Little River remembered about a blue Blazer. He wondered how Bryant's blue Blazer, which, from the old Indian woman's recollection, was not in the best mechanical condition, had managed the altitudes in these mountainous areas. His own rental car was laboring as he approached the 10,000 foot marker. Just ahead to the right of the road lay heavily wooded Alegros Mountain. The Jeep was beginning to buck as if it were gasping for oxygen, going slower and slower. Davis edged the vehicle to the side of the road to find out if there was something more than the altitude causing the Jeep to slow down.

This is no place to have car troubles, he thought to himself. Turning off the ignition, he released the hood latch, stepped from the car, and opened the hood. One thing was certain, the car was not overheating and everything looked normal under the hood. Of course, his expertise, with handling mechanical things in cars, consisted of pumping gas, changing the oil, and fixing flat tires. As Davis closed the car's hood, he casually glanced around at his surroundings. Suddenly, something moving in the distance caught his eye. Quickly, he turned in the direction of the movement. Nothing! Was it his imagination? Or, was it merely an animal running between the open spaces of the plains and back into the woods? If it were real, it had to be a good size to catch his attention at that distance. Perhaps, he thought, the setting sun casting strange creature-like shadows and the gently blowing breeze at this altitude made it appear as if something was moving in the distance. Indians have long talked of the Spirits that have roamed these lands and cast spells causing people to see things that weren't there and to lose their sense of direction. Was this the case now? No! He saw movement again and he knew he wasn't imagining it. Who could be out there? Surely, if it were human and lost they would approach him. Whatever or whoever it was did not fully show themselves nor did they try to move toward him. He had to know what he had seen.

Getting back in the Jeep, he noticed what appeared to be a trail running northeast through the sagebrush and cactus, paralleling the edge of the trees marking the boundary of the Cibola National Forest. Offering a silent prayer that the car would start, he turned on the ignition. The motor roared to life and Davis put the car in drive and activated the four-wheel drive. Cautiously, he steered the jeep around the rocks and boulders, heading to where he had seen the movement. As he approached the edge of the forest, the engine died. "Damn, now what!" he said out loud. He braked the vehicle to a stop. The car had gone about 1,000 yards down the trail and out of sight of the main road. Davis turned the key in the ignition again. Nothing but a clicking sound. He tried the lights and radio. Again, nothing. He was at a loss to explain how the whole electrical system could go dead all at once. The sputtering of the engine on the mountain road could have been explained by contaminated gas from Little River. But, that wouldn't have caused the electrical system to fail. There had to be some other rational explanation. All is not lost, he thought. Reaching into his briefcase, Davis pulled out the cellular phone he had rented from the car rental agency. It, too, wouldn't work. "Damn rental agency gave me nothing but crap everything!" he said out loud.

Davis stepped out of the car and pondered whether to enter the woods where he had seen the movement or walk back to the main road seeking help from a passing motorist. He reached back into the car to retrieve a flashlight from his duffel bag. With the sunlight rapidly dwindling, a flashlight would become important in the present situation. He tried to switch the flashlight on. Nothing! "What the hell is going on here?" he mumbled. "Dead car. Dead cellular. Dead flashlight. If I were superstitious, I would say the spirits are working overtime. This has to be a coincidence. Time to get that damn rattlesnake bracelet out of the glove compartment."

Putting on the bracelet, Davis moved away from the Jeep when he suddenly stopped dead in his tracks. A humming sound filled his ears. It sounded like a motor. Was this the humming sound Mattie spoke about back at the restaurant? Which direction was it coming from? Slowly, he turned to get a better fix on where the sound came from. It was coming from the forest. How could that be? he thought. Forgetting the importance of getting back to the main road before it became dark, he moved closer to the forest. The sound continued at the same intensity. No louder, no softer. The last light of day cast an eerie glow across the landscape. He reached the edge of the trees and immediately realized the thick forest was too dark to be trekking around in when one was completely unfamiliar with the surroundings. The sound continued. Davis wanted to know what was causing it and where it was coming from. However, he had to get back to the main road.

As he reached the main road once again the stars were shining brightly in the night-time sky. Based on the number of cars he had seen on his ride up from Horse Springs, he knew his chances of finding someone traveling this road at night were limited. As he searched for even the slightest glow of light in either direction, he realized the humming sound was still in his ears. Again, as he strained his ears to identify the source of the sound he looked toward where his car stood. The hair on the back of his neck stood on end. Davis, for the first time, was becoming frightened. He observed a pulsating bluish glow from deep in the forest. The owner-waitress of Mama Bs had told him about how spooky it was out in these parts and about the bluish glow people often saw across the Plains of San Agustin. Davis had put little credence on what Mattie had told him about such things. Actually seeing the glow with his own eyes, coupled with the strange electrical failure of his car, cellular phone and flashlight, set Davis to wondering. Was there a connection? Were there evil spirits lurking out here trying to keep inquisitive people from where a mysterious tribe of Indians once lived? Or was it something else?

A faint glow of white light coming out of the north on the horizon became brighter and brighter. Davis was frozen in place. As the light came over the horizon, he finally realized it was the headlights of a vehicle heading south. Heart pounding, he stood in the middle of the road to stop the oncoming vehicle. The tow truck came to a screeching halt, almost hitting him as he stood his ground.

"You crazy, man?" a voice rang out from the driver's side of the truck.

"Sorry, but I had to make sure you saw me," Davis said excitedly.

"Who could miss you, you crazy bastard. I could have killed you. What the hell are you doing out here without a car?"

"My Jeep's down there," Davis said, pointing down to where he left the car.

"What's it doing down there way off the road? You have a blowout or an accident?"

"I was checking out something off the road when my car all of a sudden went dead."

"That sure sounds like a stupid thing to do at this time of night." The portly man behind the steering wheel of the tow truck stepped down onto the pavement. He was 70-ish, with dark skin, deep-set eyes and long black hair pulled back into a braided pony tail. "Whereabouts is that car of yours?" Davis walked to the edge of the road and pointed in the direction of the Jeep. The tow truck driver shined his high intensity flashlight beam in the direction Davis was pointing. The beam wasn't strong enough to completely illuminate the Jeep, but the shadow of a car in the distance was evident. "Okay, hop in the truck and we'll ride down there and take a look."

The truck lumbered down the side of the sloping uneven terrain, bumping both occupants from side to side until coming to a stop immediately behind the Jeep. Both men emerged from the truck and went around to the driver's side. The high beams from the truck cast an eerie silhouette against the nearby trees. The truck driver was the first to speak. "Why don't you get in and try to turn the engine over?" Davis slid behind the wheel, turned the key, which he had left in the ignition, and the engine started immediately.

The truck driver gave Davis a funny look. "Hey," exclaimed Davis, "I'm telling you the truth. This engine was deader than a doorknob, and this flashlight, here, was also dead." Davis flipped the switch on the flashlight and a bright beam shot up into the truck driver's eyes. Davis turned the light away from the driver's face offering an apology. "Sorry about that, but this damn flashlight wasn't working either. I just can't explain it."

"What else you got there that didn't work before?" asked the man with the braided pony tail.

"My cellular phone wouldn't work either."

"Try it now, my friend."

Davis reached for the phone on the seat and flipped it open. Pressing the on button, he saw the display light up. "What the hell! I know you think I'm crazy, but everything went dead."

"No, mister, I don't think you're crazy. I am a Navajo and I can tell you the spirits can play any trick they want on anyone they want at any time. Very powerful spirits in this area. I feel them now. They are watching us. Tell me, did you see or hear anything after your car went dead?

"Yeah! I actually came down off the road because I could have sworn that I saw something large moving at the edge of the forest. When I got down here, everything went dead. Then there was this humming sound like an engine running somewhere beyond the trees."

"Perhaps you are too close to what the spirits are protecting. They are warning you to stay away. What is it that brings you to this place?

"I'm doing research."

"Well, the spirits are not happy. You must forget your research and leave this place. Do not come back or they will use more powerful medicine on you next time. Now we must leave this place. Do you think you can drive your vehicle back up onto the road, or do you want me to tow you?"

"No, I'll be fine. But first, I have to ask you another question. When you were driving down this road before I stopped you on the road did you see a bluish glow coming from the forest?"

"Of course. It started about two weeks ago and comes and goes. Sometimes the entire Plains of San Agustin are aglow in a blue light.

"What causes it?"

"No one knows. It is just one of the many mysteries of our land we accept as being a sign of the gods that the spirits of our ancestors are among us. In fact, it gets everyone on edge and we behave ourselves lest we offend the spirits."

"You believe that crap?"

"Please do not mock our beliefs."

"Sorry. I've been told that these strange lights were seen once before, only a long time ago."

"Ah, yes. I had completely forgotten about that time. That was a long time ago. It was several years after the big war. I remember being discharged from the service in April of 1947. Coming home was a shocker to me. There were no jobs. I didn't want to go to Albuquerque to work, so I hung around here and helped out by repairing cars at the service station. I had been trained as a mechanic in the service so I knew a lot about cars. I didn't own the station then. The man that owned the station wanted to retire. He sold it to me in 1960 and my mother and I have been running it ever since."

"You got off the track there. You started telling me the other time you saw the lights."

"Oh yeah! Don't exactly remember the exact month. I just remember it was a couple of months after I got back here in April. It must have been June or July. Well, let me tell you there was the military, news reporters everywhere. At first, there were stories of UFO's and then it was denied and said to be a weather balloon. Finally, everybody got tired of the whole thing and soon forgot it, including myself. But it sure was an interesting time in these parts. I was in the military and I knew what a weather balloon looked like and this was no weather balloon."

"How can you be so sure?"

"Got a piece!"

"What did you say?" Davis wasn't sure he was hearing right.

"I said I got a piece of that so-called weather balloon."

"How could you? All that talk about the weather balloon and where they found pieces of the balloon were about a town more than a hundred miles from here."

"Sure was. Supposedly, it occurred north of the Capitan Mountains near the town of Corona."

"Then how did you get a piece of this balloon."

"Ain't no balloon, I told you. I was repairing an old truck in the garage that day and the owner asked me to mind the station while he went to lunch. These two soldiers in some sort of pickup truck drive in for gas. They're wearing uniforms and talking excitedly to each other. I couldn't help overhearing them talk when I was pumping gas. I heard them say they were tired of scouring the countryside for debris. Now two things got my curiosity. First, was the word debris. Nobody uses the word debris unless their talking about some kind of storm damage, car wreck, or some other kind of accident. I know there were no accidents or storms, especially anywhere within 100 miles of Horse Springs. Second, they were military and they weren't driving a military vehicle. Very strange, I thought. They were pretty far from where the so-called balloon was found in Corona. So how come, I thought, were these guys so far from a military base? Did it have anything to do with the strange lights we had been seeing? While they weren't looking I sneaked a peek into the back of their truck. There was a tarpaulin covering something they didn't want anyone to see. I lifted the covering and saw nothing but this metallic junk. Everything was in small pieces. It looked real interesting and I just took a small piece and put it in my pocket."

"How could you put a piece of metal in your pocket without the metal protruding out of your pocket or, for that matter, if it had sharp edges, from cutting you?"

"That's another strange thing about this metal."

"What do you mean?"

"It was metal, but it was flexible. And I could fold it into a smaller piece."

Davis looked at the Indian incredulously. "Impossible!"

"Not impossible. To this day I have never seen a piece of metal as hard or as flexible as this. And, you know what? When I took that piece out of my pocket after the soldiers left I unfolded it and there wasn't one wrinkle on it. The edges were sharp, but didn't cut me."

"Did the soldiers ever know you took that piece of metal?"

"No, they never knew."

"Did you save that piece of strange metal?"

"Won't part with it. I know it's not of this world. It's saved in a tin box on the shelf in the garage. Forgot about it for a long time until just about the time I saw those lights again. I think those lights and the piece of metal are connected."

"Would you show it to me sometime?"

"Next time you're in Horse Springs just drop in and I'll show it to you."

«Thanks! By the way, I want to thank you for your help. I never did ask your name.»

"I am called Running Horse. But my Christian name is Charles Matthews. Good thing I was coming back this way from having dropped off a car in Pie Town. At this time of year nobody drives this road at night."

"My name is Brad Davis."

"Alright, Brad Davis, where are you going tonight?"

"After what's happened, I thought I'd head back to Magdalena to have some questions answered and then pick up some extra equipment over in Socorro."

"You have two options to get back to Magdalena. Continue north on this road to Pie Town and then head east on Route 60. That's the shortest way. Or, you can follow me down to Horse Springs so I can go over your vehicle to make sure there really isn't a problem. That's where my service station is."

"I think I know the place if it's the one run by a real old lady called Little River."

Running Horse smiled. "Sounds like you've already met my mother."

"That's your mother? Well, I'll be! To be on the safe side I think I'll follow you down to the service station. It will give me an excuse to look at this strange piece of metal. Hopefully, I can find a place to stay tonight." Davis stifled a yawn. Running Horse, why did your mother laugh when I asked her why they call her Little River?"

Running Horse tried not to laugh. "That, Brad Davis, is a long story."

"Funny, she said the same thing to me. I think I might just like to hear that story someday." Davis laughed out loud. His thoughts now turned to Susan. He had better try calling her on the cellular phone. In the excitement to begin his research, he had forgotten his promise to call her. She was sure to be angry with him. Dialing the number, he anticipated what excuse he would give her when she answered. The phone rang four times. On the fifth ring he heard the answering machine pick up. "Susan, I'm sorry.........."

"Hi! I'm not home now so please leave your name and telephone number after you hear the beep. I'll return your call as soon as possible."

CHAPTER FOUR

The sun had made its way across the Sandia Mountains casting almost no shadows of the two men who emerged from the university's administration building. Trees were bursting forth with new life welcoming a new growing season. Flowers were in full bloom offering a kaleidoscope of color on the campus' many paths. The FBI agents, who had been partners for close to twenty years, were totally engrossed in their own thoughts as they got back in their car, oblivious to the signs of spring all around them. Fred Smith and Jack Osborne were an unlikely pair. Fred, the older and taller of the two at six feet three, was a West Point graduate. At fifty-seven years of age he still maintained his military- perfect posture and bearing. His silver gray hair, blue eyes and good looks often served him well in his role as a government agent. It enabled him to charm his way in and out of many tough situations.

Jack was the more talkative of the two FBI agents. Slightly balding and three years Fred's junior, Jack was just a shade under six feet. His tendency to put on weight easily was the reason he was always on some kind of diet. Unlike Fred, who joined the Bureau following his four-year tour of duty in military intelligence, Jack was a CPA. Following graduation from Bowling Green, Jack earned an MBA degree from Northwestern. It was during his graduate studies that he found time to pass the CPA exam.

Both men, assigned to Washington headquarters, lived in the Virginia suburbs. Fred, who had three children, was divorced and pledged to never marry again after a fifteen-year stormy marriage to his childhood sweetheart. Jack, with one married daughter and a son in his senior year at Georgetown, lost his wife to cancer in the spring of 1991.

"I can't believe they assigned us this case." Jack was the first to speak as they drove through the stone columns marking the Sandia Estates development.

Fred shook his head. "For the first time in a long time I quite agree with you. Damn it, you would think we were more important than to be assigned ET work. There are a lot of goofball agents who would kill to get a bullshit assignment like this. What about Billy Stiles who thinks he had an abduction encounter? Why us? Stiles is well qualified for an assignment like this."

"I agree with you on that count, but remember how everyone at the Bureau was treating him like he was a nut!"

"Sure I do! Remember, they had all the shrinks in DC look at him? He spent a lot of time at Walter Reed and at Bethesda under a microscope and they all declared him physically fit. He even subjected himself to lie detector tests and passed."

Jack laughed out loud. "Of course he passed the lie detector tests. He's so crazy he really believed it happened!"

"Did you ever talk to Billy about his experiences?" Fred looked over towards Jack to read his expression." Jack shook his head no. "Well, I did. He and I had lunch while you were out sick one day last year. Now, mind you, I don't believe this shit, but show me some hard facts and you might, I said might, convince me. However, I don't think Billy is crazy or that he's lost it. His record is top notch with the agency with many citations for bravery above and beyond. That's the reason the agency assigned him to menial office tasks instead of retiring him after his pronouncements about his experiences. Like I've already said, this is the type of assignment he should have gotten, not us!"

Jack stopped Fred from continuing. "Look, there's the house, 10256 Cottonwood Road."

"That's the address we were given," Fred agreed.

The one-story ranch house sat back about fifty yards from the road under the shade of a lone, towering oak tree. Fred slowly edged into the driveway, parking behind a maroon Chevy Caprice.

"Nice new car." Jack said, getting out of the car first. He waited for Fred to join him on the pathway before walking to the front door. "I always thought college professors weren't paid much and had to drive around in ten year old Fords." Getting no response to his comment, Jack looked at Fred. "Shall we knock or ring the bell?"

"Does it matter?" Fred shrugged. "We're going to scare the shit out of this guy when he opens the door and sees the two of us."

"Yeah! That's what I like most about this job; flashing my badge, letting them see the shoulder holster, and just plain scaring the living shit out of ordinary law-abiding citizens. It always makes me think everyone has something they're hiding and they've been finally found out." Jack smiled an evil smile.

"You're a sicky! Okay, ring the bell and get this over with," Fred sighed.

A bespectacled man with a full beard and a head of hair that looked like it had just been frazzled from an electric shock came to the door. From the expression on his face it was obvious he was startled at the sight of the two men on his doorstep.

"Yes, can I help you?" asked the man, dressed in dungarees and baggy sweater.

Fred and Jack showed their identification. Fred asked the question. "Sorry to bother you, but are you Professor Timothy Beal?"

"Yes! Is there something wrong?"

"No, sir. We're with the FBI. I'm agent Smith and this is agent Osborne."

"Well, what is it I can help you people with this time?"

Jack chimed in first. "You are an archaeoastronomer and work at the University of New Mexico?"

"That's correct. But what's that got to do with why you're here to see me?" Professor Beal relaxed and smiled. "I haven't stolen anything from any of my digs, you know."

Fred forced a smile. "No, it has nothing to do with anything stolen, but it has something to do with the kind of research you do. We know about your work over in Chaco Canyon and read about your deciphering some unusual cave drawings about celestial events and the tie-in with the Anasazi Indians."

"That's true Agent Smith. I discovered many such petroglyphs throughout the southwest. The one to which you are referring is the one at Penasco Blanco showing a crescent moon, an exploding star and a hand."

"Yes, that's the one," Fred responded. "That's part of the reason we want to talk with you."

"Gentlemen, excuse me for being so rude." The professor motioned both men to enter his home. "Please come in, take a seat, and make yourselves comfortable. Can I offer you something to drink?" Both men politely declined his offer. "My wife is out shopping and won't be back for a couple of hours, so you can be assured we won't be interrupted and you have my undivided attention."

Jack leaned forward on his seat. "You served on Project Blue Book, did you not, Professor?"

"Yes. That was a long time ago and it was only for a short time before they decided to cancel the project in 1969."

"I know that, Professor." Fred interrupted. "Even though you served on the project during the last few years of its existence you had some very strong feelings about the project and voiced strong opposition to the program being canceled. In fact, you and a handful of other Project Blue Book members have continued to stay in touch through meetings and correspondence. Our files say you and this informal group have actually continued to investigate sightings and other unusual phenomena."

"Has the FBI been spying on me?"

"Well, sir," Fred continued, "on such matters of vital national interest, we've been keeping tabs."

"I would call that outright spying and an invasion of my first amendment rights. And, your spy files will show that we have done nothing illegal, immoral, or anything that would jeopardize national security."

Fred tried to calm the professor, who was becoming agitated. "Sir, I want you to know the Bureau is supportive of your efforts and wants to enlist your expertise. That's why we're here!"

"Oh!" The professor relaxed from his defensive posturing. I can see from both your expressions you want to know if I believe in such things. UFO's! Aliens from other planets! Little green men! The answer is yes! But you already know that. The agency most likely has a very extensive file on me." The professor paused and studied the expression on the two agents' faces. Nothing! "I have investigated enough sightings and oddities that can be explained rationally or logically 90 percent of the time. But that remaining 10 percent that can't be explained makes me believe there is the possibility of visits by intelligent life from somewhere other than this planet. Have I had a ride in a space ship? No! Have I talked to aliens? No! Have I seen physical evidence that we have been visited? Yes! Now, let's get to the heart of the matter and the reason for your visit."

Jack started to answer, but Fred held up his hand to signal he would take the lead on this discussion. "Let's say we've been asked to investigate an occurrence and we would like to get your expert opinion."

"What occurrence are we talking about?"

"Here in New Mexico, out in the vicinity of the Plains of San Agustin, a bluish glow can be seen for miles around. Also, a strange humming sound. We asked the military to check it out and they've come back saying there's nothing to it and that we should forget about it."

"So, if the military has said they've checked it out and there's nothing to it, why is the FBI still investigating?"

"Well, if there was nothing to it why are you and your informal UFO group so interested in investigating this matter?"

"I don't follow you."

"Oh, come now, Professor. We were sort of suspicious of the military casually passing it off and we started looking for answers elsewhere. And guess what we found?"

"Alright, I'll play along with your silly little game. What did you find, Agent Smith?"

"Baby Blue!"

The professor's facial expression did not change. "Baby Blue?"

"No sense pretending you never heard of Baby Blue, Professor. It's the name your group uses on the Internet to discuss sightings and investigations. During the last year you held three meetings, one in London, one in New York, and one in Houston. Would you like me to give the addresses of where those meetings took place?" The professor stared at Smith and shook his head no. "Your group has expanded from the original six Americans to now include an additional American, two Russians, a German, a Dutchman, an Englishman, and one Australian."

The professor shifted his gaze back and forth between the two agents as if he were waiting for them to draw their guns and arrest him. "There is nothing illegal in what we're doing, you know." Smith and Osborne shifted uneasily in their seats as if they were teachers that just caught a student cheating during an exam. "Our group is only interested in verifying the authenticity of sightings and other strange phenomena. We perform a valuable service by investigating these strange occurrences and documenting all our evidence. It is available for any government to see, if they want. But, it just so happens that this government and a number of governments around the world don't want to be bothered because a long time ago they passed off extraterrestrial visits as something only for the crazies. By the way, did you gentlemen know one of your own agents is a member of our group?"

"Billy Stiles." Jack Osborne said matter of factly.

"That's how we accidentally came across your group on the internet." Fred Smith continued.

The professor stood up, running his hands through his hair as he walked to the baby grand piano sitting in the far corner of the room. Making a motion as if he were running his fingers backwards over the keys, he forced a smile. Finally, after what seemed like an eternity of silence, which, in reality, was a little more than a minute, he spoke. "You guys amaze me! The government amazes me! Don't you or the government have anything better to do than spy on a group of people who conduct scientific investigations for a hobby? What really amazes me is the fact that the government abandons a project devoted to these type of investigations because they feel it's a bunch of hogwash and then they turn around and spend time and money spying on people who are investigating things they say have no validity. Has everyone gone insane? Okay, okay! Let's proceed on the premise that our government and its security agencies are totally insane. Next, let's talk about FBI agent Stiles. No one in our group has ever met Billy Stiles personally. He's only a name and a voice, having talked to him several times on the telephone. If the FBI knows and is interested in us, why didn't they assign him to come talk with me about this matter?"

Fred, rubbing his chin with his hand responded, "He's been assigned desk duty until further notice under the Director's orders."

"They think he's crazy because of what he said about his abduction, don't they?" The professor blurted out. "No matter. Stiles shared his so-called adventure with us on the Internet and we all know as much as there is to know about the incident."

"Does your group believe Stiles' story?" Jack Osborne asked.

"As with all the investigations our group carries out we keep an open mind. Based on his reputation Stiles certainly qualifies as one of the more credible witnesses. For my benefit would you share with me just how you became aware of Stiles' association with us?"

Fred loosened his tie and unbuttoned the top shirt button. "It really was an accident. Every one of his fellow agents was giving Billy room to breathe and just avoiding the subject altogether. Our desks, Jack's and mine, are pretty close together in a bullpen sort of office arrangement. This one afternoon about a year ago Billy was working on his computer and the phone rang. After a few quick 'Yes, sirs!' he hung up the phone, threw on his jacket and raced toward the boss' office. In his rush, he forgot to get out of the document he was in and close down his computer. That's an agency directive you don't ignore or you'll be taken to task for it. We're paranoid about keeping secrets from each other if we're not working on the same cases. Jack, here, being the good boy scout, saw Billy's screen was still on so he asked me if we should shut it down. 'That's your call, I told him. Me, I'm playing by the book and not touching his computer.' Jack told me to screw myself and went over to shut down Billy's computer." He was grinning from ear to ear as Fred was recounting the story. "You want to finish the story?"

"Sure!" Jack continued to smile. "When I went to shut down

Stiles' computer, I couldn't help but notice what was on his screen. My first reaction, after quickly reading the first paragraph, was that this was something Fred and I should take a look at the whole document. I immediately saved the document to the public file and then exited the document and closed down Stiles' computer. Then, I rushed back to my computer, went into the public file and copied the document onto my personal disk. Immediately, I deleted Stiles' document from the public file. That way there was no trace of it being any place other than his own file. Next, I checked the backup files to make sure there was no trace there. As I had hoped, it hadn't been in the public file long enough to copy itself into the backup file."

The professor returned to his chair, shaking his head in disbelief. "You guys are unreal. You've been entrusted to protect our national security and your actions are as criminal as a lot of people behind bars."

"It was not intentional dishonesty!" Jack said indignantly. "Our training has ingrained in us to be suspicious and on the lookout for the bizarre and unusual. What I saw qualified as being just that! That very night Fred and I went to my home and reviewed the document on my home computer. It was the complete story on his abduction that he relayed via the Internet to your group."

"Alright, let's get back to why we're here," Fred cut in. "Remember, we were talking about the strange occurrences out in the vicinity of the Plains of San Agustin."

"Gentlemen, I am aware of these strange goings on which have been taking place for the past two weeks," the professor responded, posturing himself into a more comfortable position in his chair.

"What's your opinion, then?" Jack spoke before Fred could ask the question. Fred gave Jack a disapproving glance.

"Since I haven't seen first-hand the glow, as you call it, I can't give you an educated answer. However, these strange lights, or glow if you prefer, have been an on and off thing for close to fifty years. Did you realize that?" Both men shook their heads no. The professor continued, "Ever since the testing of the atom bomb here in the deserts of New Mexico during the early forties we have experienced strange happenings. Do both you men have the highest level security clearance?"

"Yes, but only on a need to know basis," Fred answered.

"You've heard about the Roswell file, I assume, and that those files can't be accounted for. I've never seen all the documents associated with that file, but I know that one particular part of those files that still exists is buried somewhere deep in the Pentagon. If it were uncovered, it would still be classified as Top Secret and would be protected from the Freedom of Information Act."

"We only know about the possible contents of the file through hearsay," Fred answered honestly.

"Having worked on Project Blue Book I received the highest level security clearance. Members of that project all had the same security clearance and were allowed to review numerous documents in that 1947 Roswell incident file before they supposedly disappeared. What

I am about to tell you is contained in those documents that members of Project Blue Book reviewed. The government, specifically the U.S. Air Force, feels that what happened back then should remain a secret so as not to cause a worldwide panic. Everyone was led to believe the initial announcement about pieces of a spacecraft being found were the result of an overactive imagination and that, in reality, those pieces were actually part of a new highly scientific weather balloon. Stories were rampant about pieces of a spacecraft and of alien beings actually being found. The military did a good job of finally convincing everyone it was the result of a few people with overactive imaginations. Eventually, interest died out and the media went on to other stories.

"I'm going to tell you a strange, hard-to-believe story that is absolutely true, so help me God! It was no balloon. There were those stories about alien beings who were said to be about three and a half feet tall and of a greenish color. Those stories were denied. So were the stories about military flights in the middle of the night transporting the alien bodies between Roswell and St. Louis Army Air Force Base. Supposedly, soldiers involved in the event were ignorant to some extent. However, I have seen those so-called green aliens and I will tell you without any hesitation that what I saw were not beings, but some sort of robots."

"Oh, come now professor, robots!!" Fred and Jack said in unison.

"You heard me right!"

Fred shifted uneasily in his chair. "We had been told these aliens are real and that they are frozen to preserve them."

"Yeah, and they're in a heavily guarded hangar at Langley Air Force Base, next to the hangar storing the stealth bomber," Jack added.

"If you gentlemen, with your security clearance, wanted to check it out you would find there *is* something at Langley, but not three little green aliens. I'll tell you what's really in that hangar, but I first need to tell you about some things that weren't included in Project Blue Book, which, by the way, was preceded by two other projects on this same topic. I can't recall off the top of my head the name of the first project formed shortly after the Roswell incident, but I can tell you Project Grudge was the name of the UFO file before it was renamed Project Blue Book. And, of course, you know officially that Project Blue Book was canceled in 1969. Unofficially, information gathering about unidentified sightings is still going on. The first known time that a bluish glow was seen in New Mexico was one day following the first test of the atomic bomb. Everyone dismissed it as some sort of airborne residue from the bomb's fallout. It was the first time that those humming sounds were heard that you spoke of earlier. Those sounds have been heard all throughout New Mexico for the last fifty years. I have always said our atomic tests woke up the universe and space travelers have been visiting New Mexico ever since. I did promise to tell you what was in that Langley hangar. Are you ready for this? It's a six-foot plus humanoid with reddish skin and, yes, he's on ice. Now that I've told you all my secrets why don't you tell me what it is you need my help with."

General Nathaniel Eaton Brantfield, retired three star Air Force general, lived in a one story stucco building with a flat roof, and large rectangular windows framed by wooden shutters. The pinkish-brown house was surrounded by a foot-wide concrete wall of the same color. A brown-colored steel gate at the front of the house was the only entrance into the walkway leading up to the double etched-glass doors of the general's home. The home had been built just prior to his retirement in the mid-seventies. Many locals were curious why a general of such prominence and rank would choose Magdalena as his retirement community.

It was a well-known fact that the general had spent almost thirty years at Roswell. The last twenty had been exclusive oversight of a super secret project, or so it was rumored. It was also known his wife came from a very prominent, wealthy New England family. They could afford to live anywhere. And so, the general and his wife were the subject of much town gossip, speculating why they settled in Magdalena. Up until the time of her death, she spent more time away from Magdalena than she did living in her retirement home. She would go away for months at a time, leaving the general to live by himself. One year she left around Memorial Day and didn't return until Christmas. A woman of regal bearing and elegant manners,

Catherine Brantfield died tragically in a head-on collision with a tractor trailer on her way to the airport five years ago.

The general deeply mourned his wife's death and had become more reclusive as time went on. His contact with other residents of the small town was minimal except for Sheriff Cooper. As time passed after his wife's death, the general started to make more frequent and longer lasting trips out into the Plains of San Agustin. Since his official retirement from the Air Force in the seventies, he had made at least one trip a week out there, rarely staying overnight. Since Christine's death he began going two or three times a week, often not returning until the next day. During the past two weeks, his trips to the Plains became more frequent and it was obvious to everyone he was staying away longer. While the locals thought it odd, they paid little mind to the general's eccentricities. After all, the trips were something the general had been doing for years. The only difference was that they were becoming more frequent and lasting longer. When asked by Mattie one day if everything was okay, he replied by telling her to mind her own business. The word got around quickly and as long as the general had his health and appeared normal in every other respect, the townspeople left him to live his life any way he wanted.

The only two people who had anything to do with the general were Sheriff Cooper and Big Bird. They knew better than to ask if the general was alright. They knew he would confide in them if there were something wrong. The general had developed a close bond with the sheriff shortly after Brantfield's only son, Jason, was killed during the Vietnam conflict in the early seventies.

His son was a navy pilot assigned to a carrier in the Sea of Japan. He never returned to the ship and was presumed lost at sea. That was the official explanation of the Navy. Two weeks after the personal notification to the Brantfields by the Department of the Navy, a letter from Jason arrived at the general's office in Roswell. It was Jason's last letter and the contents left the general with a sick, hollow feeling that would haunt him for the remainder of his life.

According to his aide, the general became physically sick after reading the letter. When he regained his composure, resisting any help from the aide, he tore the letter into as many small pieces as he could, dropped them into the waste basket and set it afire. Months later he would confide in Sheriff Cooper of the existence of the letter and its contents. Evidently, Jason admitted to being a homosexual and that he was ashamed that he brought disgrace to the Brantfield name. His letter ended saying he loved both his mother and father and would bring no further disgrace to his family. The general took that to mean that his son had deliberately crashed his plane into the Sea of Japan.

For years after the Vietnam War he badgered high ranking Pentagon officials to investigate his son's plane crash and presumed death. Even with his clout working for him, no satisfactory answer was ever given for his son's death. The official government proclamation stood: CAPTAIN JASON BRANTFIELD'S F-19 FAILED TO RETURN TO U.S.S. CORAL SEA - PRESUMED LOST AT SEA.

The general never shared the contents of that letter with his wife. He felt it better if she never knew the truth. The death of their only son shook him and his wife so traumatically, each for their own reason, that they became even less communicative with each other. There was talk that her grief, which never left her, finally became too much to bear and that she actually, deliberately drove across the highway divider into the path of the truck. No one will ever know the truth.

"Come on in, Frank," the general responded to the knock on the front door.

"You wanted to see me, general?" asked Sheriff Cooper as he closed the door behind him. He stood in the main foyer where one could only marvel at the striking beauty of the inlaid Mexican tile floor. To the rear of the foyer was a massive sitting room with several overstuffed chairs that faced a terraced garden of cactus and a number of full-blooming lemon trees. The sliding glass doors, separating the sitting room from the terrace, were hidden into a recessed wall opening, allowing the cool breeze from outdoors to blow through the entire house. The general invited the sheriff to take a seat in this room, handsomely decorated, definitely with a masculine touch, with local Indian artwork and typical New Mexican artifacts.

"I think we've got serious problems," the general said, taking a seat across from the sheriff.

"What kind of problems?"

"Anasazi!"

"Anasazi? You mean Project Anasazi?"

"Yes, Frank, and I'm afraid we've come to that point which we knew would come someday. That someday could be now and everything we've accomplished during the last fifty years could be blown apart. We have so much more to learn."

"What makes you think Project Anasazi is in jeopardy?"

"First, there was that Brad Davis snooping around, wanting to do some research out there on the Anasazi. I heard you told him about what we found way back in '47. Damn it, Frank, have you lost your senses? We don't need any writer-type out there finding what we've been hiding all this time. Next thing we'll have the whole world beating a path to our door and messing things up! I understand he got close but turned around. I know his kind. He won't stop until he stumbles right into the middle of this project. We're going to have to deal with him right away.

"I'm sorry, General, I was just trying to scare him off. I figured most of these kind of people are scared off by their own shadow. It's my guess he's so spooked he's already on his way home."

"Maybe you're right, but I have a feeling about this one! Second problem. I just got a call from General D and Air Force military intelligence at the Pentagon saying the FBI is starting to nose around."

The sheriff moved in his chair, carefully shifting his holster to a more comfortable position. "How did the Pentagon find that out?"

"From James Phillips, the President of the University of New Mexico. He's a former government official with connections in

Washington. It seems two FBI agents were in his office earlier today wanting to talk with Professor Beal. You know him, of course! He's that arrogant know-it-all archaeoastronomer over at the university who served on Project Blue Book and deciphered the petroglyphs at Penasco Blanco. Evidently, the agents refused to tell the university president why they wanted to speak with Professor Beal. He was pissed they wouldn't tell him anything and figured it was something big. He wanted to know what it was so he called an old friend at the Pentagon. The Washington grapevine spread like wildfire and triggered a call to military intelligence from the White House."

"Goddamn! The White House! How we going to keep this quiet if the White House gets involved?"

The general stood up, straightened his shoulders and walked to the edge of the room, looking out onto the terrace. "I'm not worried about the White House. I'm more worried about those shiny-shoes, no-brainers from the agency sticking their noses into military business and blowing the lid off this operation."

"Yeah, but General, we've been covering this thing up since 1947. What makes you think they'll get anywhere now? Why are you so sure they're out here to check out Project Anasazi?"

"I'm not sure why the FBI is nosing around out here. Probably has something to do with the light show we've been having for the past two weeks. You know we have no control over the situation when they start doing their experiments. Evidently, someone has put a bug in the FBI's ear to check it out. We'll have to keep a close eye on them as well as that writer fellow. If any one of them gets too close, Big Bird will have to see that they're conveniently taken care of. Look, Frank, we have been damn lucky up to now. That's all there is to it. Pure, stupid luck! Fortunately, two years ago no one beyond yourself investigated old Sam Johnson's strange death and the weird color of his body. If that kind of thing happened anywhere else but Magdalena, you sure could have bet your ass there would have been investigations by county, state and federal officials. In fact, the Center for Disease Control in Atlanta and the EPA would all have been down here poking around a body that hadn't decomposed after being out in the desert for a week. We plain lucked out on that one. That's not to say you didn't do a good job of making it look like a pure and simple accident and normal death. We may have finally run out of luck." The doorbell rang.

"You expecting anyone else, General?" asked the sheriff as he looked toward the front door.

"I told Big Bird to meet us here. After all, he's got more at stake in this thing than you or me."

CHAPTER FIVE

"Rattlesnake bracelet worked like I said it would!" Davis had barely stepped out of his Jeep when Little River greeted him.

"It was more like I got lucky that your son was happening by, Little River," Davis laughed as he looked down on the diminutive Indian woman.

"You call it luck; I call it Indian magic medicine. You better believe that it was the rattlesnake bracelet magic medicine or else next time you may not have the magic when you need it the most. This was just a test to get you believing."

"Okay, okay, I believe! Are you satisfied now?" But Little River had already turned her back and was slowly shuffling toward the small house set behind the garage. As the Indian woman walked she could be seen throwing her hands in the air and shaking her head. Davis could have sworn he heard Little River mumbling about something evil sure going to get a hold of him.

"My mother is really something, isn't she?" Running Horse had parked his tow truck inside the garage and joined Davis who was now looking under the hood of his Jeep. "Do you know what you're looking for, Mr. Davis?"

"Not exactly! Have you got a flashlight so I can see better under this hood? The under hood lamp isn't all that powerful and I need all the help I can get to see."

"I have one right here, but let an expert take a look." Davis stood quietly as Running Horse spent about five minutes thoroughly checking every connection on the engine. "Can't find anything wrong. Maybe the altitude choked off your carburetor temporarily and then it cleared itself."

"Yeah, maybe," Davis replied, half believing what he said.

"And, then again, maybe it's those evil spirits I was telling you about."

"Thanks for your help, Running Horse. Can I get a look at that metal you told me about?"

"Sure, follow me to the garage where I have it saved."

Davis followed Running Horse to the entrance of the darkened garage. Although it was pitch black inside the garage, he could hear the whirring sound of an exhaust fan long overdue for a complete overhaul. The heavy smell of motor oil, lubricants and oily rags permeated the air.

"Don't you move until I turn the lights on, Mr. Davis." Running Horse said from somewhere deep in the recesses of the garage. "I don't want you killing yourself on my account. Ah, there we are."

Two fluorescent light fixtures suspended from the ceiling slowly blinked to life.

"That's not much light!" Davis said matter-of-factly.

"I never do any repair work at night so there's no need to have a lot of light. Most of my work these days is oil changes and tune ups. My eyes aren't too good to try to do any real repair work. Besides, there isn't much call around here. Any heavy duty repairs I send them over to Socorro car repair shops where they've got all the necessary latest gadgets to fix cars. Now, let's see where I saved that piece of metal." Running Horse checked all the drawers in the workbench that ran the width of one wall. Not finding what he was looking for Running Horse began checking the metal shelves on the rear wall where most of the supplies were stored. Not able to reach the tallest shelf, he pulled a stool over to allow him to get a better view of the top shelf. "Yes! I found it!" Running Horse said excitedly as he retrieved a rusty old Maxwell House coffee can from behind a battery. "I hid it so well I couldn't remember where I saved it." Running Horse stepped down from the stool and offered the can to Davis. "Here, you open it!"

Davis held the can and looked at it for several seconds before speaking. "Are you sure it's okay for me to look at this?"

"Sure, I want you to."

Davis wiped off the dirt and oil from the lid of the coffee can. Slowly, he lifted the lid as if expecting a snake or lizard to jump out as part of some practical joke by Running Horse. Carefully placing his hand inside the can, not knowing what to expect, Davis retrieved a grayish piece of metal and held it in his hand as he placed the coffee can on the stool. "I've never seen anything like this before in my life. Like you said, Running Horse, I can bend it any which way and it will always come back to the same smooth shape. It doesn't wrinkle. The edges are jagged, but they're not sharp."

"Let me show you something else strange, Mr. Davis."

"Running Horse, you're almost twice my age. Please call me Brad or I'm going to start calling you Mr. Horse."

"That would never do," he smiled broadly. "Now Brad, watch closely as I try to burn a hole through this metal with an acetylene torch." Running Horse lit the torch. "Hold the metal while I apply the flame."

"Hey, I'm not crazy." Davis moved away from the flame. "You put that flame on the metal and no matter where my hand is the metal will conduct the heat to my hand."

"Trust me, Brad. If you get the slightest sensation of heat drop the metal immediately. I promise I will not hurt you."

"Okay. But I'm going to hold it with the tips of my two fingers so I'll be ready to drop it quickly."

Running Horse let the blue flame touch the center of the piece of metal. Davis held the metal as far from his body as the length of his arms would allow. The flame was placed almost on the surface of the piece of metal and still no hole appeared. After one minute of trying

Running Horse turned off the torch and returned it to the workbench. Davis still held the metal in his hand.

"How did you do that?" a stunned Davis asked.

"I didn't do anything. It's the metal. It doesn't burn. You can't even burn a hole through it. It doesn't conduct heat. It's basically indestructible."

"And you say some military guys a long time ago had a truckload of this stuff. Where did they get it from? Or, was it part of some military experiment with new metals?"

"Don't think so. Remember, I told you I've had this stuff since the summer of 1947."

"1947!" Davis was shocked that he was holding something this strange that was found over fifty years ago. "Where did they find it?"

Running Horse rubbed his right ear. "My best recollection is that with all the military running around the Plains of San Agustin and all the way over to the Capitan Mountains, they had to find pieces like that somewhere between those areas."

"And you've never shown this to anyone else?"

"No, only to my mother and she wanted to use it as a placemat for her indoor cactus plant."

Davis was consumed with interest in this strange piece of metal that until today he didn't know existed. "Try to remember during the last fifty years if you can recall any strange occurrences or anything out of the ordinary."

"Like what?" Running Horse asked.

"Strange lights, noises, people, anything unusual."

"Look Brad, this is a land of a million spirits of our ancestors. There are always strange things going on. We accept them. It is part of our heritage and our superstitions. Strange lights. Strange sounds. Music. Even strange looking tall Indians are seen around these parts on a regular basis."

"Do you mean Indians from an unknown tribe spend time here on a regular basis? How can you be sure they aren't from around this area? Could they be Anasazi?"

"No way! They've been long gone from this earth. Besides, they don't look like any brothers from any tribe around these parts. Every time I have to drive up to Pie Town, and that's six or seven times a month, I would see a couple of them right around the same spot I found you today."

"What were they doing?"

"They were just sitting in a jeep as if they were waiting for someone."

"Do you see anyone else, ever?"

"Oh, sure! General Brantfield has been the most regular visitor to these parts."

"*The* General Brantfield from Magdalena?"

"One and the same. He used to spend quite a bit of time in that area, from the way folks used to tell it, when he was still in the service. Since he retired, he still would be seen up there with a small group of Indians. I always figured he liked to hunt or something.

Never really thought much more about it! Look, it's dinner time. Would you like to join me and my mother for something to eat?"

"To tell you the truth, after my experiences today I'm more tired than hungry and besides, I have to find a place to stay tonight."

Running Horse shrugged his shoulders, and said as politely as he could, "Have you taken a good look around our town? There isn't a motel within thirty miles of here and even if there was I wouldn't recommend you stay there. You can sleep on the couch in our place."

"I appreciate your generous offer for both food and lodging, but if it's okay with you I'll sleep in the back of the Jeep tonight and get an early start back up to the area where we met today."

"Are you sure you really want to do that, go back up there, I mean?"

"Sure do! Remember, I came out here to research and write about the Anasazi and try to unravel the mysteries surrounding this area. You never know what I'll find. Maybe I'll find something interesting, like your piece of metal."

"You may find more than you can handle. I have a feeling the spirits are already angry with your presence here. I have no quarrel with what you do, but the spirits are a different matter." Running Horse, his face frowning, was issuing Davis a warning.

"What is it that you are afraid of? Is there something you don't want me disturbing?"

Running Horse took the piece of metal back from Davis, put it in the coffee can and placed it back on the top shelf. He then gestured toward the garage door. "All throughout this land the spirits of our ancestors are buried in sacred ground. Some areas are more sacred than others according to our legends. The area you want to go is where those strange Indians have been disturbing sacred ground for far too long and I feel the spirits have reached their limit on patience. I sense you are a good person and intend no harm. However, when the spirits are angry they will take their vengeance on anyone and anything in the way, no matter how good a person is."

"Thank you for your concern, Running Horse. I'll be very cautious and on my guard and promise not to desecrate any graves or sacred land. By the way, what do they call this area we are talking about?"

After turning out the lights in the garage and locking the doors behind them, Running Horse pointed to the north and said, "The Land of Great Spirits is what they call it. I recommend you do not venture into that area again. Wear your rattlesnake bracelet, Brad Davis. You are going to need all the special magic the spirits can conjure up. You may park your Jeep alongside the garage so the lights from any cars or noise from the highway will not bother you. Goodnight, my friend. May the good spirits of the Navajo protect you from the evil spirits that roam our land." With a wave of the hand Running Horse turned and walked back toward the lights from the house he shared with Little River.

Davis moved his Jeep alongside the garage, still dwelling on the piece of metal he had seen and touched, as well as the warning from Running Horse. He knew all Indians, as well as many nationalities, had superstitions that they fervently believed in. Davis wasn't much on superstition. His feeling was that people make their own bad luck and then pass it off as an accident or conveniently blame bad fortune as a result of some silly superstition. Indians were different though, as he found out in his studies of their many cultures. He would take Running Horse's advice and be extra cautious.

Davis finished his can of Chocolate Royale Ultra Slim and laid out his sleeping bag on the rear floor of the Jeep. He zipped up the bag and placed his head on the small pillow he had brought along. A thousand questions were racing through his mind. What was he getting himself into? Where did that piece of metal come from and did it have anything to do with his theory that there was a connection between the Anasazi, Mayas, Incas and Aztecs? Could the strange Indians Running Horse described possibly be Anasazi? Have they suddenly returned as mysteriously as they disappeared centuries earlier? Was there some connection between these people and visitors from somewhere out in the vast void of space? And what about the piece of paper with the strange inscription that someone placed under his windshield wiper. Was there a connection? Should he show the paper to Running Horse and see if he had any idea as to what the inscription could mean or who would have placed it there? The questions did not get answered as Davis, exhausted, fell into a deep sleep.

"Come on in Big Bird!" The general's commanding voice called out.

Big Bird nodded to both the general and the sheriff seated in the great room. "What's so urgent that you call me away from my tribal duties?" Big Bird demanded, showing his displeasure for being summoned.

"Mind your tongue, my Indian friend!" The general, using his military reprimanding voice, only referred to Big Bird as his Indian friend when he was annoyed. "There's something going on you and your friends need to be aware of."

"I am not stupid, general! Of course I know what's going on. We've got a nosy person poking around under the pretense he's researching the Anasazi. In fact, he was as close as I ever want to see him get. I don't know how much he saw on the edge of the woods, but he did get close enough to the southern pathway leading into the complex. His car's power failure got him turned around. If Running Horse from Horse Springs hadn't shown up when he did we might have had some real trouble. Hopefully, we can get this Davis fellow pointed in some other direction."

"For your information, Big Bird, Frank ran a background check on this Brad Davis and found he is legitimate. It seems he is a well-known researcher and writer who wrote for *National Geographic* until recently when he gave notice to come out here and write about the Anasazi. He has some impressive writing credentials to his credit and graduated with honors from New York University. There's no record of his serving in the military." The general motioned Big Bird to take a seat beside him. "We've got bigger problems than this writer. I just finished telling Frank about the FBI beginning to get interested in our secret. Let me tell you what I've told him and then I'm going to tell you how to best handle this situation so it doesn't get out of control."

Taking a seat alongside the general, Big Bird responded, "I'm listening!"

The next day dawned without much light as the sun was obscured by a heavy covering of clouds. A light drizzle was falling. Davis opened his eyes and looked at his wristwatch, surprised that he had slept until almost seven o'clock. He sat up and remembered where he was and then complained to himself about how long he had slept. The windows of the Jeep were blurred from the rain which was now falling a little harder. Through the blur on the side window Davis could barely make out the dark shadow moving toward his vehicle. A tap on the window and a voice calling his name, Davis realized it was Running Horse. Exiting from the rear of the Jeep, he was greeted by the Indian with the short ponytail.

"Please come to the house and have a good breakfast before you begin your journey." Running Horse spoke to Davis as a father would talk with a son. "I want you to wash up first. It may be some time before you eat a normal meal and have the opportunity of bathing."

"Thank you, Running Horse.," responded Davis as he closed the rear door of the Jeep. "I'll take you up on just a cup of coffee and pass on the washing-up. Actually, I plan on only spending today up there doing some preliminary exploring and then returning to Magdalena for supplies."

"You won't find the kind of supplies you need in Magdalena. You'll have to go over to Socorro for them. In any event, it's a good idea to spend only a day up on the mountain. I would strongly recommend you never stay in that area at night."

As Running Horse poured Davis his cup of coffee, he tried to assess what motivated this writer to brave the perils of dealing with the ghosts of the *ancient ones*, the term by which Navajos referred to the Anasazi.

Brad Davis was a dreamer. From the time he first entered school his teachers all branded him a foolish daydreamer. Born into a middle-class family living in the Torresdale section of Philadelphia, Davis was the only son of Grant and Lillian Davis. His favorite subject was geography and his daydreaming was of faraway places he would love to visit someday. He knew the capitol of every country of the world and of every state in the United States. Ask him the name of a mountain, a river, an odd sounding city and he would immediately tell you the name of its country. Davis' other love was creative writing, which grew out of his spirit of adventure. His teachers would wonder at this young man, who seemed not to be paying attention or caring for schoolwork, and yet had the ability to write marvelous stories of faraway places that he had only visited in books or in his mind.

Growing up in Philadelphia offered Davis many cultural opportunities. He took advantage of every chance he could to visit these special places. A loner, he did many things on his own. His parents never knew where he was or what he did on Saturdays, holidays or during his long summer recess from school when he would leave the house long before anyone else was awake. He loved the Philadelphia Museum of Art and the main public library where he would scour books on faraway places. It allowed him to take his school time daydreaming to new heights as he read about the mysteries of the pyramids and other wonders of the world.

This same love of adventure and exploration at an early age was the catalyst in his senior year of college that finally led him to his interest in the Anasazi Indians. While he never dreamed of actually being able to visit and write about such mysteries, Davis always felt writing of some form or another in advertising was his true calling. When he finally realized in his last year of college that he would rather write and explore more than anything else in the world, his life took on new meaning.

Davis' mind was set to wondering about many things following his college graduation. He remembered all the library books he had read that dealt with unexplained mysteries that baffled mankind. It was more than fascination with the pyramids of Egypt. He wondered about the connection with those pyramids and those found in Mexico, Central and South America. What was the explanation for Stonehenge in Great Britain, Newgrange in Ireland, the giant statues of Easter

Island, Machu Pichu in the Andes, the strange figures carved on the landscapes of Peru and Chile that could only be seen from a great height? All these things were of interest to Brad Davis and it was this interest that led him to finally narrow down his choices of what he wanted to do with the rest of his life.

His attention focused on an American mystery. Where did the Anasazi come from? Where did they disappear to? There were so many similarities among all these nations and yet, there were differences in how they farmed and hunted, their religious practices, and their attitudes about fighting. Davis was most intrigued with something he discovered in his research at the University of New Mexico, just before embarking on his latest quest. His research uncovered something he hadn't known before: approximately one-sixth of all the uranium deposits on earth can be found in this region of New Mexico and huge deposits of coal can also be found in the San Juan Basin.

Deep in the recesses of his brain was always the nagging possibility that maybe these ancient civilizations had help from someone or something more powerful and more intelligent. That someone or something came from another world and was far more advanced than even our present-day world. It was this possibility that he wanted to explore. If he were lucky, he might find the answer to many unexplained modern-day riddles. Were these huge deposits of uranium and coal the reason the Anasazi lived in this region? Was it the fuel that powered the spacecraft to and from our planet? Until now this kind of thinking was mere fantasy, but Running Horse had presented testimony and physical evidence of a material that did not originate on this planet. Davis was bursting at the seams to begin searching for the answers.

"Brad Davis, if I had more courage I would like to accompany you on your trip to the Land of Great Spirits on Alegros Mountain," Running Horse said, as he cleared Davis' cup from the table.

"Alegros Mountain!" Davis responded in a surprised voice. "I thought I was at Mangas Mountain!"

"Guess you got mixed up like that other fellow who took a wrong turn and headed up into the wrong mountain, thinking he was at another mountain," Running Horse chuckled. "Sorry, I didn't mean to poke fun at your mistake. It happens all the time out here. People take roads thinking they're going one place and actually wind up at an entirely different location."

"Mangas, Alegros! Either way, I'm heading back alone up to the mountain where you found me. This is something I have to do on my own. And, as you have said in your own words, it could be very dangerous. It's bad enough I have to look after myself, but to worry I might be the cause of something bad happening to you is a responsibility I cannot accept. No, thank you, my friend. I'll tell you what I will do though. Give me your telephone number and if I get in trouble I'll call you on my cellular. Is that a deal?"

Running Horse looked troubled. "Brad, someday I will have the courage to join you on your quest, but for the time being, I will remain concerned for your safety. Please promise you will call me if anything unusual or out of the ordinary happens."

"I promise," Davis said as he excused himself from the table and headed toward the door. "Thank you for the coffee and please convey my best wishes to your mother." Davis closed the door behind him and headed for the Jeep.

"Is he gone?" a raspy voice called from the back room.

"Yes, mother, he is gone."

"The spirits spoke to me last night and told me there is nothing we can do to stop him. He must battle with the spirits on his own without any interference from us."

"I know, mother. I heard you talking with them during the night. Did your spirits say if he would be alright out there?"

"Don't know! I woke up before they gave me an answer."

CHAPTER SIX

Davis pulled off the road at the exact spot where he had been the day before. It had taken more than forty-five minutes to take the short trip because the drizzle at this altitude had turned into a frozen mist that made the road icy and treacherous. This time the Jeep's engine did not stall out. Carefully, he edged his vehicle down the sloping incline stopping where he thought he caught a glimpse of shadows late the evening before. Davis pulled the hood of his parka over his head as he exited the Jeep.

Although it was only nine in the morning, the freezing fog was enveloping everything, making visibility extremely difficult. A cold wind, coupled with the freezing mist, was beginning to give Davis a headache. He was only a few feet from the edge of the forest and yet, in the heavy fog that suddenly blanketed the entire area, he could barely make out where the tree line began. Another few feet and he was among the trees. Taking a few steps beyond the entrance into this thick forest, he felt strangely warm after having experienced severe body chills outside the forest. He also noticed the fog did not permeate the forest. Very strange, he thought. Only a few feet from the freezing drizzle and fog into the woods and he was now quite warm. He looked toward the tops of the trees to see if he could see daylight. There was none and yet the light, in what should be a darkened forest, was quite good.

Davis unzipped his parka and removed the hood that had covered his head. He had a very strange feeling. There wasn't a sound to be heard in this thickly blanketed forest of trees. No smell from the pine trees. No sound of animals being startled in their attempt to get away from this stranger walking among the trees. Why were there no birds chirping? It was almost as if the trees were the only living things in this strange place. Am I treading on some sacred Indian site that even the animals know enough not to inhabit? Was there any truth to those silly stories and superstitions that the Indians talk about?

Before taking another step, Davis thought about how far away he was getting from where he had entered the forest. He checked his watch and took the compass from his pocket to get an accurate reading on which direction he was heading so he would be able to find his way back out of this place. The dial on the compass was spinning out of control. Davis shook it to see if there was something wrong with it. Still, the compass dial would first spin one way and then spin in the opposite direction. It was as if a giant magnetic field were giving the compass fits. Disgusted, he returned the compass to his pocket.

He had to have a way to mark his trail back to where he had left his Jeep. Taking a hunting knife from the case strapped to his belt,

Davis began marking trees as he progressed deeper into the woods. As he continued his journey Davis felt as if he were moving closer to the source of the draft of warm air that he was feeling. He stopped, suddenly realizing that he had been walking for over an hour but his watch showed only five minutes had elapsed. How could that be possible? Was his watch broken? Was his mind playing tricks or was that a clearing up ahead? He took a few steps forward, listening for any kind of sound. There were no sounds, only a very low hum beyond the clearing. The sound became only slightly louder as he got closer to the clearing. The humming sound was barely audible, almost as if it were an air-conditioning unit set on the lowest setting.

"Wait a minute!" he said to himself. "Now, I recognize that sound. It's the same sound I heard when I visited Habitat, the experimental environmental station outside of Tucson. It was the sound of a self-contained air purification system." Davis was perplexed by this sound he heard that should not be in a place like this. He remembered someone talking about a secret project General Brantfield was responsible for. Was this it? Why would such a secret project be set up in a remote site like this? Davis stepped from the forest and into the clearing.

"My God in Heaven!" he exclaimed. Davis could scarcely believe his eyes. He sat down on the ground overcome with both shock and excitement looking out on this sight that appeared before him. How could this place be? He sat there for what seemed an eternity, looking all around him, taking in every detail, marveling at the sight before him. Here, in this canyon, surrounded by a forest on one side and a sandstone cliff wall on the other, was a miniature city of at least two hundred homes. There seemed to be four or five short streets, crisscrossing each other, lined with one-story modern adobe dwellings. No two houses were the same color. There were street lights on every corner. Beyond the houses was the steep cliff wall where ancient dwellings could be seen, as perfect as if they were just built. How could that be? Davis thought to himself. The dwellings looked untouched by time.

All of a sudden two things became apparent. First, this town or village was totally deserted. Second, he noticed that the light in this clearing appeared to be very strange. Davis finally looked up to see why the sun was casting such a strange light over this whole clearing. What he saw completely took him by surprise. It appeared as if the entire area was covered by some sort of translucent dome, cutting down the direct rays of the sun. Somehow or another this strange living area was a controlled environment. "That's the sound I heard," Davis said to himself. "What is going on here? Who or what is in control of this place? Where are the people?"

Davis stood up and moved down the side of the sloping hill leading to the first street of homes. He decided to be brave and knocked on the front door of the first house on the block. No one answered and yet he could see lights on. Next he tried a second house. Again, no one answered the door. He moved from house to house and still no one answered the doors to houses that appeared to have someone or something living in them. Moving to the next street, Davis again tried to get a response from several houses.

Getting his courage up, he decided to try the door on one house after receiving no response to his knock. It was unlocked. Slowly he opened the door and entered what appeared to be an American family home, complete with furniture and appliances. It had a combination living room-dining room, a kitchen, two bathrooms, and two bedrooms. But no sign of people!

Davis moved to the next house. Again, he found the house fully furnished and all the signs that someone was living there. Looking at his watch he realized it had stopped running. His watch showed the same time as when he had checked it in the woods. It hadn't changed. Not able to accurately tell time, Davis guessed he spent a great deal of time on the mountain and decided he had better start back if he wanted to reach Magdalena before dark. He was more anxious to investigate the cliff dwellings, but that would have to wait until another day. He decided to try one more home before heading back to his vehicle. Making sure no one was in the house, he entered leaving the front door open should a quick escape be necessary.

Davis decided to snoop around a bit. He discovered fresh food in the refrigerator, pots and pans, dishes and the cupboards full of packaged and canned goods. No doubt about it, he thought, someone is living in these houses. But, who? And where were they? Davis opened a door off the kitchen where he expected to find a laundry room or a pantry. Instead, he found a stairway leading down to what he assumed was a basement. A cool, damp breeze blew up the stairwell. Davis, who had spent many research hours in caves, knew that the smell he detected was the damp smell of a cave. His keen sense of hearing detected a low frequency humming noise, evidently made by some sort of electronic equipment coming from somewhere deep within the recesses of this cave. He immediately closed the door and headed for the front door. Making sure no one was around, he exited the house, closing the door behind him, and ran for the opening in the woods where he had entered this unusual place. Taking one last look, Davis retraced his path back to where he had parked his Jeep. Only on his return trip up through the woods to his vehicle did he realize how steep the incline had been on the way down to the strange town in the mountain.

His Jeep started right up and Davis was on the road north to Pie Town and then east to Magdalena. Checking his watch, he remembered that it had stopped running earlier that day. To his amazement, he found that his watch was now running again, showing the time to be six minutes past nine. The clock on the car's dashboard showed that it was 5:15. He had many questions that needed answers and believed General Brantfield was the one man who could supply those answers. The only question in his mind was, would the general give him those answers? Davis kept going over and over what he had seen. How did that dome get there? Who placed it there? Was it the government? Visitors from another planet? A lost race of the Anasazi? What about the stairway leading to the caves? Should he call Running Horse and tell him of his discovery? No, he reasoned, it was better that as few people as possible should know of his discovery. He would call him and tell him nothing happened and that he was heading to Magdalena to get a room for the night.

Davis thought about Steve Bryant's writings covering his discovery over two years ago. Was this the same place, the same discovery? Did Bryant intentionally mislead people about where his discovery was located so as to keep his find all to himself? Or had he really become disoriented. Bryant had said his discovery was in the Mangas Mountains, between Aragon and Horse Spring. Did he really believe that? I remember Little River saying Bryant took the wrong road. Could he have really found this place? Maybe, Davis thought, he had found Bryant's discovery. Could Bryant's disappearance be connected to his having found this place? Davis promised himself he would search the cliff dwellings on his return trip for any trace of Bryant having been there.

"Hello, Running Horse? Yes, it's Brad and I'm fine. I promised I would call you on my cellular. No, I didn't have any trouble up there and I didn't find anything," he lied. "Look, I'll call you soon! What? Thank you and tell your mother I appreciate her worrying about me, too!" Davis pressed the off button on the telephone. He could see the lights of Magdalena in the distance and breathed a sigh of relief that this day would soon be over.

Magdalena's only motel made Albuquerque's Days Inn seem like a four star hotel. Aptly named the Magdalena Motel, the motel was nothing more than one of those old single bungalow types of cottages that existed along the main road leading to Florida in the thirties and forties. Those days were a thing of the past now that Interstate 95 stretched from Maine to Miami and travelers have their choice of Holiday Inns, Marriotts and Motel Six, to name but a few. All those cottage style motels must have been shipped out west to towns like Magdalena, just waiting for a new interstate highway to be built.

Before heading to Cottage Number Six, Davis felt he needed a substantial meal. He walked the one block to Mattie's restaurant, knowing she didn't close until eight o'clock.

"Well, I'll be, look who found his way back to our beautiful little town!" Mattie greeted Brad Davis with a big smile.

"How you doing, Mattie? I see Big Bird hasn't convinced you to sell yet."

"No way, young fellow. I'm not ready yet."

"I'm starving! What can you recommend for dinner?"

"It's the end of the day and there isn't much of anything left, except the blue plate special-meat loaf today."

"I don't care at this point, as long as its food."

"Okay, be right out with the blue plate special."

Davis looked around the small restaurant to see if he recognized any familiar faces. For the late hour, there were still about ten to twelve people finishing their meals. Over in the corner he thought he recognized the old timer who filled his tank with gas on his first arrival in town. The man was slumped over the table snoring loudly, but unnoticed by the remaining diners. Mattie returned with his dinner.

"Something to drink?"

"A nice, hot cup of coffee would be great. Mattie, let me ask you a question."

"Shoot."

"How can I get in touch with General Brantfield?"

"You don't! He only gets in touch with people he wants to get in touch with."

"Does that mean I have no chance of ever getting to meet with him?"

"No! If he figures you got something important that's of interest to him, you'll hear from him."

"Well, can you get the word to him that I have something important to discuss with him?"

"Don't have to tell him. He has ways of just knowing everything."

"Anyway, if you do happen to get a chance to speak with him, can you please let him know."

"Okay!"

"By the way, isn't that the old man who pumps gas across the street?"

"Yeah, that's him. He gets rip roaring drunk late every afternoon, comes over here to have a cup of coffee to sober himself up and then falls sound asleep."

"Isn't that bad for your business?"

"Nah, everybody knows old Jake and feels sorry for him. I haven't got the heart to throw him out. I let him sleep on the cot in the shed out back. He's harmless. He's been that way since something scared the sense out of him about ten years ago. Everyone's tried to find out exactly what caused his traumatic condition, but no one could find out anything. Even old Jake can't remember or he doesn't want to and drowns himself in booze every day."

Davis finished his meal, thanked Mattie and headed back to his room. The first thing he did when he settled into the room was try Susan's telephone number. On the fifth ring, again he heard, "Hi! I'm not home right now. After the beep please leave your name and number and I'll return your call as soon as possible."

He slammed the phone down. "Where the hell are you, Susan?" A knock on the door brought Davis to his feet. "Who's there?" No answer. Again, another knock on the door. "I said, who the hell is there?" Davis was getting agitated, as if was being bothered by some prankster who refused to identify himself. If he were in New York City or Miami, he was sure it would be a robber after his money. But here in Magdalena!!! Swinging the door open Davis was surprised to see Sheriff Frank Cooper. "Sheriff, it's you! Why didn't you answer when I asked who was at the door?"

"I'm sorry Mr. Davis I didn't hear you. I had my two-way radio up to my ear and I didn't hear you. Sorry about that."

"What can I do for you Sheriff?"

"Have you got the emergency vehicles on the way out there?"

The sheriff spoke into his radio. He returned his attention to Davis. "Sorry, we got a bad wreck out on the Interstate and I'm trying to help the state police coordinate getting emergency vehicles to the accident scene. One of my deputies is handling the police end of the emergency. I'll be joining him shortly. You were asking me what I wanted. Well, it seems General Brantfield would like to have a meeting with you."

"Can it wait until tomorrow morning sheriff? I'm dead tired and need some sleep."

"Afraid not! The general wants to see you now and when he asks me to bring somebody to him I follow his orders."

"Do you work for the general?"

"You might say I work for all the citizens of Magdalena."

"All right, you convinced me. I'll follow you over in my Jeep."

The ride took no more than five minutes and the sheriff escorted Brad Davis through the front door, down the foyer and into the great room.

"May I offer you a drink, Mr. Davis?" A voice asked from behind a desk in the far corner of the room.

"No, thank you, general."

"So, what is it that is so important that you needed a meeting with me, young man?"

Davis stood facing the general who did not get up from his chair behind the desk. "How did you find out so quickly that I wanted to talk with you?"

"I have my ways. So, I'll ask the question again!"

Davis didn't want to tip his hand about everything he had seen in the last twenty-four hours. He would first ask him about the Roswell incident and, based on his initial reactions, he would then ask other questions. "No need to waste your breath. I'm out here doing research on the Anasazi Indians and a theory I have about their connection with other ancient Indian civilizations."

"Mr. Davis, I am a retired Air Force General and have no knowledge about long forgotten Indian civilizations other than the fact that Indian artwork fascinates me. If you look around my house you will see evidence of that interest."

Casually scanning the room as the general spoke, Davis was mesmerized by the strange tapestry hanging on the wall behind the general's desk. It depicted many small scenes of people blending into a larger scene of cities from what looked like something out of the future. The oval tapestry, which he estimated to be at least eight feet in circumference, had geometric designs circling the outer edges. "That's an interesting piece of artwork on your wall there. Where did you get that from?"

"A friend's gift to me," the general responded, ignoring Davis' question of the origin of the artwork. "Now, Mr. Davis, let me tell you again that I am not an expert on ancient Indian civilizations nor do I really care. My life was spent in the military and I only know about military matters."

"Well, it so happens I think you are in possession of information that could possibly lend credence to my hypothesis."

"And what would that information be, my friend?"

"I want to know everything there is to know about the 1947 Roswell incident."

"Oh, that silly nonsense again." The general removed a stack of papers and placed them in the desk drawer. "I've said it before and I'll say it again. There was no flying saucer! It was a weather balloon."

"Excuse my irreverence, General, but I think you're full of shit and have been covering up the real story for over fifty years. Don't you think it's time you began telling the truth?"

"Young man, I am becoming quite angry at your insinuations. Why don't you believe me like everyone else has believed me all these years? Roswell is ancient history. The media back in '47 got carried away with the ranting of one man who was sure the balloon was a UFO."

"Why then did Sheriff Frank Cooper, who was under your command at Roswell back during the incident, say to me it was no balloon."

"Frank said that? He's always been a practical joker. Don't believe everything you hear, especially from Frank. He's getting on in years and he's bored with his job, so he tries to liven things up once in a while."

"How do you explain the metal the military collected back during that time?" Davis could scarcely believe his own ears that he had asked this question of the general.

The general, getting up, moved from behind the desk and stood in front of Davis. "Metal? What metal are you talking about?"

"I've seen it general! I've touched it! It's tangible evidence from your 1947 incident that we have been visited."

"Someone has been playing a trick on you, Mr. Davis. I know of no such metal."

General, you know all about this metal that won't burn and can be bent to any shape and then returned to its original form."

"I'm sorry, son. Again, I think someone's having fun playing a trick on you. There's nothing more for us to discuss, so I believe you should leave."

Davis knew full well that the General was lying and to ask him about the strange city in the mountain he had just visited would also be met with denial. He was about to mention the piece of paper with the strange inscription but thought that this was neither the time nor the place to broach the subject. There would be another day when he would face off against the general. "General, there are other things I know about and I promise you that they will be investigated and written about. And if it just happens to blow the lid off some secret thing you've been hiding all these years, so be it. If you ever decide to level with me, I'm sure you'll find a way of getting in touch with me."

"Goodbye, Mr. Davis."

Davis' Jeep pulled away from the general's house as Brantfield dialed the sheriff's office.

"I'm sorry, sir, the sheriff is at the scene of an accident," the dispatcher informed him.

"This is General Brantfield! Patch me through to the sheriff's car at once."

"Yes, sir, General, sir!"

Within less than a minute the sheriff was on the other end of the line. "Frank, when you get finished with that accident haul your ass over here as quick as you can."

"Anything wrong, General?"

"Don't ask questions! Just get your ass over here, pronto!"

CHAPTER SEVEN

American Airlines flight 455, a continuation of flight 273 from Newark, arrived in Albuquerque at 5:35 p.m. mountain time, more than three hours behind schedule. The intermediate stop in Chicago turned into a longer-than-expected stopover when O'Hare was closed down for a strong line of thunderstorms and tornadoes moving through the area. The airport was closed for two hours and by the time it reopened it was another hour before flight 455 left the runway.

Susan Adams was not happy. She had expected to arrive in Albuquerque much earlier allowing time to register at a hotel, get her bearings, and then begin the task of tracking down Brad Davis. Following Susan's abrupt announcement to her editor the evening before, she had immediately gone home to her apartment on East 67th Street. On the taxi ride home, she had a feeling that things were not going to go smoothly on her two-week trip to New Mexico.

Arriving home, she checked the telephone answering machine for messages. There were two. "One of these messages better be from you, Brad Davis, or I'm going to give you the tongue lashing of your life when I find you!" Susan exclaimed angrily to an empty apartment. The first message was from the dry cleaners saying her clothes were ready to be picked up. The second message was the one she was waiting for.

"Sorry, Susan, I've gone and done it again. I forgot to call you this morning when I was checking out of the motel. You know how I am. I get so excited about setting out on these adventures that I lose my sense of responsibility to you. Please forgive me. I love you so much and yet I continue to do dumb things where you're concerned. I really did remember to call you, only it was much later than I promised. In the future, I'll make every effort to get rid of this bad habit. For your information, I'll be running around in the area of the Plains of San Agustin and the Mangas Mountains. Once I find a base to operate out of I'll give you more details of where I'll be. Love you! Talk to you soon!"

"You'll never change, damn you!" Susan shouted at the answering machine. Susan knew Brad Davis, no matter how well intentioned he was, would always be Brad Davis: dreamer, explorer, writer par excellence, researcher, intelligent, kind-hearted, fun-loving, people-oriented, all the things Susan thought she wasn't. Since their relationship first began at *National Geographic*, Susan would often confide in Davis about how unattractive and dumb she thought she was. This from a woman who graduated at the top of her class at Wellesley.

Davis would become exasperated with Susan and her feelings of inadequacy and he would take every opportunity he had to tell her how gorgeous and smart she was. Susan wanted to believe him, but had this deep sense of not being good enough. Somewhere in the deep recesses of her brain she would try to analyze herself to determine why she had these feelings. The answer she would come up with every time was immediately dismissed from her head. No, she would reason with herself, it was not her father's constant prodding her to excel at everything, not praising her for the things she did well as a youngster. Deep down, she knew her father loved her dearly, but he had never openly demonstrated that love. He was embarrassed when she would run up to him after he returned from work every day, throw her arms around him, kiss and hug him. Beginning in her teen years and continuing until her father passed away suddenly from a massive heart attack last summer, Susan took this lack of affection as displeasure with her.

Several times before his death Susan came close to confronting him about their relationship. She wanted to clear the air between them. She wanted to know why he seemed to have a better relationship with her two younger brothers than he did with her. There were so many things she wanted to discuss with her father before he died. The telephone call from her mother that sultry July evening announcing her father's death caught Susan completely by surprise. Her father was so healthy all his life. This was some sort of cruel joke he was playing. Death! "Impossible!" she cried out to her mother over the phone. "He can't be dead! We have so many things we've got to talk about. He can't do this to me!" But there was her mother, sobbing over the telephone, saying, "I'm sorry, Susan."

At the funeral, Susan had a hard time dealing with her anger at her father for dying while at the same time handling the family's grief. Several days after the burial, while Susan was in her old bedroom packing to return to New York, her mother came into the room.

"Susan, I know how much you loved your father and yet you always felt he was displeased with you. I know you will find this hard to believe, but your father loved you very much and did nothing but brag about you to everyone he met since the day you were born."

"Yeah, well he had a funny way of showing it!" Susan angrily responded.

"Dear, your father was one of those people who didn't know how to express his affection openly. He was the same way with me. He would get embarrassed if I hugged or kissed him in public. It didn't mean he didn't love me. It was just the way he was." Susan's mother pleaded for her daughter's understanding.

"But, Mom, even as a little kid he wasn't a warm person with me. How do you think that's made me feel all these years?"

"I know, dear."

"No, you don't know, Mom. That's why I've had these feelings of inadequacy all these years. I'm mad at Dad because we never talked about this. Now, he's dead and he'll never know how I felt. I'm going to have to live with this the rest of my life. Damn him! Damn him!"

"Susan, he knew very well that there was this miscommunication between the two of you and he had hoped that one day soon the two of you would have a long talk," Mrs. Adams said softly.

"Great, Mom! Dad's dead, I'm miserable and we never did talk. Just great, Mom!"

"Susan, please don't hold any ill-will against your father. He did his best to be a good husband, a good father, and a good provider for our family. He had his shortcomings as we all do. I loved him with all my heart and I'm going to miss him terribly." Nancy Adams began to cry. "I'm as angry with him as you are. How dare he leave me at this time of our lives when there were so many good years left before us. He was planning on retiring to Florida in five years where he promised to spend all his spare hours with me in doing the things we like best. We had plans and now I am alone." Susan's mother continued to cry.

"God, Mom! How selfish of me to think only of myself about Dad. Please forgive me! I know how much you loved him and how you're going to miss him. We'll both miss him, each in our own way."

Mrs. Adams handed Susan a sealed letter with her name written across the front of the envelope. "I found this letter addressed to you in the safe when I was looking for your father's will. There were four letters altogether, one for you, one for me, and one each to your brothers."

"What's in it?" Susan asked, placing her mother's hands in her own.

"I don't know dear. It's a letter for your eyes only. I've already read mine and can only guess what yours says."

"What do you think it says?"

"You'll have to read it yourself, Susan. I'll leave now so you can have some privacy to read your father's letter." Mrs. Adams rose from the side of the bed where she had been seated and moved to the door. She looked back at Susan, who had already begun to open the sealed envelope, and quietly closed the door behind her.

Susan had no idea what to expect in the letter. She removed it from the envelope, unfolded it, and began to read. As she read, tears welled up in her eyes, trickling down her cheeks. As she finished the letter, folding it and carefully placing it back in the envelope, Susan began to sob, realizing for the first time that her father thought she was something special.

Susan picked up her luggage from the baggage claim area on the lower level of the Albuquerque airport. It was now almost six fifteen and she still had no idea where she would be spending the night. Her first chore was to get a rental car. The young woman at the Avis counter suggested the Best Western motel immediately outside the airport entrance.

After registering at the front desk, Susan was escorted by the bellman to her no smoking room on the second floor. Albuquerque was two hours behind New York time, so even though her heavy eyelids told her it was time to go to bed in New York, Susan wasn't ready to call it a day. She decided to check her apartment's answering machine in the hope that Brad had called again.

"Susan, Susan, where art thou? Are you out having a good time without me? Listen, I left you a message yesterday and I hope your machine is working. Got to tell you, there's some strange things going on out here. My theory on the Anasazi could possibly be true. It's exciting and at the same time scary. Can't wait to talk to you about this. I still am moving around and not staying in any one place. Let me give you the name of a possible place you can reach me in an emergency. Be sure to give me a couple of different times to contact you so I am sure to get hold of you.. The place is called Mama Bs and it's in a town called Magdalena. The owner's name is Mattie. Love you! Talk to you soon!"

"Now we're getting somewhere," Susan said excitedly. She unfolded the map the rental agency had given her and searched for a town called Magdalena. Placing her finger on the small dot, she said out loud, "Gotcha, Brad Davis!"

It was almost two a.m. when Sheriff Cooper arrived at General Brantfield's house. The accident had happened in the southbound lanes of Interstate 25, a mile north of the U.S. 60 cut-off. It had taken over six hours to clear. A multi-vehicle accident between a camper and a school bus carrying Indian children back from an all-day outing in Albuquerque, it had caused a massive traffic jam. The initial crash had started a chain reaction accident involving twenty vehicles strewn across the interstate, with a number of vehicles ending up in the gully. Emergency vehicles from as far away as Albuquerque assisted state and local police in clearing the highway and transporting the injured to hospitals in Socorro and Albuquerque. Frank Cooper was exhausted and not in any mood to be dealing with an angry General Brantfield. Those who knew the general were well aware of his mean-spirited disposition and his sudden outbursts of temper. The sheriff, who had served under the general at Roswell, as well as being a police officer in the community where the general resided, had been publicly reprimanded and humiliated by the general many times. But still a strange bond existed between the two men, transcending any long-lasting hard feelings.

General Brantfield responded to the doorbell and motioned the sheriff into the house. "When I tell you to get your ass over here right away, I mean instantly, not four hours later." The general pointed his finger at the sheriff as he admonished him.

Shrugging his shoulders as if indifferent to the general's admonition, the sheriff walked through the foyer into the great room and across to the wall bar. Pouring himself a Dewar's, he added a few ice cubes from the small bar refrigerator, slowly stirring the ice cubes with his finger. Turning toward the general, Frank Cooper stared silently at the figure that followed him into the room. Both men said nothing, playing a waiting game to see who would be the first to speak. The general, his eyes narrowed and his upper lip contorted into a sneer showing his displeasure, was waiting for the sheriff to respond to his outburst for being late. Taking a sip from his glass of scotch, the sheriff felt the warmth of the liquid begin in his throat and continue down to his stomach. The biting taste and warmth were exactly what Frank Cooper needed. The rage building in the general could not be seen in the semi-darkened room. "Cheers!" the sheriff said as he took another sip from his glass.

"I'm not in the mood for any crap, Frank!" the general, extremely agitated, shouted at the sheriff.

Frank Cooper calmly turned away from the general, placed his drink on the bar, and then turned back to face the figure at the far side of the room. Slowly the sheriff moved closer to the general, coming within a few feet of him. The sheriff, looking the general straight in the eyes, was trying to read this man he had known for over fifty years. Did this old man still have all his faculties? Or was he finally losing it? Was he still trying to be the general, demanding obedience from one of his soldiers? The general's eyes did not provide any answers. "General, you were my superior officer in the military, but we have been friends far longer," Frank Cooper said softly without a hint of animosity. "I am a police officer and have a responsibility to the community and its citizens. I will not drop everything or neglect my duty to answer your every command. Tonight there was a horrendous accident that had to be taken care of. Three young Indian children are dead and five others were seriously injured. I came as fast as I could when everything was cleared up. In fact, I'm so tired I can't think straight. I should have gone straight home. Instead, I came to see you as requested. I'm here and I'm not offering any apologies for being late. So, what the hell is so important that I'm standing here at this hour of the morning?"

Brantfield took a few steps back, weighing how Frank Cooper had responded to him. Slowly the general brushed past Cooper and opened a diet soda. The tenseness in the general's body had eased and his face became less taut. Drinking from the can, the general finally spoke. "Well, you do have a set of balls, Sheriff Cooper." A raised eyebrow and a slight smile were evidence that the general was more at ease. "I needed to talk with you about our writer friend. When you brought him here several hours ago, he was about to question me about something. He abruptly dropped his questioning and made some veiled threat about exposing something. One thing he does know about for sure is the metal found at the crash site in 1947. I don't know how he could have possibly found out about it, unless there's someone else out there who recovered a piece of the wreckage and showed it to him. In either case, I think he knows more than he's letting on or has stumbled onto something he can't explain without our help. We can't afford to have him running around and finding out about Project Anasazi. You, Frank, will have responsibility for taking care of him any way you see fit. He must be taken care of just like those two people who got too close the last time. And, I don't want a repeat of the fiasco surrounding Mattie's husband two years ago. That Sam Johnson's body incident almost blew the lid off this project. We can't afford to have that happen again."

Frank Cooper took a deep breath. "If you remember general, I really had nothing to do with what happened to those people. And, you'll also remember I didn't agree with your original solution to that matter. Luckily the matter resolved itself without any help from us. For the record, I don't agree with what you're planning now."

"Project Anasazi is vital to our national security!" shouted the general.

"I don't happen to agree with you, General. We're talking about a fifty-year-old secret that can't be kept a secret any longer."

"It has to!"

"You're wrong, general! I think our visitors are back to take their families home."

"What are you talking about? They can't be back! Big Bird hasn't said anything about their returning at this time! He always said that they would be back on the exact day and time of their 75th anniversary. That's twenty-plus years away. The reason for their returning precisely at that time has something to do with the planets being aligned exactly as they were in 1947."

"Can we be sure it's the same people?" The sheriff asked. "They did tell us there were another five galaxies in the expanse of the universe and there were at least twelve planets they knew were inhabited. Before their planet exploded in 1054 earth time, most of the survivors had colonized another planet called Dacon, in their own galaxy."

"Frank, Frank, listen to yourself! Do you forget I know more about these people than you do? I don't need to be reminded of their history!"

"I'm sorry, general, I was thinking maybe some of the original inhabitants of the exploding planet didn't make it to Dacon and instead colonized another planet."

"And, if you remember, Frank, they told us six of those planets were well behind in their development compared to Earth. They had not yet traveled to or investigated the remaining six. From their sophisticated communications systems they were able to detect some form of life on those other six planets. And they have recently told us that centuries later, in our time period vernacular, those planets have not yet reached the technological level of Dacon."

"Well anyway, several hours ago while out taking care of the accident we saw UFO's pass over us, heading toward Alegros."

"How many?"

"Two, maybe three."

"Who all saw them?"

"Everyone stuck on the highway saw them. People were scared and pointing up at them. Those UFO's were making no attempt at not being seen. The news radio programs are all carrying stories on the sightings. People have been calling police switchboards all over the area ever since they were first sighted about 11:30. My greatest fear is that the TV stations will pick up on this story and start nosing around trying to tie these sightings in with the glow that has been seen across the Plains of San Agustin. So, we've got more trouble than our friend." The sheriff moved toward the foyer.

Grabbing the sheriff's arm, the general issued an order. "I still want Brad Davis taken care of. He's a real threat and we can't afford to have his meddling cause us any additional problems. Find a way to get him away from this area. And if it takes a drastic measure, so be it! Big Bird and I can take care of any visitors and give the media the old run-around. Just remember, Frank, you may be the sheriff, but you still draw military pay for your involvement in Project Anasazi. You have a military duty to uphold."

Frank Cooper forcibly removed the general's grasp from his arm. "I will have no part in your plans, General!"

"I issued a command, soldier!"

"Screw you, general, sir!" Sheriff Cooper opened the front door and walked out into the brisk morning air toward his police car. A new day was dawning as the sun slowly began to cast its morning glow on New Mexico.

He did not hear the general exclaim, "You will obey my orders or I will initiate disciplinary action against you myself!"

CHAPTER EIGHT

Fred Smith and Jack Osborne sat drinking coffee in a corner booth of Denny's on Washington Avenue, 10 blocks east of the university campus. "Fred, I don't know why you suggested meeting the professor for breakfast at this god-awful hour of the morning." Osborne whined in a sleepy voice.

"Look, the sooner we get on with this assignment and put it behind us the better off you and I will be," Smith chastised his partner. "I would sure as hell like to be back home in Virginia commuting to the office on the Metro and doing boring things other than chasing down strange lights and noises in New Mexico. This professor character gives me the creeps. I don't like his type. He's probably taken a trip on one of these UFO's and his body been taken over by aliens."

"You watch too many science fiction movies," Osborne laughed. "Hey, do you remember that Rod Serling guy who used to have that TV program years ago?"

"Sure, I used to watch it all the time, when I was home. It was called *Twilight Zone.*"

"That's it! Do you remember one show about these aliens that came down in their flying saucer and got people on earth interested in visiting the aliens' planet?"

"That was a really stupid story," Fred Smith said. "The show ended with all the earthlings lining up and boarding the spacecraft and Rod Serling saying that the earthlings were unaware the aliens planet was running out of food and soon that shortage would be over."

Osborne laughed. "What do you think, Fred? Is Professor Beal one of them?"

Before Smith could answer, the professor was at the table greeting them.

"Sorry to get you up this early, professor." Fred Smith said apologetically. Jack Osborne nodded his head in concurrence.

"Nonsense! Actually, when I'm out on a dig my day begins at four allowing me to review the finds of the day before and plan for the upcoming day. Have you had breakfast yet?"

Both agents shook their heads. Osborne was the first to respond. "We've only been drinking coffee. We wanted to wait for you to arrive before ordering."

"Thank you. I'm starved" The professor said as he looked over the menu. "What are you two going to have?"

"Grand Slam," both agents said in unison.

"Ah, it sounds as if you have experience eating breakfast at Denny's!"

"On our government expense account, eating at Denny's, Wendy's,

Miami Subs and Burger King is mandatory," Smith responded with a chuckle.

"Grand Slam, you say. Oh, here it is. Grand Slam includes two eggs, two pancakes, bacon and sausage. Wow! That seems like a lot of food!"

"The price is right, professor," Jack Osborne responded.

"How's that?" asked the professor.

"Two dollars and ninety-nine cents, plus coffee and juice, if you want it," Fred said quickly.

"Okay. I'll have the same. I can't pass up on a bargain, can I, especially when my government is going to treat me to breakfast? Now I ask you, when was the last time you received a treat from the government?" The smirk on the faces of both agents was not missed by Professor Timothy Beal.

The waitress took their order, asking if anyone wanted juice or more coffee. The two government agents pointed to their cups indicating they wanted a refill. The professor politely asked for a cup of tea and then was the first to speak after the waitress' departure. "Since you've enlisted my assistance to help you unravel these New Mexican mysteries, I'll take the lead and lay out our plan for the next few days. Is that the way you want it?"

"Since you're the expert in these parts, that's the way it has to be. However, if there is any kind of trouble, get out of the way and let us do what we do best," Fred Smith said sternly.

"Agreed!" Professor Beal responded.

"Good!" Smith said.

"Great!" Osborne added.

The black Ford Bronco with the heavily tinted windows pulled into General Brantfield's driveway. A tall, thin young man, dressed in jeans, denim shirt and a leather jacket emerged from the driver's side of the vehicle. Quickly, he moved to the passenger side to open the door for the figure already emerging from the car.

"You three stay here!" ordered the barrel-chested man in the dark blue suit to the two men seated in the back seat and to the thin man holding the door. "I'll talk to the General alone and fill him in on everything that's been going on. When we're finished, we'll get a bite to eat down at Mamma B's." The balding man in the blue suit walked to the door of the house and rang the bell. It was six o'clock in the morning.

Signs of weariness showed on General Brantfield's face as he extended his hand to shake the colonel's hand. There had been no sleep for the general since Sheriff Cooper left his house. The responsibility for keeping Project Anasazi a clandestine operation for the last fifty years had taken its toll. After years of secret- keeping, administering the project obviously had become too much for the general in his eightieth year. He knew the man standing before him now, Colonel Wally Parker of Air Force intelligence, was the man to take his place as head of the project. General Brantfield, at this moment in time, was ready.

"Can I offer you a cup of coffee?" the general asked as both men took seats facing each other in the small kitchen dinette.

"Thank you, no. I'm sorry to have asked for this meeting so early in the morning, General, but there are a so many things happening that we need to develop a quick strategy to get the media and the general public calmed down. In order to assist your eventual successor on this project it is imperative that we work together and get everyone's attention diverted away from all of New Mexico and onto other matters."

"Yes, yes, that's very critical," the general nodded his head in agreement.

"First things first, though. Do you know the compound has been compromised?"

"Damn, that can't be!" The general moved forward in his chair, arms folded and leaning on the table.

"Afraid so! My men and I have just come down from the mountain and there is evidence that someone marked a trail on the southern side of the mountain through the trees to the edge of the compound. On careful examination we found a fresh set of tracks leading down into the compound and in and around the houses. The markings on the footprints don't match any of the compound residents' footprints. Do you have any idea who might have gotten into the area?"

"There's only one possibility! Brad Davis, that damn nosy writer who is out researching Anasazi history to write a book on his theory."

"What theory is that?"

"Mind you, I got this second hand from Sheriff Cooper, but it's my understanding he's trying to find a link between the Anasazi, Incas, Mayas and Aztecs."

"I don't understand, General."

"Davis feels there is a connection among all those Indian civilizations, and their sophistication, knowledge, building techniques at some point in history. Therefore, he reasons, they had to come from somewhere else."

The colonel, getting up from his chair, poured himself a cup of coffee and sat down again. "You know, General, that's not a new theory. Many people in the past have speculated about those civilizations and how they were able to have such advanced knowledge and mathematical skills. The only difference between us and those speculating astronomers and archaeologists is that we really know the answer. We have living, breathing proof right up there in the mountain."

"Damn you, Colonel!" the general shouted, shaking the table and spilling the colonel's coffee. "Don't you realize that Davis with his nosing around can be the one individual to start the ball rolling uncovering all our work?"

"Yes sir, I know that very well!" the colonel answered, as he wiped up the spilled coffee with his napkin. "And as you already know, we've also got the FBI sticking their nose around, coupled with the fact that the media has picked up on the sightings last night. Time is running out on all fronts. It seems our visitors have returned. Do you have any idea why, general?"

"Evidently they're ahead of schedule. We always knew they would return to retrieve the members of the 1947 expedition. They just happen to be a little early. We knew some of them would stay and work with us, but the majority would return to Dacon."

"You say that like there is a possibility that might not be the plan anymore."

"Yes, I'm not so sure any of them will be staying, colonel." The general sighed. "In fact, the way things are going no one may ever get the chance to succeed me on this project. Project Anasazi will be history."

"What makes you say that, General?" the colonel asked quizzically.

"Well, what started out last year as mild disagreement with our philosophy on the part of a few Daconians has recently spread to more of them in the colony. They have become disillusioned with the future course of the planet and feel we are no longer an earthly power that is able to control this world. I guess the downing of TWA Flight 800 was the final straw. They say even in our own country there are elements that want to bring down the government. Crime is rampant all over the world as a result of drug use. Since they first arrived, we have fought in Korea, Vietnam, and Iraq, and have had police actions in Panama, Grenada, Somalia, and Haiti. Wars continue all over the planet unabated. Political and religious unrest continues in the Middle East, Bosnia, South Africa, almost any place in the world you can name.

"General, the military establishment is truly sorry about TWA Flight 800. It was an accident."

"Accident my ass!" the general fired back. "It's the exact same thing that happened several years ago over Maryland when your people, using a weapon designed by our visitors, destroyed the Marines' White House helicopter. I, in my own mind, could never figure out if it was an accident or a real attempt on the President's life. Luckily, the President's plans changed and he wasn't aboard. This wouldn't be the first time some misguided military officials have tried to take over the country."

"Hold on general! I want you to know the microwave weapon your friends built was not intentionally used against the airplane. It was an unfortunate accident, which the American public must never find out about. As you probably heard and read, a navy vessel off the Long Island coast was simulating the use of the weapon, practicing and targeting all planes leaving JFK. U.S. military jet fighters do the same thing every day, using American airplanes for simulated target practice. Some malfunction in the ship's computer caused the microwave burst to fire on the targeted TWA plane. People who claim to have seen the flare of a rocket were partially right. What they saw was a micro burst of the microwave weapon. It's the government's newest secret weapon, as you well know, which will make the nuclear age obsolete. As far as the White House chopper incident, let's say that was an accident also. The only unfortunate thing about that incident was the fact that the four marines weren't burned to death, leaving no evidence. A forensic evidence expert, conducting the autopsies, found strange burn marks on the dead men's skin that were inconsistent with chemical or aviation fuel burns. You, general, know what caused those burns."

"Our friends at the compound are not stupid, colonel. It is for these reasons they refuse to offer any further assistance or provide us with knowledge that would enable the U.S. government to become the dominant power on this planet. They have always wanted us to work out our own problems with the resources we have here on earth. They will not interfere with the destiny of the earth. Quite truthfully, it was never their intent to share their advanced knowledge of weapons. Rather, they only agreed to provide us the wherewithal to curtail the arms race on earth."

"Further, they have been instrumental in helping us develop cures for major diseases and, as you know, they have shared their advanced technological knowledge. Undoubtedly, you have read in my reports that over the years their planet eradicated all diseases eons ago. It is the primary reason for their extremely long lives."

"Just which one of them gave you that garbage about no longer wishing to help us?"

"Colonel, the same one who has served as their spokesman for the last fifty years. Big Bird! He is an original descendent of the first visitors from their planet. Not wanting to help us is the least important thing we have to worry about right now. I'm sure I can talk some sense into Big Bird, but first we have to divert public and FBI attention away from this area."

"I thought you wanted to take care of that writer, too?"

"Right, Colonel! It looks as if you are going to have the responsibility for getting rid of that nuisance. I gave a direct order to Sheriff Cooper several hours ago to do just that. He refused to obey my order. Can you believe that sonofabitch? After all we have been through since 1947. He disobeyed my order. Do you have a problem with getting Davis out of the way, colonel?"

"No sir! Consider it done. In the interest of national security we will do what is necessary to ensure that the country's best interests aren't compromised."

"Ah, music to my ears!" the general smiled. "But remember, get him out of the way without resorting to anything deadly. I don't want any more deaths on my conscience."

"Good morning, Albuquerque, this is KBAL radio and you're on the air!"

"Hey, good morning, Lou! I listen to your show every morning and wouldn't miss it for anything."

"Well, thank you, listener. What's your name and your question?"

"My name is Vinny Duffy and I wanted to ask you what you think those strange lights were last night out over the western sky? They sure looked like flying saucers to me."

"Well, it seems as if everyone agrees with you, Vinny. If you heard our six o'clock news you know it's the talk of New Mexico. It seems everyone has seen those strange lights. From what I hear, police switchboards were lit up all over the state. We're told that the air force has said they couldn't confirm any sightings. Nothing showed up on their radar, they said. Probably some atmospheric conditions that made it appear as if there were UFOs. Are you listeners buying this junk from the government? Next, they're going to tell us it was a weather balloon, just like in 1947. Come on, listeners, the lines are open. Let me know what you think!"

Sheriff Cooper turned off the radio in his patrol car and turned up his police radio. All was quiet at six forty-five in the morning as he drove toward Brad Davis' motel. The sheriff knew if the general wanted Davis taken care of, the job would be done by someone. But that someone was not going to be Frank Cooper. This Project Anasazi was not something he had freely volunteered for. He had no choice when he was given orders by the general to be part of the project. It was something that just happened. He had been paid two thousand dollars a month on top of his sheriff's pay for the last ten years.

His involvement with the project began in the summer of 1947 when he was paid an extra five hundred dollars a month on top of his regular military pay. When he left the military and began working on the police force his Project Anasazi pay increased to one thousand dollars a month. He knew about the mountain compound and its residents, but really didn't know what went on there. His job was to keep the public away from the area and handle any outside problems that might arise. His confrontation with the general earlier in the morning finally made him realize that his principles to uphold the law and protect human life were more important than the project. Hence his decision not to let any harm come to Brad Davis. He reached the motel and immediately proceeded to Davis' room, knocking on the door.

"Just a minute!" the voice on the other side of the door called out. "Who is it?"

"Sheriff Cooper!" came the reply.

Opening the door, clad only in pajama bottoms and with shaving cream on his face, Davis was visibly surprised by the sheriff's visit. "What is it this time, sheriff? Does the general want to talk some more?"

"I'm sorry to bother you at this hour of the morning, Mr. Davis, but I need you to get dressed and come with me."

"I'm afraid not, sheriff. I have more other pressing plans that I have to take care of."

"You don't understand, Mr. Davis. You don't have a choice."

"Excuse me, sheriff? I don't have a choice? What the hell do you mean I don't have a choice? Have I done something wrong?"

"No, sir! I just think it's in your best interest if you come with me voluntarily."

"Well, sheriff, like I've already said, I've got more important things on my agenda."

"Please Mr. Davis, don't make this difficult for me."

"Look, sheriff, if you don't tell me what's going on I'm not going anywhere with you."

"Afraid I can't tell you anything. It's for your own good."

"Goodbye, sheriff."

"I'm placing you under arrest. Now get dressed and come peaceably."

"On what charge are you arresting me?"

"Resisting arrest will do for starters and I'm sure I can come up with a few others."

"Alright, I don't know what your game is, but I'll come along. Can I make a call to my lawyer in New York before you take me in?"

"No. You'll get your chance to make the one call you're entitled to down at police headquarters. I want you to get in your jeep and follow me into town."

Davis washed the shaving cream from his face and hurriedly dressed. He followed the sheriff out of his motel room and got into his car. "Don't worry, Sheriff, I'll follow you and promise I won't try any funny business." The drive to the small building housing the sheriff's office and one jail cell took all of two minutes. Davis was extremely perplexed at this sudden turn of events. All he could think about was the valuable time he was losing playing this game with the sheriff. Was General Brantfield behind this escapade, he thought? After all, he took on the general a few hours ago and it was obvious the general was hiding something from him. The general's agitation had been quite obvious.

The sheriff had parked his car and was moving toward Davis' car. He motioned Davis to get out of the car and move around to the passenger side. "Give me the keys to your vehicle, son," the sheriff said.

"What are you up to?" Davis asked, confused.

"Just get in your car. I'm going to be doing the driving." The sheriff ordered.

"Wait just a minute," Davis responded emphatically. "I thought we were going into your office so I could make a telephone call?"

"I didn't say which sheriff headquarters I was taking you to" the sheriff said as he slid behind the wheel of Davis' car. Tossing his police hat onto the back seat, he started the engine. "Okay, let's buckle up. We're going to take a little ride."

Colonel Wally Parker and his three men finished breakfast and returned to their vehicle. They had been given their orders for the day as they sat quietly talking and eating their breakfast at Mattie's place. Once outside they entered the black Ford Bronco, all except the colonel, who walked the block to the sheriff's office.

"Good morning!" the colonel greeted the lone man seated behind the desk.

"Good morning to you sir," came the reply.

The sheriff's office was in the front part of an old adobe style building which had long ago been slated for demolition, ever since Amnesty International convinced the government in Santa Fe to condemn the jail cells. The human rights group said the cells, which had no sinks or toilets, were unfit. There never was much use made of the cells, except to let one of the locals sleep off a heavy night of drinking. Sheriff Cooper was offered new offices in city hall, complete with two jail cells with running water and toilets, but he steadfastly refused to make the move. "Someday," he would always say.

"Yes, I'm looking for the sheriff."

Bones Laughlin stood up and moved to the front of the desk. Standing six-foot five and so lean it was a wonder the young deputy sheriff could keep his gun belt from sliding down over his hips. "Sheriff's not in. I expect he'll be back in about two hours. Can I help you?"

"Maybe you can. I was looking for a friend of mine who was traveling out this way. Being this is a small town you might know where I can find him. His name is Brad Davis."

"Yeah, I think I heard the sheriff talking about him. In fact, I think the sheriff had some kind of sheet on him. Let me look in the drawer here."

"He's not in any trouble, is he?"

"Oh, no. The sheriff did a background check on him. Sometimes we do that on strangers that show up in town and stay around for a while." Retrieving a folder from the top drawer, the deputy sheriff read out loud. "Yup, here it is! He's a writer doing some research out here. He used to work for *National Geographic*."

"Yes, yes, I know all that, Mr. Laughlin. I told you he was a friend."

"Oh, yeah, right!"

"Do you know where he might be staying or the kind of vehicle he's driving?"

"There's only one motel in town, the Magdalena Motel. Let me check the report here for a vehicle. Okay, here it is. It's a rented car out of Albuquerque. The vehicle is a Jeep Cherokee with New Mexico license plates AMR456."

"Thank you, deputy, you've been a big help." Colonel Parker walked back to the Bronco and got in alongside his driver. He turned to the two men seated in the rear seat. "We're going to drive by the motel where this Davis is staying and see if he's there. Then we're going to ride over to Socorro where you two will rent a car and then track down this guy. Ideally, we want to wait until he's out riding in his car and then have him become a road fatality. Once you've done that, take the car back to the rental agency and get rid of it. Then take a plane and head back to Washington and wait for further orders. Okay, let's see if our friend is at the motel." Driving past the Magdalena Motel there was no sign of Davis' Jeep Cherokee. The colonel motioned the driver to drive on. "We'll find him later. Let's get you two a rental car."

It was close to eight o'clock when Big Bird showed up at the general's house. Instead of his usual pony tail Big Bird's hair was shoulder length, neatly shaped and combed. He wore a colorful red, blue and grey headband with the figure of an eagle prominently in place on the front. A tan buckskin jacket covered a multicolored Navajo shirt. His jeans hung just right on his cowboy boots, the back part of the leg sitting just below where the boot and heel meet.

"Big Bird, I'm glad you're here!" The general greeted the Indian cordially. His voice was a little hoarse and his usual formal bearing was missing this morning.

"General, are you all right? You look and sound weary."

"Weary. That's a good word for it, Harold." He rarely called Big Bird by his first name, only in times when he was worried about something.

"What is troubling you, my friend?"

"Your family is back."

"That is true!"

"Have you spoken with them yet?"

"Yes, as we always speak. As we have spoken all my life."

"No, no, don't talk mumbo jumbo to me! I know you have ways of communicating with them without them being around. I mean in person."

"Not until the sun sets today will I meet with them."

"Why are they back so soon, Harold? They're not expected for a number of years."

135

"It is not too soon for them, Nathaniel. It has been over fifty years since their visit to Roswell and they have decided, once again, the time is right. They are back to take those who wish to return to the land of their fathers."

"But, why now, almost fifty-two years to the day?"

"They decided it was time that our people leave this planet to live in harmony in our land. There is no harmony here. I doubt if there ever will be. We have tried to provide you guidance in bringing peaceful changes to the world. We have been trying to help you eradicate disease on this planet by offering our experience in uncovering natural roots and herbs to conquer disease. Dacon has been a disease free planet for a long time. We learned to use what was found naturally in our forests and oceans. Unfortunately, Earth has a different environment and my people have been working diligently these past fifty years to work with those things found naturally here on earth to cure your diseases. It has not been easy."

"I know that and we have appreciated all your efforts. But I'm afraid you're all going to go away and leave us. You and I both know of the growing discontent among your people in the compound. I know the world is a troubled place, but look at all the good your work has done over the years. Please, please, I beg you to let them stay a little longer."

"That's not my decision, Nathaniel. Remember, I am born of this earth, but I am also one of them. If it is ordained that all my brothers are to return to Dacon, it shall be so. If it is permitted, those who wish to stay may stay. It may be ordained that I must leave also."

"Can't you talk to them and convince them to stay?"

"Nathaniel, Nathaniel, have you not listened to my brothers when they have talked with you lately? They look around and see a world that is no better than the day they arrived. They came in curiosity and stayed with the hope of improving this world. Fifty years later they see things worse than when they arrived. All my brothers are asking to leave."

"Is there no way I can convince them to stay?"

"None, my friend. I must go now. I have been summoned."

"What do you mean?"

"It is time for my meeting!"

"How do you know they want you now? You said they were going to meet with you tonight."

"We will talk later."

"Wait! Big Bird, tell them I wish to meet with the leader of the exploration team from Dacon."

"You will, general, you will!"

CHAPTER NINE

The New Mexico State Police Headquarters in Socorro was located a block off Interstate 25 on Hazel Street in downtown Socorro. The building was a one story structure which housed offices on the first floor with the basement serving as a temporary jail for drunk drivers and those guilty of other minor offenses waiting to be transported to the county jail. It had taken Sheriff Cooper a little over a half-hour to drive from Magdalena to the state police headquarters. He knew his friend Captain Gerard would hold Davis in jail long enough for him to try to find a solution to his problem. He was hoping to talk the general into changing his mind about Davis being a threat. As long as he could keep him off the streets for twelve hours the sheriff felt Davis would be safe. Sheriff Cooper parked the Jeep Cherokee in the police lot behind the building. Both men entered the building through the rear door and proceeded to the dispatcher at the front desk.

"Is Captain Gerard available?" the sheriff asked.

"Sure, he's in his office down the hall," the dispatcher replied, never looking up from the paper he was reading.

"Thanks." The sheriff motioned Davis to follow him down the

hall. The door to Captain Gerard's office was open and the slightly balding man standing at the filing cabinet with his back to the door didn't hear the two men enter his office.

"Hey, Stan, you must be losing your hearing," Sheriff Cooper called out to his friend.

"What?" Gerard, turning and recognizing Frank Cooper, reached to shake his hand. "Well, hello, Frank, it's good to see you. Sorry, I was so engrossed in filing these UFO reports I didn't hear you come in. By the way, thanks for your help on the interstate. What brings you over this way?"

"I was hoping you would keep an eye on Mr. Davis for me."

"You mean like in a jail cell?"

"Exactly."

"Sure. What did he do? He doesn't look like the criminal type."

"He's not. I just want him held in protective custody until I get back here within twelve hours."

"Protective custody!" Brad Davis shouted at the sheriff. "So that's what this is all about. Well sheriff, I don't need protective custody and I demand my one phone call."

"Here, use the phone on my desk." Captain Stan Gerard pushed the telephone toward Davis.

"Hope you're there, Susan." Davis said to himself as he dialed her New York number. After several rings the recording came on and Davis immediately hung up. "Damn!" he said out loud. "I need to make another call since there was no answer on my first call."

"Sorry, Mr. Davis," Sheriff Cooper said as he placed his hand over the phone, pushing it away from Davis. "You've had your one phone call."

"Hey, Frank, let him make another call," Captain Gerard interjected. "It's no big deal and you yourself said he was here for protective custody."

"No, he's had his one phone call. Now please, Stan, lock him up. I'll be back before the end of the day to pick him up."

"Okay, Frank, but you had better be back by five o'clock or I'll set him free." Captain Gerard motioned Davis to follow him out of his office and down the hall to the door leading to the cells in the basement.

"I strongly protest your locking me up, sheriff, and you can bet your ass I'm going to press charges for false arrest and unlawful imprisonment." Davis looked the sheriff straight in the eyes as he voiced his unhappiness at this set of events. The sheriff said nothing, holding a blank stare, as Davis followed Gerard down the hall.

The two Air Force intelligence men had rented a Ford Taurus from a local rental car agency in Socorro. They were assured they could drop the car off at the Albuquerque airport without paying a drop-off charge. It was close to nine o'clock when the Taurus turned off of Interstate 25 and headed west on Route 60, back toward Magdalena. About two miles ahead of them Sheriff Cooper was returning to Magdalena in Davis' Jeep Cherokee. A half hour earlier, after leaving state police headquarters, the sheriff had stopped for breakfast at the McDonald's across the street. Following a sausage McMuffin, hash browns, and a cup of coffee he returned to Davis' vehicle. Getting behind the wheel, Frank Cooper found he was uncomfortable wearing his gun belt. He unbuckled his holster and carefully placed it alongside his hat on the back seat where he had placed it when he began the drive to Socorro. Placing his unfinished second cup of coffee in the holder on the console he started the engine and began the drive back to Magdalena. As he drove, he thought about Davis and how he disliked putting the writer in jail, but given the present circumstances, it was his only option. Taking a sip of coffee, he convinced himself it was the right decision and put the matter out of his mind. Looking down at the speedometer the sheriff realized he was doing close to eighty. Quickly, he eased up on the gas pedal and reduced his speed to the legal limit of sixty-five on Route 60.

The car being driven by the military intelligence men was exceeding the speed limit by twenty miles an hour and was slowly catching up to the car being driven by Sheriff Cooper. Their directive was to get back to Magdalena as quickly as possible, find Davis and eliminate him. Killing was not difficult for these men as they had been involved with covert military operations in Panama, Grenada, Somalia and other hot spots around the world.

Recently, they had been part of an advanced group of military sent to Haiti by the UN. Their special assignment as part of this group was to ensure the peaceful reestablishment of former Prime Minister

Jean-Bertrand Aristide as the lawful ruler of the island nation. US undercover operations called for them to quietly and methodically take out key opposition leaders in the present government, thus paving the way for the return of the exiled leader. With execution style precision, they quietly assassinated their targets, making it look as if the victims were killed by locals.

Their justification for carrying out the executions was that justice would be well-served by bringing peace back to Haiti. After all, they reasoned, it was in the best interest of US national security to bring Aristide back to power in Haiti. The US didn't want communism getting a foothold in another Caribbean country. And so, the military men killed easily in Haiti and they knew someday they would kill again in the name of national security.

The driver of the Taurus spoke first. "Hardly any traffic today."

"Yeah," replied the broad shouldered man in the passenger seat. "The only other car we've seen for the last ten minutes is that car up ahead of us."

"Guess it's not tourist season yet. I've only counted three cars and a truck coming the other way. By the way, when we get back to Magdalena what kind of vehicle are we looking for?"

"Jeep Cherokee, why?"

"Just curious. It seems you see a lot of those kinds of vehicles these days. Broncos, Blazers and Jeeps everywhere. The automobile manufacturers sure did a good sell job on the American public getting them to switch from station wagons to these utility vehicles. See what

I mean?" The driver pointed to the vehicle in front of them. "There's one of them Jeeps right there ahead of us. It sure would be our lucky day if that was the vehicle we were looking for so we didn't have to go all the way back to that hick town."

"No, we couldn't get that lucky." The passenger leaned forward in his seat to get a better look at the Jeep. "Why don't you get a little closer look?"

The driver accelerated to get within a hundred yards of the lone car in front of them. "Have you got the license number of that Jeep we're supposed to find?"

Reaching into his jacket pocket, the passenger pulled out a slip of paper with the license number. "Now, don't get your hopes up. Chances are a million to one of this being our target." Unfolding the slip of paper, he read out the license number. "New Mexico plate AMR456."

"Hey, that could be our car," the driver said excitedly.

"Nah, you're only hoping it's our target. It's wishful thinking on your part."

"Well, I'm going to get closer so we can get a better look at that license plate."

"Bingo, Mr. Lucky!" the passenger shouted as he shifted his weight forward in the seat. "Buy your lottery ticket now! This is your lucky day!"

The driver slowed down letting a distance of a hundred yards separate the vehicles. "How do we go about taking him out? Do we ram him and force him off the road or do we shoot him in the head?"

"No, no" the passenger responded to the driver's question. "We don't want it to look like a killing resulting in an investigation. I say we shoot out his tires making him to lose control and crash. If the crash doesn't finish him off, we'll take a tire iron and smash his skull. It will look like he died of a blow to the head when the jeep crashed."

"Okay, you're the boss on this one. It's your call."

"Since you're driving and I'm the better shot, I'll take care of the dirty work. I'll be able to get a better shot at him from the passenger side as we pull up alongside him."

"Are you ready?"

"Yeah, there doesn't seem to be any other cars on the road right now. Go for it!" the passenger said, as he pulled his semi-automatic from his shoulder holster and rolled down the window.

Slowly, the Ford Taurus pulled out to pass on the two-lane road, carefully avoiding abrupt moves that would cause the driver of the Jeep Cherokee to become suspicious. The Taurus inched up slowly until the front bumper was aligned with the rear bumper of the Jeep. "Ready?" the driver asked. "Let me move up a little more so you can get a clear shot of the front and rear tires on the drivers' side. As soon as you take the shots, I'm going to slam on the brakes so we don't get hit by the Jeep when it loses control."

"I'm ready," the passenger said as he leaned the gun on his forearm resting on the window ledge. The road was flat and no traffic could be seen coming from the distance, allowing the Taurus to pass without having to worry about oncoming traffic. There was no traffic behind them either.

Frank Cooper had been checking his rearview mirror for the last five miles, watching the car that had been slowly catching up to him. His years of experience taught him always to be cautious and on the lookout for strange behavior. There were plenty of opportunities for the car behind him to pass yet the car made only one attempt to get close and then backed off. Maybe he was being paranoid, he thought. It was probably some old driver who just felt comfortable staying being behind another car way in this remote area. Old people, he reasoned, felt the need for such security when they were driving out here.

He watched as the car now pulled out to pass and begin to overtake him. He sighed a sigh of relief. Strange feeling, he thought, as he caught a glimpse of the two people in the rearview mirror. He followed the vehicle's movement with his eyes as it moved from his rearview mirror into his side view mirror. They certainly weren't old people. Suddenly, through his side view mirror, he saw a gun pointed at him. Instinctively, he reached for his gun which was not there, but on the back seat where he laid it earlier. "Damn!" he said out loud. Putting his foot to the gas pedal and swerving into the path of the passing car, Cooper hoped to make the gunman miss his mark. Two shots rang out in quick succession, both shots immediately finding their target. With both tires blowing out almost simultaneously, it was impossible for Cooper to control the Jeep. It rocked and swerved from one side of the road to the other. He had all he could do to keep his hands on the steering wheel. The driver of the Taurus immediately slammed on the brakes, attempting not to get hit by the Jeep's maneuvering to regain control. Both Air Force intelligence men watched the Jeep go through its dying gyrations before finally crashing through the guardrail, tumbling down the embankment into the dry gully below, coming to a rest on its top. Fire immediately engulfed the crumpled Jeep. The Ford Taurus pulled to the side of the road above where the jeep burned.. Both men looked down dispassionately at the fiery scene.

"Think we should check and make sure he's dead?" the gunman asked.

Just then the burning Jeep exploded, a large fiery cloud rising over the vehicle. In the distance the two military men saw a vehicle approaching from the direction of Socorro. Not wanting to be found at the scene they jumped into the vehicle and headed back to Socorro. "I don't think we have to worry about him anymore," the driver said, grinning from ear to ear. "Let's get the car back to the rental agency."

Susan Adams had checked out of the Albuquerque motel early. She was dressed in jeans, cardigan sweater and boots, prepared to hike around the New Mexico mountains until she found Brad Davis. Eating a quick breakfast at the motel restaurant, she was eager to be on her way. The Buick Skylark she rented had seen better days. The speedometer read 32,457 miles, but the car rode and handled like it had just completed the Baja Road Rally. She didn't want to waste time exchanging the car, but she vowed to lodge a complaint when she returned it.

Looking at the roadmap the rental car agency had given her, Susan traced the route she needed to take to reach Magdalena, a small dot west of Socorro on Route 60. Brad's last recorded telephone message had mentioned he could be traced through Mama B's in Magdalena. Route 60 was clearly marked as an exit off of Interstate 25 which made it easy for her not to get lost. Being a city person, she did have a habit of easily getting lost in strange places.

The car had been traveling along Route 60 at a leisurely pace since leaving the interstate when she saw dark smoke rising ahead. The further she drove west the darker the smoke became. Up ahead she saw a large dirty car speeding away towards Magdalena from where dense smoke was rising from a gully below the highway.

Pulling the car to the side of the road, Susan got out of the car and walked to the edge of the road, gasping at what she saw below, a crushed, blackened overturned vehicle, barely recognizable, was smoldering, billowing black smoke into the air. A few flames licked at the remains of what once was a jeep.

Susan quickly scrambled down the side of the ravine hoping somehow to find someone who might have survived this accident. The smoke was still too thick for her to get too close and peer into the wreckage. She scouted the sage brush and cactus on the side of the sloping hill leading down to the gully, hoping to find someone who may have been thrown clear. Nothing! Just then she heard a voice from up on the highway.

"Hey, lady, what happened?" a short, fat, bald man dressed in dungarees and a brightly colored flannel shirt asked.

"I don't know," she replied. "I just got here and saw this car burning."

"How long ago do you think it happened?"

"My guess is no more than ten minutes. I saw the smoke from a few miles back."

"Me, too," said the bald man, "I was driving east on my way to Albuquerque when I saw the smoke. I'm going back across the road to my car and call the state police on my car phone. Can you see anyone in the car?"

"No," Susan replied as she felt a cold chill run down her spine. "If anyone is in there, he sure as hell is dead." Susan walked around the car at a safe distance to see if she could find any sign of life.

The short man was back, now joined by a few other people driving by who stopped to see what the commotion was all about. "Police said they'd be here in five minutes."

Susan climbed the embankment back to her car.

"Were you in that car, lady?" One of the onlookers asked. Susan merely shook her head no and opened the car door, sliding in behind the steering wheel, closing the door behind her. The four or five people continued to gawk at the vehicle below, talking among themselves about the cause of the crash and whether there was anyone still inside the car. Susan was nauseous at the thought that someone had died in the crash, probably a horrible death by burning. As a reporter she had seen death before many times, but it was never easy for her. She knew the awful stench of burned flesh, which, strangely, she didn't detect at this wreck. One night as a cub reporter she had covered a tenement fire in Harlem where three children had been trapped in their fifth floor apartment and all burned to death. She was allowed to follow the firemen into the burned out apartment after the fire was out. Those three charred corpses piled one on top of another in front of the window was a sight that still haunted her dreams. And the smell! That same smell did not come from this car and she couldn't understand why, if someone had been trapped inside the vehicle. Susan, white as a sheet and perspiring profusely, did everything in her power not to throw up. A knock on her window brought her back to the present.

"Hello, are you okay?" the state trooper asked through the closed car window. "May I talk with you, please?"

Susan was too weak at the moment to get out of the car. She rolled down the window. "Yes, officer, how can I help you?"

The gentleman over there said you were the first one on the scene here."

"That's right!"

"Did you see what happened?"

"No. I saw the smoke from a distance and stopped to see what was causing it."

"Did you see any other cars nearby or shortly after you first noticed the smoke?"

"I don't remember seeing any other cars in front of me or for that matter, passing me."

"What about coming from the other direction? Somebody driving extremely fast?"

"My brain is a little foggy right now and I can't really be sure of anything."

"I was just trying to find if there may have been another vehicle involved in this accident and they left the scene. Are you all right, miss? You look a little pale."

"I'll be alright. This sight has been a little unnerving. Wait a minute! I do remember something! There was a four-door car, very dirty, that was pulling away from here as I arrived."

"Did you happen to get the license number?"

"No," Susan shook her head weakly.

"Okay. I'll ask some of the other people here if they saw such a vehicle. Right now I suggest if you live around here you go home."

"No, I'm from New York."

"Then, miss, I really recommend you find yourself a motel and get some rest until you feel better. Where you headed?"

"To Magdalena. I hope to meet up with my boy friend."

"Look, there's a small motel there. Why don't you spend the night until you feel better. If you don't feel well enough to drive I can get someone to drive you over to Magdalena."

"No, thanks, I'll be fine."

"Okay, but before you go, I need to have your name and address for my report. I'm also going to question the gentleman who called in the accident. Maybe he can recollect seeing any speeding cars heading west."

As Susan finished talking to the trooper, a loud voice called out. "Hey Deke, it seems you got yourself a nasty mess down there."

"Hey, Running Horse, what are you doing so far from home?" The trooper asked.

"Heard about the call over the scanner on my way to pick up a car north of Socorro. I figured I could make some money going both ways. Maybe I could tow your wreck over to headquarters and then pick up my other vehicle."

"Sorry, Running Horse, not this time. We'll need a flat bed after the coroner gets here. You can't tow that wreck the way it is."

"Well, let me go down and take a look at it anyway. Hello, miss!" Running Horse smiled as he addressed himself to Susan, still seated in her car. "My name is Running Horse."

"Hello, Running Horse. My name is Susan Adams."

"Were you in the wreck?"

"I'll tell you the whole story later," the trooper interrupted. "She's not feeling well and I think she should be on her way."

"Sorry, miss. Glad you weren't in the wreck."

The trooper thanked Susan and sent her on her way. He then joined Running Horse climbing down the embankment to the remains of the smoldering vehicle. Reaching the overturned vehicle, Running Horse circled the blackened wreck, inspecting it closely and then examining the scorched license plate. He let out a loud "Yiiii."

"What the hell is that for, Running Horse?" the astonished trooper asked.

"I recognize the vehicle."

"What do you mean, you recognize it? Do you really know who owns this car?"

"Yes! It's what's left of a Jeep Cherokee and I can still barely make out the license plates...AMR456."

"Don't jump to conclusions until I get verification from motor vehicle." The trooper pulled out his two-way radio and barked a request. "This is trooper Danzig. Can you get a make on a vehicle for me?" The police officer provided the dispatcher with the information she needed. In less than five minutes Danzig's radio came to life. "Have you got that information?"

"Yes, we do," the dispatcher responded. "The vehicle is a rental out of Albuquerque. Name of the renter is Brad Davis."

"Thank you, dispatch. Is that who you thought it was, Running Horse? Was he a friend of yours?"

"Sort of! I can't believe he's dead. He must not have been wearing his rattlesnake bracelet."

"Oh, don't tell me your mother is still peddling that silly superstition?"

"You keep making fun of our beliefs. Not being of Indian blood you could never understand the power of the Indian spirits. If Mr. Davis was wearing his bracelet, he would still be alive."

Trooper Danzig smiled. "Running Horse, take my word for it, anyone in that car, bracelet or not, is dead."

"I have a heavy heart and cannot stay any longer."

"Yeah, there's no sense you hanging around here. Not much any of us can do except pick up the pieces. Look, I'll be here for awhile waiting for the medical examiner and getting the wreck out of here. If I come across anything unusual or can give you more information I'll give you a call. In the meantime, can you stop by headquarters and drop off my preliminary report to Captain Gerard. I'd really appreciate it. Thanks."

Running Horse placed the trooper's report on the front seat of the tow truck. He walked back to the edge of the road taking one last look down at what had been Brad Davis' Jeep. So many dreams lost, he thought. He offered a prayer to the gods, asking them to allow Brad Davis to be a hunter, letting him join with other warrior braves in the next world. Running Horse waved goodbye to Susan as he returned to his truck. Starting his engine, he headed for Socorro, chanting an Indian prayer for the soul of Davis as he drove.

CHAPTER TEN

Running Horse drove the twelve miles to Socorro at a leisurely pace. Many things were running through his mind. This has been a week of strange occurrences: the lights and sounds across the Plains of San Agustin, meeting Davis and his story of his car losing power, and now an accident that takes his life. Did all these things have something in common with the piece of metal that he had shown Davis? Was there some connection? Did he anger the gods by showing the metal to Davis?

Running Horse knew he was not capable of finding the answer by himself. He was thinking of having a meeting with the tribal council in order to make sense of these things. On second thought, he hadn't met with the tribal council in more than thirty years, and maybe this wasn't the right topic to discuss with them, at least not at this time.

Parking the tow truck on the street in front of state police headquarters, Running Horse walked through the front door, waving and smiling weakly at the dispatcher seated at the front desk. He continued on down the hall to Captain Gerard's office. The captain was talking on the two-way radio. He motioned Running Horse to take a seat and holding up one finger, indicating he would be with him in one minute. Placing the radio back in its charger, Gerard greeted Running Horse.

"Running Horse, it's good to see you. How long has it been since we last saw each other?"

"Too many moons, Captain," Running Horse responded.

"Yeah, I guess you're right. It was over at the county rodeo eight months ago. That *was* many moons ago. What brings you over to these parts?"

"I was headed over here to tow a car back home for a local who was in an accident last week. On my way I came upon an accident out on Route 60."

"Oh, you mean the one Danzig is handling."

"Yes, and he asked me to drop off the preliminary report to you since there was a rental car involved and someone needed to alert them."

"Right. Don't know much more than the fact there was a wreck out there. Danzig called it in when he arrived on the scene. He'll probably be out there for some time so now with his report we'll be able to notify the car rental agency. That way they can get someone to investigate from the insurance side."

"That Jeep Cherokee sure didn't look much like anything after it ended up in the gully and burned. I recognized the car and knew the driver."

"How's that?" the sheriff asked, surprised. "Was he a local?"

"No, he was a writer out of New York I met when he had car trouble. He came out here to do some research on the Anasazi for a book he was going to write."

The sheriff stood up abruptly. "That's a coincidence! I have a fellow under lock and key that's a writer doing some Indian research. I don't think there could be two people doing the same kind of work. What was his name?"

"Brad Davis!"

"That's impossible, Running Horse!" the captain said as he moved to where Running Horse was seated. "A young fellow named Brad Davis is sitting in a jail cell downstairs."

"That can't be, Captain!" Running Horse stood up and faced the captain. "I know that was the car Brad Davis was driving!"

"Well, Sheriff Cooper brought him over here this morning and asked me to keep him in protective custody until he picked him up later today."

"Protective custody? What for?"

"Don't know. He wouldn't explain."

Running Horse grabbed Gerard's arm. "You don't think the sheriff could have been driving that vehicle?"

"I'm not sure! But there's one sure fire way to find out. Sergeant, go down and bring up Mr. Davis from his cell." Captain Gerard called out. The sergeant returned within a few minutes followed by Brad Davis. "Thank you sergeant. Mr. Davis, you know Running Horse here, I presume?"

"Sure do! How are you, old friend? What are you doing way over here? You couldn't possibly have come over here to bail me out."

Running Horse, excited at the sight of seeing Davis alive, put his arms around him, giving him a strong hug. "I am so happy to see you alive, my friend."

"Whoa! Go easy on the joy and hugging. You almost choked me to death. Now, what's this about being glad to see me alive? What's going on?"

Before Running Horse could respond, Captain Gerard held up his hand for both men to stop their conversation. "Mr. Davis, I have to know how Sheriff Cooper got you over here. Did you come in his police car?"

"No, he left it in front of his office in Magdalena. Why, did something happen to the sheriff?"

Captain Gerard sat down behind his desk and reached for the telephone. "Before we jump to any conclusions, let's call over to his office and see if he's there." Gerard dialed Sheriff Cooper's number.

"Magdalena Sheriff's Office, Deputy Laughlin speaking."

"Bones. This is Captain Gerard over in Socorro."

"Hi! How you doing, Captain? I was about to call you, looking for the sheriff. One of your troopers, Danzig I think his name was, called over here for some help on a highway accident. I couldn't oblige because I'm all alone over here until the sheriff gets back. Have you seen him?"

"No, that's why I was calling you."

"Has something happened to him?" Bones Laughlin inquired in a concerned voice.

"Don't know. Do me a favor and check outside and see if the sheriff's car is parked outside."

"Don't have to! I can see it through the window. He left it there earlier when he drove off in that writer's car. He said he'd be back within two hours and I'm still waiting. Are you sure something hasn't happened to him?"

"I'll call you back, Bones, when I know something more on where the sheriff is. In the meantime, if you need backup on anything, just give a holler." Gerard hung up the phone slowly.

"What is it, Captain?" Davis and Running Horse asked in unison.

"I'm afraid to think of the possibility that it could have been Frank Cooper in that car."

"Would you mind telling me what the hell is going on?" Davis demanded. Has something happened to my Jeep and Sheriff Cooper?"

The captain motioned for both men to take a seat. "Sergeant, I don't want to be interrupted for awhile." Gerard called out as he closed the door to his office. After Running Horse and Captain Gerard finished telling Davis about the accident, Gerard pulled a note pad from his desk. "Okay, gentlemen, something very odd is going on here and I want to know what the hell it is. I'm going to be taking it all down, so don't leave out anything, no matter how trivial you may think it is. Let's begin with why Sheriff Cooper wanted you under protective custody, Mr. Davis. What was he protecting you from?"

"Damned if I know. He whisked me out of my motel room this morning. He refused to answer any of my questions."

"Were you involved in something or did you see something that he thought you should be protected from?"

"No! The only strange thing about it was the fact that the night before I met with retired General Brantfield and he was upset with me."

"*The* General Nathaniel Brantfield of Roswell and 1947 fame?"

"One and the same!"

"What was he upset about?"

"Don't know. Could have been something else was bothering him and he just got angry at me because I was around at the time."

"I didn't know he was still alive." Gerard stopped writing for a minute.

"He's still alive!" interjected Running Horse. "Very strange man and he spends a lot of time around Alegros Mountain."

"How do you know that, Running Horse?" Gerard asked as he continued writing.

"That's my territory and I'm driving that road between Pie Town and Horse Springs all the time. Sometime he's alone and sometimes he's with some Indians in a jeep."

"What do you think he's doing there?"

"Don't know. He's been doing that for as long as I can remember. Now that I think about it, I remember seeing him up there when he was still in charge of Roswell Air Base, what used to be called 509th

Army Air Field, and ever since he was supposed to be retired. That's strange, isn't it?"

Gerard turned his attention to Brad Davis. "Mr. Davis, do you know anything about Alegros Mountain and why the general would be up there?"

"No, can't help you there, captain," Davis lied.

"Brad, tell the captain how we met when you had trouble with your Jeep up there and then you went up there again the next day," Running Horse prodded Davis.

"Not much to tell, really. I was almost to the top of the mountain headed to Pie Town when the car went dead. Everything electrical wouldn't work. Then Running Horse showed up and the car started right up. Running Horse checked my Jeep out at his service station and found nothing wrong. Guess it was just a tough climb for the car and it choked out. Haven't given it a second thought since."

"What about the next day, Mr. Davis. Did you go back up there?"

"Sure. Remember I'm out here doing research on the Anasazi for my book."

"Did you find anything when you went up the next day?"

"Nothing, I'm afraid."

"What about your vehicle? Did you have any more trouble with your vehicle?"

"No."

"In your meeting with General Brantfield last night, just what did you discuss?"

"I wanted to ask him if, in his travels around the area, he came across any old Anasazi sites, Davis lied.

"Are you sure that's all you discussed?"

"Positive," Davis lied again.

"That doesn't sound like something that would have caused the general to get angry at you. All in all, I don't think the sheriff was trying to protect you from him. It must have been something else. Try to think, Mr. Davis, is there something else you did or said since you came out here that made the sheriff think he had to protect you?"

"Like I said, captain, nothing."

"There's something strange going on here. Running Horse, what do you think?"

Running Horse shrugged his shoulders. "Can't imagine what would have made the sheriff do that to Mr. Davis."

"Damn!" Gerard banged his clenched fist on the desk. "Too many weird things happening around here."

"What weird things?" asked Davis.

"The strange lights out over the Plains of San Agustin, the humming sound getting louder, and those UFO's last night."

"What UFO's are you talking about?" Davis leaned forward in his chair.

"Didn't you hear the radio and television news reports this morning?"

"Hardly. Sheriff Cooper pulled me out of the motel room before

I even finished shaving. He barely let me get dressed. Tell me about them."

"Not much to tell. I didn't see them myself, but supposedly our switchboard lit up all night long with people calling in wanting to know what was going on. Those were the reports I was filing this morning when Frank brought you in here. Evidently, there were two or three UFO's sighted last night, depending on who you can believe. Regardless, there were enough sightings by upstanding citizens to make you say that everyone can't be seeing things. Albuquerque airport and Kirkland Air Force Base said they didn't have any blips on their radar. Air Force people over at Alamogordo said they saw nothing and could find no trace of any UFO's. They said people were probably looking at a planet and if you look at long enough it appears to move. Knowing the U.S. Air Force and their record with such things, I would say something was really flying around up there last night."

"It's been some time since we have had sightings here in New Mexico. The latest one I remember was one of our troopers right here in Socorro, along with hundreds of other local folks, saw this strange craft come down just beyond town. They all said there were two people dressed in white suits and funny looking helmets walking around the craft, then climbing a ladder into the space vehicle. Next thing you know, the trooper said, the craft made a low whining sound, lifting to about 500 feet and then heading off in a westerly direction. We all speculated about it for a number of years until one day we got to see what the U.S. moon landing craft looked like. Almost everyone who saw the so-called UFO years earlier remarked how much the moon landing craft looked like what they saw that night. The way I figure it, the government was testing that craft out here and didn't want anyone knowing what they were doing. Typical! And the only other time I remember was in 1947 when the military boys said it was a balloon and not an alien space craft that crashed. I was just a kid back then, but I remember my father talking about it. He said a public relations man for the military first issued a news release about a UFO crashing and finding parts. The next thing you know the military is putting a lid on everything, saying that it was a weather balloon."

"The media wouldn't let it alone, but after a while they gave up and everyone forgot about it. Not my father! Not to the day he died! He said he saw a piece of the UFO wreckage, a piece of strange metal that he had never seen before." Brad Davis and Running Horse both shot each other a glance. "Why did you two look at each other when I mentioned the metal? You know something about this metal I'm talking about?"

"No," Davis answered quickly. "It sounds so outrageous! A piece of metal from a UFO?"

"Yeah, stop pulling our legs, captain."

"Oh, so you don't believe me, huh? My father never lied and he had no reason to make up such a story."

"If you say so, captain."

"Forget it, and get the hell out of here, the both of you." Captain Gerard smiled as he gestured the two men out of his office. "I can't hold you any longer, Mr. Davis, so you're free to go. I'm finished taking notes on your case. Besides, I've got too much work to do to be farting around with the likes of you two. Mr. Davis, leave me a telephone number where I can reach you if I need you."

"I'm staying at the Magdalena Motel."

"Stay out of trouble!" All three men exchanged handshakes.

"Running Horse, keep those Indian spirits of yours in check. And thanks for bringing in the report. See you again." The telephone on the captain's desk rang as the men were leaving. Both Running Horse and Brad Davis stopped and turned to the man answering the telephone. "Would you please repeat that!" Gerard cupped the mouthpiece of the phone and waved both men off. When Davis and Running Horse were out of the office, Gerard resumed his conversation on the phone. "Alright Danzig, give that to me again! Well, how do you explain a burning car, upside down in a gully, in the middle of nowhere, and nobody inside the vehicle? It's bloody impossible! Did you check all around the perimeter to see if someone was thrown clear of the vehicle? Someone had to be driving! Keep checking until you find someone or something!" Gerard hung up the telephone, pushed himself away from the desk and turned to look out the window behind his desk. "Damn," he muttered, "New Mexico should be called the Land of Mystery instead of the Land of Enchantment! Where did Sheriff Cooper disappear to?"

Brad Davis and Running Horse left state police headquarters by the front door. Running Horse was the first to speak. "Captain Gerard was right. Something strange is going on and I don't like it. You're not going back to that motel." Running Horse took Davis by the arm. "You're coming home with me. Get in the truck."

"Wait a minute!" Davis said. I haven't had a thing to eat all day and I'm starved. What do you say if I treat you to a Big Mac and fries across the street at McDonalds? We need to talk before we go anywhere."

"Since its lunchtime and I'm hungry also, let's eat."

Both men walked quietly across the street, lost in their own thoughts. They ordered their food and sat at a table in the front part of the restaurant. Both unwrapped their sandwiches, looking out toward the tow truck parked in front of the state police headquarters. Before taking his first bite, Davis leaned across the table and said softly. "Are you thinking what I'm thinking?"

"About the piece of metal Gerard talked about?"

"You don't think our glancing at each other made him think we knew anything about the metal?"

"I think your answer about us thinking he was a bit crazy satisfied him."

"Okay, Running Horse, you're the resident expert on the metal and some history about it. Do you think there's a connection between the metal, the UFO's last night and what I saw up in the mountains?"

"Right now, I don't know what to think."

"Before I tell you about my experience on Alegros Mountain, I want you to tell me what you think about Sheriff Cooper getting killed in my Jeep?"

"I don't think it was an accident and I think someone may have thought you were driving the vehicle."

"That's nonsense!" Davis said nervously playing with his sandwich.

"It's a distinct possibility and you'd better start looking over your shoulder." Running Horse responded.

"What are you talking about?"

"I got a good look at that vehicle of yours down in the gully. If there had been an accident with another car, chances are the other car would have stayed around."

"Maybe not." Davis took a sip of his coke. "Suppose they got scared when they saw how bad the wreck was and took off?"

"That would make sense if there was evidence of being rammed by another car. But the dents in the side of the Jeep got there as the vehicle rolled down the embankment. There was no visible damage anywhere indicating it came in contact with another vehicle."

"Maybe you couldn't tell the difference."

"You forget I make my living from towing wrecks and repairing cars. This one was different. I didn't like the looks of it from the start."

"Maybe the sheriff fell asleep at the wheel. He told me he was up late last night clearing a wreck from the highway."

"No, I can't believe that." Running Horse leaned closer to Davis and in a soft voice said, "Now tell me what you didn't tell Captain Gerard."

"What are you talking about?"

"I know you weren't telling the truth to him about your conversation with General Brantfield."

"How do you know that?" Davis smirked.

"Again, it's a feeling. I had a suspicion you were going to go back where you broke down that first time we met. And you did!"

"Yes."

"And, did you discover anything?"

"I discovered something very strange that I couldn't explain. Now that I know of the UFO's last night and the strange metal you have, just maybe, all these things have something in common. And I think the general is involved or knows more that he lets on."

"It makes sense that they could all possibly tie together and that's what the general is afraid of. Whatever you said to the general put a fright into him and I think he told the sheriff. The sheriff, fearing the general may do something drastic, brought you over to Socorro."

"That doesn't make sense."

"Oh, no? You've heard me say that I've seen the general and military men up in that vicinity. I think there's a big military secret about that place. I always get bad vibes about that place. It's something more than just spirits."

"You're suspicious as hell."

"Exactly what did you discover on Alegros Mountain and what did you tell General Brantfield, Brad? You must trust me! I can help you," Running Horse pleaded.

"Alright! I found a village of houses deep through the woods in a clearing. On the far cliff wall I saw what looked like cliff dwellings."

"Nobody has ever mentioned there being such a place with houses and cliff dwellings." Running Horse took the last bite of his sandwich. "Are you sure of what you saw?"

"I'm not making this up. There were a number of houses, maybe 200, and nobody was living in them."

"Of course nobody lives in them. It's too remote and the elevation is 10,000 feet. You would have to be crazy to live in a place like that. On the other hand, if someone were trying to hide out, it would be a helluva place to stay."

"You don't understand. There was some sort of shield over the whole area. When I went into several of the houses, they showed signs that people were living in them. I found stairs leading down to what appeared to be a cave."

"Sounds like you've been smoking something powerful. Did you go down the stairs and check it out?"

"No, but I plan to go back. There was something else very strange about that place. I know I spent a long time up there and yet my watch never changed time. When I got back to the Jeep my watch said 9:05 and the car clock said five-fifteen."

"So maybe the battery in your watch went dead."

"Explain why my watch is working perfectly now?" Davis showed Running Horse his watch. "I haven't replaced the battery. The watch started running again when I got away from the mountain."

"I'm sure there is a rational explanation for your watch stopping. On the other hand," Running Horse smiled, "there are some powerful spirits up there. Now hurry up and finish eating. I've got to get you back to my place just in case the sheriff's death was no accident and the car crash was meant for you. We must try to sort this whole mess out and find out if there's a connection between what you found on the mountain, the UFO visit, the sheriff's death, and most especially, the metal, circa 1947."

"What about the vehicle you came here to tow?"

"Tomorrow is another day!"

CHAPTER ELEVEN

The blue Ford Taurus carrying three men passed the accident scene as the burned-out Jeep was being placed on a flatbed truck. Minutes before, an ambulance had made a u-turn on the narrow two-lane highway and headed east toward Socorro. A New Mexico state trooper waved on the few passing vehicles that slowed to get a glimpse of the blackened Jeep and to speculate on what had happened.

"Hey, professor, you think a flying saucer scared the driver off the road?" Fred Smith said laughingly.

"Not funny," Professor Beal responded in a serious tone.

"Don't pay any attention to Fred, Professor, he's only kidding," Jack Osborne added, turning to the professor, who was seated in the back seat. "How much further until we get to where you found these new Anasazi ruins?"

"It will take us about two hours to get to the top of the mountain and then another thirty minutes or so down to the base of the mesa," the professor answered.

"Where exactly did you say this place was located?" asked the driver, taking his eyes off the road momentarily.

"Mangas Mountain. Just stay on Route 60 through Magdalena to Datil and then take Route 12 south through Horse Springs. About five miles this side of Aragon there's a cutoff we'll take. I'll let you know when we get close."

"Mangas! That's an interesting name for a mountain, professor. Was that an Indian original or a white man's?"

"Will you stop with the nonsense, Fred, and just drive," Jack said, somewhat annoyed.

It was close to eleven o'clock when Susan arrived in Magdalena. She was still upset at having seen the accident earlier that morning. Food was something her stomach couldn't handle at the present moment. But she did remember Brad's message saying to check with Mattie at Mama Bs restaurant in Magdalena. She needed to find him as quickly as possible. He always had a calming influence on her and she was desperately seeking that comfort right now. Mama Bs was not hard to find in this small town. After parking the car she entered the restaurant: certainly not the Four Seasons, she thought, but quaint. Sort of what she expected way out here in the New Mexico wilderness. Walking across the linoleum floor Susan sat on one of the stools at the counter. There were only a couple of people in the restaurant. An old couple, obviously tourists passing through the area, who looked like they didn't belong in this setting, and a half-dozen old ladies drinking coffee at a back table.

"Can I help you, miss?" a voice asked from a half-opened door leading into the kitchen.

"I hope so!" Susan answered wearily.

"What's the matter, miss? Are you okay? You look terrible, if I do say so myself."

"Oh, I'll be alright, thank you. I've just had a long drive from Albuquerque and I saw a bad accident on my way here."

"Yeah, I heard about that a little while ago. Don't know more than it was a Jeep and whoever was inside that vehicle didn't have a chance. Ain't the way I want to die. Can I get you something?"

"Just a cup of tea, please."

"You got it." Mattie took a cup out from underneath the counter and cleaned the inside with her apron. She poured the hot water into the cup and handed Susan a tea bag. "Milk and sugar?"

"No, plain is fine, thank you."

"What's a single woman doing riding way out here alone? Ain't you got no husband?"

"No, I'm single, but I do have a steady."

"Well, you're too pretty for him to be letting you run around these parts by yourself."

"Actually, I'm here to find him."

"What did he do, run away from you or something?"

"No, he's out here on business..........."

Before Susan could finish the sentence Mattie interrupted. "What kind of business?"

Susan took a deep breath to hide her frustration in not being able to finish her sentence. "As I was about to say, he's out here doing research."

"Don't say."

"Yes. In fact, he gave me the name of a someone called Mattie that I should contact. He said she would know where to find him."

"Hey, that's me! You say your boyfriend gave you my name?

"That's right! Susan nodded her head yes.

"Say, miss, your fellow's name wouldn't be Davis, would it?"

"Yes! Yes! You know him then?"

"Sure. Good looking fellow. "Yeah, I can see you two sure do make a nice looking couple."

"Do you know where I can find him?"

"I haven't seen him today, but he was in here last night and had dinner. Surprised he didn't show up for breakfast this morning. Maybe he got up early and started looking for those Indian dwellings again."

"Do you know where he's staying?"

"Only one place in town, Magdalena Motel down the block."

"Thank you! Thank you! How much do I owe you for the tea?"

"It's on the house. Don't you think you should eat something? I'm sure you'll feel better. Besides, I don't think you'll find him there."

Susan didn't hear what Mattie said as she grabbed her handbag from the counter and rushed to the door, bumping into a tall Indian as he entered the restaurant.

"Well, she sure was in a big rush," Big Bird said as he smoothed his rumpled jacket. "Did you chase her out of here?" He asked laughingly.

"No. She's evidently that writer's girlfriend from the east and I told her he was staying over at the Magdalena Motel."

"You mean Davis?" Big Bird said surprised. "What's she doing out here?"

"Looking for him. Why are you so interested?" Mattie wanted to know.

"No reason." Big Bird turned and headed for the door.

"Hey, where are you going? You just got here."

"I just remembered I forgot something. Look, I'm supposed to meet a fellow by the name of Wally here. Will you tell him to wait for me. I'll be back shortly."

"Does this Wally have a last name?" Mattie called out as he rushed out the door. The door had already closed behind Big Bird.

Once outside he looked to see where Susan was going. He caught a glimpse of a small figure with blond hair turning the corner. Walking quickly, Big Bird reached the corner to see her heading for the motel. He watched from a safe distance as she entered the motel's office.

"Yes ma'am, may I help you?" The stoop-shouldered old gentlemen with a cardigan sweater asked from behind the desk.

"Yes, please. I would like to know if you have a Brad Davis registered here?"

"We're not allowed to give out information like that, miss. It's against the law."

"Is it against the law to provide that information to his wife?"

"Wife? I thought Mr. Davis was traveling alone."

"Oh, so you admit that Mr. Davis is staying here!"

"Well, yes, but I'm still not at liberty to divulge his cottage number."

"Look, mister, he called me yesterday and told me to meet him here. I forgot what cottage number he told me he was in. If you don't give me the number I'll knock on every door in this place until I find him."

"No need to get upset, miss. I'm sure it'll be okay if I give out his cottage number. And, if you weren't his wife I'm sure he'd be mad that I didn't give out his cottage number to a pretty lady such as yourself. Let me check the register here." The old man ran his finger down the list of names in the register. "Ah, yes, cottage number six. I don't think you'll find him in though."

"Why not?"

"I saw him and the sheriff leave here together at seven this morning."

"What was he doing with the sheriff?"

"Can't say, miss. I'm sure you'll find the sheriff at his office and you can ask him yourself."

"Where's his office?"

"Let me show you." The old man walked to the front door and

pointed in the direction to where the sheriff's office was located. "Just beyond the second street there and down around the corner is where you'll find him." Big Bird did an abrupt about face as he saw the motel clerk pointing in his direction. He entered the Indian trinket shop pretending to be buying something as he watched Susan walk by the store. He followed her, staying well behind, until she entered the sheriff's office. Within a short time Susan came out of the sheriff's office and started walking back toward her car parked in front of Mama B's. Getting in the car, she checked her watch and turned the ignition. Big Bird, following on foot, watched as Susan made a U-turn and headed toward the motel and parked her car in front of cottage six. He concluded Davis' girlfriend was going to check into his room.

Big Bird wanted to know what she was really doing here and how much of a threat she was going to be. He decided to check the sheriff's office and the motel office to find out what kind of questions she was asking. His first stop would be the sheriff's office.

"Hello, Bones," Big Bird called out to Deputy Laughlin who was on the telephone with his back to the door.

Turning to see who came into the office, Bones Laughlin greeted the tall Indian. "Hi! How you doing, Big Bird?" The deputy held his hand over the mouthpiece as he gestured for Big Bird to take a seat. "Be with you in a minute." He whispered as he took his hand off the mouthpiece. "Yes, dear, I know you fix lunch for me every day and

I come home to eat. I just can't go home now. The sheriff's not back and I have to stay here and watch over things. No, dear, I can't lock up the office and come home. Sorry, dear, someone came into the office and I have to take care of them. Talk to you later. Bye! Now Janie, don't be getting mad at me. I'll call as soon as I get some free time. Bye!" The deputy hung the phone up. "Sorry, Big Bird, the little woman just doesn't understand things sometimes. What can I do for you?"

"Two things, Bones." Big Bird stood up. "First, where is the sheriff?"

"I really don't know. In all my years of working for Frank he was always in the office at seven in the morning. That's the arrangement we had. He'd come in early and I would come in at nine. Today when I came in there was a note on the desk saying he had to take care of some special business and would be back by ten or ten-thirty. He still hasn't shown and I haven't heard one word from him. That's not like him."

"You have no idea where he went?"

"Yeah, I got a call a little while back from Captain Gerard over in Socorro, asking if Frank's car was here. I asked if something was wrong and he said he'd get back to me later."

"Maybe he came back and didn't come into the office."

"That's not likely since the car was parked out front when I got in this morning. You said you had two questions?"

"Yes, that woman who was in here a few minutes ago. What did she want?"

"She was hoping to speak to the sheriff. I told her he wasn't in. Said she was Davis wife and was looking for him. Wait a minute! She did say something that was kind of funny."

"What do you mean, funny?"

"She said the man at the motel said he saw Davis and the sheriff leaving the motel together at seven this morning."

"What would they be doing together, Bones?"

"Beats me, Big Bird. The sheriff never told me anything."

The telephone on the desk interrupted the conversation. "Excuse me Big Bird. Maybe it's the sheriff. Hi, Captain Gerard, what's up?"

Big Bird moved toward the door, whispering, "Tell the sheriff to give me a call when he gets back."

"What? That can't be true, captain." Big Bird hesitated a moment before opening the door. Bones Laughlin signaled for Big Bird not to leave. "My God, that's awful. I just can't believe it. There's no doubt? Okay, I'll talk with you later."

Big Bird moved closer to the desk as Laughlin hung up the phone and slouched in the chair. In a quivering voice, the deputy said, "The sheriff is presumed dead!"

"What do you mean Frank's presumed dead? How?" Big Bird shouted in a surprised voice.

"Auto accident about twenty miles east of here on Route 60. I guess that was the accident I got a call to handle. Seems the car went over the side, down into a gully, where it exploded and burned. The fire was so intense it didn't leave much of anything except melted bullet casings, probably what was left of a gun."

"That's not a positive identification, Bones."

"I know, but the person who rented the car was in jail at Socorro."

"I don't understand."

"Captain Gerard said Frank showed up there early this morning with Brad Davis and asked to have him put in protective custody. So, Davis couldn't have been in the car! Furthermore, Gerard said the sheriff was driving Davis' car. Even without positive identification of any remains they find in the vehicle it's pretty certain it was Frank in that car. Remember, he never came back here, and he never did call. I'm afraid the sheriff is really dead!"

"Oh, shit!" Big Bird whispered softly.

"What was that you said, Big Bird? I didn't quite hear you."

"Nothing, Bones. Did Gerard say how it happened? Was he run off the road?"

"They really don't know how it happened. From the few witnesses that showed up at the wreck, no one saw anything."

Big Bird frowned. "Look, I've got to be going. Sorry about the sheriff. He was a good man. It's a shame that he had to die that way."

Big Bird left the sheriff's office and headed for Mama Bs. There was no need to check out the motel at the moment. Susan Adams could wait. He had more important items that needed to be addressed.

If Colonel Parker›s men did the dirty deed, they got the wrong man. Things were not going right as far as Big Bird was concerned. He needed to find out if Parker›s men were involved. Also, was the intended victim suspicious? Would he be hard to find? Susan Adams was Big Bird›s ace in the hole. She could be used as bait if necessary. Time was getting short and there were many things still left undone. The descendants of his ancestors would not be patient. They had a timetable that had to be met. He entered Mama Bs and looked around the restaurant. There, at a far table with a window view, were Parker and his skinny assistant. Big Bird sat down facing the two men and signaled for Mattie to bring him a cup of coffee.

Parker was the first to speak. "I was watching you through the window walking up the street. You look like a man who's carrying the weight of the world on your shoulders. Relax, everything's been taken care of and we have no more worries."

"Wrong, my friend!" Big Bird stopped talking as Mattie placed his coffee on the table.

"Anything else, Big Bird?" Mattie asked.

"No, thank you." Big Bird looked up at Mattie and faked a smile.

Mattie headed back toward the kitchen. Colonel Parker leaned over the table and smiled. "I guess you didn't hear me, my Indian friend. My men called from the airport and said our nuisance friend is no more."

"In case you didn't hear me, White Eyes, I said wrong!" There was controlled rage in Big Birds voice.

"What the hell are you talking about? Wrong what?"

"Your clever aides took out the wrong man!"

"Impossible! We never make mistakes! I got a call from my men before they boarded a flight back to Washington. They shot out the tires on the Jeep Cherokee driven by Davis. He was driving along Route 60 coming from Socorro. They made sure he was dead. The car fire finished him off permanently."

"You goddamned military assholes! Its people like you who your government put in a position to police the world and all you do is create havoc and destruction. There's no hope for this planet and that is why I have instructed my people to end Project Anasazi and return to our own world. We will not be a part of your plans any longer. My people will leave very soon."

"Calm down, friend! You're talking gibberish.. And keep your voice down," Parker said sternly. "You still haven't said what makes you think we took out the wrong man."

"You killed one of the true patriots of this land, and you did it in such a way we couldn't save him."

"You're talking in riddles, Indian."

"You killed Sheriff Frank Cooper. My people can do many things, but we cannot bring a burned body back to life."

"The sheriff?" The colonel shifted uneasily and then leaned back against his chair, arms folded. "That's impossible! Are you absolutely sure?"

"Yes! He that writer fellow over to Socorro, placing him in

protective custody in the jail over there. Sheriff Cooper was driving Davis's Jeep back to Magdalena when your men killed him by mistake."

"Well, that's a shame and we're really sorry. Sometimes mistakes are made. We'll find Davis and finish the job."

"No, I have decided! There will be no more killing! There need be no more sacrifices for this project. The project is ended."

"Look, Big Bird, I don't think you understand what's going on here. Right now the general runs this operation and he says it will continue and has instructed me to insure that the project doesn't come to an end."

"No!" Big Bird shouted and slammed the table with his fist.

"Is everything okay, Big Bird?" Mattie called over to the table.

"Sorry for the disturbance, Mattie, everything is fine." Big Bird waved an okay sign toward the counter. He turned back to face the colonel. "Over the years the general has been a very stubborn man, but when push came to shove, he finally saw my way of thinking. He is old in terms of earth years and very tired. He will see that what I am saying must come to pass now."

"Big Bird, I think you and I should finish our conversation outside where we can talk a little more freely." Parker motioned for the three men to get up from the table and walk outside. "We left the money for the check on the table, Mattie." He smiled and waved goodbye. Once outside, Colonel Parker and his aide walked side by side to the colonel's car. "Hop in, Big Bird. You can sit up front and I'll sit in the back. My driver will take us all out to the mountain compound where we can talk this out and settle things like intelligent beings."

"There is nothing to discuss. Plans have been put in motion and there is no turning back."

"Are you telling me, Big Bird, that you refuse to cooperate any longer?"

"Ah, you are finally getting the message, Colonel."

"It's a shame you feel that way, Big Bird," the colonel responded sarcastically. A real shame. I want you to know I will be taking over Project Anasazi from the general."

"There is nothing to take over. We are folding our tents, as my Indian brethren would say," Big Bird said firmly.

"Your tent is being folded as of this instant!" Parker said with a sick laugh.

A muzzled, soft, popping sound was heard as a bullet entered the base of Big Bird's skull. He slumped forward as Colonel Parker unscrewed the silencer from his service revolver. "A real shame, Big Bird. Pull off the road up ahead there in that clump of bushes and we'll toss the body out there," the colonel ordered his driver. The vehicle stopped. The driver got out from behind the steering wheel and moved around the front of the car and opened the passenger side door. He looked around making sure no other people or cars were in the vicinity and then pulled Big Bird's limp body from the car. Rolling him over with his foot he positioned his body under a juniper tree.

"Let's get out of here." The colonel shouted. The colonel's vehicle headed back to town and General Brantfield's house. About one hundred yards from where Big Bird's body had been dumped, a lone car, which had been following at a safe distance, waited until the colonel's car was long out of sight. The car moved to where moments ago Colonel Parker's car had been parked. The two occupants of the car emerged from the vehicle and retrieved Big Bird, lifting him carefully and placing him on the back seat. Quickly, the car started up and headed for Alegros Mountain.

Susan sat in the chair beside the bed trying to decipher Davis' notes. It had been almost a half hour since she convinced the motel clerk to give her a key to cottage number six. Once inside she found his razor and shaving cream sitting on the sink as if Davis had left in a hurry. Clothes were strewn across the unmade bed. It was evident the maid had not yet tried to clean the room, or if she did, one look told her she would pass on this room for the time being. Susan continued to page through Davis' notebook, stopping and pondering some of the strange notations he had made in the margin. After finishing the last page she closed the notebook, wondering what kind of craziness Brad Davis had gotten himself into this time. Before her mind could suggest an answer of its own, a soft knock on the door interrupted her thought process.

"Yes? Who is it?"

"A friend," came the muffled answer.

Susan got up from the chair and peeked through the curtains to see who was at the front door. A lone figure, definitely Indian, stood waiting for Susan to answer the door. He wore a brightly colored shirt tucked in at the waist of his brown leather pants and a sleeveless brown suede jacket. His black cowboy hat could not hide the unusual skin tone of his face. A string of multicolored beads draped around his neck rested on his chest. The reddish-brown boots he wore had a design of a rattlesnake and a coyote stitched into the leather. Not your everyday modern Indian, Susan thought. A shiny metal object on a silvery looking chain around the Indian's neck, resting below his voice box, caught Susan's attention. She couldn't really get a good look at it. The Indian was standing in the shade and yet the object appeared to reflect sunlight. She moved closer to the door. "What do you want?"

"I bring you a message." the voice on the other side of the door responded.

"A message from whom?"

"All I can say is that a friend has a message for you, Miss Adams."

"How do you know my name? Is the message from Mr. Davis?"

"No, but it concerns Mr. Davis."

Susan was getting nervous. Where was Brad when she needed him? There was a strange Indian outside the motel door who knew her name. How could this person know she was staying there and knows her by name. She was not one to become easily frightened, but she was having trouble trying to remain calm. The motel clerk said

Davis left with the sheriff early in the morning. It was now a little past twelve noon and neither the sheriff nor Davis were around. And what about the strange notes Davis had scribbled in the notebook's margins? Is there something sinister going on? Her mind continued to race trying to make sense out of this strange visitor at her door. "Tell me what you want."

The calm voice on the other side of the door again tried to convey that he had a message for her. "I must talk with you, please let me in."

"Not on your life, Buster. You have something to tell me, tell me through the door."

"Please, I mustn't be seen talking with you. Open the door so we can talk."

"Think again. I'm not opening this door to anyone."

"Your life is in danger and....." The Indian's conversation ended abruptly.

Susan waited for what seemed an eternity to hear more from the voice outside. When she looked out the window the Indian was gone. Slowly, she opened the door to see if he were anywhere around. He was nowhere to be seen. A car had pulled up in front of the cottage next door. Two people could be seen hugging and kissing through the windshield. Matinee time, Susan thought. The approaching car must have frightened the Indian away. "I wonder what the hell that was all about," she said out loud. She made sure the dead bolt was engaged in the door and then returned to the chair and began reading Davis' notes one more time.

CHAPTER TWELVE

General Brantfield was sitting on the chaise lounge on the rear patio eating a tuna fish sandwich he had made for lunch. He had loved tuna fish sandwiches ever since he and his wife were first married, even though they could afford to eat anything they desired. To this day, it was his favorite sandwich. A great deal had taken place in the last twenty-four hours and the general was trying to collect his thoughts and put everything in perspective. He was quite proud of the fact that as an octogenarian he still possessed a sharp mind.

Over the years he had watched many of his contemporaries lose their mental abilities, unable to remember things that should not be forgotten. He watched as men and women much younger than himself deteriorated mentally and physically. He attributed his own prowess to the physical and mental exercises he conducted daily. A five-mile brisk walk every morning as the sun rose over the distant mountains in the east provided him the zest to keep on living forever. His once a week treatment at the mountain compound also had a lot to do with his youthful appearance and vigor. Playing mental games was another one of the tricks he devised to keep his mind sharp.

"Good afternoon, General!" Colonel Parker's surprise appearance on the patio startled the general.

"How the hell did you get back here without me hearing you?" The general snarled at the colonel. "Don't you ever startle me like that again! Do you understand that, colonel?"

"Sure, sure, General, but I have some news that you need to hear." The colonel's lack of respect for the general was obvious in his tone of voice.

It was not missed by the general. "Look, you son of a bitch, you may not like me, but I'm still your commanding officer on this project and you better show my rank some respect."

"Look, old man, I didn't come here to take any shit from you." The general's mouth opened wide in surprise, caught off guard by the colonel's flippant attitude. "In case you don't know it, your days are numbered as head of this project and things have been set in motion by the Pentagon to finally retire you." The general sat dumbfounded as the colonel continued. "It's obvious you've been head of this project too long. All of a sudden Big Bird starts calling the shots saying how he's going to bring the project to an end. He tells us his people are going to pack up and head for the great blue yonder. I don't think so, General. I've already taken care of the head Indian so he can't give us any more orders."

The general stood up and walked toward the colonel. "What are you talking about? Has anything happened to Big Bird?"

"Relax, Pops." The colonel gently pushed the general back down in his chair. "Big Bird was becoming a nuisance and I decided it was time for him to join his ancestors here on this planet." The general sat stunned at what he was hearing, unable to utter a word. "I came to give you another piece of bad news about the sheriff."

"What about the sheriff?" The general asked weakly.

"He's dead! It seems he had an unfortunate accident out on the highway."

"You bastard!" The rage was building in the general. "Did you have anything to do with that accident?"

"Not me, General. But two of my men witnessed the accident. If you remember you asked me to take care of Brad Davis because he was becoming a nuisance. Well, I agreed with your decision and decided to eliminate him. Not because you ordered it, mind you, but because as the next head of Project Anasazi I didn't want anyone around who could possibly mess up this project. Your sheriff buddy didn't have the guts to carry out the elimination of Davis. In fact, he took him to Socorro and placed him in protective custody over there. The sheriff was evidently driving Davis' vehicle when he had his accident. Such a shame."

The general sprang from his chair, lunging at the colonel in an attempt to choke him. "You murdering, crummy, bastard. I'm going to kill you myself."

Grappling with the general, the colonel easily overpowered the old man and threw him to the floor. "You old fool. Isn't it strange that you wanted someone taken out? No qualms about removing someone like Davis and then you become this mighty and holy figure protesting the death of Big Bird and the sheriff. How do you figure that, General?"

"I'll see you burn in hell before I let you get away with killing Frank Cooper and Big Bird." The general raised himself from the floor and sat on the chaise lounge. He hung his head and murmured, "I'm sorry, Frank, old friend. I never wanted to cause you any harm," he moaned softly.

"Too late for sentimentality, General. Things have changed and there's one more change that has to be made."

"And, what's that, Colonel?"

"You are finally going to retire from this project."

"Like hell I am. I will decide when that day is. And if you think this is over, think again. I'm going to contact General D at the Pentagon and let him know that you've overstepped your bounds. I'm not retiring and I'll be damned if you or anyone else like you replaces me on this project or any other project. I'll see to that personally."

"I hate to disappoint you, General, but General D has already appointed me head of the project. He was hoping to convince you to retire, but that possibility seems quite remote at this time. So I was given the authority to deal with you on your retirement as I see fit."

"I don't believe a word you're saying." The general tried to stand but was forcibly restrained by the colonel's aide who had entered the patio from the side of the house, unseen by the general. "What the hell are you doing, Colonel? Don't you realize who you are dealing with?" The general felt a pin prick on the back of his neck. "What the hell was that? What did you do to me?" The aide stepped back holding the syringe to his side.

"General, you have just been given a sedative that will solve all our problems."

"Sedative, hell! What did you inject me with?"

The colonel smiled. "It's like a sedative. First you will feel your body going limp and then you will get very sleepy. Slowly you will drift off to sleep, never to worry about the project again. Actually, you'll never have to worry about anything ever again." The colonel and his aide both laughed out loud.

"Why are you doing this? What was in that injection?" The general's body was becoming limp. His head fell back against the headrest of the chaise.

The colonel motioned for the aide to prop the general's feet on the lounge. "Relax, general, it will be all over for you very shortly."

"You won't get away with this, colonel." The general's words were becoming slurred.

"Oh, but I will, General. You see, when they find your body and perform an autopsy they'll find no trace of anything. The cause of death will be listed as heart attack due to old age. Isn't modern chemical warfare wonderful? We developed this unique chemical that can be administered by injection or in gas form. It's a nice way to eliminate your enemies painlessly. We can get away with so many things these days." The general made one last attempt to move from the chaise. He could not move. He looked up at the colonel with contempt in his eyes and then slowly his eyes rolled back in his head, his body going limp. Colonel Parker smiled at his aide and said to Lieutenant Nelson, "Check his pulse."

"There is none, Sir."

"You've done a fine thing here today, Nelson. I'm going to recommend you for promotion to captain as soon as we get back to Washington. Right now, we've got to find Brad Davis and Susan Adams. They're next on the list."

The skinny aide, who would soon be Captain Robert Nelson, smiled broadly.

The trio of men had reached their destination high in the Mangas Mountains. Professor Beal had taken the lead as they carefully made their way through the forest of juniper trees. As they emerged through the clearing the professor pointed to the steep, red colored mesa that stood before them, rising above the surrounding trees. From their vantage point all they could see was the eastern side of the sheer mesa. It appeared as if some internal force of nature thrust up the mountain of red clay from within the earth, pushing it higher than the forest.

"Gentlemen, we have arrived," the professor said excitedly.

"And where the hell might that be?" Fred Smith wanted to know.

"I don't see anything," observed Jack Osborne.

"That's because you don't know what you are looking for," Beal responded. "Isn't it beautiful! Come on and I'll show you how truly magnificent these people were." The professor motioned for the two FBI agents to follow him through the small clearing to the northeastern edge of the mesa. At this point the trees grew close to the walls of the cliff, making it difficult for the men to move easily.

"I hope you know what you're doing, Professor," Smith, from his position of third in line, called out.

"Just a little further and we'll be there." Professor Beal encouraged his followers. The trail snaked back through the trees and then out again to where there seemed no place else to go.

"This is a dead-end!" Agent Osborne shouted out in frustration.

"Not quite, my friend. Do you see this rock here?"

"How could we miss it?" both men responded in unison.

"Just watch what happens when I place both hands at the edge of this huge ten-foot rock." The rock swung out as easily as if it had no weight at all, exposing a gently sloping path leading upwards inside the mesa.

Smith and Osborne stepped forward to touch the rock and were amazed how easily it moved. Smith was the first to speak. "I don't understand how a rock that large can move so easily."

"You evidently didn't study physics or if you did, you have forgotten your experiments," the professor answered in his teaching voice. "It has to do with weights, balances and counter-balances."

"Wait just a minute!" Osborne joined in. "This is impossible! We're talking about a tribe of Indians that was last seen in the late

1200's. That's over seven hundred years ago, and I'm not sure it was the last thing they did before they disappeared. In any case, how in the hell did they have the knowledge and the tools to accomplish this feat?"

"That is the sixty-four thousand dollar question, my government friends. You see, another part of this puzzle is that the Anasazi excelled at astronomy, but they were not known as mathematicians. If that's really the case they had to have help from someone. That help could have come from the Mayas or for that matter, up there." The professor pointed toward the sky.

"Can it, professor," Smith waved his hand at the professor. "I think I can buy into the Mayas having something to do with it, even though over one thousand miles separated them. Recently, I read in the *Washington Post* that a group of archaeologists studying in Central America came across some evidence that indicates the possibility there was contact between the civilizations. But extraterrestrials? Forget it!"

"Mr. Smith, do you have a personal theory on the pyramids, Stonehenge, Easter Island, Newgrange in Ireland, Machu Pichu, strange drawings throughout South and Central America, and the strange markings on the ground in Peru that can only be seen from the sky?"

"No, I can't explain them, but I do know about the markings in Peru. Some quack has a theory that they are markings for space travelers to land there. Utter nonsense!"

"Keep an open mind, Mr. Smith. Back to our physics lesson. Do you know about Fahata Butte?" Both men shook their heads no. Fahata Butte sits alone in a valley at the southern entrance to Chaco Canyon. It is a 480-foot high butte that served as a holy place for the Anasazi. At the top of that butte is an astrological marvel called a Sun Dagger which precisely measures the movement of the sun and moon throughout a nineteen-year cycle. The three architecturally designed stone slabs that mark and measure the movements each weigh two tons. The sun and the moon shine through these slabs onto a spiral carved in a rock. At precisely noon on any given day a light dagger shines on the spiral corresponding to the exact time of year. While that is a marvel in and of itself, how about the fact that these stone slabs of enormous weight were placed in a precise position to mark the passing of the sun and moon? Amazing, isn't it? Theories? Sure, I've got a couple of my own, but I'll keep them to myself for the time being so people won't think I'm crazy. Okay, enough of the physics and astronomy lesson. Let's move on up into this place. There are more interesting things I want you to see."

Osborne, who had taken a few steps into the walkway, had a question. "There are no lights in here and you have only your one flashlight. How do you think you're going to see in here?"

"Not to worry, Mr. Osborne. In fact, we won't even need the flashlight. This walkway, which is about two hundred yards long going half way up the inside of the mesa, was engineered in such a way to be just within a few feet of the cliff wall. Every three feet there is a two-foot rectangular opening, allowing light to enter the walkway. Let me lead the way."

"I'll pass on joining you on your journey inside a mountain," Osborne said. "But, professor, I have one question that needs to be answered."

"You're going to ask me how I found this hidden door and what lies beyond? Is that correct?"

"Yes, and how did you know what I was going to ask?"

"It's logical! I was out exploring one day last fall, not searching for anything. It's my way of relaxing. I remembered seeing this mesa when I was sail planing and thought I saw an opening in its south face. It was impossible to get a good look from the plane so I was determined to investigate. It was a fascinating sight from the air and it just looked like it was inviting me to check it out. When I first explored this site I realized it was the same place an explorer named Bryant had talked about finding a couple of years back. He wrote about his finding in one of the scientific magazines."

"How did you come upon the door?"

"Purely by accident. I had reached this point and needed to rest, so I placed my backpack on the ground and leaned against the rock. The rest is history. It's a shame you don't want to join us to see for yourself the marvels of what I discovered."

"Like I said, professor, not this time. Somebody has to stay behind and watch your rear." Osborne was adamant about remaining behind.

"Hey, there's nothing to be afraid of. I've been here before."

"All the same, professor, I'll wait for you right here at the entrance."

"Have it your way, Mr. Osborne."

"Are you sure you don't want to come along?" Fred asked.

"I'm absolutely sure. Have fun!"

The two men slowly moved along the pathway leading upwards inside the red clay mesa. Smith had to rest and catch his breath every few minutes. He was not used to the thin air at this altitude. Besides, his leg muscles were cramping up on him, which was typical for people in sedentary jobs who didn't exercise regularly. On his frequent stops Smith would peer out through the openings that served as windows for the walkway. He marveled at how clearly he could see the forest below. With each successive step upward he got a better view of the distant surroundings. What especially intrigued him was being able to see peripherally on either side of the cliff wall. Looking ahead, Smith could see that the walkway was coming to an end. All he saw was a solid wall and no way out except the direction from which they had come. The professor took out his flashlight and searched the wall.

"What are you looking for, professor?" Smith asked.

"There is a door opener here somewhere on the wall," the professor answered. "I just have to find it. These amazing people thought of every precaution to protect themselves. Ah, here it is." The professor pushed what looked like a spot on the wall, which, in reality, was a three-inch piece of the wall that retracted into the wall when pressed. Silently the panel in front of them moved sideways into the recesses of a much larger wall. They entered a large circular, brightly lit, windowless room with walls covered with hundreds of drawings. The artwork seemed to be depicting a continuing story from one side of the room to the other. The walls rose about thirty feet to a ceiling that seemed as if it had been sanded smooth. On the far wall, about twenty feet high, was a pictograph of a crescent moon and a star. It was similar to the one found at Penasco Blanco. About fifty feet from the crescent moon pictograph was a series of smaller pictographs of strange geometric designs. The room with no windows was as bright as sunlight. The intense light came from strange looking thin coils that ringed the room where the walls met the ceiling. On the opposite side was a small doorway leading out of this room into what seemed to be some sort of ancient waiting room. At the base of the walls were what appeared to be stone slabs that probably served as seating. In the center of the chamber was a stone table which reminded Fred of a table in a doctor's waiting room where one could find the latest reading material. However, in this case the table was bare except for some strange markings.

"How do you explain this place, professor? asked Smith.

"I haven't been able to come to any conclusions yet. But I will. This is definitely the room Steve Bryant wrote about in his article. The only thing that has me puzzled is the fact that he talked about using his lantern and flashlight. If this light were here then he wouldn't have needed his lantern. On the other hand, maybe someone was watching him and controlled the lights. Those lights almost look as if they came off the Starship Enterprise." The professor tried to make a joke of the matter. "Seriously, though, it doesn't look as if it came from a period over six hundred years ago. Indians only had fire for light. I just don't know what to make of it. Sure does send a shiver up your spine, doesn't it? Let me show you some more unusual things."

"If this is the same place that this guy Bryant talked about, do you think there really was someone watching him?"

"I can't answer that."

"Well, Professor, what about now? Do you think someone's watching us?"

"I can't answer that either."

"That's a real comforting thought! What about the table and those markings?" Fred was hoping the professor would have some down to earth explanation.

"Never saw anything like it before. It's one of many things that need to be looked at closely. I need to bring one of my colleagues who specializes in ancient languages up here to check it out. But not until I have finished with my research. Then and only then will I be ready to tell the world of my find."

Professor Beal walked across the cavernous room followed by the FBI agent. They walked to the small doorway at the far end of the room which was the only way out except for the sliding door from the walkway. There were no smells of any kind in this place: no smell of dampness, burned out ashes, or of anything else. This place had no smell at all! Every other place the professor had ever explored had a smell or aroma all its own. If for no other reason, this place should at least have had the smell of nothing having ever been there. Not this place. Beal wanted to ask his companion's opinion about this, but decided against it. As Smith followed Beal through the doorway leading out of the large room, he noticed that it suddenly turned dark behind him. Abruptly he turned to see if he had imagined that the lights in the large room had gone out. It was dark. The only light came from the opening at the far end of the passageway they were in, which was no more than fifteen feet from the great room.

"Hey, Professor!" Smith called to Beal.

"Yes, what is it?"

"The lights! The lights went out!"

"Open your eyes and you'll see there's plenty of light ahead of us."

"No, no! I'm talking about the lights in the room we just came from."

"Oh, yes. I forgot to mention that there is some sort of device that turns the lights on and off when we enter or leave that room."

"You knew about that?"

"Yes, but I haven't had time to determine what makes it work. I haven't figured out the lighting system yet so how am I going to figure what turns them on and off. Someday I'll come back with some electrical engineers and let them find the answer. But again, like I've said, only after I've completed my studies of this place. My interest is in finding evidence of these Indians and their studies of the solar system." The light at the end of the passageway came from the sunlight streaming into the large opening in the southern end of the mesa. "Watch your step. The passageway ends here and it's a drop of about twenty feet. There is a ladder which leads down to the next level. What you are seeing before your eyes is amazing. It is a perfectly preserved cliff dwelling that no one has visited since the Anasazi left here centuries ago. Except Steve Bryant and me, of course."

The two men, emerging from the rear of the cliff dwelling, carefully made their way down the ladder onto the floor of the dwelling. Professor Beal estimated the size of the room to be three hundred feet high by two hundred feet wide and one hundred seventy-five feet deep. It was situated more than five hundred feet above a small canyon that stretched for miles in a southerly direction. A distinct advantage of this location was the ability to see for long distances down the length and breadth of the canyon. "Nothing has changed since the last time I was here. For your information, this is one of the smallest cliff dwellings I have ever explored. Most of the dwellings have anywhere from fifty to well over a hundred pueblos. Can you believe that no one else has found this place?"

"No, I can't believe it." Fred had never seen anything like it in his life. He stood in one place and turned in every direction to marvel in this awesome sight. There were about ten pueblos at different levels set in the southerly side of the mesa where once a tribe of Indians had lived and called this place home. Gathering his composure he moved up alongside the professor as they examined one pueblo after another. "Must have been small people, professor."

"By today's standards, they were. Nothing has been disturbed. Their eating utensils haven't been destroyed by the ravages of time. Here, look at this plate." Beal picked up a plate from the floor of what was once a dining room. He blew the dust from the plate and handed it to Smith.

"Wow, I'm handling something from the past, something real Indians used. Hey, Professor, I don't understand why it looks like everything is intact and as if the people left in a big hurry. Why are all these utensils still here?"

"The looters are the ones that destroy these places and until now they haven't discovered this place. I would like to keep it that way."

"You've got my word, Professor. I can't believe the view these people had. How come we couldn't see this opening from down below?"

"We were looking at the eastern side of the mesa and this opening is on the south side. Now, come, I want you to look at these markings on the outside of each of the dwellings." The professor pointed to the outside doorway of the closest dwelling, at about eye level, where there was a strange marking. "What do you make of this, Mr. Smith?"

"I don't know, professor. You're supposed to be the expert."

"True, but I've never seen Indian markings like this before. Here, here, look at this one. I made a sketch of this the last time I was here. I've gone through every known book on Indians and Indian markings that was ever printed. Nothing! What do you think it looks like?"

"Well, this is going to sound funny, but it reminds me of an astrological sign. It's definitely not one of the ones we know, but maybe they had their own signs."

"That's very good. I thought so, too. However these signs couldn't possibly belong to anything we're familiar with. On the other hand,........"

"Wait a minute, professor," the FBI agent interrupted the professor before he could finish his sentence. "You're not going to start talking space nonsense again, are you?"

"We'll finish this conversation later." The professor gave a weak smile. "Let me show you the kiva I found on my first trip here. Now mind you, I was alone and I didn't want to go down there by myself. But now that you're with me we can both go down."

"What's a kiva, professor?"

"It's a ceremonial chamber room where the living communicate with the dead. Most of the Indian tribes had some sort of ritual ceremonial chamber where they would smoke, get high and communicate with the spirit world. The Anasazi were one of many tribes who had kivas for these sort of things. It was thought that the Anasazi crossed over to the other world through these kivas."

"Did they actually communicate with the dead spirits?"

205

"I'm sure they thought they did."

"Do you think it was the stuff they were smoking?"

"Probably."

Both men descended the hand-cut stone stairway to the floor of the kiva. The professor was the first to reach the bottom of the ten-step stairway. Immediately, the fifty-foot circular room became dimly illuminated as if someone had thrown on a light switch. Turning off his flashlight, the professor was the first to talk. "What the hell is going on here?"

Fred had reached the bottom of the stairway and exclaimed in a loud voice, "Holy shit! Where did the light come from?"

The professor looked back at the agent. "Can you believe this! Look up at where the light is coming from." He pointed to the small coil that circled the room between the ceiling and the wall. "It looks like the same type of lighting coil we saw in the main room upstairs. The only difference is that the light is dimmer here. What do you make of it, Mr. Smith?"

"Beats the hell out of me. Are you sure someone hasn't been here and wired this place for lighting?"

"Hardly. I tell you that no one has been here since it was abandoned more than six hundred years ago. That's a fact. And, if you take a good look at the light you'll see it's nothing like we've ever seen before."

"What made it turn on by itself?"

"My guess is some type of sound sensitivity triggering device."

"Installed by Indians more than six hundred years ago? Give me a break, Professor. I wasn't born yesterday."

"Who said anything about Indians?"

"Oh!" Fred answered nervously.

The two men moved about the room examining the lighting and the smooth, barren walls of the kiva. Stone slabs, about a foot in thickness, were placed against the wall around the circular room. They rested on stone supports positioned every two feet.

"The slabs were where the Indians sat during their ceremonies," the professor said matter of factly.

"It's very impressive, professor. I can't get my mind off these lights. You know I'm no expert, but I've seen enough cowboy and Indian movies and I always remember seeing places where Indians had places to put fire torches for light. Throughout everything up stairs and down here I haven't seen one place where they would have placed torches."

"That's a very good observation, Mr. Smith. And, you're right, of course. It is very strange. Why don't we sit down for a moment and see if we can imagine what it must have been like to be part of their ceremony."

The two men sat down next to each other. As soon as they were seated the room lights dimmed to blackness and a strange swirling white light rose from a square, perfectly shaped smooth stone in the middle of the room. The white light, almost like a spotlight, reached from the floor to the ceiling. The men were too startled to utter a sound or look at each other. They were transfixed at the image that began to appear in the white light. A male figure took form in the smoky soft white light. He stood well over six feet tall and was dressed in clothes that were not of any time period that the professor was familiar with. On his head he wore a silver headpiece that looked like something out of an old 1930's Buck Rogers movie serial.

His clothes were definitely not period piece Indian clothes. The figure wore a one-piece suit made of a shiny material that was difficult to describe. Only his hands and face were not covered by these clothes. Attached at his waist was some sort of device that looked like a modern day pager, except it had blinking lights that alternated between red, green, yellow and blue. His shoes looked more like ski boots than anything else. A silvery object on a chain around the figure's neck glowed. It rested just below the voice box.

The figure began to speak and neither the professor nor Fred Smith understood the language being spoken. They turned to look at one another and became a little bit frightened at what they saw taking form throughout the room. Seated all around were half naked Indians smoking and conversing with the figure in the light. They spoke in soft reverent tones. Fred Smith sat paralyzed with fear. Only the professor had the wits about him to stand up and start investigating these apparitions. He stood in front of one of the Indians checking to see if he were real or an illusion.

The seated Indian appeared as if he did not see the professor. Slowly, the professor circled examining each one of the Indians seated around the room. They appeared real, but yet not one of them seemed to recognize the professor's presence. All the Indians seemed quite elderly, the professor reasoned. He dared not reach out to touch them lest he disturbed them and have a spell cast upon him. It had to be some trick of the mind, some illusion that the spirit world was conjuring up to get him to leave this place forever. He looked back at Fred Smith who sat wide eyed and frightened, unable to move.

The professor walked to the center of the room to determine where the light was coming from. He reached out to touch the figure. His hand went through the light and the figure. He bent down placing both hands over the stone. Light continued to swirl from ceiling to floor. The figure's speech was uninterrupted by the professor's actions. He stepped back to find the source of the light. There was none. It is some sort of hologram the professor reasoned, but how? Now, the professor was getting nervous and a little bit frightened. He moved back across the room to get Fred so that they could leave this place quickly. Smith was not there. In his place was an old Indian, like all the others in this room.

"Smith, where the hell are you?" The professor yelled. Instantly, the room that was dark immediately became extremely bright at the sound of his voice. The white light in the middle of the room with the tall figure disappeared as did all the seated Indians. Fred was nowhere to be found in the room.

"Probably scared out of his wits and hightailed back to his partner," he said out loud. Worrying for his own safety, or was it his sanity, he started back toward the stairway to take him out of the kiva. Suddenly, he had the courage to satisfy a curiosity he had about this place. As he climbed the stairway he called out in a soft voice, "Okay, you can come out now, I'm leaving." Immediately, the lights once again dimmed and the room slowly returned to total darkness. The figure in the white light returned and so did all the Indians seated around the room.

CHAPTER THIRTEEN

A little over an hour had passed since Lieutenant Nelson had administered the fatal injection to General Brantfield. A dusty old Chevy Caprice pulled into the driveway of the General's house. Two tall Indian looking men emerged from the car and walked around to the back of the house. Calling out to the general, both men waited at the back gate for a response. After several attempts to get a response from the general, they unlatched the six-foot gate and entered the rear courtyard. Immediately, they saw the general stretched out on the chaise lounge as if he were sleeping. One of the men leaned over and shook the general gently, trying to wake him without frightening him.

"Shartumo. Shartumo." There was no response from the general.

The second man spoke to the first. "Eisa yogum blisci?"

"Shartumo qlork nesi vighha!" the first man answered while reaching out to touch the general. He placed his hand on the general's forehead. "Rzeengig!" He then placed his finger on the side of the general's neck searching for a pulse. "Shartumo eis tkulld!"

While the first man lowered the back on the chaise lounge to allow the general's body to be prone, the second man went into the house and returned with several blankets. Carefully, they wrapped the general's body in the blankets and carried him to their car. Within minutes the car was on its way to Alegros Mountain.

Neither Brad Davis nor Running Horse had much to say on the way back to Horse Springs. The drive in the non-air-conditioned tow truck was an ordeal on this unusually hot day. Each man was lost in his own thoughts about what had transpired on this day that was only half over. Davis desperately tried to think back over the course of the last forty-eight hours trying to make sense out of the events that had taken place. First it was the discovery on Alegros Mountain, then the confrontation with the general, followed by being whisked away by the sheriff. And now, the sheriff's death in his vehicle. Was it an accident? Or was it a part of a plot the sheriff was trying to protect him from? If it was truly an accident, what really happened out there on the highway? Were there witnesses? Suppose it wasn't an accident? Was he the intended target? Was the sheriff a victim by mistake? So many questions and so few answers.

Maybe, Davis thought, it was time to put aside his original reason for coming to New Mexico and start investigating what was really going on out here. His research on the Anasazi could be put on hold until he cleared up the present mystery in which he had gotten himself involved. He remembered Captain Gerard talking about sightings of UFO's over New Mexico the night before. Evidently, the sheriff knew

about them but never mentioned the sightings on the ride to Socorro earlier that morning.

Who could forget Running Horse's story of the strange goings on during the summer of 1947,especially the piece of metal he kept as a souvenir. Was there some secret the government was keeping from the American public about 1947? Again, so many questions and so few answers. He was thankful that Susan wasn't with him. That was one worry he didn't want to have. It was bad enough he had to worry about taking care of himself with all the strange things going on out here, but worrying about Susan was something he didn't want to have to deal with.

"Brad, are you awake?" Running Horse reached across the seat and placed his hand on Davis' shoulder.

"Yeah. I was lost in my thoughts there for awhile."

"Are you sure you're okay?"

"Thanks, Running Horse, I'm fine, really."

"Good. We'll be home in five minutes. By the way, since we're going to be spending some time together I think you should know everybody who knows me real well calls me Charley."

"Charley! How do you get Charley out of Running Horse?"

"My formal name is Charles Running Horse Baxter. You can't go to white kid's school without having a real American sounding name."

"So, what's wrong with that name? It's nothing to be ashamed of."

Running Horse laughed. "Oh yeah? How would you like all the kids making fun of your name, calling you Charley Horse?"

A slight smile crossed Davis' face. "I guess it would be hard for little kids not to make fun."

"After I beat the crap out of everyone who made fun of my name no one dared to call me anything but Running Horse."

They both laughed out loud. They were still laughing as the tow truck pulled into the service station where Little River had just completed filling a car with gas. Her eyes lit up when she saw Davis getting down out of the truck.

"Were you two laughing at me?" Little River asked, shading her eyes from the bright sun.

"No mom, we weren't laughing at you. Actually, I told Brad the story about the kids in school making fun of my name."

"That's not a funny story. Besides that was a long, long time ago. Don't you have any current stories to tell? Never mind! Hello, Mr. Davis. Are you still wearing the bracelet?"

"Yes ma'am!"

"Good! I'm really worried about you. The spirits have been telling me some pretty scary things and you'll need all the protection you can get." Little River removed a tissue from her skirt pocket and wiped the sweat from her brow. "How bad was the damage to your Jeep? Are you hurt any? Running Horse, what did you do with his vehicle?" Little River replaced the tissue in her pocket.

"Mom, it was destroyed in the accident, but you knew that already. Why do you continue to play those games?"

"I wasn't in the car. Sheriff Frank Cooper of Magdalena was in the car when it had the accident. He was killed."

"Sorry to hear about the sheriff, but glad it wasn't you. I would say your bracelet is working overtime keeping you safe. Maybe I should have charged you more for that rattlesnake bracelet. Are you two hungry?"

Running Horse and Brad Davis followed Little River back to the house behind the garage. "Don't pay no mind to my mother's sassiness. She means well." Running Horse whispered to Davis.

"I heard that young man!"

"Heard what, Mom?" Both men started laughing uncontrollably once again.

Little River turned and looked at her son and Davis with a scornful eye. She shook her head, turned and entered the house. "We're having rabbit stew. You like rabbit, Mr. Davis? Don't matter, that's what you're getting, like it or not."

Running Horse continued to laugh all the louder as they entered the house. "Sounds like she's adopted you, Brad," Running Horse said with tears running down his face from laughing so hard.

Following lunch, Little River excused herself and disappeared into the back bedroom to take her afternoon nap. She was thanked for the wonderful meal and hospitality as she closed the door behind her. Running Horse went to the refrigerator and removed two Coors

Light beers from the bottom shelf. Twisting off the caps he offered one to Davis while he took a sip from the bottle he saved for himself.

"Okay, there's something going on between those two ears of yours, Brad. Do you want to talk to me about it?"

Davis pushed his chair from the table and crossed his legs. "As a matter of fact, I do. I need to go back up into the mountains and see if I can find that place again. I want you to come with me so I can show you I'm not crazy."

Running Horse took another long sip from the beer bottle, running his finger around the mouth of the bottle. "Mind you, I'm not afraid of anything. However, it will take quite a few beers to get me to go with you." Running Horse placed his beer bottle on the table. "I'm an old Indian who is very superstitious and believes in the spirit world. Maybe I should start working on my courage right now." He retrieved two more bottles of beer. He held them up to make sure Davis was interested in joining him. Davis responded by shrugging his shoulders affirmatively.

"Perhaps, we should continue our talk and drinking outside," Davis whispered so Little River wouldn't hear him.

"Excellent idea. I don't need my mother lecturing me on going up to the mountain with you. She has this thing about being able to see the future and knowing a great many things before they happen." Running Horse continued to talk as both men made their way outside to the garage. "The older she gets the more predictions she makes. I think it has something to do with the fact that she is so close to becoming a spirit herself that she believes they talk to her all the time. With her energy she'll be around for another twenty years driving me crazy. Now, don't get me wrong. I love my mother." They had reached the garage office and both men sat down, beers in hand, and made themselves comfortable. "It's just that sometimes she's downright scary. Do you know that since the first time she met you she has had this terrible premonition about you?"

"You're kidding!" Davis responded incredulously.

"True! I swear on my father's grave. She believes in spirit magic, especially with that rattlesnake bracelet that I'm sure you think is ridiculous." Davis smiled and took a sip of beer. Running Horse continued, "She felt so strongly about you needing protection she would have given you that bracelet for nothing. My mother may have told you this before, but the Navajos are great believers in protecting sacred burial grounds with rattlesnakes. As a Navajo myself I hold those same beliefs."

"Now you tell me that your mother would have given me that bracelet for nothing," Davis kidded.

"Seriously, she has talked to me of her concern about you. Want to hear something scary?"

"Are you sure I can handle it, Running Horse?"

"Please be serious, Brad."

"Sorry," Davis responded sheepishly.

"I didn't just happen to be on the road where your car went off the road. My mother was boiling water for her tea this morning and suddenly dropped the kettle, letting out a cry in her Navajo tongue. I was outside pumping gas when I heard her. I expected to find her dead on the floor. Instead, she was standing there shaking like a leaf. She said your car had crashed over a guardrail and was burning. She told me the exact spot where the car went over. That's one of the scary things my mother does. I also want to warn you she already knows about Alegros Mountain and that you will be caught up in whatever or whoever is up there. She has said that there are some pretty powerful spirits up there."

"Are you afraid of those spirits, Running Horse?"

"With each sip of this beer I'm getting braver and braver. When do you want to go up there?" Running Horse took a long, slow swig from the bottle.

"Now is as good a time as any!" Davis reached out for Running Horse's hand. They clenched hands and smiled at each other. Words were not necessary to describe what both men were thinking.

Susan had cleared Brad's clothes from the bed, neatly placing the pants and shirts on a hangar. She then lay on the bed, propping two pillows under head, and began, for the third time, reading Davis' notes. Drifting off into a deep sleep, she was suddenly awakened by a knocking on the door. Sleepily, she sat up, checked her watch, and realized she had been sleeping for almost two hours. It was almost one-thirty in the afternoon. The knock on the door came again. Susan slowly placed her feet on the floor and stood up from the bed. She rubbed her eyes and straightened her blouse and skirt. Running her hands through her hair she called out, "Is that you, Brad?"

"Miss Adams, may we speak with you? It is very important" a voice outside the door responded.

Susan pulled aside the curtains and saw two Indians standing by the door. One of them was the same Indian who had tried to get her to open the door earlier. The second man was dressed identically as the first man. He, too, wore the strange glowing object around his neck. "What do you want?" Susan demanded to know.

"We must speak with you. Please open the door."

"Go away, please. I don't want to be bothered. If you don't, I'll call the motel manager to get the police."

"That won't be necessary. We have come to take you to Mr. Davis."

"You know where he is?" Susan began to let her guard down.

"Yes! He asked us to bring you to him."

"If that's the case, why didn't you tell me that before when you were here?" Susan asked, still suspicious.

"You never gave me the chance before some strangers showed up. I didn't want anyone seeing us so I left to tell Mr. Davis you wouldn't talk to me."

"Why didn't he come himself?"

"Danger!"

"What kind of danger?" Susan was still hesitant to trust these two men.

"There is danger because of what he knows."

"What does he know?"

"Please, Miss Adams, we can answer all your questions in a place of safety. We must go now. It is imperative!"

"Why should I believe you?" Susan still wasn't convinced that these men were sent by Brad.

"How can I convince you that you have nothing to fear from us?"

Susan thought for a moment and then decided on what to ask. "What is Mr. Davis working on out here?"

"Mr. Davis is a writer of some renown and has a theory about the Anasazi and a connection to other civilizations."

"Yeah, that's partly true. What else?"

"If you are referring to a connection to other galaxies....."

"Okay, okay, one more question. If Mr. Davis sent you, tell me what he told you about me.

"He said you would be difficult to convince being a reporter and especially since you were a New Englander."

Susan opened the door. "That's good enough for me. Do I need to bring anything with me?" Susan looked around the room to make sure she wasn't going to leave anything important behind.

"No. Please follow us to our car and we will take you to him." The two Indians walked to their dusty, old Chevy Caprice parked in the shade of an old oak tree at the far end of the motel driveway.

Closing the door to the cottage, Susan began to follow the Indians to their car when she suddenly stopped dead in her tracks.

For a moment she thought this car looked like the very car she saw speeding away from the accident scene earlier that day on the highway. Reasoning that her imagination was getting the better of her, she moved quickly to where the two Indians were getting into the car. She glanced toward the motel office and saw the motel clerk peering out the office window, watching her leaving. The car with the three occupants headed out of the parking lot, through town and then onto Route 60 heading towards Alegros Mountain.

About five minutes later the black Ford Bronco carrying Colonel Parker pulled into the driveway of the motel. The colonel instructed his driver to remain in the vehicle while he checked to see if Davis and his girlfriend were in their cottage.

"May I help you, sir? Would you like a room for the night?" the motel manager asked politely.

"No, I'm looking for two friends of mine, Brad Davis and his girlfriend. Are they registered here?" Parker was abrupt in his questions.

"Oh, you mean Mr. and Mrs. Davis?"

The colonel frowned. "Yeah, yeah, I guess that's who I mean. Well, are they here?" The question was curt.

"Well, Mr. Davis has been gone since early this morning. He went away with Sheriff Cooper and hasn't returned. His wife just left not more than five or ten minutes ago with a couple of strange looking Indians in their car.

"What do you mean strange looking?" Parker was becoming impatient.

"They didn't exactly look like all the other Indians around here. It was almost as if they tried to look like regular Indians but they weren't. I can tell the difference. Maybe they were from Arizona or Utah." The motel clerk tried to hide his nervousness at the questions being asked by this stranger. "Oh, another thing I remembered about these Indians. They both had some sort of glowing object hanging around their neck."

"Shit!" The colonel was suddenly aware who the two Indians were. "Do you know which way they went when they left here?"

"No, sir. Can I ask who you are and what this is all about? Have they done something wrong? Are Mr. and Mrs. Davis in some kind of trouble?"

"None of your business, mister! It's nothing for you to concern yourself with and if you know what's good for you, you'll forget that I was ever here. Do you understand me?"

"Yes, yes, sir!" the motel clerk responded in a weak, frightened voice.

The colonel hurried back to the car and slammed the door behind him. "Damn! Damn!" he said in an angry voice.

"What's the problem, sir?" his driver, Lieutenant Nelson asked.

"They're out of the compound and that means they're up to something no good." The colonel was practically screaming at his driver.

"Who are we talking about, sir?" Nelson asked, already knowing the answer.

"Wake up, Nelson!" Parker was angry at his driver for asking the dumb question that he already knew the answer to. "You damn right well know who I'm talking about. It's those damn aliens from the mountain. I had given strict orders for them to stay confined to the compound. Somebody is going to get their ass chewed out for this."

"What do you think it means, colonel?"

"I think it means we better backtrack our steps and get Big Bird and the general's bodies before these characters start working some of their freaking magic." The angriness in the colonel's voice was being replaced with fear. "Let's check out the general's house first and retrieve his body and then we'll go and get Big Bird's body. We have to find and dispose of them before they find them."

CHAPTER FOURTEEN

"General Darlington, good afternoon, sir." The voice on the telephone was cordial, yet very firm. "This is Mitch Kaminsky. The President has instructed me to tell you that he would like to see you in the Oval Office at 1400 hours, one hour from now." Mitch Kaminsky was a slightly overweight man, less than six feet tall with a full head of closely-cropped white hair. A close confidant of the President, Kaminsky had been placed in charge of national security when the President first took office. He had cut his teeth in government working at the CIA under Allen Dulles many years ago. The oldest member of the President's senior staff, his many years of government service qualified him as an expert in government affairs. It was this experience and the respect he commanded from members of Congress that made him an invaluable aide to the President on national security matters. His tough but fair attitude with members of the media endeared him to top network brass. On any given Sunday you could tune in one of the networks and find him being interviewed on *Meet the Press* or any number of other public affairs programs.

"Two o'clock! I'm sorry, Mr. Kaminsky, but I've got a meeting scheduled at that time with some of my top Air Force staff."

"Shall I tell the President you can't make his meeting then?"

The voice at the other end of the telephone was heard to take a deep breath and the sound of a muffled expletive. "Er...." the voice hesitated.

"I'm sorry, general, I didn't quite hear your response?"

"Look, Mr. Kaminsky I have a very important meeting that I must keep. Do you have any idea what the President wants to see me about?"

"Yes, General, I do, but I'm not at liberty to discuss the matter over the telephone. Let me tell you it is of the utmost importance that you be prompt." Kaminsky's voice was commanding.

The general was still hedging. "Who else will be at this meeting?"

"Just you, me and the President. If you're entertaining the thought of showing up late, I must remind you that you serve at the pleasure of your Commander-in-Chief, the President, who can easily find a new head of the Air Force."

"Okay, Mr. Kaminsky, I get your message loud and clear. I'll be there on time." Five-Star General Elliott Darlington, or General D, as he was referred to in military circles, was a career military man. A member of the first graduating class of the Air Force Academy in Colorado Springs, Darlington was assigned to teach at the Academy following his first two-year tour of duty, and he remained there until the mid- sixties. President Johnson, delivering the commencement address at the Academy in 1964, first met General Darlington at the graduation luncheon. The President was taken with the general immediately and offered him a special post as an advisor to the White House. From that time on, General Darlington, with offices at the Pentagon, quickly rose through the ranks, winning political favor with a number of influential senators and congressmen. It was President Bush who had a hand in promoting Darlington to his present position in charge of the Air Force at the Pentagon and as a member of the Joint Chiefs of Staff. "Captain Bork, come in here!" the general shouted into the intercom.

"Right away, sir." the voice on the other end replied. The eight-foot wooden door opened into the mahogany paneled office adorned with military memorabilia, including a replica of an F-15 that sat on the general's desk. The captain approached the general and stood at attention as he spoke. "Yes, sir. How may I be of service, sir?"

"Cancel my 1400 hours meeting and reschedule it for 1630 hours. Make sure you tell those two men that I expect a full accounting of their activities with Colonel Parker. I want you to call down and get my car out front. I've been summoned by the President. I can't believe the damn President has the balls to call a sudden meeting without giving me more notice. Does he think I sit around here with nothing to do except wait to be summoned by him?"

The grandfather clock in the hallway outside the Oval office was chiming for the second time, indicating that the general had indeed arrived in time for his meeting with the President.

"Hello, general. How are you?"

"Fine, thank you, Mary. And how are you and the family?"

"Well, thank you." Mary Finley had been the appointments secretary for the President for almost two years. She replaced a young thing the President had brought from his home state. After almost six months the First Lady had the leggy, single blonde fired. The First Lady took control over her replacement and Mary was her first and only choice. "You can go in now, General. He's off the telephone."

"Thank you, Mary." Before the general reached the door, Mitch Kaminsky opened it and invited the general in. They shook hands as a formality. It was not a strong handshake. "Mr. President, so good to see you."

"Good afternoon, General Darlington." The President didn't especially like the general. From his personal dealings with him in the past the President found the general, with all his connections to the old Washington establishment, to be pompous, arrogant and a manipulative individual. Not many Cabinet members held the general in high regard either. "Let me get right to the point of why I called you here on such short notice. We need to discuss a matter that has come to my attention involving national security."

"And what might that be, Mr. President?"

"Don't get cute with me, general!" The President was obviously angry. "I'm talking about New Mexico and all these UFO sightings, glowing blue lights throughout central New Mexico and some supposed humming sound."

"Yes, sir. I've had Air Force tracking radar and planes out of Alamogordo trying to come up with something sir, but we've been unsuccessful."

"That's pure unadulterated bullshit, general, and you know it!" The general played with the braid on his hat as the President continued talking. "We're the most technologically advanced country in the world and you give me an answer that is no answer. If your radar and planes can't find these so-called UFO's, then how come our spy satellites that can read a license plate from one hundred and sixty-five miles above earth can't get a reading on them."

"I don't have an answer for that, sir."

The President slammed his fist on the desk. "I want an answer now! Today! Is that understood, general?"

"Yes sir, Mr. President!"

"I've had several phone calls today from some New Mexico congressmen and one senator asking what the military was doing about this. All they get is a runaround from Air Force brass out there. I do not need to add this situation to all the problems I'm handling. It's bad enough my foreign relations programs are under attack in both Houses and my personal legal problems keep mounting. I do not need this country scared shitless about UFO reports."

"Yes sir, I understand, sir. I'll do my best to get to the bottom of this, sir."

"You bet your ass you will because I'll have your job if I'm not satisfied. And another thing, I want some answers on something that Mr. Kaminsky has been briefing me on."

"What would that be, Mr. President?"

"Go ahead, Mitch, you ask him." The President walked over to where his National Security Director was seated.

"General, what do you know about Project Anasazi?"

The general's face remained expressionless. "Excuse me, Mr. Kaminsky, what was the name of that project again?"

"Project Anasazi!" Kaminsky angrily fired back. "You know damn well......."

"You can cut the act, general," the President interrupted. "We know you have full knowledge of this project. In fact, we know a lot more about the 1947 Roswell incident than you give us credit for." The President had walked across to the other side of his desk and was now standing in front of the general. Mr. Kaminsky was over in the top-secret file room at the Pentagon earlier today when he came across this single file that somehow was lying on the bottom of a file drawer with rows of other files strung out over it. Evidently, all these years no one took the time to check out every file in this one particular file cabinet." Turning around, the President reached down and picked up a deteriorating brownish manila folder and waved it in front of the general. "Have you ever seen this file before, general?"

"No, Mr. President, I swear to you I have never seen that file, but I can probably guess as to the contents." General Darlington shifted uneasily in the chair.

"Mitch, why don't you enlighten the general on this matter." Turning away from the general, the President returned to the leather chair behind his desk.

"Let me be perfectly candid, general. We were not looking for this file. The President and I had no knowledge of its existence. I went down in the basement file room at the Pentagon because of an Associated Press story that appeared in today's *Washington Post*. After reading the article I was curious about the missing documents concerning the Roswell UFO reports. Perhaps, I thought, they may have gotten buried among some top secret files which were not released as part of the Freedom of Information Act. Did you read this AP story, General?" The general shook his head no. Kaminsky handed the general the article. It read:

ROSWELL UFO REPORTS
APPARENTLY DESTROYED

ALBUQUERQUE, N.M. (AP) - *Key military documents on the so-called Roswell Incident, cited by UFO buffs as an alien crash, were apparently destroyed without authorization decades ago, a congressman said Saturday.*

Rep. Steve Schiff of New Mexico said a General Accounting Office report shed no new light on the 1947 crash and showed that important documents are missing.

"Documents that should have provided more information were destroyed," Schiff said.

Schiff said the GAO estimates the information was destroyed more than 40 years ago.

The Air Force has said that the wreckage was probably a balloon launched as part of a classified government project to detect Soviet nuclear weapons.

The GAO report, released Friday, said that two government documents are the only official records remaining of the crash near what was then the Roswell Army Air Force Base.

For nearly half a century, the mysterious crash has fueled speculation about aliens in the New Mexico desert, Cold War secrecy and a government cover-up.

"The debate on what crashed at Roswell continues," the GAO report said.

It said the Roswell base's administrative records from March 1945 through December 1949 and its out-going messages from October 1946 through December 1949 were destroyed.

Those messages, internal military communications, would have shown how military officials in Roswell explained what happened to their superiors, Schiff said.

The weather balloon story has since been discredited by the Air Force itself, which last year said the wreckage was probably a balloon launched as part of Project Mogul. The project was a highly classified effort to detect Soviet nuclear weapons using balloons that carried radar reflectors and acoustic sensors, the GAO report said.

The general finished reading the article and handed it back to Kaminsky. "What have you got to say about Roswell and those missing documents?" Kaminsky asked in an authoritative tone of voice.

"Very interesting, but nothing that we all haven't heard before," the general responded.

"Alright, General, let's talk about what I found in this Top Secret file cabinet in the basement. Among several files in this cabinet I found this file which was marked **Presidential Orders1947**. I broke President Truman's seal and opened it. You know what I found in this file?"

"No, I don't, Mr. Kaminsky."

"I found an internal memorandum detailing the 1947 Roswell incident and the subsequent cover-up by the Army Air Force. According to the memo, there really was a UFO landing, with pieces strewn over a wide area. Roswell sent out all kinds of troops to pick up these pieces and retrieve three alien bodies. The military establishment back then denied it was a UFO and perpetrated a story of a new type of weather balloon. It took awhile, but the public finally bought the story. The cover-up took place between the military and this office right here. President Truman himself is the one who gave the orders for Project Anasazi. It also mentions the creation of a task force code named 'Majestic 12.' The report also says there are two secured rooms at Roswell full of notes and files on what this project is really all about. Tell me, general, what the hell is Project Anasazi and who were the individuals who comprised 'Majestic 12?' Are Project Anasazi and the 'Majestic 12' still in existence? And, are those files still in Roswell?"

Folding his arms, the general cleared his throat, a clear indication he was very nervous. "Let me see if I can shed some light on this matter. As you know, I assumed this position during President Bush's Administration. Since 1947, there have been five generals in my position, each of them knowing about the project and passing on the information to his successor."

"Did President Bush or any other President have knowledge of this project?" The President interrupted.

"To my knowledge only Presidents Truman, Eisenhower and Kennedy were advised of this project."

"Why was that, do you think?" Kaminsky asked.

"Truman, for the obvious reason, sanctioned the project. I understand Eisenhower and Kennedy believed in UFO's and obtained the information because of their interest. If you remember, sir, it was President Kennedy who kicked off this country's space program. I would say he had more than a casual interest in space exploration."

"Why was no other President briefed?" an angry President asked.

"Sir, I was told from the day I was first made aware of this project that only three people, at any given time, were to have this knowledge so as not to cause panic and interrupt the project's work."

"Who are the other two besides yourself?" Kaminsky wanted to know.

"The head of Air Force Military Security, who at the present time is Colonel Wally Parker. The other individual, who actually has overall responsibility for the project, is retired General Nathaniel Brantfield."

"Brantfield? Wasn't he one of the officers in charge of Roswell at that time?" both the President and Kaminsky asked at the exact same time.

"Yes. He lives in New Mexico and was second in command at Roswell in 1947 when the incident occurred."

"How the hell old is this guy?" Kaminsky asked incredulously.

"He's in his eighties."

"Eighties!" The President stood up. "What the hell is this project that we have an eighty-year-old man running? I want to know right now what this project is all about!"

"Project Anasazi is about UFO survivors who are helping our government by using their advanced knowledge to develop new medicines to combat diseases on earth, among other things."

"Survivors!" The President slumped down in his chair.

"Are there really aliens living on earth?" Kaminsky edged forward in his chair. "Have you seen them?"

"No sir! Only General Brantfield has had direct access to them. It's only been during the last year that Colonel Parker has gained limited access. That was our agreement with these people. They would help us as long as they could do so without interference from our government. This is why it has been such a hush-hush operation."

"I'm pissed you haven't advised me of this project. As your Commander-in-Chief, you had an obligation to inform me of this threat to our national security." The President was now talking at the top of his voice.

"Excuse me, sir, but I don't see this as any threat. They've been here for over fifty years." Darlington wiped the sweat from his brow.

"Any foreign government, whether it's from somewhere on this planet or from any other planet for that matter, that takes up residence in our country and receives military help is my concern. Do I make myself perfectly clear?"

"Yes sir, Mr. President."

"I can't believe this has been going for over fifty years and no one, except a select handful of people over the years, has known about it." Getting up from his chair, the President began to pace. "I believe you said they were working on developing medicines, among other things. What other things?"

"Advanced propulsion systems, stronger metals, advanced communication techniques, things like that, sir."

"Things like that!" the President responded sarcastically. "How has this thing been funded all these years?"

"No government money has been spent to fund this project that I know of, sir."

"How could that be possible?" Mitch Kaminsky listened intently, letting the President do all the talking. The President continued,

"They have to be receiving funding from somewhere. Where do you think it could possibly be coming from?"

"I don't know, sir. If they're such an advanced civilization I would think they're capable of being very self sufficient."

"That's a lot of crap! Somebody or some group has to be financing them. I want you to find out. Maybe there's someone else we don't know about in government or in the private sector who is assisting them financially."

"I really don't think that's the case, sir."

The President pointed his finger at Darlington. "I don't give a shit what you think!" he said angrily. "Find out, and get back to me with an answer. Do you think the House and Senate Appropriations Committees might be supporting it through some creative bookkeeping? And then again, the 'Majestic 12' may have put something into operation back in the late forties that we still don't know about. Is that possible? I want all these things checked out."

"Yes, sir, I'll get on it right away," General Darlington said in a commanding voice.

The President, still with a slight trace of anger in his voice said, "I still can't believe all of this. Where are these people?"

"In a mountain southwest of Albuquerque."

"Does the mountain have a name, General?"

"Yes, sir! Alegros Mountain, sir!"

"Mitch, I want you to make some notes of our meeting here with the general. Just for our eyes only."

"Yes sir, Mr. President," Kaminsky answered.

The President continued to interrogate the general. "How many people are we talking about out there?

"Close to three hundred."

"Three hundred! That's incredible! Where do they sleep? How do you feed them?"

"They have homes that they constructed for themselves and as far as food is concerned, they supply their own."

"How?"

"Like they do on their own planet, an advanced method of hydroponics."

"By the way, where do they come from?

"A planet called Dacon in a galaxy beyond our own star system."

"What do they look like?"

«Actually, they›re like us, except their skin has an unusual color.»

"You mean like our own Indians?"

"Yes sir."

"What about a space ship?"

"Actually sir, there was a smaller scout ship and a larger craft that carried over 500 people. The scout ship was destroyed in 1947 and what was left was in a million pieces. The pieces were all gathered and stored in an underground cavern near where they are living. The larger craft left some of their people behind when it was decided the craft would have difficulty returning to their planet if they took everyone back with them."

While the President was angry with the general, he was at the same time fascinated with what he was being told. "I need to see the records on this project that are stored at Roswell."

"That's going to be impossible, Mr. President. They were stored in Hangar 84 at Roswell Army Air Field and a fire in 1953 destroyed all those records."

"Was it sabotage or an accident?"

"They never were able to solve that case, sir."

"General, I want you to bring this General Brantfield to the White House. Since he is the only one who sees these people on a regular basis I want to talk with him. Do you know who the twelve people who comprised the 'Majestic 12' are or were?"

"I did at one time, sir, but they're all dead except one and he's in a nursing home somewhere in the Midwest. He was a nuclear physicist and worked on developing the atomic bomb."

"Find out where he is and see if he's well enough to come to Washington. If he can't, I'll send Mitch to talk with him. One last thing I have to know."

"Yes, Mr. President."

"General Darlington, now that we know there are really live aliens out in New Mexico who arrived here by some sort of UFO, do you want to tell me the truth now about your radar and plane sightings out there?"

"Yes sir, Mr. President, I believe I can give you and Mr. Kaminsky the true story about the Air Force's findings and my thoughts on why the aliens have returned."

General Darlington had spent an uncomfortable two hours in the hot seat in the Oval Office. He was not happy on his ride back to the Pentagon. His driver pulled into the underground garage, letting the general out by the main door to the complex. Entering his security code he proceeded past the military guards, heading up to his office to prepare for his next meeting with members of Colonel Parker's task force. He never did tell the President the whole story about what was going on at the compound in Alegros Mountain. It was something that, if known by the President, would have blown the lid off the entire project operation and the President would have him court-martialed. No, it was a subject he would never tell the president or anyone else in the government. Some secrets inside the military establishment were best left as secrets. The general's main worry now was how to keep the President at arm's length on this project while deciding what he should do about letting General Brantfield meet with the President. First, he had to have the two men assigned to Colonel Parker report on the project's latest developments. It was almost time for his meeting with the two men at 16:30 hours.

The black Bronco pulled into the driveway, coming within a foot of the garage door of the general's house. Parker and Nelson emerged from the vehicle at the same time. Walking around to the side of the house, they opened the gate leading to the back patio.

The chaise lounge was facing toward the house and the fact that the general's body could not be seen immediately did not alarm them. Approaching the lounge they immediately saw that the general's body was not where they had left it.

"We did leave the General on that lounger, didn't we, Nelson?"

"Yes sir! Don't you remember I propped his feet up?"

"Yeah, but what the hell happened to his body?" The colonel curled his lip between his teeth. "Did you make sure he was dead?"

"Colonel, he was deader than a doornail! There was no way he could have survived that dose."

"Then where the hell is his body? He sure as hell didn't get up and walk away."

"Maybe somebody came and found him and took him away."

"That is a distinct possibility! The only explanation is that those two Indians the motel clerk saw probably had something to do with it. We haven't been gone that long and besides anyone other than those aliens finding his body would have called the sheriff's office. There would be someone around checking out things. No, there's something strange going on here and I plan to find out what it is."

"What do you mean strange, colonel?"

The colonel, lost in thought, didn't hear the question. "Let's check where we dumped Big Bird's body and make sure it's still there.

It took fifteen minutes for the colonel's Bronco to reach the spot where they had hidden Big Bird's body. Lieutenant Nelson was the first to call out.

"Hey colonel, I don't see his body."

"Get out and check real good! It better be there!" the colonel said angrily as he opened the door and stepped outside the vehicle.

"He's not there, colonel!" The anxiety in Lieutenant Nelson's voice was evident. "It's like we never placed his body there. Do you think he wasn't dead?"

"Believe me, lieutenant, he was dead!" The colonel stood looking at the ground where the body had been placed. "Check and see if you find anything unusual in the vicinity." Walking back toward the road the colonel bent down to examine a set of tire tracks. "Nelson, come over here."

"Did you find something, colonel?"

"Yeah! Bend down here and tell me what you see."

The lieutenant bent down where the colonel sat on his haunches examining the dirt. Pointing at a set of tire tracks he asked, "Do you mean this set of tire tracks?"

"Yes! See anything unusual?"

"I see two distinct sets of tire tracks that look like they were made recently."

"That's very good, lieutenant. What else can you tell me?"

The lieutenant looked back at the Bronco's tire treads and then back to the spot they were examining. "One set is definitely made from the Bronco, sir. But, the other set is definitely not from the Bronco. Do you think there was another car here that maybe picked up Big Bird's body?"

"I'm positive that's what happened." The colonel stood up and the lieutenant did the same. "I'm also convinced whoever took Big Bird's and the General's bodies were one and the same. In fact, those individuals also took that Adams woman from the motel."

"What makes you say that, colonel?"

"When we were at the general's house I noticed a fresh set of tire tracks in the dirt driveway. The outside treads were smooth as if the front wheels were out of line. At the time I remembered seeing that same set of tire tracks at the motel when we were looking for the girl. That's why I had said there was something strange going on while we were back at the general's house looking for his body. And now that same set of tire tracks is here. Coincidence? I don't think so. It's those damn Indians from the mountain. There's no doubt about it. We're going to pay them a visit. First, though, I think it's time we pay the deputy sheriff another visit and track down Mr. Davis. We know he's still alive. Maybe he can provide us some answers as to what the hell is going on out here."

It took ten minutes for the two men to reach the sheriff's office in Magdalena. "You stay here while I check with the deputy and see what he can tell us about our friend." The colonel closed the car door and walked the few steps to the sheriff's office. He found Deputy Sheriff Bones Laughlin hunched over, typing on a Packard Bell word processor. "Hello there!" he greeted the deputy.

Looking up from the keyboard the deputy returned the greeting, "Oh, hi, how you doing, sir!"

"I'm Colonel Parker and I was wondering if you could help me locate a friend I was supposed to meet here at noon today. I thought he said to meet him at Mama B's, but he never showed up. He's staying at the motel and has been gone since early this morning."

Standing up, Bones Laughlin moved to shake the colonel's hand. "Pleased to meet you, colonel. Are you in the military now or are you retired? I only ask that because you're not in uniform."

"Actually, I'm on vacation passing through."

"What's the name of your friend?"

"Brad Davis."

"Sure. I don't know where you'll find him though."

"Why is that?" the colonel asked, frowning.

"Well, Captain Gerard over at the state trooper headquarters in Socorro told me that the sheriff brought Mr. Davis over there early this morning for some kind of protection. The captain said he let Mr. Davis go when he heard the sheriff was dead."

"Did he say where Mr. Davis went?"

"No. Would you like me to call over there and find out if they can give me any more information?" Parker nodded his head. "I know he never showed up back at the motel. A little while ago I called over there to see if he had returned. Oh, but you know that already, don't you? You know, I was curious if he could shed a little more light on why he and the sheriff went over to Socorro. Something else is odd too. His girlfriend was waiting over there for him and suddenly she took off with two Indians."

Parker was becoming impatient. "The telephone call, deputy, please."

"Right. Sometimes I just talk too much and don't know when to stop."

"Deputy!"

"I'm dialing now. Hello, this is Deputy Sheriff Laughlin over at Magdalena. Can I speak with Captain Gerard, please? He's not there. Well, maybe you can tell me about that Davis fellow who was over there earlier today. Yeah, that's him. I wanted to know if the captain knew where he went. Some friend of his is trying to meet up with him. Good. Thank you!" Bones Laughlin hung up the phone and smiled. "You lucked out. Mr. Davis left with Running Horse late this morning and the dispatcher overheard them talking about going back to Running Horse's place."

"Who is this Running Horse?" The colonel wanted to know.

"He and his mother run a small service station and towing business over in Horse Springs. You can't miss it. It's right on the main road."

Colonel Parker reached out and shook Bones Laughlin's hand. "You've been very helpful, deputy. Thank you!" Without another word the colonel abruptly turned and left. Getting back into the Bronco he barked an order. "We've got some unfinished business at Horse Springs. Then we'll be going to Alegros Mountain."

"Horse Springs?" the lieutenant, asked surprised.

"You heard me right! Horse Springs! It's time you meet our visitors!"

CHAPTER FIFTEEN

Professor Beal made his way to the top of the ladder leading out of the kiva. Taking a last look back, he saw the cavernous room had once again become totally dark. He moved toward the opening in the cliff dwelling looking out onto the narrow valley below. His thoughts were of Fred Smith. One minute he was there, the next minute he was gone. Had the spirit world gobbled him up? Nonsense, he thought. Spirits and ghosts were something that only existed at Halloween.

His years of studying archaeoastronomy had made him a cautious scientist, weighing all the facts and coming to plausible conclusions. There is a reasonable explanation for everything that takes place in the universe. A logical order exists that means everything can be explained by cause and effect. Of course, this was his scientific reasoning, but many people didn't buy into it. However, his work on Project Blue Book for the government exposed him to phenomena that couldn't easily be explained. He and his colleagues documented many sightings and so-called extraterrestrial encounters that could be explained ninety-five percent of the time. And then there was the five percent that just couldn't be explained. But did that mean he believed in UFO's, spirits and ghosts? Hardly! He always considered himself a cautious skeptic. Until today, that is! What he saw today in this cliff dwelling in the kiva defied logic. How could an Indian tribe that inhabited this place more than six hundred years ago have the technology to create holograms and utilize a lighting system that was far superior to today's electric lighting systems? All of this five hundred years before the invention of the light bulb! He was trying to be logical again. There had to be some other explanation, he reasoned. His thoughts were interrupted by thunder in the distance. A light rain had begun to fall. It was time for him to leave this place, before he became trapped by the impending storm. He moved away from the cliff opening, turning toward the ladder that led up to the opening where he and Fred Smith had entered this cavernous room of cliff dwellings. Suddenly, a movement from high above the near wall caught his eye.

"Hey, professor, wait for me!" Fred Smith cautiously moved from a narrow opening in the cliff wall down steps that were carved into the sloping walls toward the professor.

"Where the hell did you disappear to?" Beal shouted up at Smith.

"Wait until I tell you what I found!" Smith was talking excitedly at the top of his lungs. The professor reached out for Smith's arm and helped him down the last few steps. "I don't give a good damn what you found. You gave me a terrible scare when I couldn't find you in the kiva."

"Look, it wasn't my fault! I'm sitting there watching you poke your hand through that figure in the middle of the room when all of a sudden the wall behind me gives way and I find myself in this room full of all kinds of treasure."

"What the hell are you talking about? Room? Treasure?"

"Yeah, a huge room filled with things I've never seen before. Strange things that don't seem like they belong on this planet."

The professor released his grip on Smith when he reached the last step. "You're not making sense."

"Look, professor, nothing in this place makes sense. The futuristic lighting, Indian spirits and what looks like space suits...."

"Space suits?" The professor could hardly believe his ears.

"Like nothing you have ever seen before and a lot of other things I couldn't make out what they're used for. Here look at this metal-like tablet I found with strange writing on it. Looks like the same kind of writing we saw on the walls outside the dwellings, except it looks like a saying or message of some kind." Fred pulled the soft metal piece from his pants pocket and handed it to the professor. "It's really something, isn't it?"

The professor took the piece of metal and examined it very carefully. "This is a very exciting discovery. The metal is soft but yet extremely durable. I don't know of any metal like this on earth. You're right, Mr. Smith. The writing does look like the same kind of lettering used outside the entrance to the dwellings. I don't know of any writing system that looks like this." The professor looked at the specimen carefully trying to recognize any kind of letter he may have seen before.

•❄🏳✌• •🖘🖘🦺 •••☺✪ ☼🖘•🏳☼•🖘• •🦺❄🏳🖘❄•••🖘 🏳🖘
••☺••• ••🏳•• ❄🏳✌❄✌ •✌🦺• 🏳🖘🖘✠•☺🏳☼•🖘• 🏳✌✝🖘🖘🖘❄
🏳•☼ ☺✌🦺• ❄🏳 ☺🏳•☺🖘🖘☺❄🏳☼🏳•🤙🏳❄🏳🖘 •🏳🦺❄•🦺•••
❄🏳 •🖘❄❄☺🖘✌🦺• •☼🖘✌❄🖘🦺🖘• 🖘•••☼🖘•• ❄🏳🖘•☼
•🏳•☼✌🤙🖘✌🦺• ☼🖘•🏳•☼•🖘🖘☞•☺🦺🖘•• ••☺☺ •🖘 ☼🖘•🖘••🖘☼🖘•
☞🏳☼ ✌☺☺❄••🖘•

The professor started to hand the metal object back. "I can't make heads or tails of this thing. Do you mind if I hold onto it?" Smith shrugged his shoulders and gestured for the professor to keep the strange looking object. "When we get back to the university, we'll get some experts to try and decipher it. Tell me more about this room"

"The room was all lit up by the same kind of lighting we saw in those other rooms. I tried to get back to where you were but that entranceway evidently only worked one way. I looked around for another entrance and I think there was one, but I just didn't know how to make it work. Then I noticed steps carved in the stone going right up to what looked like an entranceway. That's how I got out of there. It was a short tunnel leading right back out to this room. The steps inside that room are just like the ones I climbed down on this side. Come on, follow me and I'll take you back to the room."

The thunder was much closer now, echoing throughout the cliff dwelling. The rain had begun to fall harder. The professor stood debating whether to take Smith up on his offer. "Mr. Smith, what you are telling me is fascinating and I am anxious to see these things you talk about. But right now I'm worried about that storm coming this way. This time of year these storms can be ferocious and turn narrow gullies into raging rivers. I think it best that we leave this place for the time being, pick up Mr. Osborne, and head back to the car before we're caught in a flood and get stranded out here overnight. Tomorrow is another day. On our walk back you can try to describe some of the other things you saw in that room."

"Alright, but I wanted to tell you I think I found another way out of this place."

"What are you talking about?"

"Just off to the side up there where I came into the opening of the cliff dwelling, I found another narrow tunnel. I could feel a strong breeze coming through it, like there was an opening at the end of the tunnel."

"That's great. Most likely it was the tunnel Bryant found to enter this place. Come on, tell me more as we walk."

By the time they reached the entranceway where they had left Jack Osborne hours earlier, it was pouring rain. Osborne called from the shelter of trees some twenty yards away. "What the hell took you guys so long? I was about ready to go back and get a search team to look for you."

Smith and the professor ran through the drenching rain to join Osborne. "Jack, wait until I tell you what we found up there. I'm going to score some points with the director when I tell him what we've uncovered at this place. You can bet your ass the President will want to hear our story personally. He'll probably give us a medal."

"Slow down, Fred, and talk some sense to me." Osborne raised both hands gesturing Smith to talk slowly.

"Look fellas, I would love to stand here and revel in your new found success but I better remind you we have a long, narrow gully to cross to get back up where we parked the car. With the rain coming down this heavy, this area has a tendency to flash flood. Believe me, you don't want to get caught in one of our famous New Mexico flash floods. So let's hold the chatter and get a move on. Follow me carefully and stay close."

All three men gave up their shelter and began the journey back to where they had parked the car. Carefully, they made their way along the narrow foot path paralleling the woods. "Okay, here is the tough part" the professor called out as thunder resounded throughout the mountainous terrain. The wind was now beginning to blow. "We've got to cross through this narrow gully heading back up the mountain for the next hundred yards. If you feel the ground rumbling underneath you at any time run like hell up the side of the gully. If you see a wall of water heading toward you don't try to out-run it. You have to get up the side of the gully or you won't survive." As the three men made their way for the first twenty-five yards a small trickle of water had become a heavy flow rushing at them through the gully.

They were having difficulty maintaining their footing and as a result were making slow headway. "I don't like the looks of this, guys!" the professor yelled back at his two companions. The wind had picked up in intensity making it more difficult for them to move quickly through the area. Lightning seemed to fill the sky continuously as the thunder shook the ground beneath their feet.

"Hey, professor, I'm not sure, but is the ground shaking from the thunder or is it something else?"

"Something else, I'm afraid!" the professor yelled back at the two men trailing him. "We're almost out of here. See that huge boulder up ahead on the right. We have to get there quickly. Hurry, hurry!"

The urgency in the professor's voice gave Smith and Osborne the added adrenaline they needed to fight their weariness. The two FBI agents could see that the gully just below the boulder took a sharp turn and they knew they were almost out of danger. "What's that roaring sound I hear?" Smith shouted to the professor who was about five yards ahead of him halfway up the steep incline.

"Hurry up! There's a wall of water heading this way," the professor screamed back to the two men. We're almost to the boulder where we'll be safe."

The professor was the first to reach the safety of the boulder as the roaring sound became louder. The flow of water was rising beneath Smith and Osborne as they struggled to reach the safety of the boulder where the professor waited for them. Smith was the first to join the professor as the water continued to rise in the gully. Osborne was partly submerged in the rising water and was desperately grasping for something to hold onto. Both the professor and Smith reached down, each grabbing Osborne's hands and pulling him to safety above the rising water.

"We should be safe here," the professor said in a reassuring tone. All three men clasped hands in a joint hand shake congratulating themselves that they had reached safety. The roar of cascading water drowned out their voices as they tried to communicate with each other. As they turned toward the roaring sound of the water, still clasping hands, all three were swept away in a rush of water pouring down from twenty feet above their heads.

Mitch Kaminsky sat back in the overstuffed leather seat and took a long sip of his Absolut vodka martini. The waitress returned with the bowl of peanuts Mitch had asked for and set them on the glass table in front of him. He thanked her as he reached for a handful of peanuts, placing them one at a time in his mouth. A tap on his shoulder from behind stopped him from reaching for another handful.

"You should know better than to leave your back exposed. You're supposed to have enough sense to sit with your back to a wall." The voice was that of FBI Director Everett Weaver.

"Hey, Ev, good to see you. Glad you could make my meeting on short notice." Kaminsky stood and shook hands with his long time friend, motioning him to sit, taking the leather seat close to his. "As far as your concern about my sitting with my back to the wall, thank you, but forget it. I'm not paranoid like you. Besides, I'm too old to give a damn."

"Just the same, Mitch, you might live a little longer if you were a bit more cautious. Now, tell me what's this all about? Why the sudden urgency?" Everett Weaver was a career agent with over thirty years service. His last assignment before being appointed by the President and approved by Congress in '93 was head of the New York City office of the Bureau. He was a no-nonsense, loyal and dedicated government agent who would lay down his life for his country.

"The grapevine has it that you have some agents nosing around out in New Mexico. Any truth to that rumor?"

"Sweet Jesus, Mitch, if you wanted to talk serious business you could have picked a better place for our meeting other than the public bar at the Jefferson!"

"That's the beauty, Ev. Nobody would ever guess we were talking about important things like UFO's."

"Shit! Don't say that so loud!" Everett whispered, leaning close to Kaminsky, looking around the open room. "You know Peter Jennings stays here and a lot of the ABC news staff from around the corner drink here. That's all we need is for those media people to get hold of a story like this."

"Ev, look around you. There are two people sitting at the bar deep in conversation with the bartender and two women by the window comparing their shopping acquisitions of the day. None of them are within earshot, so stop worrying."

"I guess you're right, but all the same, next time pick a better spot to talk about stuff like this."

"Agreed!" Kaminsky smiled and Weaver became less tense. "As I was saying, UFO's."

"Okay! As you probably read in the newspapers and saw on television, there are some strange things going on out in New Mexico. Sightings, strange lights, sounds, all taking place, as I understand it, in and around a place called the Plains of San Agustin. We assigned two of our Washington agents to quietly nose around out there and see what they could come up with."

"And?" Kaminsky asked.

"Look, let me say this first, Mitch. I don't give much credence to this UFO crap, but I have an obligation to at least investigate. The two men I have out there have latched onto an archaeoastronomer who has spent his whole life studying Indian civilizations in the southwestern part of the United States."

"An archaeo what?" Kaminsky laughed.

"Archaeoastronomer. It's someone who studies past civilizations in terms of astronomy. At least, I think that's what they study."

"I'm sorry I asked. Go on, tell me more about what your agents have uncovered."

"There's nothing to report yet. I heard from them yesterday and they said they met with a Professor Beal from the University of New

Mexico who was going to take them out to a new Anasazi find in the mountains. They'll check in tonight with more information."

"Do you think there's some connection between this Indian find and the UFO sightings?"

"Can't imagine why there would be!"

"Would you like another drink, sir?" The waitress had finally returned to take a drink order.

Kaminsky returned his empty glass to the waitress' tray. "I'll have one more of the same. What do you want, Ev?"

"Glass of your house white wine will be fine."

The Director of National Security waited to speak until the waitress had returned to the bar.

"Ev, I want you to call me as soon as your men report in."

"Is there something I should know about?" Ev Weaver helped himself to a handful of peanuts.

"It's so big it could cause a national panic." he said softly.

"National panic! What the hell are we talking about, Mitch?" Weaver asked in a hushed, but concerned tone.

"Here are your drinks, gentlemen." The waitress had returned and both men fell silent. "Vodka martini and a white wine." She placed the drinks on the table. "Will there be anything else right now, gentlemen?"

Kaminsky held up his hand to indicate there was nothing else they needed at the present time. "No, thank you," he said cordially. The waitress smiled and returned to the bar. Both men reached for their drinks at the same time and took long sips. "Ev, I've just come from a meeting with the President and General Darlington."

"Darlington! The color in Weaver's face, already a ruddy color, turned even redder. His bushy eyebrows narrowed as Weaver contorted his angular face into a deep frown. "That blue-suited bastard has given me more fits in the last year and a half than I've had from all the military during my career."

"What's the problem?"

"During the last twelve months I've asked him on several occasions to have his people check on some strange calls we've gotten from people saying they've seen UFO's. These calls came from all over the country. We asked him to have his radar installations give us a readout. He yessed us to death and then never got back to us. When I confronted him on it, he said there was nothing to it and figured there was nothing to report to us. He's a freaking liar!" Weaver's voice was becoming angry. "Then, the other day I asked him to check on sightings in New Mexico. He was told to get back to me within two hours. Nothing! That's when I dispatched my men to New Mexico. I tell you, Mitch, we have got to get that bastard out of the Pentagon. Please have the President order me to investigate him and get some dirt on him. It really would be a pleasure."

"Calm down, Ev. His arrogance and lying are part of why the President wanted to see him. Have you ever heard of Project Anasazi?" Weaver shook his head no. "How about the 1947 Roswell incident?"

"Come on, Mitch. You trying to pull my leg? That's ancient history. Of course, the story in the *Washington Post* the other day still has the weirdoes talking government cover up. They still think we were visited by aliens and the government has their dead bodies hidden somewhere." Weaver reached for his drink and held it to his mouth.

Mitch Kaminsky picked up his glass and set it on the armrest of the overstuffed chair. "Ev, the aliens are alive and well and living in New Mexico." Everett Weaver looked at Mitch Kaminsky in astonishment and quickly emptied his wine glass.

It was close to seven p.m. when the National Security Director's chauffeur-driven limousine pulled into the Pentagon's underground garage. He had driven Everett Weaver from the Jefferson, dropping him off at Mr. K's restaurant where the FBI Director was meeting his wife for dinner. The marine guard saluted smartly and asked how he may be of service. Kaminsky told the guard he had a meeting with Brigadier General Darlington.

"Do you know where the general's office is, sir?"

"Yes, thank you."

"Please, sir, I must ask you for identification and to sign in. Regulations."

"No problem." Mitch Kaminsky displayed his ID, signed the register and headed down the corridor to the elevators in the east wing. On the third floor, room E312 was about four doors down from the elevator. Entering the office he was greeted by Captain Bork who was seated behind a word processor. He stood and saluted Mitch.

"Good evening, Mr. Director. Would you like to see the general?" Bork knew better than to ask the National Security Director if he had an appointment. He knew the director's visit was unexpected.

"Good evening, captain. Yes, I would like to see the general."

"Yes sir! Please wait here, sir, and I'll tell him you're here." Bork knocked on the general's door and let himself in, closing the door. Less than fifteen seconds had elapsed when Captain Bork opened the door, escorting two air force noncoms from the office, while at the same time, inviting the Director to enter. The two noncoms excused themselves, passing in front of Kaminsky as they left the general's office. Colonel Parker's men had no idea who this individual was that had cut their meeting short. They reasoned it had to be somebody very important for the general to have reacted the way he did when Captain Bork quietly informed him of his visitor's name.

"Ah, good to see you again, Mr. Kaminsky. To what do I owe this visit?"

"Just following up on our conversation in the President's office and trying to put some loose ends together." Kaminsky took a seat in front of the general's desk without being asked to sit. "I didn't mean to disturb your meeting."

"Oh, you mean those two who were leaving my office when you arrived? No problem. We had finished with our business and they were leaving anyway. Those two men are on Colonel Parker's staff and recently returned from being with him out in New Mexico. They were filling me in on Colonel Parker's progress."

"Progress? What progress is that, General?" Kaminsky picked up the F-86 model on the general's desk, examining and placing it back on its stand.

"Parker is officially replacing General Brantfield as head of Project Anasazi and I sent him out to become more familiar with the project." Darlington, who had been standing the entire time, sat down behind his desk and pulled out a cigar. "Care for a cigar, Mr. Kaminsky?" Kaminsky shook his head no. "Do you mind if I smoke, then?" Again Kaminsky shook his head in the negative.

"You didn't tell us about replacing Brantfield when his name came up in our meeting this afternoon."

"I'm sorry, Mr. Kaminsky. I thought I had mentioned it."

"He's one of the reasons I'm here. Have you been able to get hold of him to tell him the President wants to see him?"

"There's was no answer at his house when I had the captain call. When Parker checks in with me later tonight I'll instruct him to tell the general to catch the first plane to Washington. Is that okay with you?" Darlington reached into his top side desk drawer and retrieved a lighter, not paying attention to Kaminsky's response to the question. Flicking the lighter several times, taking several deep puffs, the cigar's red tip glowed brightly.

Taking a small note pad from his suit jacket pocket Kaminsky flipped through the pages until he came to the notes he had taken at the earlier meeting with the President and the general. "Have you been able to get a lead on the nuclear physicist in the Midwestern nursing home?"

"Actually, I haven't had time since getting back from the meeting with the President. It's been one meeting after another. I'll get on it first thing tomorrow morning."

"General, I find that difficult to believe. You have at your disposal many intelligence people who could come up with that information within an hour's time."

"That's true, Mr. Kaminsky, but the fact of the matter is I didn't think the President meant immediately."

"That's exactly what he did mean. How could you not consider a direct order from the President a top priority?" General Darlington took the cigar from his mouth, tapped the ash into the ashtray, and continued to nervously tap the cigar as Kaminsky continued to talk. "General, let me save you the trouble of providing me with information on Milton Goldberg."

Darlington, placing the cigar in his mouth and taking a deep breath clearly exhibited a surprise look on his face. Slowly exhaling, he said, "How did you know the man's name was Goldberg? I never mentioned him by name during our meeting."

Kaminsky displayed a sly smile. "No pun intended, general, but it doesn't take a nuclear physicist to discover who this man is, his whole life history, and the name of the nursing home in Grand Rapids where he's confined. One of the interesting things we discovered about this man is the fact that he and Robert Oppenheimer absolutely despised each other. Oppenheimer, a product of Nazi Germany, and Goldberg, a Jew from Nuremberg, who was able to escape before the slaughter, were two Germans that put aside their differences to work together. You know what else, General? I was able to obtain this information in less than an hour. My question to you is, 'How come you couldn't do the same thing?'"

General Darlington, saying nothing, stared at Mitch Kaminsky, taking the cigar from his mouth, holding it in his hand as he rested his elbow on the armrest of his chair.

"One final thing, General. The President has instructed me to inform you that Project Anasazi is being taken out of your hands as of right now. The President has given me responsibility for this project. Further, I have enlisted the FBI's help in this matter. The Director will be working closely with me and you are not to have any communication with anyone, military or otherwise, involved with this project. However, you are instructed to contact Colonel Parker and have him report to my office within forty-eight hours. Is that clear?"

"Who do you think you are, Kaminsky?" Darlington, who had been seething the entire time Kaminsky was talking, finally let his temper flare. "You can't come in here and give me orders on a project that was assigned by a former President." The general, face flushed, veins popping in his neck, was now standing and shouting. "This office has been responsible for Project Anasazi since 1947. Do you realize I'm head of the U.S. Air Force and a member of the Joint Chiefs of Staff?"

Kaminsky rose from his chair and moved toward the door. "Take it up with the President directly, general, if you have a problem with his Presidential order. No need to see me out, thank you." Kaminsky left, leaving the door open behind him, the general standing red-faced behind his desk.

CHAPTER SIXTEEN

Finding Running Horse's service station in Horse Springs was an easy task for Colonel Parker and his aide. They pulled their Ford Bronco past the fuel pumps, parking on the far side of the garage. The sun hung low in the western sky, casting a golden glow, slowly giving way to a crimson color that bathed the distant mountains in a surreal landscape. As the two men emerged from their vehicle a little old Indian woman approached.

"What are you two doing over there? You can't park there! You have car troubles? If not, you'll have to move your vehicle."

Colonel Parker, trying his best to act friendly, asked, "Is Running Horse around?"

"Who wants to know?" Little River, with good reason, was suspicious of these men.

"An old friend." As the colonel spoke with the woman, distracting her attention, Lieutenant Nelson checked inside the garage.

"My son doesn't have any friends the likes of you," Little River said sarcastically.

"Well, if Running Horse is your son, you haven't been doing a good job as his mother, knowing who his friends are." By this time Nelson had made his way to the house, entering it and finding no one else around. He returned, signaling to Parker that nobody else was around. "In fact, we have another friend who is with your son. His name is Brad Davis." Little River showed no sign of recognition at the mention of Davis' name. Parker finally lost his patience with Little River and grabbed her by the arm. "Look old woman, I need to talk with your son and Davis. Now, where are they?"

Little River whimpered as Parker tightened his grip on the woman's tiny arms. "I don't know where my son is and that is the truth. Besides, I wouldn't tell you if I did know. Let go of me." Parker squeezed her arm even harder. "Stop that, you're hurting me. If you don't stop hurting me I'm going to put a Navajo curse on you. And when my son gets back he's going to take care of you two real good."

Nelson had come up behind the frail Indian woman and grabbed her by the other arm. Lifting her by both arms, Parker and Nelson carried Little River into the garage office where they pushed her into a chair against the wall. "I'm losing patience with you, old woman. Where the hell are those two?"

Little River spit in the colonel's face. He took the back of his hand and slammed it hard across the woman's face knocking her off the chair onto the floor. The woman, blood trickling from her mouth, shouted up to the men. "A curse on you both!"

"Alright, Nelson, I'm going to put some gas in the car. You work on her until she tells us what we want to know." Nelson walked outside the garage and moved the Bronco over to the gas pumps. As the colonel pumped gas he could hear Nelson working the woman over. Within a few minutes the tank was full. He didn't hear any more noise from the garage. As he moved to the front of the vehicle to clean the windshield, Nelson approached the Bronco from the garage, rubbing his knuckles.

"Well, what did she say?"

"I'm sorry, colonel. She sure is one tough old Indian woman. I'm afraid I didn't get anything out of her. But it's logical her son and Davis have to return here sometime. We can wait until they show up."

"No, we'll come back and take care of them later. Right now, we had better get ourselves up to the mountain and inform our space visitors that they have a new boss. We are also going to find out what our friends did with the general's and Big Bird's bodies. I am in charge now and they will have to answer to me for everything." The colonel smiled.

"Colonel, are you sure our visitors are responsible for taking the bodies? Maybe someone else found them."

"Lieutenant, I have no doubt they took the bodies. I'm curious what they did with them. Maybe they're going to use their bodies for some scientific experiments in the name of humanity. We'll see! By the way, did you finish the old lady off? I don't want her around to identify us."

"Don't worry, Colonel. I beat her so bad I think she's already dead. She was bleeding pretty bad from her mouth and the crack on her head."

"How did she crack her head?"

"Her head slammed against the wall with the last good hit I gave her. She didn't have a pulse when I checked. If she's not dead yet, she'll bleed to death in a matter of minutes."

"Good work, once again, lieutenant! Let's head up to the mountain." Parker walked around to the passenger side of the Bronco and climbed in while Nelson entered the vehicle on the driver's side. They turned to each other and gave a thumbs-up signal.

Davis and Running Horse had left the tow truck parked alongside the woods more than two hundred yards from the road. Running Horse felt a little better about this adventure knowing it would be difficult for anyone to spot the truck. Davis felt Running Horse was being overly cautious. He had convinced Running Horse the likelihood of anyone else being up there was extremely remote. They entered the woods at the approximate spot where Davis had entered two days earlier.

"How far did you say it is to the opening where you saw this village?" Running Horse asked nervously.

"I thought I knew the first time, but I discovered that my watch for some unknown reason had run slow at first, then stopped altogether. It was impossible for me to measure the distance by time."

"Not as crazy as what you told me you saw up here. I'll tell you again Brad, I'm not too enthusiastic about being here with you. There's one simple reason I got to be an old Brave."

"Yeah, what's that?" Davis said, half laughingly.

"I've never been known to be a brave Brave." Both men laughed quietly.

They had been walking through the woods for more than a half hour and Davis' frustration level was building. "Damn it, I know this is the same direction I went in the last time."

Running Horse placed his hand on Davis' shoulder. "If everything you told me about this place was as you remember, it should be here. Are you sure you headed due north when you entered the woods?"

Davis stopped and leaned against a tree. The altitude was having a direct effect on his breathing. "Why am I having more trouble breathing this time than the last time I was here, Running Horse?"

"I'm no doctor, but it probably has something to do with being nervous this time. When you are nervous your heart beats faster, causing blood to flow faster and you take deeper breaths. Then, your lungs need more air and you start huffing and puffing. Besides, I don't think you're in such great physical shape."

"Thank you for your diagnosis, Dr. Horse. But I am not nervous," Davis said breathlessly.

"Okay, you're hyper then!"

"Will you stop it, please?" Davis tried to force a smile. "Let's continue in the same direction for a little while longer." Davis pushed himself away from the tree and began walking.

"As you wish." Running Horse shook his head, resigned to a fruitless journey.

All of a sudden Davis stopped and held up his hand. "Do you hear that humming sound?"

Running Horse moved up alongside Davis. "Yes, I hear something."

"What does it sound like to you?" Davis looked at Running Horse.

"It sounds like a pipe organ in a great cathedral where the air is coming through the pipes before you hear the music."

Davis smiled when he heard Running Horse's explanation for the sound. At least it made Davis feel as if he wasn't crazy. "Well I don't know if that's how I would have explained it. But, at least you hear it, too. It's a heavy vibrating hum."

"Isn't that what I just said, Brad?" Running Horse raised his hands in the air expressing disdain for Davis. "That's the sound a pipe organ makes."

"Okay, okay! No arguments! Why can't I see an opening through the trees?" Davis was becoming agitated. "It was at this point I heard the humming sound and I found an opening into a clearing."

Running Horse placed both hands on Davis' shoulders. "Calm down, we'll find it."

Both men moved around, first straight ahead for one hundred yards and then to the west for almost one hundred yards and finally to the east for one hundred yards.

"I'm beginning to think I've lost my mind." Davis rubbed his forehead in frustration.

"I don't think you have lost your mind, my friend." Running Horse tried to console Davis. "It is at times like these you need to have your mind and body become one. My ancestors' wisdom on such matters is worth following."

"More hocus-pocus talk, Running Horse! Talk in plain English to me."

"You have much to learn of the Indian ways, my friend." Running Horse was not offended by Davis' remark. "There is a way for mind and body to become one, but you must believe. Indians believe strongly in their ability to meld the two together. As a result, they are capable of seeing what is, what has been, and what will be. It gave my ancestors great courage in facing battles with the white eyes. Today, they use these powers to come to grips with the modern world, not dwelling on what a powerful force we were in times forgotten. They also see the day when they will once again be a mighty force. Unfortunately, there are many Indians living on reservations throughout this country who remember the past, but do not use the gifts of their ancestors. They have become sad, bitter, and hostile and have given into the spirits of the white man's medicine, liquor and drugs. It is a sad time for many once proud Indian nations, but I have hope. And, my friend, I have hope you can use your hidden powers to remember where this opening in the forest is. Now, close your eyes and let your mind and body become one." Davis frowned, giving a suspicious look at Running Horse. "Do it!" Running Horse commanded softly.

Startled, Davis closed both eyes for a few seconds and then slowly opened one eye to see if Running Horse was watching. "I really feel stupid doing this, you know."

"Quiet! Keep both eyes closed and concentrate. Remember back to the first time you came to this place."

"Am I allowed to talk out loud and converse with you while I do this?" Davis was trying to take the situation seriously.

"Yes. Think hard about that first time. What do you remember about your surroundings? Awaken your inner self and get in touch with your senses. Concentrate!"

There was no conversation between the two men for a short time. It was Davis who spoke first. "Damn! I do remember something!"

"Good!" Running Horse continued with his encouragement. "What do your senses tell you?"

Davis, eyes closed tightly, brows furrowed, lips pursed, was beginning to remember. "There were no birds! That's right, there were no birds in this forest. Isn't that strange?"

Running Horse smiled. "Of course you did not hear birds in the forest. There are no birds at this altitude. But remembering about birds is good. Keep trying. There are other things you will remember."

"You're right! I remember a smell, the heavy smell of juniper was suddenly gone."

"I do not understand," Running Horse said quizzically.

Davis continued, "During my entire walk through the forest of pinion and juniper trees the smell of juniper was overwhelming. It was a wonderful smell, as it is right now. The smell right now is present, but it is not as strong as before. I also remember the smell was not where the opening was to the village. Why would that be, Running Horse?"

"Perhaps, there were no trees there."

"No, they were there!" Davis' answer was emphatic.

"Maybe you thought they were trees and it was something else."

"What are you talking about?"

Running Horse paused before answering immediately. "Sometimes we think we see things because our mind says that is what we are supposed to see. In reality, the mind has been tricked into seeing something that is not real."

"Running Horse, you're talking crazy."

"Think about it, Brad. Have you ever seen a magician create an illusion?"

"Sure, David Copperfield and Doug Henning do it all the time. I've seen Copperfield on television make the Statue of Liberty and a jet plane disappear."

"Did they really disappear?"

"Of course not!" Davis, eyes still closed, chuckled.

Running Horse became serious. "I think someone has created an illusion here and you accidently saw beyond the illusion."

"That sounds absurd!"

"Not if you are hiding something and don't want anyone finding what it is you are hiding. Strange things have been happening around here for the last two weeks. Remember, the UFO sightings in this area?"

Davis opened both eyes and looked directly at Running Horse. "You don't really believe in such things, do you?"

"Remember the metal piece I showed you in my garage?"

"Sure!" Davis shrugged his shoulders.

"If there are creatures capable of creating a metal like I showed you, I think they are capable of creating an illusion to keep people away from where they may be hiding. From what you have told me of this place it is impossible for normal people to live in such an environment. It is too isolated. There is no water. There is no food. No one has seen anyone shopping or traveling in the area that would qualify as little green men from outer space. Yet, you have told me this place exists. I believe you. But, for what purpose and for whom does this place exist? We must find the answer, you and me, together. Is there anything else you remember?"

Davis was still trying sort out in his mind what he heard from Running Horse. "Yes, I do remember the ground was no longer crunchy from fallen branches and dead leaves. In fact, it was smooth. Look, up ahead there the ground is different." Davis pointed to a spot about ten yards north of where they stood. Running Horse stuck his hand out stopping Davis from proceeding further. His face took on a strange look. He had begun to speak saying, "The trees ahead look strange, as if they were a painted canvas." He stopped speaking and stood motionless.

Davis didn't pay attention to his expression or his movement. He only heard Running Horse say something about a painted canvas. Turning back, to look at Running Horse, he noticed that the Indian seemed transfixed where he stood. "Hey! What is it? What's the matter?" Running Horse didn't respond. Davis became alarmed. "Are you okay? Are you afraid of what's up ahead?"

Running Horse began to speak softly. "We must leave this place at once."

"Come on now, Running Horse, you're not going to tell me the spirits are scaring you off."

"Not those spirits, my friend. The spirit world of my ancestors is calling for my mother's soul to join them."

Davis grabbed Running Horse's arm. "What are you talking about?"

Tears were welling up in Running Horse's eyes. "Two evil spirits of this world have visited my mother. She is near death in the garage. We must go to her at once."

"What are you talking about? How do you know that?"

Running Horse took Davis by the arm and began leading him back through the woods where they parked the truck. "There are certain things you cannot know or understand because you are not of Indian blood. What I have told you about my mother is true. This I know as her flesh and blood. We will go now and come back to this place another day."

CHAPTER SEVENTEEN

It took more than forty minutes for the black Bronco carrying Colonel Parker and his aide to reach a well-hidden dirt path ten miles east of Pie Town on Route 60. They were both oblivious to the fact that they had actually passed within two hundred yards of where Running Horse had parked his tow truck on the road leading to Pie Town. It was now dark as the black Bronco headed east on Route 60 after having passed through Pie Town. There were no other vehicles on the road, allowing Lieutenant Nelson to put on his high beams to see the road better. Colonel Parker placed his hand on Nelson's right arm, signaling him to slow down. Pointing to a cutoff on the right side of the road, Parker motioned the driver to turn and follow the dirt road heading south into Alegros Mountain. The Bronco moved slowly over the bumpy road, bouncing both men back and forth, until about five miles deep into the woods where the road ended. They stepped from the Bronco looking around for the entrance into the compound. Parker and Nelson had both been to this spot only once before. Only Parker had been allowed beyond the cleverly concealed opening.

"Colonel, I don't recognize any of the landmarks," Nelson said as he shined his flashlight on the trees that surrounded them on all sides except on the road behind them. "I've never been up here at night."

Parker was feeling the cold and pulled his jacket up over his long neck. "These damn people keep changing things!"

"All I see is trees and more trees." The lieutenant, also feeling the cold at this elevation, was blowing into his hands trying to keep warm. "I can't see any opening."

"Of course you don't see any opening. That's the way they planned it. Look for something out of the ordinary."

"Like what?"

"Wavering or shimmering lines among the trees."

"I'm sorry, Colonel, but I really don't understand. It's just too dark to see anything beyond the headlights and this flashlight really isn't much help."

In an exasperated tone, the colonel replied, "Our friends are using a hologram to confuse us. That's why if you see any unusual shimmering it's probably our opening."

Both men tried in vain to find an opening in the dark night illuminated only by the car's headlights and one flashlight. Suddenly, two tall figures appeared from the shadows to the right of the Bronco announcing their presence to Nelson and Parker who were standing illuminated in the glare of the headlights.

"You are to leave this area immediately!" one of the figures who had fully emerged from the shadows spoke sharply. The other figure remained partially hidden in the shadows.

"Hey! Don't you dare ever sneak up on me again!" the colonel, shielding his eyes from the lights, barked at the figure. "Do you know who I am?" Parker asked defiantly of the figure dressed in brown leather pants, brown suede jacket with no sleeves, and black hat. A glowing object hung from the figure's neck.

"We know very well who you are, Colonel Parker, and we still demand that you leave now. You are not welcome here!"

"I'm afraid you're not getting the point, my friend. I have replaced General Brantfield and now I'm in charge of you people and this project." Parker's anger was evident.

"The project is over, Colonel. No one is in charge anymore."

"Look, you son of a bitch, you are here as guests of this country and as such you will obey my orders." Colonel Parker removed a service revolver from his shoulder holster and pointed it at the tall figure. As the figure stepped toward Parker, the colonel aimed the gun and pulled the trigger. It would not fire. Parker desperately tried again to make his revolver fire. "Nelson, something's wrong with my gun. You shoot this bastard where he stands."

Nelson removed his gun and aimed it at the figure standing in front of the colonel. It too, would not fire. "Sir, my gun won't work either."

Parker, frightened by his inability to handle the situation, took two steps back away from the tall figure. "What the hell kind of power do you people have that can control our weapons?"

"You are not a good man, Colonel Parker! It is not for me to punish you for your evil deeds. Some day you will answer to a higher authority."

"Did you have anything to do with the disappearance of Big Bird and General Brantfield? What about the woman from the motel?"

"Time for you to leave this place, colonel." The tall figure stepped back into the shadow.

"I want to talk to your leader!" the colonel shouted toward the figure in the shadows.

"Colonel, don't you think we ought to leave? That guy and this place are spooky," Nelson pleaded with the colonel.

"Not until I find that opening and get inside," Parker responded. The colonel had no sooner uttered those words when the lights of the car and the flashlight dimmed and went out. "Now what the hell are these guys doing? Nelson start the car and try the lights again."

The lieutenant got in behind the steering wheel and tried to turn the motor over. The engine did not respond. "It won't start, colonel."

"Alright, aliens, you win this time. I'm leaving, but I'll be back. You can bet your ass I'll be back and then you'll see who's in charge." The flashlight and the headlights slowly came back to full strength and once again shone brightly. Parker got into the passenger side of the Bronco. Try the engine now, Nelson." The engine roared to life and Nelson turned the vehicle around and headed up the dirt road to Route 60 at a faster pace than when he entered. Neither man said a word.

Running Horse had his foot to the floor urging his tow truck to go faster. Brad Davis had made sure his seat belt was securely fastened as the ride down the mountain was swift. The truck took the turn from the mountain road onto Route 12 on two wheels. Davis was skeptical of Running Horse's vision of his mother being in trouble. But he had seen enough strange things since he came to this land to keep an open mind. The darkened service station lay ahead.

"See, Brad, the station is dark!" Running Horse said excitedly. "It is never dark! My mother always keeps the place lit up like a Christmas tree. I knew something was wrong."

"Maybe you're worrying for nothing." Davis tried to reassure Running Horse.

Bringing the truck to a screeching halt outside of the garage, Running Horse jumped from the cab and ran into the darkened office. Davis was right behind him. "Mother! Are you in here?" In the blackness nothing could be seen. Running Horse felt along the wall nearest the door for the light switch. Finding it, the room became dimly lit. There on the floor, at the far end of the office lay the crumpled body of his mother, her head laying in a pool of blood. Her face was barely recognizable. Running Horse let out a cry as he bent down to lift his mother's head into his arms.

"My God!" Davis said out loud. "Who the hell would do this to an old woman?"

Running Horse did not hear Davis' question. His Indian friend cradled his mother in his arms as he chanted softly above a whisper.

"Running Horse, is she.....," Davis was almost afraid to ask the question. "Is she dead?"

There was no response from Running Horse. Davis bent down and felt for a pulse in the woman's scrawny arms. Next, he checked the carotid artery in the woman's neck for a pulse. "Nothing! I get nothing, Running Horse! I'm afraid she's dead!"

"She is not dead!" Running Horse yelled at Davis as he rocked his mother in his arms. "There is warmth in her body. She is not ready to join her ancestors."

Davis moved away from Running Horse. Trying to appease his Indian friend he asked, "Where is the nearest hospital?"

"We are too far from doctors and hospitals out here. The nearest one is in Socorro and my mother would never permit it."

"No disrespect intended, Running Horse, but she doesn't have much say in the matter right now. If we're going to try and save her life the hospital in Socorro is our only hope."

"My mother hates modern doctors and hospitals. If I were to take her to such a place she would have my hide. If she were to die in a hospital she would haunt me for the rest of my days. No, I know of a place on the outskirts of Pie Town. There is a medicine doctor there who works at the clinic. He is a Navajo from the Alamo Navajo Indian

Reservation north of Magdalena. Maybe he is still there at this time of night. I now have no choice but to take my mother there. Will you join me, Brad Davis?"

Leaning down to help Running Horse lift Little River, Davis looked his friend in the eyes. "You ask the dumbest questions."

Running Horse forced a smile. "Go to the house and get me a blanket and a clean towel. I need to wrap her head in the towel and keep her warm with the blanket."

Davis returned within a few minutes and assisted Running Horse attend to his mother. "Let me drive so you can hold your mother."

"Good! Let us go then!"

The President was working late in the Oval Office. Since his meeting with Mitch Kaminsky and General Darlington, the President had been involved in one round of meetings after another with different members of his Cabinet on various routine matters pertaining to affairs of state. The urge to mention the Roswell incident was very strong, but he felt there was no need to alarm any one of his cabinet heads about what he had learned earlier that afternoon. Hopefully, the matter, left in the hands of Kaminsky, would be handled properly without too many Washington insiders learning of aliens living in New Mexico before he had time to sort out this whole mess. It was ten o'clock and the President was getting restless. He had been waiting for Mitch Kaminsky to report back to him on his meetings with the

FBI Director and General Darlington. There was a knock on the door. "Come on in, Mitch!" The President called out.

"Good evening, sir!" Kaminsky entered the room and closed the door behind him. "How did you know it was me?"

"There's no one else I asked to be in my office at this time." The President got up from his chair and moved to the front of the desk, shaking Kaminsky's hand. "How did your meetings go?"

"The general was not too happy about being relieved of his responsibilities on Project Anasazi. He let me have it."

"Sorry I had to put you through that, Mitch."

"No problem, Mr. President." Kaminsky took a seat.

"Did the general get a hold of General Brantfield in New Mexico?"

"Darlington said he had tried calling several times, but there was no answer. I really don't believe him, so I had an old friend of mine, who is retired out that way go out to his house. He left a message on my answering machine that Brantfield wasn't home. My friend did mention that the house looked like he should have been around. He said it looked as if he left unexpectedly. The front and back doors were both open. He felt that was a little unusual."

"What do you make of it, Mitch?"

"Well, my suspicious nature says General Darlington has something to do with Brantfield not being there. This Air Force fly boy of ours has the ambition and the inclination to take over the whole operation from Brantfield."

"Do you think he might have had Brantfield removed already?" The President moved to the window and gazed into the nighttime sky.

"Anything's possible with this man. I know he's got two of his intelligence people out there."

"What are they doing out there?"

"Taking care of Brantfield, I suspect." Kaminsky replied sarcastically.

The President turned from the window. "You know, you might be right. I want Ev Weaver to put surveillance on Darlington and I want you to find those two Air Force intelligence men and bring them back to Washington. Now, what about the nuclear physicist who lives in the Midwest?"

"Again, I got the run around from the general. Luckily, I had my staff check him out and I found him in a nursing home in Grand Rapids. His name is Milton Goldberg. With your permission, I plan on going over to Andrews Air Force Base, take a plane out there and interview him. I understand he's too sick to be moved."

"Sure, that's a good idea. Take a tape recorder with you so we get everything he says. I don't want to miss a single thing. Next item on the agenda is what you found out from Weaver."

"Believe it or not, the director has two men out there investigating these strange goings on."

"Did he know anything about Project Anasazi?"

"No, Mr. President, but he does now. He should be calling here any minute to tell you about his latest conversation with his agents. They report in every night giving the director an update."

The President smiled. "That old son of a gun never ceases to amaze me. I'm sure glad we have someone like Everett Weaver as the Director of the Bureau." The phone on the President's desk rang twice before he picked it up. "Hello! Yes, you can put him through." The President covered the mouthpiece and whispered to Kaminsky. "It's Weaver. Yes, good evening Everett. Thank you, I'm fine. And yourself? That's good. I have Mitch Kaminsky sitting here with me and he told me you would be calling. Let me put this on the speaker so we both can hear you." The President pressed the hands-free button on the phone. "Can you hear us, Everett?"

"Yes, sir, I can. Hi again, Mitch!"

"Hello, Ev. What did you hear from your men?"

"I haven't heard from them yet. They check in with me directly every night at seven. This is the first time since they've been out there they've missed a call. It's not like them. I still wanted to call you both as promised. Do you have any suggestions as to how you want to handle this?"

"You're speaking on your secure phone at home, aren't you?" The President was worried for a moment until he was assured their voice signals were being scrambled on the secure phones.

"You know me better than that, Mr. President."

"I'm sorry, Everett." the President apologized. "Knowing what you do about this situation, I want you to give this your top priority, but I do not want a massive agency response."

"No, sir, but I have already called in one of my agents who is knowledgeable in this area. His name is Billy Stiles and at one time was involved with Project Blue Book. He's already on his way to New Mexico."

"How much did you tell him, Ev?" Kaminsky asked.

"Absolutely nothing. He was told to track down Smith and Osborne and get back to me quickly."

The President returned to his chair. "Everett, it sounds as if you are doing everything properly. Check in with this office when you hear anything from those agents or of anything else you find out from your men."

"Yes, sir, I will. Goodnight, gentlemen."

"Good night! Good night!" The President pressed the release button on the phone.

Kaminsky rose from his chair in front of the President's desk. "What if I mobilize a small force of elite military personnel to patrol that area out there?"

"Mitch, I don't want to start a panic that begins in New Mexico and spreads to the whole world. How big a force are you talking about?"

"Probably about two hundred men on the ground and about two or three helicopters to patrol the air over this area."

"No, Mitch, I don't want uniformed soldiers scaring the hell out of everybody and I absolutely do not want military helicopters flying around all over the place."

"You don't understand, sir. This is a very remote area and I would have the military dressed in civilian clothes, driving pick- up trucks. They would be spread out around the area once we pinpoint exactly where these aliens have their base of operations. The helicopters would be civilian and flown by military personnel."

Clutching a pencil with both his hands, the President was tense. "Can you put this together with people you can trust?"

"With my life!"

"How fast?"

"I can have everything in place by sundown tomorrow night."

"Do it!" The President stood and shook Mitch Kaminsky's hand.

Montgomery Street was one of those picturesque tree-lined streets that often appeared on postcards depicting a typical street in the Georgetown section of Washington; expensive row homes set back from the cobblestone roadways where bicyclists and pedestrians mingled freely. Mitch Kaminsky had parked his Chrysler New Yorker on the street in front of his home and had notified Andrews Air Force Base that he would need a military plane to take him to Grand Rapids within the hour. Putting a fresh set of clothes in his overnighter, he placed it by the front door and then returned to the kitchen to make a few last minute calls.

A dark blue compact turned onto Montgomery Street from Tully

Avenue and moved slowly past Mitch Kaminsky's house. The two occupants of the car looked to make sure Kaminsky was still inside and that his car was unattended by any kind of security. At the end of the street the car made a U-turn and headed back toward their target. They double parked the compact alongside Kaminsky's car. Both men checked up and down the street to make sure no one was walking or watching their movements. The occupant on the passenger side of the car reached down to retrieve the package he had placed on the floor between his legs. He opened the door and moved to exit the car.

Mitch Kaminsky had finished making his last call and was hanging up the telephone when a thunderous explosion rocked the walls in his house, blowing out almost every window on both floors. He dropped the telephone and rushed to the front door, stepping out on the front porch to see what had happened. The whole neighborhood was bathed in an orange-red glow from the fire of several automobiles parked on the street, as well as several row houses. He could feel the heat of the fire against his face. One car could be seen standing on its end, leaning against one of the houses that was totally engulfed in flames. The houses on either side of where the car had parked were a blazing inferno. A crowd had formed quickly and was trying to help the people in the burning houses. Kaminsky ran back into the house and dialed 911. The next call he made was for a taxi to meet him a block away. A final call was made to an aide to come and handle the mess at his house.

CHAPTER EIGHTEEN

The tow truck with Brad Davis driving sped along the mountain road toward Pie Town. The altitude always made driving a little bit sluggish on the upward climb to the top of the mountain. Davis had his foot to the floor and still the tow truck slowly lumbered up the incline. He looked apologetically at Running Horse for the slow progress they were making. Without saying a word, Running Horse, who had traveled this road many times and experienced the same difficulty, merely stared off into the clear night sky. His mother's head rested on his lap, her feet resting on Davis' lap. They were approaching the top of the mountain, just five miles outside of Pie Town when a bright light seemed to be coming straight toward them on the road ahead.

"Damn crazy driver with his high beams on!" Davis yelled out. The lights were filling the entire front of the truck cab with a blinding brightness. "I can't see!" Davis was also having trouble steering the truck as it suddenly began vibrating uncontrollably. The beam was now intense. Pulling the truck to the side of the road Davis realized the motor had died and the vehicle no longer had headlights. Running Horse and Davis continued to shield their eyes.

"That's no ordinary light! If I didn't know better, I'd say it was evil spirits playing games with us! No time for that now!" Running Horse spoke, his voice angry.

The truck continued to vibrate as if some giant hand was shaking a toy truck. The light was creating considerable heat in the cab of the truck. Davis placed his hand on the door handle, trying to open the door. He let out a loud yell and quickly removed his hand from the handle. Looking at his hand, he saw a burn mark imprinted on his hand. "Son of a bitch!"

"What's the matter?" Running Horse asked as he cradled his mother, supporting her head with one hand as he placed his other hand on the dashboard trying to steady himself in the gyrating vehicle.

"I burned my hand on the handle. Whatever that is out there it caused all the metal parts to heat up."

"It's some bad medicine outside trying to get in here."

"Tell you the truth, Running Horse, whatever it is it's scaring the living daylights out of me, but I've got to know what it is."

The light, with the intensity of a strong searchlight, had been blinding them through the windshield. Now, it seemed to rise in front of the truck until the light was no longer shining directly into the truck. Instead, it now seemed to be shining directly down on them from above. Outside the truck the entire area was being bathed in a bright bluish glow. The interior of the truck was fully lit from above.

Davis, while fearful of this unknown encounter, was determined to investigate and have his curiosity satisfied. Carefully, he tried to touch the door handle with one finger. Finding it had cooled, Davis placed his full hand on the handle and opened the door. He jumped down from the truck, shielding his eyes from the bright lights above him.

"You stay put!" Davis said in a commanding voice to Running Horse still seated in the truck, which had stopped vibrating.

"Don't worry, I'm in no hurry to go out there!" Running Horse said in a voice barely above a whisper. "What do you see?"

Davis looked to see where the light was coming from. "Holy shit!" A chill ran through his body.

"What? What?" Running Horse wanted to know.

"You're not going to believe me! You're going to have to see this for yourself!"

"No, that's okay, Brad, I believe you! I believe you!"

"Sitting smack dab over us about five hundred feet up is some kind of space ship." Davis' voice seemed calmer.

"Space ship? Have you been smoking some of my mother's special tobacco?"

"No! I'm not hallucinating! It's not moving and I can't hear any motor sound. Son of a bitch, I think we're having an encounter."

"Encounter? You mean like in the movies? An encounter of the third kind?"

"I hate to bust your bubble, but encounters of the third kind refer to having direct contact with alien beings. At this point I have no desire to meet with any strange creatures from another planet." Davis continued to look at the spacecraft hovering above him.

"Okay, okay!" Running Horse was not about to argue with Davis. "How big is it and what does it look like?"

"Great! You want me to give you a description of this thing that's probably the size of an aircraft carrier and blinding me! All I can make out is the strange outline of a huge craft! Why don't you come out here and take a look for yourself?"

Running Horse, in no rush to join Davis, secretly was hoping it wasn't a UFO. "You think it's some military type of aircraft that the government has under wraps and nobody knows about?"

"Running Horse, will you get out here and take a look at this thing!"

"I can't leave my mother alone. Besides, we need to get her some help! Remember?"

"Of course I remember. Evidently you have forgotten the truck has no power at the present moment with this thing hanging around us."

"Alright, alright!" Running Horse carefully placed his mother's head on the seat. He stepped from the vehicle and slowly looked toward the craft above. "You're right, it's difficult to make out any sort of shape with that blinding light. One thing for sure, it certainly is too large to come from the spirit world! Brad, besides the spotlight coming from the center of that thing can you make out any other details?"

"No. But my big question is "Who the hell are they and what are they doing up there looking down on us?""

Running Horse moved around to where Davis stood. "Do you really think it's from outer space?"

Davis still shielding his eyes turned to face Running Horse. "Look, you're the one who told me about the strange goings on out here in 1947 and showed me that metal piece. What else could it be? Didn't we hear talk about UFO sightings last night?"

Before Running Horse could respond a tall figure emerged from beyond the glaring light and stood before both men. Running Horse and Brad stood transfixed at the dark figure, silhouetted in the light with a glowing disk hanging from his neck.

"Do not be afraid." the dark figure spoke in soft, slow tones. "I have come to help Little River."

Davis was unable to speak or move. It was the first time since his trip to Costa Rica that he was frightened speechless. Doing research on ancient ruins in the remote mountains several years earlier he had lost his footing and fell off a steep cliff. If it hadn't been for his agility and his quickness to grab an overhanging branch from a tree he would have fallen to his death. But this was a different type of fear that froze him to the spot where he stood. He couldn't even force himself to look at Running Horse who stood dumb struck, his eyes glazed, at the sight before him.

Slowly, the figure moved closer to the men and continued to speak. "My people know of you both and that we have nothing to fear from men with brave and pure hearts. Brad Davis, we know of your quest for answers to questions that you of this land have asked for many earth years. Soon, you will have answers which will lead to more questions that cannot and will not be answered. Running Horse, you truly are a son of your ancestors. There are many things that have been passed down to you of which you know nothing. It is deep within your living spirit. Someday, you will know all things and be proud of your once living ancestors, of a time that has long since passed on this planet. With that knowledge you will experience sadness because this is a different time in the evolution of the universe. No longer can things be as they once were. Little River knows all things in her mind. We will take care of her so that she may live to see the dawn of a new day of our once proud people."

Billy Stiles, driving into the Sandia Estates development, glanced at the sheet of paper where he had written the street address of Professor Beal. More than twelve hours had passed since he was asked by the director to track down agents Smith and Osborne. FBI agent Stiles caught the last flight out of Dulles, arriving in Albuquerque around midnight. He had checked into the airport Holiday Inn and immediately gone to bed. He rose at four-thirty fully rested. On the plane he had familiarized himself with the work Smith and Osborne were doing out in New Mexico. Now he wanted to go over his notes one more time before beginning his search for the two agents who failed to report back to the director. For the last ten years Stiles had been assigned to routine work behind a desk. He knew that everyone in the Bureau thought he was crazy. He blamed only himself for his predicament. Ten years earlier he had been camping alone out in Zion National Park. After returning from dinner with a retired friend in St. George, Utah, he pitched his tent and immediately went to sleep. It was shortly after two a.m. when he was awakened by a bright light filling his tent. He thought it strange in the middle of the park that there could be a light strong enough to wake him from a sound sleep. Opening the flap to his small tent he was almost blinded by the intense brightness. Although he thought it crazy to be reaching for his sunglasses to shield his eyes in the middle of the night, he found them quickly and put them on. It wasn't much help, but at least he could tolerate the light a little better. In the distant light, through a bluish-green haze, he saw three figures coming toward him. That was the last thing he remembered until he awoke the next morning with the new day's sunlight illuminating his tent. He sat up, rubbing his eyes, trying to sort out in his mind whether he had dreamed of waking in the middle of the night or had he really experienced the light and three figures. As hard as he tried to remember anything beyond the light and the figures, he couldn't. Deep inside he had this feeling of people or something taking him to another place. He knew he experienced something that wasn't a dream. On his right arm he found what looked like a slight discoloration of skin, similar to the way one's arm would look following a blood test. There was no pain, just a discoloration and a slightly numb sensation. Upon his arrival

297

back in Washington, he made the mistake of telling Director J. Edgar Hoover of his trip to Utah and the experience. Hoover had asked him to make a report on it and provide him a copy. After several weeks of no response he approached the director and asked what he thought. Hoover told him it was interesting, but it sounded more like a tale from an agent who was suffering from stress. He advised Stiles to forget the incident and go about his regular assignments. Perplexed by such a decision that he felt warranted some serious consideration, Stiles continued harassing the Director to take his report seriously. It was then that he was assigned a desk job and subjected to a whole round of medical tests ordered by the director himself. Everyone at the agency soon learned of his story and started treating him as if he were crazy. Now, ten years later he was glad to have the opportunity, provided by the new director, to roam around New Mexico where strange things had been going on for some time.

It was seven-thirty when he knocked on the door of Professor Beal's house. Stiles and the professor, both members of the Baby Blue group, had met face-to-face several times and conversed frequently via their computers. He was looking forward to talking with the professor about the things they had been discussing over the Internet for the last few weeks. The door opened just a crack, enough for a small face to peer out on this six-foot four, large-framed individual.

"Yes, may I help you?"

"I hope so, Mrs. Beal." Stiles did not want to alarm the woman. "I'm a friend of your husband and I was hoping to find him home."

"He's out in the mountains somewhere with two other men searching for Indian ruins as he always does."

"When was the last time you saw him?"

"Yesterday morning. He left real early in the morning."

"He hasn't returned yet?"

"No," the fiftyish-looking woman, with brown hair streaked with silver, responded.

"Isn't that strange?" Stiles asked.

"Not at all. If you are a friend of his you would know he sometimes goes off for days and weeks at a time. Is there something you're not telling me?"

"Well, I do know he goes off for long periods when he's working on a dig. However, this time I don't think he was off on a dig. He was with two friends of mine from back east that he was helping. I just thought they may have come back by now."

The woman on the other side of the door was obviously tiring of this conversation. "Look, I'd love to invite you in for coffee, but I have to get ready for work. Anyway, I'm not worried about my husband, so neither should you. If I hear from him I'll tell him you were looking for him."

"That would be very kind of you, Mrs. Beal. Please tell him Billy Stiles is looking for him. Oh, by the way, do you know where he was headed with my friends?"

"He really didn't say, but I would presume he went up to Mangas Mountain where he recently discovered some sort of new Anasazi dwelling."

"Thank you very much." Stiles turned from the door and walked quickly to his rented car. He didn't hear the door close, so he assumed the woman was still watching. As he opened the car door he glanced back toward the house and could see the door still slightly ajar where a set of eyes watched him getting into the car. He knew from the tone of her voice that she really wasn't worried about her husband or then again, maybe she really didn't care. Maybe she was curious at the sight of a stranger on her doorstep at this early morning hour, making her wonder what was going on between her husband and three strangers from the east. A few blocks from the professor's house, Stiles pulled to the side of the road and unfolded a map of New Mexico. He quickly found Mangas Mountain and the roads leading out to the area from Albuquerque. His finger came to a town on the map. "Horse Springs," he said out loud. "I should be able to find myself a couple of Indian guides that can take me up to this Mangas Mountain." Stiles pulled away from the curb and headed out of Sandia Estates.

"Mr. President, Mitch Kaminsky is here to see you." The voice on the intercom belonged to Mary Finley.

The President looked at his wrist watch. "Thank you, Mary. Send him in."

Kaminsky closed the door to the Oval Office behind him and moved across the room to shake hands with the President, who remained seated at his desk reviewing some papers. "It's seven thirty in the morning, Mitch. What the hell are you doing up so early in the morning, or didn't you go to Grand Rapids last night?"

"Yes sir, I'm back with a tape recording of my brief but interesting talk with Goldberg. The guy's at death's door and sometimes he was a little bit incoherent. However, there are some interesting things he did say which could possibly be worth something."

"Mitch, have you been to bed since yesterday?"

"No, Mr. President. I caught a catnap on the ride back from Grand Rapids. Don't worry, I'm okay. My adrenaline is working overtime. I have to coordinate this thing out in New Mexico tonight. By the way, thanks for taking the call from the head doctor out at the nursing home. There was no way he was going to let me in to see Goldberg."

"I told him it was in the interest of national security and that he would be doing his country a service. Once he realized it was really me, I didn't have trouble convincing him. Alright, then, let's hear the tape." The President pushed aside the papers he had been reading.

Kaminsky placed the cassette in the tape machine on the President's credenza. "The first voice you'll hear is me starting to ask questions. The tape began running. "Mr. Goldberg, the President has asked me to talk to you about your participation in 'Majestic 12'."

"How is the President?" a weak voice could barely be heard speaking.

Kaminsky turned up the volume to better hear the elderly man's voice. "He's fine, Mr. Goldberg. He sends his best regards."

"How's his daughter, Margaret? Is she still playing the piano?"

"President Truman is resting in Missouri now. We have a new President."

"Oh, yes! I forgot for a moment. You asked me about the 'Majestic 12'. As best I can recollect it was put together by the President a few months after that UFO incident in New Mexico. I can't remember the year exactly or the place, but I do know it was after the big war."

"That's right, Mr. Goldberg. It was in 1947 and it happened around Roswell, New Mexico."

"Yes, yes, Roswell. I remember. Well, the twelve of us were put together on pretty short notice. We were called to the White House. Very, very impressive. Margaret played Moonlight Sonata for us. It was very nice. Lovely girl!"

"Please, Mr. Goldberg, try to remember who the other members of the group were and what role they played." Kaminsky tried to keep the old man focused on answering all his questions.

"It was such a long time ago I can't remember as well as I once did. I can't remember names or faces. All I remember was that besides me there were five members of Congress, the heads of the three military branches, the Secretary of State, the Secretary of Defense and one corporate executive representing private industry."

"What was the group's function?"

There was a long pause between question and answer. A voice

could be heard taking a deep breath. "We were told that a space vehicle had crashed and burned in New Mexico. There were survivors and pieces of the craft strewn all over the place. All kinds of stories were circulating when a local newspaper reported the incident. Our group first met on the very day the newspaper printed the story. The President wanted our opinion on the matter. He told us it was in the nation's best interest for us to come to a consensus on how it should be handled."

Kaminsky continued to learn more details. "How could you be sure it was an extraterrestrial vehicle?"

There was a sound of a throat being cleared. "There was this young military officer from the air base out there who was sent to talk with us."

"Can you remember his name?"

"So long ago," the voice trailed off.

"Please, Mr. Goldberg, it's extremely important. Was his name Brantfield?"

"Brantfield. Brantfield. Yes, I believe that was the name."

"What happened when you met with him?"

Again, a pause before Goldberg responded. "He showed us pieces of metal, pictures of some robot looking things and pictures of a large group of people that looked like Indians."

"Indians? Indian Indians or India Indians?"

There was a slight chuckle. "Indians, like in cowboys and Indians!"

"I want to know more about these Indians, but first let's talk about this metal Brantfield showed you. Can you describe it to me?"

"Sure, who could forget it? The military people couldn't believe their eyes. This metal bent like paper. It didn't wrinkle. It didn't burn. You couldn't destroy it. The military men all swore it wasn't anything from some secret project they were working on. I do remember that one corporate executive was curious as hell, for the obvious reason."

"Do you know where I could get my hands on a piece of this metal?"

"The military man from New Mexico took it away with him and we never saw it again." Goldberg coughed weakly.

"What happened to those robots you saw?"

"You mean those green looking things. We never saw them in person, only the photos. We were told they were being stored in a special hangar at Langley Air Force base. I can't swear to it. That's what we were told."

Kaminsky cleared his throat. "Tell me about the picture with all the Indians in it. How many Indians were in the picture?"

"There were too many in the picture to count, but I heard mention of more than 300 and they were said to have survived the crash." Goldberg could be heard wheezing. "You sure you want to hear all of this?" The tape didn't pick up the sound of Mitch Kaminsky nodding his head yes. "About a month later we instructed the military to concoct a story of a new type military weather balloon and the public lost interest. The group was called together to meet with this Indian who said he represented the space explorers."

"This Indian actually said 'space explorers'?"

"Yes," Goldberg said matter of factly.

"Was he one of them?"

"I don't think so. We asked him and he said he was born in the southwest, but these people were his true ancestors."

"What the hell did he mean by that?"

"I'm sorry, Mr. Kaminsky, but I'm really tired and need to rest."

"Please, Mr. Goldberg, just a few more questions and then I'll leave you alone."

"Five minutes more!" a third voice was heard faintly on the tape.

"Okay doctor, we're almost finished," Kaminsky could be heard telling the doctor who had stuck his head into the room. The pause on the tape was Kaminsky waiting to make sure the door was fully closed. "Please continue, Mr. Goldberg."

"This Indian was tall, good looking, jet black hair with a pony tail. He spoke perfect English. I don't think he was from anyplace other than the United States. He had a funny name, though. Let me think for a minute. It sounded like something I remembered from when I used to sit and watch television with my grandchildren. I remember now! Big Bird! His name was Big Bird!"

"Arc you sure, Mr. Goldberg?"

"Positive!"

"What did he talk about?"

"Atomic weapons and the need to keep them curtailed so that earthlings didn't blow up their own planet, contaminating the entire galaxy. He felt that the United States should become the world's policemen, keeping order with non-atomic weapons they would help us build. He volunteered to develop medicines to cure all disease and introduce us to many advanced technologies. He said his people had eradicated all disease on their planet. If we agreed, he would have his people make all these things happen."

"As far as you know, did any of these things really occur?"

"You mean, did these aliens exist?"

"No, I mean about weapons, medicines and other things. Did they help build weapons, develop new medicines, and give us some of the new technologies we have today?"

"I can't remember. They tell me since my breakdown a long time ago I haven't been able to remember many things."

"You had a nervous breakdown?"

"That's what they tell me."

"Do you know what caused it?'

"Caused it," Goldberg coughed, "I don't even remember it!"

"How about the space people?" Kaminsky was heard asking. "Did the Indian you were telling me about ever tell you where these people came from?"

"I'm sorry, Mr. Kaminsky. My mind is not as sharp as it used to be. I did know once."

"You're doing fine. What did this Indian want in return from us to for their help in building a weapons arsenal and miracle drugs?"

"They only wanted to be left alone in a remote place where they would wait to be rescued."

"Where is this place?"

A long silence followed. "That will have to be your last question, Mr. Kaminsky. I can no longer go on. We were never told of this place, only that it existed. The President and the military man from New Mexico are the only people who know where it is. The President gave it a special code name. It was the name of some long ago Indian tribe. I believe it was Project Anasazi."

"Thank you, Mr. Goldberg for your help. I know how difficult this has been for you."

"I hope I have been of some help. By the way, is Project Blue Book still in existence or has the government given it another name again?"

"What do you mean a new name again?" Kaminsky asked in a surprised tone.

"President Truman, to appease the American public, started an investigation project called Project SEIN. Later the name was changed to Project Grudge and again changed to Project Blue Book."

"You have been very helpful Mr. Goldberg. The President will......."

"Wait, I just remembered something about the 'Majestic 12'."

"What is it?" Kaminsky's voice rang with excitement.

"It was shortly after the election in forty-eight when Dewey lost to Truman. The 'Majestic 12' were invited to visit a military base in St. Louis to investigate something related to the 1947 UFO crash. Everybody connected with 'Majestic 12' took the trip except me and that corporate executive."

"How come you didn't make the trip?"

"I think I was too sick to fly."

"What about the corporate executive?"

"Don't know why he didn't make the trip."

"Mr. Goldberg, is there something about that trip you haven't told me?"

"They all died!"

"What? What did you say?"

"That damn plane crashed and killed everyone on board."

"Was it a commercial flight?"

"Of course not! Everything about this project was top secret. So, of course, it was a military transport out of Andrews."

"Can you remember anything about the crash?"

"No, only that they said it was an accident."

"Do you think it was an accident?"

"Look, they closed the books on that accident almost instantly. Who am I to contest their findings? Thank God I was not on that flight."

"What about 'Majestic 12'?"

"It was finished! There were only two of us who weren't on that plane. That was the end of the project."

"Didn't you talk to anyone about this over the years?"

"Of course not! I was sworn to secrecy by my President!"

"What about this other member of the group? Is he still alive? Can you try to remember his name? It was my impression that you were the last survivor of the 'Majestic 12?'"

Goldberg began coughing uncontrollably. In between gasps of air, Goldberg was heard to say something about California.

Mitch Kaminsky turned off the tape. "That's it, Mr. President."

"Good God! You got a lot of information from an old man who has trouble remembering anything. Good work, Mitch! What are your thoughts on the plane crash?"

"I'm a good deal older than you, sir, and I do remember reading about that tragedy back in the late forties. The crash shocked the nation. In one airline accident we lost five senior members of Congress, the top brass of the military and two Cabinet members. An investigation, as I remember it, found no evidence of sabotage. Now, hearing this story about a group called the 'Majestic 12' all dying in the crash, except for two members, makes me wonder if there wasn't something suspicious about that crash. Evidently, no one back then knew about this group, except the President."

"And maybe someone else beside the President knew about it and wanted to keep those people quiet." the President said sadly.

"That's a terrible thought, Mr. President." Kaminsky answered.

"Terrorism is nothing new to the world. The age of modern-day terrorism began with the bombing of Pearl Harbor. We raised terrorism to the next level when we dropped the atomic bomb on Japan. No, Mitch, destroying that planeload of government officials was certainly within the realm of possibility. I want you to put someone in charge of opening the books on that crash. It has to be someone who you can trust and will answer only to you. Also, we have to find out who that other 'Majestic 12' member was, and if he is still alive. If you remember, General Darlington said there was only one survivor out of the group. Did he really believe that or was he lying? I want to know."

"Okay, Mr. President. There's something else I found out about Mr. Goldberg."

"What's that, Mitch?"

"When I was leaving the nursing home where Goldberg is staying, I asked the doctor about his condition."

"And?"

"He said Goldberg's records indicate he had a nervous breakdown in the early fifties. During that time he developed a mental block about the past. It's all in his records. Over the years, he experienced several severe bouts of depression and was hospitalized."

"Where was he hospitalized each time?"

"Are you ready for this, Mr. President? Walter Reed Army Hospital."

"What are you driving at, Mitch?"

"Walter Reed! It's a military hospital. How come a civilian gets to go to a military hospital, unless someone is trying to take care of him?"

"I'm sure President Truman wanted to take care of him for his service to the country."

"Let me throw this out to you, then. How come, every time he ends one of those stays, his mind and health are worse off than when he went in? Besides, President Truman was in office only the first time he was admitted. What about the other three times? The attending doctor in Grand Rapids said his bills have been paid anonymously ever since he was first admitted to the nursing home twenty-three years ago. I think we should try to find out who paid for all his admissions at the nursing home and at Walter Reed."

"Agreed. That's something else you should have someone check out. You have my permission on that matter. Now, let's talk about those space invaders. It seems as if we have these aliens living somewhere out in New Mexico building or creating things we know nothing about. Maybe they're developing a weapon more powerful than the atomic bomb!"

Retrieving the tape from the cassette player and handing it to the President, Kaminsky responded to the President's assumption, "We don't know that for a fact. Maybe Goldberg was hallucinating a little bit."

The President moved his chair away from the desk and stood up. "Mitch, I think it makes sense. This incident happened only a few years after the end of the Second World War. Do you remember what brought the war with Japan to an end? The atomic bomb! Now, think! Who was the President who ordered the bomb?"

Kaminsky rubbed his chin. "Truman!"

"Exactly! Who was the President who created Project Anasazi?"

"Truman!"

"Right again! And, if Truman had no qualms about using the atomic bomb he would certainly buy into a program that would make the United States a super power. Especially after the horror of that war! Somewhere in New Mexico we have the wherewithal to bring peace to the world and end all wars with weapons these aliens evidently have the ability to develop. We must find out if there are such weapons. We can't afford to have China or Russia find out about these people and what they are capable of. Are we all set for tonight?"

"Yes sir! We'll commence our operations tonight at midnight."

"Mitch, do we know the exact location of this compound?"

"It's somewhere in the Alegros Mountains near a town called Pie Town. Sir, if I may say so, I think we're getting carried away with this weapons thing. What about the technology and the medicines they promised to develop for us? Isn't that more important than these weapons?"

The President laughed loudly. "Well, aren't you the caring one, Mitch! Of course, I'm interested in wiping out all disease throughout the world. But first we must make peace and let the rest of the world know that we have the ability to create peace if it is not accepted willingly. Then, we'll offer them our new miracle drugs to keep them healthy. If the threat of weapons doesn't bring us peace we can make them see it our way biologically. The miracle drugs will be like our ace in the hole. Only the protected will survive."

"Mr. President, isn't that a little drastic on your part?"

"This could be the very thing that can guarantee me a second term, maybe many more terms in office. Oh, by the way, Mitch, there was an incident on your block last night."

"Yes, I know. There was a gas explosion or something a few doors down from my house."

"It wasn't a gas explosion, it was a car bomb. The bodies were tentatively identified the as belonging to two men attached to Air Force Intelligence. Two FBI people were trailing these two individuals, who were seen earlier in the day at General Darlington's office, when the bomb went off prematurely. In fact, they were leaving his office yesterday as you were arriving to give Darlington the bad news. You probably passed them outside his office. We're convinced that car bomb was meant for you! Anyway, Darlington is history. The FBI and military intelligence are on the way over to Darlington's office as we speak."

CHAPTER NINETEEN

Brad Davis and Running Horse were still sleeping when Billy Stiles pulled into the service area to fill up with gas. After a few minutes waiting for someone to attend to his car, he leaned long and hard on the horn. The blaring noise of the horn woke the two men in the house behind the garage. Running Horse's sparsely decorated bedroom consisted of twin beds, a five-drawer dresser, wall mirror, a few pictures of his family, a poster of a long-ago concert of Santa Fe resident and jazz musician Herbie Mann, and a small closet. Running Horse was the first to sit up in his bed. He shook his head, running his hands through his hair, and then looked over to see Davis struggling to open his eyes and begin the new day. The horn from outside blared again.

"Brad! Wake up! Do you hear me? Wake up! There's something strange going on here!"

Davis, half asleep, lifted himself up on his elbows and looked over at Running Horse in the bed beside his. "Whoa! Where are we?"

"We're in my bedroom!" He and Davis were still fully clothed.

"Your bedroom! How the hell did we get here? The last thing I remember is being blinded by the light of that thing up on top of the mountain. What's going on here?"

Running Horse stood up and looked at himself in the mirror. "That's me alright in the mirror. And, that's you over in the bed. For the life of me I don't understand what's going on. All I remember is someone standing there in the bright light and talking to us. But what happened?" Running Horse looked at the clock on his dresser. "It's ten o'clock in the morning, almost ten hours after we were up on the mountain. What happened between then and now? Did we dream it?"

Davis stood up, stretched and walked to the mirror. "I don't think you and I could have possibly dreamed it all up. Holy shit! Your mother! What happened to Little River?"

Running Horse ran his hand across his forehead. "My mother! I forgot all about her! We were taking her to get some help. What happened to her? Where is she? I left her in the truck when we got out to investigate the light. My God, we've lost my mother!"

"What is all this commotion in that bedroom?" a raspy voice called out from the vicinity of the back bedroom off the kitchen.

Davis and Running Horse looked at each other in surprise. The voice got louder as Little River entered Running Horse's bedroom. "Why can't you let an old woman get some sleep?"

Running Horse rushed from beside his bed, picked up his mother and twirled her around the bedroom, out into the kitchen. "Mother! Mother! You're okay!"

"Put me down, you silly boy, and stop acting so foolishly." Little

River pried herself loose from her son's strong grip. "Of course I'm okay. Why wouldn't I be?"

Davis had joined the couple in the kitchen. "Little River, Running Horse and I found you unconscious and all beat up last night in the garage. We thought you were dead!"

"Me dead? It's going to take more than that to put me in the ground." Little River huffed.

"Mother, your face was all swollen and you were bleeding from the head."

Little River walked into Running Horse' bedroom and looked at herself in the mirror. "Come here, boy! Do I look like I have a hole in my head or a beat up face?"

"No, but you did last night." Running Horse said emphatically.

"How do you explain how wonderful I look today then?"

"Little River, your son and I found you unconscious and we took you in the truck to bring you to a clinic in Pie Town. Somehow, we never got there with you. Something happened that none of us can explain."

"Well, if you can't explain it, there's nothing to talk about and what you both say is all nonsense. I don't want to remember more than those two thugs trying to find out where you both were."

"What two thugs, mother? Are they the ones who beat you up? What did they look like?"

"Don't remember much. I had a feeling they were probably some military kind of people."

"What makes you say that, Little River?" Davis asked.

"I know how military boys act when they're looking for something. Besides, they had a military air about themselves."

"Brad, I don't like the sound of all this. UFO sightings, our encounter last night and not remembering things, and now military people looking for us."

The car horn blared loud and long again. Running Horse raced out of the bedroom into the front room. He stopped short at the front door when he realized there was a young woman sleeping soundly on the sofa. He rushed back to the bedroom, placing both hands on the door frame, and whispered, "Brad, there's a woman sleeping on the living room sofa. She looks like the woman I saw up at the accident scene."

"A woman sleeping on our sofa? Running Horse, what have you been up to now?" Little River said as she rushed out of the bedroom into the living room.

"Are you sure, Running Horse? Maybe, you're the one that's seeing things now." Davis smiled as he removed Running Horse's arms from the door frame, allowing him to pass into the living room. He had only taken a few steps toward the sofa when Davis recognized the sleeping woman. "Susan! Susan! What? How? Where?"

Running Horse followed his mother and Davis into the living room. "You know this woman?"

"Of course I know this woman! In the not distant future she's going to be Mrs. Davis."

Stifling a laugh, Running Horse replied, "Do you mean you really know this woman or are you just saying that because she's so gorgeous and it's wishful thinking on your part?"

"Hush, young man. I want to hear what this woman has to say for herself." Little River stood, with her hands on her waist, watching Susan.

Before Davis could respond Susan sat up abruptly, aware that three people were looking down on her. "Brad! Is that you? Is that really you? And aren't you the Indian I met at the accident on the highway?"

"One and the same, miss! Gosh, I had no idea who you were when I met you."

"Susan!" Davis rushed to the sofa and swept her up in his arms. "What are you doing here?"

She held onto Davis with all her strength. "Hold me tight! I'm frightened!"

Davis kissed her hard and long. "There's nothing to be frightened of here. I want you to meet my friends Running Horse and Little River. This is their house."

Susan relaxed her hold on Davis and reached to shake the hands of Little River and Running Horse. "Pleased to meet you, Little River, and good to see you again, Running Horse."

"You weren't feeling too well when we met the first time, Miss Adams. Are you feeling any better now?"

"Yes, thank you. Can someone please tell me how I got here?"

Taking Susan's two hands into his own, Davis tried to assure her everything would be alright. "That's what I want to know, too. How did you get here on Running Horse's sofa? I thought you were back in New York. I've been trying to contact you for quite some time."

"I don't know how I got here. In fact, I can't remember much of anything in the last twenty-four hours." Pushing his hands away Susan remembered she was supposed to be mad at Davis. "Listen, Mr. Davis. You've been up to your old tricks again. Not calling when you were supposed to! I was worried about you, so I took some time off to join you out here. Believe me, it hasn't been easy."

"I'm sorry." Davis responded in an apologetic tone. "But I'm still puzzled as to how you got here, in Running Horse and Little River's house?"

"I don't know how I got here. I didn't even know where you were. And, I've never seen Little River before. But I do remember meeting Running Horse at the accident yesterday!"

Davis pushed Susan's feet onto the floor, giving him more room to sit closer to her on the sofa. "Tell me, what was the last thing you remember before awakening here in this room?"

Pushing the hair away from her eyes, she looked at Running Horse and then to Davis. "Everything seems dreamlike since those two Indians at the motel said they would take me to you."

"What two Indians?"

"I don't know! Indians! That's all! They were dressed the way I would expect Indians out here to dress." Pointing to Running Horse, she said, "They were dressed like him. The only thing different about them was something that hung around their neck that glowed. It was strange looking. Like nothing I had ever seen before. I was afraid to ask them about it."

"Brad!" Running Horse interrupted. "It sounds like the same thing we saw hanging around the neck of the person we saw last night."

"You're right!" Davis remembered. "What motel were you staying at when these two Indians took you away?"

"The motel in Magdalena. I was waiting for you in your room."

"Susan, why did you go with these men if you didn't know them?"

"Look, you know I don't jump into a car with every stranger that asks me. These two Indians said they would bring me to you and there was something believable and comforting about them. Besides, here I am, with you. Maybe, they really did bring me here. I, for the life of me, can't remember anything about it."

A loud knocking on the screen door brought the conversation to an immediate halt. "Hey! Is anyone in there going to come out and pump some gas?" A large man in dungarees and a bright red parka could be seen through the open door.

"I'm coming." Running Horse stood looking out the screen door toward the tow truck parked alongside one of the pumps. "Ah, at least my truck is still here."

"Excuse me!" The voice belonged to Billy Stiles, who stood outside impatiently, looking at Running Horse through the screen door. "I'm sorry to disturb your family reunion, but can you hold the celebration long enough until after I get my car filled up?"

"I'll take care of this guy so you and your mother can talk. Susan, come on outside and we can continue talking." Davis took her by the hand, stepping outside and following Stiles to the gas pumps. "Whoops, almost forgot, I have to turn the switch on in the garage for the pumps." Davis left Susan standing with Stiles at the pumps while he went into the garage.

"You live out here, miss?" Stiles asked.

"No, I'm from New York."

"New York! Well, nice to meet another easterner out here. I'm from Washington. My name is Billy Stiles."

"Pleased to meet you. I'm Susan Adams."

"Are you out here on vacation?"

"Heavens, no! I'm tagging along with my boyfriend who's out here doing some research."

"Oh, really? What kind of research is he doing?"

"He's studying about the Indians that used to live here."

"No kidding! I have always had a fascination about these parts and the Anasazi Indians who once lived here."

Susan laughed. "Well I'll be darned! I thought there was only one Brad Davis in the world."

Stiles folded his arms and leaned against the car. "Brad Davis! Well, I'm impressed that you are a friend of his. I used to read all his

Indian articles in *NationalGeographic*. I thought I was the only one who was interested in that stuff."

Susan smiled. Davis walked up to the gas pumps, lifting the hose and placing it in the gas tank of the four-door Mitsubishi utility van. "How much do you want?" he asked?

"You can fill it up." Stiles answered. "Tell me Susan, how did you get interested in this Davis fellow?"

Davis' hands loosened on the pump handle and gas stopped flowing. Had he heard right? Was this guy asking questions about him? Could this guy be so brazen to ask such a question while he was standing there? Davis waited for Susan's answer. "You did say you wanted the tank filled?" Davis asked in a sarcastic tone.

"That's right!"

Susan was having a hard time refraining from laughing. She was watching Brad's expression as Stiles asked the question. "What do I like about Davis? Is that what you want to know? Do you mean as a writer or a person?"

"Do you know him personally?" Stiles was becoming amused.

Davis was beginning to understand what game Susan was playing. This poor chump had no idea who was pumping gas in his cars. "Would you like your windshield cleaned?" Brad asked playfully.

"Sure, you can do it after you fill the tank." Stiles said seriously.

Davis turned to look at Susan. "I thought the young lady might volunteer for the job."

"No, I'm having an interesting talk here with her right now and

I would prefer you would take care of it after you're finished with the gas."

"Yes, I know him personally. I know him so well that we're going to be married next December."

Davis grimaced at the mention of marriage. Neither Stiles nor Susan noticed.

"You're putting me on!" Stiles said laughingly, not believing Susan.

"No, I'm not! I'd like to hear what you like about Davis' writing?"

Stiles took a tissue from his pocket and cleaned his sun glasses. "I think his stories are imaginative, colorful and well researched. I would like to meet him personally. Do you think you could arrange that some time if I gave you my address?"

"What a come-on." Davis thought to himself.

Susan, still trying not to burst out laughing, responded, "I think that could be arranged."

Stiles was obviously pleased at her response. "You know, I wish Davis were out here now to help me on this assignment I have."

"What assignment is that?" Susan was curious.

"I'm with the FBI and on my way up to Mangas Mountain to look for two associates of mine and a Professor Timothy Beal. They were up here exploring a new Anasazi ruin and haven't returned yet. I'm going up there to find them with the hope I'll also get a firsthand look at a new find."

Davis was so engrossed in what Stiles was saying he forgot to pay attention to the tank. The gas, overflowing the tank and spilling all around him, got his attention quickly. "I'm sorry," he said to Stiles.

"That's okay. Don't worry about it. How much do I owe you?"

Davis returned the hose to the pump. "Fifteen forty-five. Why would the FBI be out looking around new Anasazi ruins?"

"Oh, they were out doing some exploring with a college professor friend up on Mangas Mountain. The head man wants me to find them and get them back to work."

"I know where that mountain is. It's not far from here. I could take you." Davis said with the enthusiasm of a schoolboy.

"Thank you very much, but I'm in the market to hire two Indian guides to take me up there. I'm sorry, you don't quite fill the bill."

Davis' face flushed. He was about to respond when Stiles asked another question.

"Do you know where I might find two guides?"

Brad still angry, responded, "Look, I've got more experience in these matters than any one hundred Indian guides."

Stiles laughed out loud. "You! A gas station attendant in the middle of nowhere. Get real, mister."

Davis moved menacingly close to Stiles, ready to take a swing when Susan stepped between both men. "Billy Stiles, I think it's time you officially met your gas attendant. May I introduce Brad Davis?"

"What? *The* Brad Davis! You're putting me on. It can't be! Out here in the middle of nowhere pumping gas!" Stiles stepped back and took a long look at Davis. "Go on!"

"Whether you want to believe her or not, it's the truth. I'm Brad Davis. Now, do you want some help or not?"

Susan interrupted before Stiles could answer. "Brad Davis, you are not going to go off without me again, once I've finally found you."

"Mr. Davis, can we talk?"

"Sure we can talk." He started walking back to the house, followed by Susan and Stiles. "First, Let me check on Little River and see how she's doing. Would you believe this woman was practically dead last night and this morning she's like a new person?"

"This Little River, how old is she?" Stiles was trying to make conversation.

Davis rubbed his nose. "I think she's somewhere around ninety. She's Running Horse's mother and he's seventy. So, I think ninety is about right." Davis reached the door of the house and waved Susan through the door. "Come on in, Mr. Stiles and meet the family."

Stiles introduced himself, shaking hands with Running Horse and Little River. Stiles, addressing Little River, said, "I'm glad you're feeling better. Mr. Davis told me you weren't well last night and now you're fully recovered."

Little River looked at Stiles, cocking her head to one side and then turned her gaze on Davis. "What do you mean I wasn't feeling well? Don't you know the difference between being sick and having the crap beat out of you?"

Stiles, thinking he may have blundered into a family dispute that had gotten out of hand, tried to change the subject. "I was hoping you folks could help me find some....."

Little River, still looking at Davis, interrupted Stiles. "Young man, you don't have to lie to anyone about what happened last night."

"Please folks, I didn't mean to pry into your personal lives by asking about Little River's health."

Taking Little River by the hand, Running Horse escorted his mother into the kitchen. "Mother, why don't you make us all a cup of coffee, and breakfast for those who would like some."

"I'll help." Susan said, following Little River into the kitchen.

Returning from the kitchen, Running Horse walked to the front door and turned to face both men. "Mr. Stiles....."

"Please call me Billy," Stiles interrupted.

"Okay, Billy, I'm going to tell you about a strange set of events last night that's going to put a chill down your spine." Running Horse sat in the one hard-back chair in the room, motioning Davis and Stiles to be seated on the sofa. For the next ten minutes Billy Stiles listened as Running Horse and Davis told about their finding Little River near death, the encounter, and finding themselves back at the house, remembering nothing. When he finished, Stiles was sitting on the edge of the sofa.

"Is there anything else?" Stiles was anxious to hear more.

"No, I'm afraid that's all there is to it." Davis rose from the sofa, drawn by the aroma of fresh coffee brewing in the kitchen. "However, we plan to go back up to where we were last night and try to retrace our steps."

"We plan to do what?" Running Horse replied, surprised.

"Gentlemen," Stiles said in an excited tone of voice, "I would like to join you on your trip, but first I have to find my colleagues up in another mountain, Mangas Mountain. Maybe you can help me find them and then I can go with you."

Both Davis and Running Horse looked at each other, shrugging their shoulders. Davis spoke first. "We'll have to think about that for a while."

Running Horse nodded his approval.

"I think you should hear me out before you decide not to join me looking for those men up on Mangas Mountain. Since you've been very candid with me about your experience last night, I am going to let you in on what I am doing out here and share with you a similar experience I had many years ago in Utah.

Davis and Running Horse could hardly believe what they were hearing from this government agent from Washington. Stiles had barely gotten the last words out of his mouth when Running Horse asked, "Are you telling us you believe in UFO's and alien beings?"

"There's too much evidence that can't be explained rationally. I belong to a group who has been investigating these sightings for some time now." Stiles, looking at both men asked, "And, you two, do you believe?"

Davis was the first to answer. "I have had this theory for some time that the so-called advanced civilizations on earth had to have had some extra special help. My preliminary research on the Anasazi Indians shows they had a lot in common with the Aztecs, Mayas, and Incas. All up and down North, Central and South America there are treasure troves, indigenous to one area, and yet found among all the excavations of these past civilizations. Their mathematical and architectural skills were far too advanced for their time. Look, I'm only researching the Anasazi to find a common bond and it's my intention to show a link to early visits from somewhere out of this world. If we're being visited again by some of the same people who helped these past civilizations, I want to meet them. To answer your question, I don't really know, but I hope so. The existence of aliens would answer the many questions that I've had since grade school about the Egyptians, Greeks and Babylonians. I really do hope they exist so they can help me with my research."

"Well," Running Horse leaned back in the chair and crossed his leg, "Even after last night I think there might be a reasonable explanation. I don't want to believe in UFO's and space creatures. I like to think we're still the smartest beings in the world."

"We probably are," offered Stiles. "But that's not to say outside of this world, somewhere in the vast universe, there are not beings far superior intellectually and from civilization light years ahead of us."

"I know, I know." Running Horse sighed. "Even with my doubts about last night I still remember back to 1947."

"1947? Are you referring to the Roswell incident?" Stiles asked.

"Yes." Running Horse replied.

Stiles responded excitedly. "That was about a crashed UFO and the finding of alien bodies. Of course, the government denied the whole thing, saying it was a new type of weather balloon. I was just a little kid then, but I remember being fascinated with the newspaper stories about it."

"Weather balloon! Hogwash!!" Running Horse said defiantly.

"Running Horse, I think you may want to end your conversation right now." Davis cautioned him.

"Hell, I think Mr. Stiles is trustworthy. He's not like all those other damn government people."

Davis moved over to Running Horse, still seated and put his hand on his shoulder. "Don't you think we should talk about this first?"

Stiles stood up and moved in front of Running Horse. "Is there something you care to share with me? I promise whatever it is your secret is safe with me."

Running Horse uncrossed his legs and stood up. "Yes, I want to share something with you that I have had since 1947."

As he moved toward the front door, Susan popped her head into the living room, "Hey you three, where do you think you're going? Breakfast is served."

"Be back in a jiffy." Running Horse said in a serious tone. "I'm just going to show Mr. Stiles something I've got in the garage." Before Susan could stop them the three men were out the front door and headed toward the garage.

CHAPTER TWENTY

It was a few minutes past eleven by the time everyone finished breakfast. There was a great deal of animated conversation around the table, much of the talk focusing on the events of the night before. Billy Stiles said nothing as he listened intently to what Davis and Running Horse were saying. Running Horse didn't eat much, which was unusual for him. His normal artery-clogging breakfast consisted of cereal, four eggs, a couple of slices of ham, three pieces of toast laden with butter, a large glass of orange juice and four cups of coffee. Today, he left almost everything on his plate, except for one piece of toast. His poor appetite did not go unnoticed by Davis and Little River.

"Why aren't you eating this morning?" Little River wanted to know. "Don't you feel well?"

Running Horse made a low moaning noise, rolling his eyes. "Mother, there is nothing wrong with me and it's alright to lose your appetite once in a while."

"I know when there's something bothering you."

"There is nothing bothering me other than the fact that I'm trying to think about the best way up the mountain where Mr. Stiles wants to go. You know I've been up there many times and there are a half dozen trails we could take."

Little River got up and walked to the end of the table where Running Horse was seated. Arms folded, she stood looking at him until he finally turned his gaze toward her.

"What? What is it?" Running Horse asked sheepishly. "I hate when you look at me like that."

A slight smile formed on Little River's face. "I've been your mother for a long time and I know when you are avoiding the truth."

"Mother, you know a Navajo never lies."

"I didn't say you were lying. I just said you were avoiding the truth. Now hear me out, son. You are worried about me because of last night. You can't figure out how I could have been so badly beaten and today.... it's like nothing ever happened. Well, I know the spirits were gathering to take me away. In fact, I saw them. Lots of them. All hovering around me dressed in their ceremonial Indian dress. Funny thing though, they didn't speak our language."

Running Horse took his mother's hands into his. "What are you talking about? There were only Brad and me driving you in the truck."

"Oh, but there was, my son!" Little River returned to her chair at the kitchen table. As she sat down her eyes seemed to get a glazed look as she continued to speak. "I was in the truck. There was a very bright light. The spirits came quietly and lifted me from the front seat. I could see you and Mr. Davis talking with someone in the light. I could not call out to you to bid farewell. The spirits took me into the light. It was so bright I couldn't see anything. It was very peaceful. Such a warm, comfortable feeling. Soon, I was aware of many spirits around me. I couldn't see their faces and they did not speak the language of our ancestors. Yet, I knew I was safe."

Davis, Susan, Stiles and Running Horse all sat quietly, hanging on Little River's every word. The concern of Running Horse for his mother was evident in his voice. "Are you sure of this or were you dreaming?"

"Dreaming! You think your mother makes up stories or has lost her senses?"

"No, but...."

"Hush then, and show some respect for your elders! I will grant you that everything appeared as if it were a dream. Except there was a feeling of floating. It was like my body was being separated from my mind. I could feel energy pulsating throughout my body. There was a tingling sensation, as if there was an electric current passing through me. It wasn't strong. It was more like a slight electric shock. A humming sound! Yes, I remember a low humming sound."

"What kind of humming sound?" Davis asked.

Little River closed her eyes, trying to remember the exact sound. "A vibrating sound! It is the sound one hears of someone blowing air through a musical reed before you actually hear music." Opening her eyes, Little River looked around the kitchen table. Everyone's attention was focused on the small Indian woman. "Do you all think it was a dream? Do you think me crazy? Or, do you think I met with the spirits?"

Everyone shook their heads no. Billy Stiles was the first to speak. "Little River, you are not crazy. It's the same experience I had many years ago and everyone thought I was crazy. The bright light, odd figures, a low frequency humming sound, all were part of something I had trouble remembering. There was more to recall, but I just couldn't, as hard as I tried. To answer your question, no I don't think you're crazy. Nor do I think they were the spirits of your ancestors."

Little River smiled. "Thank you."

Stiles continued, "I heard that you were beaten pretty badly, all bruised up, and according to your son, near death. Yet, we are all looking at you and you are the picture of health. There isn't a mark on you. Your face has the look of someone less than half your age. Your hands, look at your hands. They are not the hands of a ninety-year-old woman."

Little River's smile broadened as she looked at her hands. "Do you really think so? I've been told many time I don't look my age."

"Mother," Running Horse chuckled, "people said you didn't act your age. They never said you didn't look your age."

"Mind your manners, son! Maybe Mr. Stiles has something else nice to say about me!"

Stiles looked around the table, seeking affirmation to what he was saying to Little River. Everyone else was smiling except Running

Horse. He had a strange expression on his face as he looked at his mother.

Pushing himself away from the table and standing, Running Horse exclaimed, "Okay, Mr. Stiles is right! I have to agree you don't look as old as you did before. In fact, you look much younger than me, your son. How could that be? Brad, am I crazy or has my mother become younger since last night?"

Davis, sitting directly across from Little River, sat back against his chair. "My God, you're right, now that you mention it. Little River looks entirely different. It's as if her body clock has been turned back more than thirty years. That's impossible! Isn't it?" Davis looked first at Running Horse and then at Billy Stiles. "Perhaps these people, aliens, whatever you want to call them, that you met up with last night have the power to turn back our biological clock."

Stiles sat quietly, looking first at Little River and then at Davis. It was obvious from his demeanor that he was holding back what he really thought about Davis' idea.

"Hello, people, time for a reality check!" Susan said, as she threw her arms into the air. "Will you listen to yourselves? UFOs, aliens, turning the clock back, regressing our age! Get a hold of yourselves. There has to be a rational explanation for all of this. I, for one, do not believe in all this drivel."

"Susan," Davis reached out to touch her hand, "please keep an open mind. I'm the biggest skeptic that ever walked this earth. There are a number of things that I have seen and heard and experienced in the last few days that make me a little less skeptical. Running Horse, Little River and I can't account for a number of hours that we lost last night. And, another thing, what about your not remembering anything about how you got here?"

Susan pulled her hand away. "Well, that's true. But, those Indians I met and drove with to the top of the mountain were not alien beings or creatures from another planet."

"How do you know that?" Stiles asked.

"Because they were sort of nice. Neither of them had scaly skin, slits for eyes or snake-like tongues. They were very human and spoke perfect English. They didn't try to harm me. What you people seem to be caught up in is all the Hollywood nonsense generated by those movies *Independence Day* and *Men In Black*!"

Running Horse, ignoring Susan's comments, asked, "Do you remember anything after the car reached the top of the mountain?"

"Actually, no. All I know is that they said they would take me to Brad, and it seems they delivered on that promise."

"Do you think they physically did anything to you?" Davis wanted to know.

"Of course not!" Susan said angrily. "I would know if anyone was trying to fool with my parts or play doctor."

"You think so, Miss Adams?" Stiles interjected. "These same people did something to Little River and she can't remember anything."

Little River jumped up from the table. "Well, if they did any funny business with me, and me not knowing about it, and I feel and look this good, I want to be awake the next time to enjoy whatever they did."

"Sit down, Mother, and get hold of yourself." Running Horse chuckled.

"Susan, I don't want to belabor the point, but there is something about Little River's experience with these people that relates to my adventure with them many years ago. As I said earlier, everyone thought I was crazy when I told my superiors in the Bureau about my Utah trip. I would have accepted that except for one very important thing. Before my encounter, I was diagnosed with terminal kidney cancer. The most I could hope for was another year to live. I have the doctor's records to prove what I am saying. After this encounter, I returned to my doctor for a follow-up visit, telling him I was feeling much better and that my symptoms weren't bothering me anymore. Following another set of tests there was no evidence of my cancer. The doctor was at a loss to explain my complete cure. His only explanation was that I had experienced spontaneous remission. To this day, there has never been a recurrence. Strange, but true. I believe those people did something to cure me and yet, I don't remember anyone doing anything to me."

"Maybe you were misdiagnosed." Susan, leaning forward in her chair, said.

"I don't think so." Stiles replied. "Cancer specialists at both

Walter Reed and Bethesda reached the same conclusion. Another thing, which by the way I didn't tell the doctors or anyone else, was the fact that I was able to walk without a slight limp after my encounter."

"I don't understand." Davis said.

"When I was a kid growing up in Indiana, I fell out of a tree and broke my left leg in three places. It was so bad they thought I would never have full use of that leg. After many operations and a metal rod they placed in my leg I was able to walk, but with a slight limp. I walked with that limp and pain up until after my encounter. It was shortly afterwards that I noticed I wasn't walking with a limp and the pain had gone away. I thought I was just feeling okay and nothing was bothering me until I went through the metal detector at Washington National. It didn't go off!"

Running Horse, who had been listening intently, asked, "What do you mean-the metal detector didn't go off?"

"Just that." Stiles responded matter of factly. "It didn't go off for the first time in my life going through those damn machines at the airport. Do you know how aggravating that is, to be scanned all the time by the security at the airport? So, when I got to Tampa, where I was headed on assignment, I went to an orthopaedic doctor to examine me. He thought I was crazy. He told me there was no evidence my leg had ever been broken. After pleading with him, he agreed to take an x-ray. That x-ray was clean. No sign of my leg ever having been broken in three places! No metal rod! Am I crazy? No!

Those people did something to make my life better. Does that sound like people who have evil intentions? I don't think so! Do I know how they did it? No! But, I am thankful to them and would like to thank them personally. So, I am a believer. They are back and for what reason, I don't know. I just know I will meet with them face-to-face."

No one said a word for a minute after Stiles had finished speaking. Finally, Davis looked at his watch to check the time. "Damn! How is it possible we've been sitting over breakfast since mid morning and now it's a little after three?"

"No, it's not!" Little River said pointing to the wall clock over the refrigerator. "It's only been an hour we're sitting here. The time is ten minutes past eleven."

"That's not what I have." Davis answered. "Your wall clock has to be wrong."

"He's right." Running Horse said as he looked at his watch. "I have the same time as Brad. Look at your watch, mother."

"Wow, I guess you're right." Little River responded. "I have the same time as you do."

"Hold it, everyone." Stiles interrupted as he took off his watch and held it up for everyone to see. "My watch is the same as the wall clock."

"I have a different time and date on my watch than all of you have." Susan said with a puzzled voice. "My watch still has yesterday's date and the time is seven p.m. I don't understand this."

"What about your calendar date, Brad?" Stiles asked.

"That's strange. My day/date is halfway changed. That's the way it usually looks the first hours of a new day."

Running Horse shrugged his shoulders. "Sorry, my mother and I don't have one of those fancy watches with all those gimmicks. My watch is a simple Timex that only gives the time."

"I think I may have an explanation." Stiles stood up from the table. "You have all had an encounter with our friends from outer space. Something happens when you are in their presence. Time moves much more slowly. Susan's watch shows a different time than the rest of you because she probably was in their presence much longer. I had the same time problems when my encounter took place in Utah. At the time, I dismissed it as some malfunction of my watch. Now, hearing your time problems I now know that we all had our time frames altered by these people. I don't know how, but we have. I am the only one who has not had an encounter within the last twenty-four hours and my watch has not been affected. Brad, did you say you thought you might have stumbled onto their compound several days ago?"

"Yes, I'm sure of it."

"Did you notice any problems with your watch then?" Stiles wanted to know.

"As a matter of fact, I did. I thought it was curious then and tried to dismiss it as a battery problem."

"There, you see," exclaimed Stiles, "every time we are around these people they have an effect on our earth time. Somehow or another, time slows to a crawl. But, enough of this chatter, I must find those two other agents up at Mangas Mountain. Are you two still with me?"

The answer was a resounding yes from both men and Susan.

"Whoa! Wait just a minute, Susan." Davis walked around, assisting Susan from her chair. "I don't think it's a good idea for you to be going up there with us. I think it a much better idea if you stay here and keep an eye on Little River for us."

"Little River looks like she can take care of herself." Susan answered with a huff. "I want to go with you."

"Please, Susan," Davis pleaded with her, "I'll make it up to you. I promise!"

"I'll make a deal with you, Brad. I'll stay here with Little River for now, but when you return I'm going up to Alegros Mountain with all of you."

"Susan!" Davis was becoming angry.

"Brad," Stiles interrupted, "if I may stick my nose into your business, I would say it's okay for her to join us later. Think about it! All of you have had an encounter with these people before. So if we do actually run into them again, they already know you. I'm the only one they haven't dealt with on this trip and I'm the only one who would be at risk, if there is a risk."

"If you really think so, I guess there is safety in numbers."

"We'll take good care of her, Brad." Running Horse was convincing. "You can be sure of that."

"Good, now that we've settled that matter, we should be on our way." Stiles said happily. "How long will we be gone?"

Running Horse looked at Davis. "We should give ourselves at least four hours so we can get up to Mangas Mountain and return before nightfall."

"Sounds good to me." Davis concurred.

"Me, too!" Stiles added, as the three men said goodbye to Susan and Little River.

"I'm worried, Little River." Susan said after the door had closed behind them.

"Don't you worry." Little River tried to reassure Susan. "My instincts say they'll be fine. My son and the FBI man know how to take care of themselves. Your man is a different story. However, his rattlesnake bracelet is taking very good care of him."

"I don't understand."

"Sit down and have another cup of coffee and I'll explain." Little River said with a twinkle in her eye.

CHAPTER TWENTY ONE

Colonel Parker was not accustomed to being denied anything. As a military man on a fast track in U.S. Air Force military intelligence, he had distinguished himself with many courageous deeds during his twenty-five-year career. He had the ability to win his commanding officers' respect while coercing respect from his staff through intimidation. As he climbed the ladder from lieutenant to colonel, Parker was able to manipulate people at all levels of government to do his bidding. In the early years of his career he was seen as a considerate, sensitive individual. But as his career progressed, the calm, caring persona gave way to the seething desire for power that had always existed inside this man. In recent years, there were public outbursts that made his superior officers take notice. General Darlington, who was considered a control freak, took special interest in Parker, feeling he had the exact qualifications for assuming leadership of Project Anasazi from General Brantfield. It was on this basis that Darlington had assigned Colonel Parker the responsibility of going to New Mexico and doing whatever was necessary to keep the project an Air Force secret.

It was nine-thirty by the time Colonel Parker and Lieutenant Nelson finished their coffee. The new day for both men began later than they had anticipated. The previous night they had returned to their room at Magdalena's only bed-and-breakfast after the unsuccessful attempt to penetrate Alegros Mountain. Their standoff with the guardians of the compound had infuriated Parker. His first thought was to get even with those who had rebuked his authority. It was apparent General Brantfield had allowed these space visitors too much freedom and authority. Parker, feeling the General had become a government liability, had no regrets for killing him.

Immediately upon their arrival back at the motel, Parker placed a call to General Darlington's office. There was no answer. Realizing that his superior officer was enraged over the incident at the mountain and over his failure to make contact with General Darlington, Lieutenant Nelson opened a bottle of Dewar's. He poured a drink for himself and the colonel. Parker consumed the first drink in one gulp without a word. One drink led to another until both men, fully dressed, passed out on their beds.

The following morning found them, slightly hung-over, finishing their breakfast at Mama Bs. Parker looked at his watch, as he waited for Mattie to bring the check to his table. "Lieutenant, go over to Davis' motel and see if he and his girlfriend ever showed up last night. Then go back over to Brantfield's house and see if you can lay your hands on anything suspicious. I still want to know what happened to his body, just in case our friends from the mountain didn't have anything to do with it. In the meantime, I'm going to try to get hold of General Darlington again. After that, I'll stop by the sheriff's office and see if anything unusual is happening that the deputy knows about."

Nelson was sliding out of the booth as Mattie approached with the check. "Okay, gentlemen, here's your check." Mattie said.

The lieutenant, smiling and pointing to Parker, excused himself and headed for the door.

"You gentlemen have been around here for a couple of days. Did you know Sheriff Cooper?" Before waiting for an answer, Mattie continued to talk. "Terrible, terrible tragedy. He was such a nice man."

"No, I didn't know him, but I've heard of his reputation." Parker responded unenthusiastically.

"Sure has been a lot of odd things going on out here in the last few days."

"What do you mean?" Parker was suddenly more attentive.

Mattie sat down in the booth across from the colonel. Surprised and annoyed at her sitting down in front of him, he looked around the restaurant to see if anyone was watching. There were only a handful of people present and they were all engaged in the morning gossip.

"Nothing interesting happens in this town, well, at least not since my Sam died more than two years ago. Then, all of a sudden, this writer from the east shows up and things start happening."

Parker played with his empty coffee cup. "What started happening?"

"Like I said," Mattie leaned across the table and began talking softly, "this writer shows up. He seemed like a nice enough young man. Next, he and the sheriff leave early in the morning and the sheriff winds up dead. The writer never came back to his motel room. His girlfriend shows up looking for him and he can't be found anywhere."

"I don't see what you're driving at, Mattie." The colonel was playing dumb.

"She disappeared, too! She went off in a car with two Indians yesterday and hasn't been back to the motel since. Next, no one has seen Big Bird and General Brantfield. It's like they disappeared off the face of the earth. Some people are really scared. They think those sightings of UFOs have something to do with it. Maybe they were all abducted by little green people."

Parker couldn't help but smile at what Mattie was saying. "I don't think so!"

"Oh, yeah!" Mattie shot back, her voice no longer whispering. "Well, where are they? Huh? Can you tell me that?"

"No, I'm afraid I can't." Parker began sliding out of the booth, taking out his wallet to pay the bill.

Mattie walked over to the register behind the counter, followed by Parker, money in hand. "All these goings-on remind me of when they brought my husband's body back after he had been missing for a week. I'll never forget that time." Parker anxiously thrust the money into Mattie's hand in an attempt to speed up the transaction get away from this babbling-mouth woman. "Still to this day no one can figure how he could have been dead for so long and yet his body, that strange color, was so perfectly preserved. I'll never forget the look on old Brantfield's face when he came to look at my husband's body. It was as if he had seen a ghost."

Parker dropped the change Mattie had just handed him. As he bent over to retrieve the money, he showed renewed interest in Mattie's conversation. "Excuse me, what did you say about General Brantfield and your husband's body?"

"You mean how upset he became?"

"Yes."

"Why the sudden interest? You weren't paying me much mind when I was talking before. I can tell those things, you know. It comes from dealing with people in this business all my life."

"Yes, yes!" Parker was searching for words to answer the woman without arousing undue suspicion. "I'm a molecular biologist over at the university," he lied. "I've been studying the molecular properties of bodies as it relates to the foods we eat during our lifetime. You see, people eat too many foods with chemical preservatives and as a result their bodies are taking longer to decompose. We have studied exhumed bodies five and ten years after their death and are finding the body has not begun to decay because of the chemicals in the body."

347

"That's really interesting." Mattie responded energetically. "I don't think that's the case with my husband. He wasn't buried."

"Yes, that's what's so strange and makes me interested. Please tell me more about your husband's body."

"Well, initially, I was told he had broken his neck in a fall. Yet, when his body was brought to me, he had no signs of a broken neck, nor did he have any bruises on his body."

"Did they perform an autopsy?"

Mattie moved from behind the counter. "No, the sheriff signed the death certificate and wouldn't allow an autopsy. He convinced me that it wouldn't be something I would want. He said it was best we remembered Sam as he was."

"Didn't you think that a little unusual?"

"Not really. He and Sam were old buddies and it didn't take much persuasion to convince me. However, thinking back, I would like to know why there were no signs of a broken neck and why his body was that strange color. I didn't know what to make of it. The color of his body, which like I said earlier, had not decomposed after one week out in the mountains, was a grayish green."

Parker had heard enough to make him start worrying. His voice lacking sincerity, Parker said, "Thank you for sharing that story with me. I have to go now." He placed the change in his pocket and walked out the door, heading to the nearest telephone booth. Mattie's story of her husband and the general made him acutely aware that perhaps these visitors from another planet have the ability to resurrect the dead. If that were the case, he had better start really worrying and find out why he couldn't find the bodies of Big Bird and Brantfield. That they were killed, he had no doubt. Suppose these strange creatures have brought them back to life, then what must he do?

"Good morning, this is Captain Bork. May I help you?" The voice at the other end of the telephone had a military crispness.

"Captain, good morning. This is Colonel Parker. I would like to speak with General Darlington."

"Sorry, sir, the general has been relieved of his position, sir."

"What the hell are you talking about, captain?"

"Sir, this morning at 0730 hours, military police and the FBI came and arrested the general and escorted him away. There is a military guard outside of his office and the FBI is going through all the files in his office."

"What happened?"

"Don't know, sir. I do know that they are looking for you right now. They told me, if you called, to tell you to return to Washington immediately."

"What about the two aides in my office? Are they around? Did they get back to Washington and report to the general?"

"Affirmative, colonel. They did meet with the general. Unfortunately, they were killed in a car bomb explosion last night."

"A car bomb explosion! What....?."

"Excuse me, Colonel Parker," Bork interrupted the colonel, "Mr.

Weaver, the FBI Director would like a word with you, sir. Hello, hello....."

Parker slammed down the telephone. Everything was beginning to unravel. Think! Think! What did he have to do to prove his loyalty to his country and regain control of Project Anasazi? It was critical for his very survival.

"Watch your footing." Running Horse cautioned his companions. "Looks like a pretty good deluge hit this area within the past two days."

"What makes you say that?" Davis asked.

"Look down ahead of you through the narrow pass. See how the pass descends from where we are toward that distant mesa? This pass is a gradual decline and if you examine the dirt and rocks on each side you will notice the evidence left behind by a flood."

Billy Stiles stopped to catch his breath. "How could you have floods up here in such a narrow pass?"

"That is a hidden danger in all mountainous areas which are prone to flash floods. This is such a place. It suddenly starts raining in torrents and before you know it, little streams become raging rivers and narrow trails can become a cascading waterfall. I only hope your friends didn't get caught in such a predicament. From the looks of the terrain, this area was torn apart pretty good in what I suspect was a flash flood. If your friends were here, they didn't stand a chance."

"Well, I have a little more confidence in my friends being able to survive any calamity." Stiles responded, as he resumed the climb down the pass.

"We're almost at the base of the mesa." Davis said breathlessly. "This is sure a weird place for a mesa to be, right in the middle of the forest."

"No explaining geography and land formation." Running Horse laughed.

"Wow!" exclaimed Stiles. "Look at all the debris at the bottom of this trail. There are giant boulders and uprooted trees. What do you think caused that, Running Horse?"

The three men were standing side by side viewing the bottom of the pass. "Careful! That's at least a 1,000 foot drop." Running Horse warned.

"Do we have to go down there?" asked Davis.

"I would say that's Billy's call." Running Horse responded. "Billy, what do you think? Do we explore around the mesa itself or do we look to see if your friends got caught in the flood?"

Stiles rubbed his head. "You're the expert out here and I'll go with what you say."

"I say we climb down to where that debris is piled up and see if we find anything that might have belonged to Professor Beal and your friends. So far, the flash flood has wiped out any tracks or signs of anyone ever having been here. If your friends were anywhere in this vicinity and still alive, they would have made their presence known by now."

The climb down the 1,000 foot embankment to the debris pile was the most treacherous part of the journey thus far. Several times Running Horse had to help both Davis and Stiles regain their footing, lest they tumble down the mountainside. Finally, after twenty minutes of stumbling, cursing, and bruised hands and legs, the trio was within 100 feet of their destination.

"Oh, my God!" Stiles called out.

"What's the matter?" Running Horse and Davis asked.

"Look, look over there, to the left." Stiles pointed to what looked like a man's figure draped around a tree, fifty feet from the huge mound of debris. "It looks like a body."

"Hold on. Stay where you are and let me look." Running Horse made his way down past Stiles toward the tree. Reaching the tree, Running Horse used his foot to move what looked like a body.

"What is it?" Davis, who reached where Stiles was standing, called down to Running Horse.

"Bad news, I'm afraid."

"Is it someone?" Stiles asked, afraid of the answer.

"It was someone." Running Horse reached down and went through the body's pockets. He stood up and displayed a shield. "I'm afraid it's what is left of one of your friends. His body got pretty badly beaten up from being brought down here by the flood."

"I want to see for myself." Stiles said bravely.

"Please stay where you are, Billy. I'm afraid you wouldn't

recognize agent Smith. That's what the shield says, but no one would ever be able to tell.

"What do you mean?"

"It looks like the mountain lions have been lunching on him. It's not pretty. We better check out that pile over there and see if the other two are there."

Running Horse reached the pile of debris first. Stiles was the next to join him, followed by Davis. The debris consisted of tons of mountainside, boulders of all sizes and dimensions, tree branches, shrubs, and huge trees, roots and all.

"Where do we begin?" Davis asked.

"Look for anything out of the ordinary, anything that doesn't look like it's part of the mountain." Running Horse said seriously.

Stiles climbed to the top of the pile, which stood at least ten feet high in some places. Carefully, he moved across the pile, peering downwards, seeking any sight of clothing. Davis cautiously moved around the entire perimeter of the pile while Running Horse began pulling away small bits of debris from the pile.

"Hey, Brad! Come on up and tell me if this looks like a shoe." Stiles began to pull apart the top of the pile.

Davis joined Stiles and began assisting him, pulling apart the debris. "Sure looks like a shoe." They continued to dig through the rubble until they found the shoe was attached to a leg. "Damn, we've found our second body."

Within five minutes the three men had recovered the body of agent Osborne.

"Two down and one to go." Running Horse said with a sigh. "I want you two to help me pull out the bottom of this pile over on the far end. I think I saw what looked like a hand."

Lifting the body of Osborne down from the pile and placing him at the base of a distant tree, the three men began to sift through the debris for the final body. It took almost a half hour before they pulled the final body from the debris.

"I imagine this is our Professor Beal." Stiles said, wiping the sweat from his brow.

Running Horse was going through his pants pockets looking for the professor's wallet when he extracted a small piece of metal. As he stood up and examined what he held in his hands he yelled out. "Brad! Brad! Look! It's another piece of metal like I have."

"Let me see that!" Davis asked excitedly.

"Is it exactly like the one you showed me in the garage?" Stiles wanted to know.

"Sure looks like the same thing, except this one has writing on it." Running Horse said as he held up the small piece of metal for both men to see.

"Where did you say you found this?" asked Stiles.

"In the professor's pocket. Running Horse answered.

"Where do you think the professor got it?" Stiles asked as he handled the soft metal.

"Either from somewhere around here or he brought it with him from the university, hoping to find more out here." Running Horse guessed.

"I'm willing to bet he found it here and never lived to tell about it." Davis said excitedly.

"The spirits didn't want him to have it then." Running Horse said nervously.

"Billy, do you have any idea what this writing says?"

"I'm afraid not. Why don't you let me hold onto this one and I'll have someone back in Washington analyze it."

"That piece of metal with the gibberish written on it reminds me of some English gibberish I found on a plain piece of paper placed under my car's windshield wiper at the motel several days ago. Do you think there's a connection?"

"Don't know." Stiles responded. "Have you got it with you?"

Davis reached into his shirt pocket and pulled out the folded paper with the strange message. Handing it over to Stiles, he asked, "What do you think?"

"I don't have a clue. Why do you think someone gave this to you?"

"I really don't know. No one I was aware of knew what research I was doing at the university. It's all a puzzle to me."

Stiles handed the paper back to Davis. "Could be someone is trying to help you solve the mystery of the Anasazi."

"We have to find where he got it from." Davis said anxiously.

"Some other day, Brad." Running Horse responded. "It is getting late and we promised Susan and my mother we would return within four hours. By the time we get back to the house it will have been six hours since we left this morning. You have my word that we will come back another day to unravel this mystery. There is another more pressing puzzle we must solve on top of Alegros Mountain. You two place the bodies on a flat surface and cover them completely with rocks. That way the animals will not be able to feast on them. I will take care of covering the first body. When we get back to the house, we will notify the proper authorities where to find their remains."

CHAPTER TWENTY TWO

"Mr. Kaminsky to see you, Mr. President."

"Thank you, Mary. Please send him in.

Mitch Kaminsky entered the Oval Office and was greeted warmly by the President and Everett Weaver. "Sit down, Mitch. Ev got a call about a half-hour ago from agent Stiles in New Mexico. He's been filling me in on an interesting story that has been unfolding out there. Go ahead, Ev. Tell Mitch everything you've told me."

"I rushed over here to tell the President as soon as I got the call from Billy Stiles." Weaver almost sounded apologetic about not waiting for Kaminsky to tell the story. "Stiles found the bodies of our two men."

"So, that's why you never heard from them anymore."

"Right, Mitch. Evidently, they got caught in a flash flood and drowned. Professor Beal, the noted archaeoastronomer from the University of New Mexico, was also killed."

"Ev, tell him what else your agent found out."

"Yes, Mr. President, I was getting to that. It seems, by chance, my agent met up with an old Navajo Indian and a writer, who had an encounter last night with the aliens."

"Is he sure?" Kaminsky asked.

"No doubt about it. You remember this agent I sent out there said he had an encounter many years ago in Utah. He says these people experienced the same things he did all those years ago. Not only that, he came across a piece of metal out there he swears comes from one of their space ships."

"How can he be sure?"

"Mitch, he says it's indestructible! Won't dent! Won't burn! And, it has a property that allows it to be bent into any shape and then return, without a wrinkle, to its original shape. Stiles says he's seen another one, just about the same size, that's owned by the Indian. This Indian says he found it way back in 1947."

"What?" Kaminsky replied in a shocked tone of voice.

"1947! You know where I'm going with this, Mitch?"

"Project Anasazi! I know! I know!" Kaminsky replied. "Everything is tied together. All these years this thing has been such a closely guarded secret that not even the Office of the President, the State Department, the FBI, and the Secret Service knew about it. How could this have happened?"

"We think," the President interjected, "there has been a conspiracy going on for years with one mastermind behind it all." The President opened his desk drawer and withdrew a file. "Fill Mitch in on what you uncovered today."

"Well, we now know that General Brantfield has been heading up Project Anasazi from day one. His military record is unblemished. Since his so-called retirement he has lived a quiet, unassuming life in a little town called Magdalena, in New Mexico. He hasn't mingled with any of the locals since he left the military. And, all this time, he has run this project quietly. Also, we learned that the sheriff out there was a lieutenant under the general during the 1947 incident. Coincidence? We don't think so. Unfortunately, the sheriff died in a car wreck the other day. Or at least they think he did. No one has come up with a body yet, but he's among the missing. Suspicious? We don't know that for sure, but we're checking on it. Now, here's the amazing thing. We've been unable to locate the general. All of a sudden, he's among the missing, too. 1947! The general! The sheriff! UFO's! Coincidence? Again, I don't think so! Since we can't find the general, we did some checking on him. We found he has a net worth of over 10 million dollars spread out in savings and other investments in more than six states. He also owns a 1,000 acre spread just across the border south of Matamoros, Mexico. Next, we checked his telephone records. You know what we found? During the last year he's made over 300 calls to a telephone number with a northern California area code.»

"What are you getting at, Ev?" Kaminsky was anxious to hear the bottom line.

"300 calls in one year. That's quite a number of calls for anyone.

That fact intrigued us, so we checked as far back as we could on calls to that number, which, by the way. was 10 years."

"What is so suspicious about making a great deal of calls to one number over the years? Maybe, he has a very good friend who he likes to keep in touch with." Kaminsky was trying to provide a logical answer.

"No, Mitch," Weaver continued, "Brantfield made calls to that one number in California, a number that doesn't exist for all intents and purposes."

The President handed Mitch the file he had taken from his desk. "Look at these, Mitch. These are the General's records covering 10 years of telephone calls."

"I'm not following you, Ev." Kaminsky responded, frowning.

"Nor am I!" the President joined in.

Everett Weaver pulled a folded sheet of paper from his inside coat pocket, unfolding it as he began to speak. "The California number Brantfield has been calling these past years is on a list of out-of-service telephone numbers."

"You've lost me." the President said, shaking his head in bewilderment.

"Me, too!" echoed Kaminsky.

Weaver loosened his collar with one hand while holding the unfolded list with his other hand. "Early in my career I was with army intelligence, involved with special operations. Occasionally, we needed anonymous telephone numbers, ones that couldn't be traced back to any locale or individual. Those phone numbers were dead! Period! They didn't exist! We know it is possible for the government to establish such a number, without the telephone company having a record of who the number belongs to. It is selected from a database of unassigned numbers. Believe it or not, these numbers have no origin, nor do they have a terminus. These dead numbers exist only within the maze of the government's telecommunications infrastructure. They are routinely used by the various federal agencies for national security purposes. It is impossible to track them down because as I've already said, they do not exist."

The President chewed on his upper lip. "I knew the government had the capability of doing such things under the guise of national security, but how did whoever Brantfield was calling, get one of these numbers?"

"That's what I would like to know." Mitch Kaminsky, folding his arms, asked.

"Well, Mr. President, Mitch, with this new piece of high-tech equipment developed by a Silicon Valley company we got lucky. We were able to log onto our super-computer at the Agency, and using this piece of equipment we began searching all government agencies for the point of origin of that number. Unfortunately, we were unsuccessful in our multi-agency search. At the time, it had never occurred to me to check our own agency. Finally, just as a test, we did try our own telecommunications infrastructure. And, there it was! That number was assigned from inside the Bureau."

"Who issued the number?" the President asked excitedly.

"I'm sorry, Mr. President, that's the one thing that's hardest to determine. The equipment can't tell you what terminal within the Agency ordered the number. Frankly, even if it could, the responsible individual would be smart enough to program the number from a terminal other than his own. Evidently, I have someone in the Agency who is tied to all of this."

"So," Kaminsky sighed, "all we know is that the number was assigned within the FBI. We also know that Brantfield called this number given to him by some unknown person in the FBI and the number belongs to someone somewhere in northern California. That leaves us exactly nowhere!"

"Not necessarily." Ev Weaver said with a smile. You see, we were able to pinpoint the terminus of the phone number in Palo Alto.

"That's all?" the President asked, still biting his lip.

"I'm pretty positive where the telephone with that number is exactly located in Palo Alto."

Both the President and Mitch Kaminsky looked at each other. "How?" the President was the first to ask.

"We were able to narrow the terminus to a point south of Stanford University where there is a major industrial complex. There is only one employer in that complex. The name of the company is Transunion Enterprises."

"J. Barrington Foster's company?" the President called out in a surprised voice.

"JBF!" Kaminsky said, astonished at what he had just heard. "He's almost 90 years old! What would he be doing having that many conversations with Brantfield? He hated anything that had to do with the military! Do you really think he's the one that is tied in with Brantfield?"

"Yes, I do. Even though he has espoused a dislike for the military his company has made a fortune on building electronics for the government. Think about it, Mitch! J. Barrington Foster is the richest man in the world. No one has seen him publicly in years. In fact, you could call him our modern day Howard Hughes. He is chairman of Transunion Enterprises, the largest conglomerate in the world, with interests in high tech, oil, aviation, automotive, and pharmaceuticals. During the last forty-five years he has taken his company from nothing to a multi-billion dollar, privately held conglomerate. Look back over those same forty-five years and you'll remember that some of the discoveries his companies made have put him where he is today. New medical cures. New oil discoveries in places where no one else would have thought to look. New materials to make the planes he manufactures safer and more durable. He's responsible for the stealth bomber, new microchips that have outpaced every other company in the electronics industry. Automotive devices that allow cars to be more energy efficient. There are so many innovations he has introduced over the last forty-five years, I don't have time to mention all of them. Coincidence? I don't think so. Every time I try to make sense out of this thing I keep coming up with the same equation. Brantfield plus Project Anasazi equals J. Barrington Foster. Did you also know that Foster served as an advisor to President Truman from 1947 to 1949? Do you know what company's product helped us find the anonymous telephone number?"

"Don't tell me it was Transunion, Foster's company?" The President said haltingly.

"Yes. Isn't it ironic that the man we were looking for should supply us with the very equipment that would expose him? I'm in favor of bringing Mr. Foster to the White House for a little chat. Don't you think so, Mr. President?"

Yes, I agree." The President responded. "First we have to take control of Project Anasazi. Is that action still on for midnight, Mitch?"

"Right on schedule, sir."

"Good."

"Oh, by the way, Mitch, agent Stiles said he and his friends were heading up to Alegros Mountain tonight."

Kaminsky jumped to his feet. "No, no! They can't do that. They'll get in the way of our operation. Do you have a way of contacting him?"

"Yes, of course." Weaver replied. "He left the telephone number where I could reach him."

"Get him on the phone right away and stop him."

Weaver got up from his chair and moved for the telephone on the President's desk. "With your permission, sir."

"Of course, Ev." The President pushed the telephone toward Weaver.

"Hello. To whom am I speaking?"

"Me!" came the reply on the other end of the phone.

"Yes, I know it's you. Do you have a name?"

"Of course! Do you?"

"Yes. This is Mr. Weaver and I'm looking for Mr. Stiles."

"What do you want him for?"

"I want to speak with him. It's very important I speak with him immediately."

"Can't."

"Why can't I?"

"Because he isn't here right now."

"Can you tell me where he is please? I must talk with him."

"You can call back later tonight when he comes back. Goodbye."

"Wait, wait, please. When he comes back from where?"

"The mountain!"

A click and dial tone was all Ev Weaver heard after the mention of the word mountain. "Damn!" he cursed.

"Well, what happened?" The President asked.

"From the sound of that conversation I would guess you weren't successful." Kaminsky offered.

"Some crazy woman was on the phone who I couldn't make any

sense with. You're right, Mitch, I didn't have any luck getting Stiles. What's going to happen now?"

"For one thing, I'm not going to call off this operation. It has to be done tonight. Your agent and his friends will just have to suffer the consequences. Alright, now I'm going to tell you how it's going to come off. First, you should know the code name is 'Alegros' and I have arranged for members of the Alpha Force to participate.

"Excuse me, Mitch," Weaver interrupted, "but isn't that the commando group that is to be used only in rescuing embassy staff and other government officials in time of international crises?"

Kaminsky looked over at the President who nodded his approval. "Yes, it is, Ev. The President has approved of this action because it falls within the parameters of a threat to national security. The Alpha Force, assembled at Fort Bliss, will be leaving there shortly, heading for their assigned rendezvous at 2200 hours. At exactly 2400 hours we will commence operations. There will be 200 commandos on the ground and four civilian helicopters to circle above Alegros Mountain."

"How are we going to avoid scaring the people living in the area?" Weaver asked nervously.

"It's a sparsely developed and we don't expect many people will even know anything is going on. That's where I need the help of the Bureau in coordinating the New Mexico State Police and local police authorities in sealing off roads in and out of the area. I've already made arrangements for air traffic to be diverted until further notice."

"I understand there's a number of campgrounds in the vicinity."

"That's right, Ev. We already had the state police earlier today closing down the sites temporarily. How many agents do you think you'll need to help close off Route 60 at Datil and Pie Town?"

"Probably four. We'll also be checking cars turning off Interstate 25 at Socorro, heading west on Route 60. Only those cars with Magdalena as their final destination will be allowed through."

"I also want Route 12 on the south side of Horse Springs closed off. You'll need another two agents down there assisting police. How many agents do you have available in Albuquerque?"

"Four, maybe five, if I can get one of our agents back from vacation."

"Where are you going to get the other two?"

"Phoenix. They've already been alerted and on their way."

"Good! That covers all the details for now. I'm going out there to man a command post we're setting up in Horse Springs. Do you want to be part of this, Ev?"

"Are you kidding? I wouldn't miss this for the world."

"Okay, meet me at Andrews at 1700 hours."

Transunion Enterprises was situated in a campus-like setting off Mill Road, directly across from the southernmost piece of land occupied by Stanford University. Most first-time visitors to the complex often mistake the six-story sprawling structure as part of the university. The building was designed by J. Barrington Foster himself to imitate the Stanford look. He felt the university had maintained a distinctive California look from the day the first building was constructed until last year, when a new 12 story dormitory was built at the Mill Road entrance to the university. Foster wished to continue the unique university architectural style in the headquarters building of Transunion. The lobby was a two-story glass atrium that allowed sunlight to illuminate the entire area from sunup to sundown. The lobby's circular walls were adorned with Indian paintings. In the center stood a twenty-foot bronze statue of Cochise, in full Indian headdress, seated on a stallion. It was one of J B Foster's prized possessions. To the left of the lobby was a long hallway leading to Foster's office. Outside his corner office was a large private reception area where three secretaries, who attended Foster, did their work. Foster's office itself was a large room with polished oak walls. On the walls hung huge oil paintings of different Indians in ceremonial dress. The massive desk was solid oak with an antique Tiffany lamp off to the side. Behind the desk was a huge leather swivel back chair that could be turned to look through the wall of glass to a forest of cypress trees and a Japanese garden.

"Mr. Foster, there's a B. S. on the phone for you, sir." The intercom came to life. "He wouldn't give his name or state his business, sir."

"That's okay, Nancy, I'll take it." Foster answered the intercom, putting down the Wall Street Journal he was reading and picked up the phone. "Hello, Billy, do you have your scrambler engaged?

"Yes sir, I do!"

"Good! Let me turn mine on. Can you hear me clearly?

"Loud and clear," came the response.

"Alright then, what's up? I haven't heard from you in a while."

Stiles was calling from the pay phone in front of the gas station. He had thanked Running Horse and Little River for their offer to use the house phone, saying he needed privacy to make a call to his government superior. "This is the first chance I've had in a couple of days to call you. I just hung up on the Director. I have this funny feeling that the lid is about to blow off this thing."

"What have you been saying to the director? Has he found out about this project?"

"As I understand it, the UFO sightings out here in New Mexico have everybody in the government nervous. The Roswell incident is raising its ugly head again. In fact, two agents, under orders from the Director, were out in the area with a Professor Beal looking for something. All three of them are dead."

"What happened to them?"

"Nothing sinister. My best guess is that they were caught in a flash flood and drowned. Fortunately, they weren't anywhere near the compound. In fact, they were on Mangas Mountain. Most likely they found the Casabra ruins where the visitors took up residence several centuries ago."

Foster turned his chair to face the outdoors. "Do you think anyone in the government, including the Director, has learned about any of this?

"I can't say, sir. But I think the director has been talking with the President, and maybe the National Security Director." The voice on the other end paused, "Sir, I think we've got a real problem I can't avoid."

"What's that?"

"Well, I haven't been able to make contact with General Brantfield or Big Bird."

"Do you think Darlington has something to do with your not being able to contact either man?" Foster turned his chair to face his desk. Picking up a pen, he began to write on the legal pad besides the telephone. "Is Darlington making a power play and seeking to take control of this operation?"

"Could be, sir." the voice on the telephone said hesitantly. "I know he had some of his security people out here for a few days. You know what they're capable of."

"Do you think they had something to do with the disappearance of Big Bird and the general?"

"I really don't know want to think."

"Your voice tells me that's not your only concern. What else is going on?" Foster stopped writing for a moment.

"In telling the director about finding the bodies of the missing agents, I may have told him more than I should. If that's not bad enough, I've come across some people who had an encounter. Maybe I told them more than I should have, but I needed to gain their confidence to get them to tell me everything they knew. In fact, one of them has penetrated the compound and is insisting on taking the others up there to find out more about the place."

"Can't you stop them?"

"I'm afraid not. You know, Mr. Foster, all these years I've lived this double life. It hasn't been easy, working for you undercover within the government system, keeping wraps on this whole thing, maintaining a liaison with UFOlogists, and not letting on that I'm working with you and our visitors. Under military law this could be called an act of treason. Now, I have to accompany these people up there. Hopefully I can steer them off in the wrong direction."

"I strongly recommend you do!" Foster said sternly.

"Oh, by the way, there is something else you should know." Stiles paused, waiting for a response from Foster. There was none. He continued, "When the professor was found he had a piece of metal with an inscription on it."

"You mean a piece of the saucer from the 1947 crash?" Foster responded in a surprised voice.

"Yes! This Indian, named Running Horse, had a similar piece he found back in 1947. This is one of the things I had to tell the director when I talked with him about finding their bodies. I had no choice. I'm really afraid that the government hierarchy is going to start snooping around out here and there's nothing I can do to stop them."

"That really wasn't too smart, telling the Director about the metal." Foster's voice became agitated. "What's done is done! Is there anything else I should know?"

"In fact, there is, sir. This Brad Davis, who is one of the people I've been talking about, had a piece of paper with an inscription on it."

"What did it say?"

"Something to do with the time of Sillius and traveling through the continuum."

"It seems one of our friends is trying to undermine our operations. I guess it's time to visit the compound again. I'll have my jet fueled and I'll be on my way out there within the hour. Somehow or another lose your friends and meet me at the northern entrance to the compound at 10."

"I'll do my best, Mr. Foster."

"If I haven't thanked you lately for all your help over the years, let me say thank you, Billy!" Foster hung up the phone and began writing again.

CHAPTER TWENTY THREE

Parker and Nelson had returned to their room at the bed-and-breakfast, spending the remainder of the morning trying to develop a strategy for dealing with the situation that had developed at the mountain compound. One thing was sure. They needed additional firearms and ammunition to deal with the aliens. Parker, because of his rank and position in Air Force Intelligence, felt he might be able to get what he needed at Holloman Air Force Base. It was close to twelve thirty when he finally decided to make the three-hour trip to Holloman. After a quick lunch in Socorro, the black Bronco headed east on Route 380 past the Chupadera Mesa where Parker gave Nelson a military history lesson. Thirty-five miles to the southwest of their present location was the White Sands Missile Range and the Trinity Site, where the world's first A-bomb was detonated on July 16, 1945. They continued through the Valley of Fires State Park into the little town of Carrizozo. From there they headed south on Route 54 through Tularosa and on into Alamogordo.

Situated in the eastern portion of the Tularosa Basin, one of the largest undrained basins in the world, Alamogordos s 14 miles north of White Sands National Monument, a 2,220 square mile white gypsum desert. It is bounded on the west by the 10,000-foot Organ Mountains and the San Andreas Mountains, and to the east by the 12,000-foot Sacramento Mountains. It wasn't until the Second World War that Alamogordo came into prominence with the construction of Holloman Air Force Base. Since the war years the city had become a popular retirement destination.

Nelson turned the Bronco into the entrance to Holloman and slowly approached the gate. A military policeman stepped in front of their vehicle motioning them to stop. As the Bronco came to a stop, the MP moved around to the driver's side, greeted both Parker and Nelson, and proceeded to ask for their identification.

"What is the purpose of your visit, sir?" the MP asked politely as he examined both men's identification.

"We're on an unannounced inspection tour, Sergeant." answered Parker. "Why the third degree? We've never been stopped like this before and interrogated. Usually, we show our identification and pass right through."

"Sorry, sir, we've been put on heightened alert by top brass until further notice. We have to check everyone's identification entering the base. I see from your identification you are both Air Force officers. Since you're not stationed at Holloman, may I ask why you are dressed in civilian clothes if you're here for an inspection?"

"Sergeant, didn't you hear me say that we're here on an unannounced inspection?"

"Yes, sir, colonel. However, I have my orders to challenge anyone entering this base. Do you have any orders stating that you are here on an inspection tour?"

Lieutenant Nelson ignored the request and asked the next question. "Did you read the colonel's identification papers identifying us as Air Force Intelligence from the Pentagon?"

"Yes, sir, but....."

Nelson didn't wait for the MP to finish his answer. "Well, goddamn it, get it through your thick skull. We didn't come all the way out here from Washington to do some classified work and tell you what it is. Do you understand, sergeant? Did you ever consider that the reason for your heightened alert may be connected to our inspection?"

"No, sir! Sorry, sir! Can I notify the Base Commander of your presence, sir?"

"No, you can't! You are the only one we are entrusting with this matter. Can you be trusted?" Nelson asked, trying not to laugh.

"Yes, sir! I'm just doing my job, sir! I could be court-martialed for dereliction of duty for not notifying the Base Commander of your presence under the heightened alert."

Parker leaned across the seat and addressed the MP. "I want your name, sergeant. You can be assured you will not be court-martialed for maintaining national security precautions."

"William T. Webber, sir." the sergeant replied. "Am I to understand this has to do with national security, sir?"

"Sergeant Webber," the colonel said, again addressing the MP, "You are to forget I mentioned national security. Do you understand?" The sergeant nodded his head. "Maintain your vigilance during this alert. I want to commend you on the way you handle your post. I am going to notify the Base Commander of your exemplary work when we have completed our investigation. Hand me your sign-in sheet so I can comply with your base regulations." Both Parker and Nelson signed the sheet and handed it back to the sergeant. "Can you tell me how we can find your munitions officer?" Nelson asked.

The sergeant pointed to the long row of barracks beyond the guard post. "At the end of the first row of barracks you'll see a two-story building, that's the administration offices. If you take the side entrance and go up the stairs you'll find Captain Harris' office. He's the one you need to see."

"Thank you, sergeant. You've been very helpful." The sergeant saluted as Nelson and Parker drove off. Both men returned the sergeant's salute. The sergeant held his salute until Colonel Parker's vehicle had passed the first row of barracks.

Parking the Bronco in the lot closest to the side entrance of the administration building Nelson and Parker walked along the narrow path leading up to the doorway. Upon entering the building the first thing they did was to check the directory. Captain Harris' name, halfway down the list, showed his office was 2-F. Climbing the stairwell located alongside the directory both men headed down the narrow hallway until they came to room 2-F. Opening the door to the small office, they were greeted by a young, slightly balding officer seated behind a lone desk working at a computer.

"Good afternoon, gentlemen, may I help you?"

"Captain Harris, good afternoon." Colonel Parker extended his hand to the seated officer.

"You have me at a disadvantage, gentlemen." Harris replied with a quizzical look on his face, shaking the hands of Parker and Nelson. "You know my name, but I'm afraid I haven't had the pleasure of meeting you before." Captain Harris, a ten-year career man, remained seated at the desk. He was obviously ill at ease speaking to the two strangers not dressed in military attire standing before him.

"I'm Colonel Wally Parker, Air Force Intelligence, out of the Pentagon." Parker showed the captain his identification. "This is Lieutenant Nelson, who is also with Air Force Intelligence. We're here on a special project and need your help."

Captain Harris' serious look and rigid posture soon gave way to a more relaxed demeanor once he knew he was dealing with Air Force personnel. He stood up and motioned the officers to sit facing his desk. "Well, you're the first intelligence people I've ever met. I'm glad to meet you both. For a minute there I was afraid I was receiving a surprise visit by some members of Congress. Glad it's only Air Force people. If you say you're here on a special project you must have something to do with Operation Alegros."

Parker and Nelson's facial expression and body language gave no hint of their surprise at the mention of Operation Alegros. "You know about Operation Alegros?" Parker asked, pretending as if he himself knew about this operation.

"Sure! Fort Bliss said they would send someone by to pick up additional weapons, ammunition and supplies." Harris responded.

"Just how much do you know about this operation, captain?" Nelson asked, eager to learn what this operation was all about.

"All I know is that a small contingent of an Alpha Force stationed at Fort Bliss are headed up to a place that has something to do with the name Alegros."

"Alegros is a mountain, Captain. Do you know what they're supposed to do once they get up there?" Parker was as curious as Nelson to find out about this secret operation.

"Swear to God, Colonel, that's all I know."

"Listen, Captain, this is a hush-hush operation and we're trying to keep a lid on it." Parker said in a soft tone. "We hope we have your cooperation in this matter."

"Yes, sir!" Captain Harris answered quickly. "My lips are sealed and I'll make sure Sergeant Grady understands that also."

"Sergeant Grady! Who is he?" Nelson wanted to know.

Sir, he's in charge of signing out all firearms, ammunition and other armaments down at the base armory."

"It's very important Grady understand the importance of secrecy on this matter." Parker pointed to the telephone on the captain's desk. "Give him a call and give him that message. While you're doing that, also tell him we're on our way down to see him."

"Yes, sir, right away!" Harris began dialing the sergeant.

Nelson interrupted the captain as he dialed. "How do we find the armory and Sergeant Grady?"

Harris hung up the telephone as he answered the lieutenant's question. "Go down to the western end of the administration building and make a left turn. About a quarter mile you'll see the armory on the far side of the parade grounds. Easy to find." Captain Harris picked up the telephone and began dialing again.

Nelson and Parker shook the captain's hand, thanking him, and left him talking to the sergeant. Neither man said a word as they headed down the stairwell and out the door to the Bronco. Once inside, Nelson was the first to speak.

"Are you thinking what I'm thinking, colonel?"

Lost in thought, Colonel Parker took a few seconds to reply. "What? Oh yeah! There are too many coincidences today. First the arrest of General Darlington and now this Operation Alegros. Somehow or another I think the cat is out of the bag regarding our friends up at the Alegros compound."

The Bronco reached the armory in a matter of minutes. Parker and Nelson exited the vehicle, hurriedly entering the armory through a single large door at the far end of the building.

"Let me do all the talking. I want to be very careful what we say to Sergeant Grady." Parker cautioned Nelson.

The lieutenant nodded his head in agreement, not saying a word. He let Colonel Parker lead the way down the hall where they came upon an area sectioned off and enclosed by steel-mesh framing. Seated at a desk inside the fenced-off area sat a fortyish, heavy jowled man wearing military fatigues. Totally engrossed in reading the latest copy of *Playboy*, the soldier was unaware of them standing at the locked door to the weapons room. The sound of the colonel clearing his throat to get his attention brought the man to his feet immediately. Placing the magazine face down on the desk, the airman moved quickly to the door.

"Are you Colonel Parker?" the man asked.

"Yes, and this is Lieutenant Nelson. You must be Sergeant Grady."

"That's right, sir," Captain Harris said you would be coming down to see me. "I'm sorry I asked who you were, though. The captain didn't tell me you were in civilian clothes."

"He did tell you about maintaining the secrecy of Operation Alegros, didn't he?" Parker asked abruptly.

"Oh, yes sir!" Grady responded quickly.

"Good!" Parker smiled weakly as he looked around the large room full of weapons and ammunition. "You also know we're with Air Force Intelligence and we don't always wear our uniforms because of the work we do. We wouldn't be able to do our jobs effectively if we dressed and everyone knew what we were doing. That's not the way we conduct our intelligence missions." Parker's smile broadened.

The sergeant managed a slight, nervous laugh. "I fully understand, sir."

Parker moved about the room freely, walking over to a shelf

stacked with automatic weapons. "You sure do have quite a lot of supplies here, sergeant. Is this everything?"

"Hell, no, colonel!" was the sergeant's quick response. "Whoops! I'm sorry, sir. I didn't mean to answer disrespectfully."

"No offense taken, sergeant." Parker answered casually.

"As I was going to say, colonel, this room contains only a small amount of what we store here. In fact, on the other side of that steel door are about 50,000 square feet of all kinds of armaments. Would you care to see?"

"Sure, just a quick look though, sergeant. We're in a rush to get on with this operation. One thing Fort Bliss brass didn't tell us was what kind of materials you are supposed to supply for Operation Alegros."

"That's easy, colonel. I have a list over in the file on my desk." Sergeant Grady walked toward his desk to retrieve the list for the colonel. Just then the telephone on his desk rang. "Excuse me while I answer the phone. Lieutenant Nelson moved beyond the steel doors into the larger room as Parker remained with the sergeant. Hello, Sergeant Grady speaking." He held the phone with one hand as he reached into his desk drawer to retrieve the armaments list the colonel had asked for. "Yes sergeant, send them on down. Everything is all ready for them." Grady hung up the phone. "The supply truck from Bliss is on its way down here. That was Sergeant Webber at the gate."

Colonel Parker moved to the entrance of the larger supply room and saw Nelson placing several hand grenades into his jacket pocket. "Lieutenant, the supply truck from Fort Bliss is here already. That means we're way behind schedule and have to be on our way." Turning back to Grady, the colonel said in a crisp tone, "Look, sergeant, since the truck is here already we'll just pick up a couple of automatic weapons and some ammunition."

"Don't you want to wait for the truck so I can give you everything all at once?" Grady asked.

"No, just give us two of those weapons on the shelf and the appropriate ammunition and we'll be on our way."

"Okay, colonel." Grady was surprised at the urgency of Colonel Parker's command. The sergeant turned away from the two men and removed the requested weapons from the shelf. Placing the weapons on the counter Sergeant Grady handed the colonel a pen and an authorization form. "I need you to sign for these before you leave. Besides, I thought you wanted the list of armaments Fort Bliss required?"

Parker handed the form back to the sergeant. "No, sorry, haven't got time! The Pentagon brass will eat our ass if they find out we're so far behind schedule." Parker faked a smile. "Get the Fort Bliss crew to sign for all the stuff at one time."

"But, sir!" Grady stammered.

"That's an order, sergeant!" the colonel responded in an agitated tone.

"Yes, sir!" Sergeant Grady saluted as Colonel Parker and

Lieutenant Nelson, ignoring the salute, started down the hallway leading out of the armory.

Getting quickly into the Bronco, both men threw their weapons and ammunition on the back seat. Nelson, behind the wheel, started the engine, backed out of the parking lot, and headed for the main gate. They passed what they were sure was the truck from Fort Bliss. Reaching the gate, stopping long enough to sign out of the base, the black Bronco was headed back to Alegros Mountain. Neither of the two men knew what the remainder of the day held in store for them, but they were sure they could handle it.

Billy Stiles hung up the phone and turned to exit the phone booth when he was greeted by Brad Davis. "Hey, Brad you startled me! I didn't expect anyone to be waiting outside the booth for me. You want to use the phone, too?"

"No, I just came to check on you since you were gone for so long."

Stiles looked at his watch. "Wow!" he said. "I hadn't realized I was talking for twenty minutes. So, what's the urgency on checking me?"

"Actually, Little River is the one who sent me to get you. She and Susan have set the table and dinner is ready. You've seen Little River in action; you know how demanding she can be. She told me to come get you and that's what I did. She has me jumping at everything she says."

Stiles chuckled. "Yeah, she can be pushy. Look, do you mind

telling her I'm not really hungry and I would like to sit out here and enjoy the last moments of daylight?"

"You tell her yourself. I'm not ready to have her get angry at me."

"Oh, never mind! I guess I should eat something since it could be a long night on the mountain." Billy Stiles put his arm around Davis as they both walked back to the house.

"Billy, do you mind telling me why you couldn't use the phone in the house instead of the telephone booth alongside the highway. We wouldn't listen to what you were saying."

"I had to talk to the FBI Director and tell him about the two missing agents we found today. It was a little uncomfortable for me to talk about two of my friends being found dead. I didn't mean to offend anyone."

Davis had a suspicion Stiles wasn't telling the whole truth. It was hard for him to believe that it took twenty minutes to talk about the dead agents. Davis had had this nagging feeling from the first time they met that there was more to this man than what met the eye. "I was always curious about something." Davis remarked casually.

"What's that?" Stiles asked.

"When agents are calling in about sensitive matters how do they protect themselves from anyone listening in on their conversation?"

"Hey," he said jokingly, "Are you trying to find out about our secrets?"

"Why not?" Davis joked back with a Russian accent.

"Okay, I'm going to let you in on how we secret agents work.

When we call into a special telephone number, I provide the person answering the phone with a coded pass word. They in turn give me a code. The phone is then converted electronically into a secure line so that no one other than the two parties talking can hear what is being said."

"Amazing." Davis responded. "It's so James Bondish!"

Both men entered the house laughing, greeted by Little River, who was holding a large soup ladle in one hand and a carving knife in the other. "How thoughtful of you two to finally join us for dinner." She said sarcastically.

Running Horse came up behind his mother and carefully relieved her of the knife as Davis and Stiles entered the house. "Sorry, my mother can be a little intimidating at times, especially when both hands are holding lethal weapons." Running Horse said with a whimsical grin.

As they all sat around the table Little River made sure no one began eating until an Indian prayer was said to give blessing for the food they were about to eat. At the conclusion of the prayer, Running Horse was the first to start eating.

"Okay, listen up everyone." Davis said. "After we finish dinner, it's my plan to head out for Alegros. Eight o'clock is my drop dead time for leaving. All of us need to bring some extra clothing for warmth and several flashlights. Running Horse and I will show Billy and Susan where we were yesterday before we had to leave the mountain. That's as good a spot as any to find our way into that compound. Any questions?"

"What about my mother?" asked Running Horse.

"She's staying here." Davis answered.

"I don't think so!" Little River stood up and slammed her fork on the table. "I'm not staying around to have those two goons come back and beat me up. It will be safer up there with whoever those people are and, of course, you."

"Mother!"

"Don't you 'Mother!' me! Just sit there and eat your food. I'm going with you and that's that!"

Running Horse hung his head in embarrassment at being chastised by his mother. Susan, Davis and Stiles looked at each other, rolling their eyes, trying to conceal their amusement.

CHAPTER TWENTY FOUR

Major Robert Beardsley and Lieutenants Jack Dugan and Tom Conway joined Captain Tom Becci, the pilot of the civilian four-seat Bell Ranger helicopter on the flight from Fort Bliss Military Reservation to Horse Springs. The four military men, dressed in street clothes, were responsible for setting up the Alpha Force's staging area outside of Horse Springs. In order not to draw attention to their helicopter as it headed northwest toward the Alegros Mountains, Becci received clearance to maintain an altitude of eleven-thousand feet, flying over sparsely populated areas. The helicopter passed over Lake Lucero south of Alamogordo, just skirting the southern boundaries of White Sands National Monument, then across Elephant Butte Reservation on the Rio Grande River. After passing over the Black Range, Becci slowly nudged the controls of the chopper taking it to his approved altitude as it crossed the 9,220 foot Pelona Mountain on the Continental Divide, barely skimming the tops of the pine trees. The tiny town of Horse Springs, situated at an altitude of 9,490 feet could be seen 20 miles in the distance across the Plains of San Agustin.

Major Beardsley, who had been studying a map of the terrain, pulled out his flashlight as the final light of day disappeared beyond the distant mountains. "That's probably Horse Springs up ahead there." Beardsley pointed to the lights ahead and then focused the flashlight's beam to a small dot on the map. "Yeah, that's got to be Horse Springs. There are no other lights for miles around."

"Where do you want me to put the chopper down, sir?" Becci asked the major.

"I'm sure these folks out here aren't used to hearing much noise, so I recommend we then head up north, setting this thing down about two miles south of the town. We don't want to startle anyone, nor do we want people asking questions we can't answer. I'll keep a lookout for you, sergeant, as we get close and I'll tell you the best place to land."

"You've got it, sir," Becci responded, as he slowed the craft's speed and maneuvered the helicopter to a more southerly course.

"Wow!" Conway, seated in the back on the right side, exclaimed as he pressed his face hard against the helicopter's rear-side window. "Did you see that?"

"See what?" asked Dugan, who was seated beside Conway, looking out the other window.

"Out there to the northeast, there was like a bluish glow that lit up the ground." Conway answered, cupping his face with his hands, still straining his eyes out the window.

"Oh come on now, Lieutenant, you must be seeing things." Beardsley jokingly responded.

"I didn't see anything either." Becci said seriously. "But I'll tell you what I did see. For a second there all my instruments went wacky."

"What are you talking about, sergeant?" Beardsley asked as he looked over at the instrument panel in front of Becci. "Looks fine to me."

"It is now, sir."

Suddenly, the helicopter began rocking violently as if some invisible force were pummeling the craft. The dials in front of Becci began to spin erratically, first one way, then the other. As the rocking continued Conway yelled out, "There it is again. Do you see it? Do you see it?"

As Becci fought to control the helicopter's erratic behavior Beardsley, Conway and Dugan were trying to grab hold of anything they could to prevent their being tossed around like a bowl of Jell-O. This time everyone looked in the direction Conway was calling attention to. Becci took his eyes off the spinning dials for a moment to see if he could affirm some strange, unseen force causing his chopper to gyrate wildly, all the while fighting to control the rocking helicopter. Turning his full attention back to controlling the craft and monitoring the instrument panel, Becci asked, "What the hell is that about?

"Don't know!" Beardsley answered. "Why don't you turn this thing around so we can have a good look at what might be causing it?"

"Are you sure that's wise, sir?" Becci asked with a hint of fear in his voice. "I'm having trouble with these instruments and keeping the chopper under control. I don't want us getting into trouble we can't get out of. Maybe I should just set us down while we're still in one piece."

"Negative, sergeant. Your concern for our safety is noted. Now turn the chopper around and let's check it out."

Before Becci could respond Conway called out, "It's gone. It stopped!"

"Hey, my instruments are all right again and we've stopped bouncing around." Becci said, smiling and turning toward the Major. "You still want me to go find the source of the glow, sir?"

"Damn right! I want you to take us up there and have a look at whatever caused that phenomenon. Head up in the direction and see if we can detect anything strange." Beardsley ordered.

The helicopter took a northeast heading reaching a point 12 miles from the Plains of San Agustin where they first saw the glow and had trouble with the instruments. Nothing! Following the major's orders the helicopter circled the area for another 15 minutes looking for signs of anything unusual. No glow. No rocking. No instrument problems.

"Explain to me exactly what you saw, lieutenant? Beardsley asked

Conway, straining his eyes to see out into the night sky, seeing only the very distant lights of Albuquerque.

"I don't know if you'll believe this or not, major." Conway responded, still peering out the window.

"Try me!"

"It was the ground that seemed to be pulsing with a bluish glow. First, very faint and then building to a bright blue continual glow, all within a few seconds time span."

"Did it have form or a recognizable shape?"

"No, sir. It had no definite form."

"Could you determine how large an area it covered?"

"It all happened so quickly, but I would venture to say it seemed to cover an area as wide and as long as the size of the plains on our terrain map."

"Are you telling me that glow covered the entire Plains of San Agustin?"

"If that's what these plains are called, yes sir, I am. In fact, I could have sworn the glow extended off into the northern horizon, as far as I could see from up here. What do you make of it, sir?"

"I haven't the foggiest notion." the major answered. "Okay, we've wasted enough time here. Let's head back to our primary destination. We'll try to get a handle on this later."

"Major," Dugan asked, "Do you think what we saw and experienced has anything to do with Operation Alegros?"

"Don't know, lieutenant. Could be. All I know is we're to be briefed by two top government officials out of Washington, and we're to take our orders from them. Until that time we can only speculate."

The helicopter had reached its primary destination. "Sir, how close to the road do we want to be?" Becci asked, turning on the spotlights located beneath the chopper.

"About a hundred yards is as close as I want to get for the time being. Do you see that clearing down there? Place the chopper down right in the middle." Turning to the two men in the back seat, Beardsley gave them instructions on how he wanted the command tent set up. "Becci and I are going to do a fly-over of Alegros Mountain and the surrounding terrain to get a better idea of what we're going to be dealing with up here. Then, we're flying over to Albuquerque to pick up the two Washington big shots who are arriving on a private Lear jet. We're supposed to pick them up near one of the private hangars in order not to arouse any suspicion. We'll also fuel up there. Figure, at the latest, we'll be back here somewhere between 2100 and 2130 hours."

Dugan and Conway looked at each other, nodding approval to their commanding officer. Beardsley, a career officer and a graduate of the Citadel, had always carried a self-imposed stigma of not being able to get into West Point. He had been born to working class parents in the small paper mill town of Covington, Virginia, where he received little recognition for his outstanding scholastic aptitude and athletic ability beyond Bath County. As a result, the more influential Virginia politicians were able to get their candidates from the larger urban areas of the state accepted for the limited number of openings at West Point. It was during his senior year of high school that he realized his dream of attending the Academy would never be fulfilled. The six-foot muscular youth with the crew-cut decided after a school visit that the Citadel would be his best choice for realizing a military career. It also allowed him to attend school in the South, providing him the opportunity to visit his parents and high school sweetheart during vacation time. Mary Beth Livingston, a gorgeous green-eyed blond cheerleader and high school senior homecoming queen, became Mrs. Robert Beardsley the day after his graduation from the Citadel. Following his tour of duty in Germany five years earlier, Beardsley asked for reassignment to the Alpha Force at Fort Bliss. His request was granted and he was assigned there following the intensive training required of all Alpha Force members. He did not see his wife or three children for six months as he trained in the jungles of Guatemala and, Brazil and in the frigid conditions of the Arctic Circle. Upon his return to Fort Bliss, he was immediately shipped out to assist U.S. forces during the Haitian crisis. The last two years had been relatively quiet for the major and he was excited to participate in his first top-secret assignment since Haiti.

"Okay, Major," Becci said as he signaled for Beardsley to get back into the helicopter. "Dugan and Conway have all the necessary equipment out of the chopper and we're all set to get out of here."

"Good!" Beardsley, stepping up into the chopper, patted Becci on the back and called back to the two men they were leaving behind. "We'll be back in no time! The two squads of men assigned to us should be here by the time we get back. Have them stand down and wait for my return. By that time we'll have more information to provide everyone with a complete briefing."

The major never heard their response as the helicopter whined to life. Becci and Beardsley waved a salute to the two men as the helicopter lifted up into the darkness of night. Both men were wearing their headphones to better communicate with each other and to listen for any important transmissions on the chopper›s radio.

Becci had first met Beardsley when he transferred to Germany from Fort Drum in upstate New York. They became close friends immediately and their wives, lacking family in a foreign country, also became inseparable. Becci, still built like a wrestler, a sport he excelled at in high school and junior college, was blond, brown eyed, Italian, and quick tempered. There were many times during his two-year tour in Germany that Beardsley had to intervene to save Becci's military career from self-destruction. It was Becci's fierce competitiveness and loyalty that Beardsley most admired. When he informed Becci of his desire to join the Alpha Force, the captain asked the major to have him reassigned. During their six months of training the two men became even better friends, depending on each other for support and comfort.

Davis checked his watch. It was a few minutes past seven.

He stood filling Stiles' Mitsubishi with high-test, waiting for the remainder of this newly formed expedition to come out of the house. "Hey, everyone, let's get going." Davis yelled back at the house as one by one, Susan, Stiles and Little River stepped out of the front door. Running Horse was the last to leave the house, checking to make sure the lights were all turned off. "Hold your horses, Brad," Running Horse responded in his loudest voice, closing the door behind him.

"Aren't you going to lock the door?" Susan asked, as she watched Running Horse walk toward the group.

He laughed as he answered her concern. "This is the wilderness of New Mexico. Who do you expect to steal from me?"

"Crime is everywhere!" she said, raising her finger in a chastising gesture.

"New York has not come to this part of the world." Running Horse answered as he reached Susan. Putting his arm around her shoulder he continued, "We have nothing worth stealing anyway. Besides, there are no locks on our door."

Susan and Running Horse had reached the vehicle where Davis was placing the hose back on its holder on the pump. Stiles and Little River waited to be told where they were to sit inside the vehicle. "You mean to tell me anyone could go into your house anytime and take whatever they want?" Susan, who had three locks on her New York apartment, asked in an astonished tone.

"Our friends," Running Horse continued, "often do come when we are not there and help themselves to whatever they need."

"Well, isn't that stealing?"

"No! It is the way of my people. We help each other. They always leave something of value in return. They would not take anything if there were not a need. We are a proud people with a long history of tradition. Luckily, my mother and I have always had enough of everything. The gods have been good to us and we are fortunate we are able to help our brothers."

Susan shook her head in amazement. "We so-called civilized people have a lot to learn from the first inhabitants of this beautiful country."

Running Horse merely smiled. "Brad, I have the blankets, some extra clothing, flashlights and extra batteries."

"Throw them in the back of the vehicle." Davis replied, again checking his watch. "Since I know where we're going, I'll do the driving." Stiles said nothing, merely nodding his head. "Running Horse, you sit up front with me. Billy, you and the ladies sit in the back. Running Horse, do we need to turn off the electricity to the pumps?"

"We'll do it when we return. I often leave them on in case someone needs gas while I'm not around."

"Last chance for anyone to back out!" Davis turned to see the reaction of the two women. No one responded. "Okay, we're off on Brad's great adventure." Davis turned the key in the ignition and the engine roared to life. Turning his headlights on, he placed the automatic gearshift into drive. Slowly Davis edged the Mitsubishi onto the deserted highway and headed for the road leading to Pie Town. Everyone knew that this road would take them on a journey of uncertainty and possible danger. The extra weight of the five passengers caused the utility vehicle to sway a little more than normal. Davis drove slowly and cautiously as if he feared what lay ahead of him. Visiting the site this time was not like his previous visit with Running Horse. On this trip he had Susan and Little River to worry about. He knew Stiles could take care of himself.

It had been almost thirty minutes since they left the gas station. Davis slowed the Mitsubishi down and put on his high beams as he approached the site where he had turned off on two other occasions. He looked at Running Horse for reassurance that this, indeed, was the right place. "You agree this is it?"

"You bet it is!" Running Horse agreed emphatically.

Davis turned the vehicle onto the pathway leading down the steep incline. He was following the tire tracks left by his last visit. "Hold on everyone. It gets a little rough here."

Billy Stiles, seated directly behind Running Horse, leaned over the front seat. "What are you doing here? We're supposed to be going over to Pie Town and then heading east on Route 60!"

"What!" Brad Davis and Running Horse said out loud in unison.

Immediately, Stiles realized he had made a clumsy mistake and tried to rectify the slip-up. "Brad, I thought you told me you had broken down on Route 60 and entered the Alegros Mountain woods from the north."

Davis, his mind racing a mile a minute, was trying to give Stiles the benefit of the doubt concerning what he said to the FBI agent about this location. He was sure he had never mentioned approaching the mountain compound from Route 60. How could he have mentioned it if the thought never entered his mind that there might be more than one way into the compound? Davis had this nagging suspicion that Billy knew more about this place than he let on. In fact, maybe he's been in the compound, entering from Route 60. Feeling that Stiles might have accidently tipped his hand, Davis tried to allay Stiles' fear that he was onto him. "You know, Billy, I might have said that in error. I apologize. You probably think I've said a lot of crazy things that didn't make sense ever since we met."

"Not at all." Stiles said, sitting back in the seat, not believing a word Davis said. He knew Davis was smart enough not to fully trust him anymore. "Anyway, maybe I just thought you said you entered from Route 60. It really doesn't matter. I do remember you saying that it took you at least a half hour of walking before you reached the edge of the compound."

"You got that right!" Davis smiled weakly, trying to see the expression on Stiles' face in the rearview mirror. The Jeep stopped at the edge of the forest at the exact spot where he had parked before. "This is it! Everyone out! Billy, get the flashlights and extra batteries from the back, please."

Running Horse walked around the front of the Mitsubishi to

398

where Davis was standing. Making sure Stiles was out of voice range, Running Horse whispered, "You believe that bullshit he gave you?"

Davis shook his head no. "Keep your eye on our friend. There's more to this guy than meets the eye. There's something suspicious about a phone call that takes twenty minutes and has to be made out of our earshot."

Running Horse didn't get a chance to respond as Stiles moved from behind the vehicle and approached both men. "Here you are, gentlemen," Stiles said. "One flashlight each for everyone and one set of extra batteries. I've given the women their flashlights and batteries. By the way Brad, can I have my car keys back. I'd feel more comfortable knowing they were in my pocket."

"Sure thing!" Davis replied, as he reached into his pants pocket, retrieved the car keys and handed them back to Stiles. The FBI agent had some ulterior motive for wanting the keys in his possession, thought Davis, but he was not about to let on that he was suspicious of every move Stiles might make from now on. "Susan!" Davis called out to where she stood pulling an additional sweater over her head. "What are you doing back there?"

"I'm cold and I'm putting on another sweater under my jacket." She answered in a chattering voice.

Little River had joined the three men standing in front of the Mitsubishi waiting for Susan. "Okay, I'm ready."

"Mother, what are you doing wearing that old Indian blanket?" Running Horse asked as he pulled up the collar around his coat.

"Why don't you wear another sweater under your coat like Susan is doing?"

"Hey! Who is the parent and who is the child here?" Little River shook her hand at Running Horse, who turned away from his mother as she spoke.

Susan had now joined the group. "I'll lead the way." Davis said, taking command of this expedition. "Follow close behind each other so no one gets lost in the dark." One by one they followed Davis through the narrow trees leading deeper into Alegros Mountain. They had only been walking for ten or fifteen minutes when he stopped to identify a sound he heard from above. "You hear that?" he asked.

"It's a helicopter!" Stiles was the first to answer as he glanced at his watch. "7:45!" he said to himself.

"I haven't seen helicopters up here in these parts for a long time." Running Horse said, looking up, straining to see where the sound was coming from.

"Do you mean to tell me in this day and age that helicopters aren't a common sight out here?" Davis asked.

"Oh sure! Every now and then we would see one. But nothing like the air traffic we saw back in 1947!" Running Horse answered, remembering those days when the military had great numbers of small planes scouring the area for debris from a fictitious weather balloon. He smiled as he remembered the small piece of metal from the government's imaginary weather balloon.

Stiles looked at his watch again. The sound of the helicopter made him anxious. He knew his meeting with Foster was set for 10:00 p.m. Maybe Foster was early so he could spend some time with Anjou to find out what he knew about the disappearance of Big Bird and General Brantfield. Stiles had taken the trailing position when leaving the van, in order to quietly slip away before anyone realized he was gone. He looked at his watch again. It was time.

The Bell Ranger had approached Alegros Mountain from the southeast, barely two hundred feet above the pine and fir trees below. Becci turned the helicopter to the east, shining its searchlights on a deserted campground below. Beardsley requested Becci to crisscross the entire top of the mountain until they found something, anything that would make sense out of Operation Alegros.

"Tom, have you got the infrared heat sensors on?" Beardsley asked.

"Sure do, major." He responded, pointing to the luminescent small box that sat on the floor between them. "See, there's nothing out there. What do you think this thing is all about? It's just plain desolate out there. Nothing but woods and more woods. It's so densely forested I can't see between the trees with my lights. Major, I've crisscrossed this whole mountain twice and there's no sign of anything. Don't you think we've wasted enough time and we should be heading toward Albuquerque? I need to get some more fuel in this thing."

"Maybe you're right, Tom." Beardsley sighed. "Let's take one more look over at the southwestern end which is the only area we've missed."

Becci made a 45 degree turn toward the southwest, maintaining his 200-foot clearance above the trees. "Hey major, look at the screen. The heat sensors have picked up five warm life forms." Becci placed his finger on the screen showing the five blips.

"Those are five life forms alright. Wait, look at that! A few seconds ago all five dots were moving in single file in a northerly direction. Now, only four are moving north and one has moved away from the others, moving in a more southwesterly direction. What do you make of that, captain?"

"I don't know, sir. Do you think this has anything to do with this operation?"

"I don't see how five dots on a screen could be something that they need an Alpha Force to take care of."

The chopper reached the edge of the forest and its spotlights picked up the outline of a vehicle. "Look. There's a car parked over there." Becci called out as he moved the chopper around, slowly descending until the craft was less than fifty feet from the ground, hovering directly over the parked vehicle. The spotlights focused on a white Mitsubishi van.

Beardsley pulled a pen and notepad from his pocket and wrote down the license number. "Don't know if that vehicle and those five people down there have anything to do with anything. For all we know they could be campers that weren't cleared out of the area.

We'll find out what Operation Alegros is really all about and then we'll take appropriate action to remove them from the mountain. Let's head up to the Albuquerque airport, get some fuel, and pick up our government VIP's."

"Do you really think they're campers or are they part of the mystery of this project, Major?" Becci asked as he lifted the helicopter from fifty feet to an altitude of 2,000 feet, turning toward a northeast heading and an eventual altitude of 12,000 feet. Beardsley, lost in concentration, did not answer Becci. The dim lights of Datil and Magdalena could be seen ahead with a brighter glow coming from Socorro to the east. What looked like pinpoints of light from the flat terrain of the San Agustin Plains were in reality window lights from the scattered laboratories throughout the restricted area. The large mass of lights further north of Socorro were the city lights of Albuquerque, barely visible on the northeastern horizon.

A lone figure emerged from the woods, headed toward the white Mitsubishi and watched as the helicopter turned off its spotlight and lifted into the darkness of the night. Billy Stiles had spent enough time in government work to know a military helicopter when he saw it. There were no military markings on the chopper that Stiles could see, but all the same, he was, by nature and agency training, suspicious. He knew time was running out on this project, and quite possibly on his career with the FBI. The engine of the white van turned over and the vehicle headed up the dirt road to the main road leading to Pie Town.

CHAPTER TWENTY FIVE

"How much further, Brad?" Susan called out with a trace of weariness in her voice.

Davis, who had been leading the group from the start, stopped and turned to answer Susan. Little River and Running Horse also stopped, aiming the beams from their flashlights to the ground. "I feel we're very close." Davis answered, trying to hide his displeasure with Susan's impatience, while at the same hiding his frustration with not having found the opening. "Hey, wait a minute! Where's Stiles?"

"He was here a few minutes ago. I know he was right behind me," stated Running Horse.

"Damn, I knew I shouldn't have given him back the keys to his vehicle," Davis said angrily. "Without him we're stuck out here in this godforsaken wilderness."

"I guess your suspicions about him were well founded," Running Horse answered.

"What are you two talking about?" asked Susan.

"Remember when we were turning off the road and Stiles started to ask why we were turning off here?"

"Yes, Brad, I remember, but I don't remember anything unusual about his answer. He said he simply was mistaken."

"Sorry, Susan. Billy Stiles knows more about this area than he was letting on."

"Agreed." Running Horse responded. "My Indian instinct says that our so-called friend didn't tell us everything he knows. When he had to make that call from the pay phone in front of the house, I offered him the opportunity to use the phone in the house and he politely declined saying it was government business. However, I was watching him when he was making the call and he held up some kind of device to the mouthpiece of the phone and then returned it to his pocket."

"That seems perfectly normal to me," said Susan. "He is an agent and..."

"Ah, yes," interrupted Running Horse, "but he did tell us that when he makes government calls he uses a code word that automatically scrambles conversations with the receiving party. It's my guess he used a portable device to speak with someone other than his office."

"We all basically agree," Little River interjected, "that Mr. Stiles didn't tell us everything, just enough to get us to open up to him about our experiences. A real clever fellow. His story about having an encounter in Utah, his cancer disappearing, and the metal rod in his leg were all probably made up to get information out of us. Let's forget about Mr. Stiles and get on with our expedition. I'm getting cold."

"Running Horse," Davis said as he moved closer to where Little River was standing, "You, your mother and Susan bundle up real good and stay put for a few minutes while I try to see if I can find the opening again. I promise I'll return in a half-hour whether I find it or not."

"Do you really think that's a good idea, Brad?" Running Horse asked. "Wouldn't it be better to leave the two women while you and I scout ahead?"

"No, I want you to stay and keep your mother and Susan warm. I don't want to leave the women alone. Now stay put! I don't want to have to go and start looking for all of you. Remember, we're without transportation out here."

"Okay, we'll sit right here until you get back. Just hurry up."

"Look, Brad, I'm not happy with being left behind here. My journalistic instincts say we're possibly onto the biggest story of my life." Susan said, through chattering teeth.

"Don't worry, Susan, I'll share the rights to my story with you," Davis laughed.

"Okay, wise guy, but hurry back," Susan responded, resigned to the fact that no matter how much pleading she did, Brad wouldn't change his mind.

Little River made a slight grunting sound as she sat and leaned against a rotted tree trunk. "Got your bracelet?"

Brad Davis smiled and waved as he moved away.

It was a minute past 8:00 p.m. mountain time when J.B. Foster's Gulfstream taxied up to the small hangar at the private airport in Socorro. He knew the drive from the airport would take close to an hour and a half. This was a trip he had made many times during the last fifty years, always under the cover of darkness. Socorro had grown during the years, with more and more retirees finding the climate and laid-back lifestyle to their liking. Once he had passed the hospital and National Guard armory beyond the western limits of the town, however, nothing had changed. Outside the few more inhabitants of Magdalena and Datil, the main road to Alegros Mountain and the compound were the same. He smiled, remembering that it was he who suggested this remote and desolate area as a worksite for the visitors from somewhere else in the universe to President Truman and Air Force intelligence officials.

J.B. Foster, a graduate of Stanford, was an electronics genius who began his career on a top secret government project in New Mexico, where he teamed with nuclear physicist Milton Goldberg. Together with a team of world renowned scientists, they worked on the development of the atomic bomb and the earliest testing at White Sands. His work developing the bomb guidance system for the Enola Gay brought him in close contact with senior military officials at Roswell Army Air Base. One of these senior officers was Nathaniel Brantfield, with whom he became fast friends. Following the war, Foster joined the Howard Hughes Aircraft Company, signing over his patent rights to Hughes for a substantial sum of money. Hughes, recognizing Foster's talent, had him working on development of better navigation systems for military and commercial airplane use. Midway through 1946, Foster and Hughes had a falling out over the ownership rights to a number of inventions Foster had patented for Hughes Aircraft. Mutually agreeing that a long, drawn-out law suit would only make their lawyers richer, Foster signed over his remaining rights with the provision that Hughes would allow him to open a competing business. Thus Transunion Enterprises was born.

Within a year's time, Foster had acquired a number of small electronics firms and built a company that was worth more than fifteen million dollars, a large sum of money in those days. *Forbes Magazine*, in an April, 1947 cover story, profiled the meteoric rise of the country's newest successful entrepreneur. Several months after the magazine article, Foster heard from an old friend, who he hadn't seen since leaving New Mexico. Shortly before midnight on July 5th the phone call came into Foster's California residence.

"Hello!"

"JB, it's Nathaniel Brantfield!"

"Nathaniel! How the hell are you? What are you up to these days? Are you still in the military?"

"You know me, JB," Brantfield laughed heartily. "I'm military to the core."

"So, to what do I owe the honor of your phone call at this time of night?"

"Look, JB, I am sorry to call at this hour, but I've got a situation that the President wants handled immediately."

Foster could sense the urgency in Brantfield's voice. "So, what does that have to do with me?"

"It's of such a top secret nature that I can only trust a few individuals. Based on our past friendship, and your background and clearance level, I think you'll find this right up your alley."

"Okay, you've got my attention. What is it?"

"I don't want to discuss it over the phone, but I will tell you it has something to do with a local newspaper story saying an unidentified flying object crashed on a ranch out near the base."

"Ah, yes! I heard something on the radio about it today. Knowing the government, they want to cover it up! Right?"

"Exactly! Can you meet me at the White House at 8:30 a.m. tomorrow morning?"

"What? Do you realize there's a three hour time difference and it's already midnight here on the West Coast."

"I know. I know, I'm sorry!"

"Nathaniel, the time difference, and the fact no commercial flights are available at this hour of the night, I don't see how I can make it! I'll probably have to charter a plane, but it's going to take at least eight to ten hours to get there. Can't you make the meeting for one or two o'clock?"

"Can't! The President has ordered me to his office at nine and I'm not about to call him at this hour of the morning and ask for a delay.

Tell you what I'll do, I'll meet with the President as scheduled and ask for a second meeting for two o'clock with the both of us. He'll probably buy that! Now, please get busy to find a way here for that meeting. See you at the White House."

As Foster, the man who was a few months away from celebrating his ninetieth birthday and yet had the look and energy of a man half his age, headed out of the airport onto Route 60 in the rented white Buick Regal he had arranged to have waiting for him, he recalled that late night phone call from Brantfield more than fifty years ago. For a large sum of money, he had successfully convinced a private pilot friend to fly him to Washington. President Truman, the man who had made the ultimate decision to drop atomic bombs on two Japanese cities several years earlier, thus ending the war, was not what Foster had expected. From newspaper photographs and his voice in radio broadcasts he had conjured up a mental picture of a mean-spirited, uncaring individual, with no redeeming virtues. Foster's first impression upon meeting the President was that this man was not at all as he had imagined him to be. He found the President to be charming, impish, and very warm-hearted.

"J. Barrington Foster! It is a pleasure to meet you."

"Thank you, Mister President! The pleasure and privilege are all mine."

"No, *thank you*, Mr. Foster! I sincerely appreciate your coming on such short notice, but we have a serious situation which could become a national calamity if word leaks out. First, let me say I am familiar with your work on the development of the bomb and I read the *Forbes Magazine* story about you. You have very impressive credentials. Has Brantfield told you anything about what happened near Roswell on the night of July fourth?"

Brantfield, who had been standing beside the President since Foster entered the Oval Office, quickly interjected, "No sir, because of security I did not tell him much over the telephone."

"Gentlemen." The President motioned for the two men to take a seat on the couch.

Both men sat beside each other as the President took a seat in the sofa chair facing them.

Looking at Brantfield, the President asked, "Would you like to fill him in now?"

"Yes sir! JB, if you remember I told you something crashed on a ranch near the base in Roswell. Well, now we're changing our story to say it was a weather balloon."

"Was it a weather balloon?"

"Of course not! It is some sort of flying object with intelligent life from another world."

"You have to be kidding me!"

"I'm afraid not, Mr. Foster," The President responded. "From what Brantfield tells me there were two objects. One crashed with no survivors, and the other landed to pick up the pieces and check for any sign of life. Brantfield is responsible for starting a dialogue with these people, and hopefully, they can be of some use to us. We cannot let any of this leak out to the press or public. We're just getting the nation back to normal following the war, and the last thing we need to do is panic everyone. We're going to cover this up and we're going to create a committee of loyal and tight-lipped Americans to go along with our plan. This committee will be appointed by me to go through the motions of investigating the furor this incident has caused. For the record......there was no alien space ship! There are no bodies! Do you understand? It was a weather balloon! I have many regrets for my decision to bomb Japan and I will not do another thing that will cause my administration to be put under a microscope! The American public must be kept in the dark. I will begin immediately putting together a group of 12 individuals to evaluate how we can utilize these interplanetary travelers to make sure our nation is the world leader in space technology. JB, I am asking you to become a key member of this committee. Is there anyone else you personally think should serve on this committee?"

"Only one, Mr. President. His name is Milton Goldberg. I worked with him at White Sands. He has a fascination with nuclear energy and always talked about using nuclear energy power for peaceful purpose, including the development of rockets that will propel man to the moon and beyond."

"Sounds exactly like a person we need on this committee. Please talk to him and see if he would like to become a member of the 'Majestic 12'."

There was no traffic in the Socorro area, especially at this time of night. He knew the ride out to the compound would be boring and uneventful, as always. It was after nine as his car approached the town of Datil, nothing more than a small dot on the map where Routes 60 and 12 converge. He could see the headlights of several cars parked on the side of the road up ahead. Slowing down, he cautiously approached the parked cars where he could see a state trooper vehicle, a black Ford Taurus, two Jeeps, and what looked like an army truck, but with no military markings. As he passed through the intersection of the two highways, he counted two state troopers, two individuals in plain clothes that were most certainly government men, and about fifty well-armed military types carrying automatic weapons. Billy Stiles was right, he thought, the government is onto Project Anasazi. Foster slowly moved past the group, as everyone turned to look at his vehicle, but no one made a move to stop his car. "Dammit!" he said out loud, "Everything is coming unraveled." Foster was sure the word had not been given yet to close off access from Route 60 to the compound entrance or else he would have been stopped. He found it difficult to believe that anyone even knew where the entrance to the compound was. In any case, he had to meet with Stiles, Anjou and the compound residents to ensure his empire did not crumble.

"Albuquerque this is November Charley 987. Do you copy?"

"Roger November Charley 987. We have you on radar and have been awaiting your call. Please tune to 54 point 7."

"Thank you Albuquerque. Switching to 54 point 7. This is November Charley 987."

"Roger, November Charley 987. This is Albuquerque tower. I have you in sight. Traffic is light at present time; you are cleared to land on runway three from the west. Turn left on taxiway, just short of runway eight, then proceed to Cutler Aviation. Your guests have arrived and are awaiting your arrival at Hangar 25. A fuel truck is standing by. When you have refueled and boarded your passengers, please contact ground control".

"Thank you, Albuquerque!" Captain Becci maneuvered the helicopter to a straight-in approach to runway three, descending from an altitude of 9,000 feet to 6,000 feet. As the chopper reached the threshold of the runway Becci lowered the craft to 10 feet above the ground, hovering momentarily before slowly moving down the runway. As the craft approached the taxiway intersection, Beardsley pointed to the large Cutler Aviation sign and the row of hangars at the southern end of the airport. He maneuvered the helicopter towards the row of hangars using the spotlights to find Hangar 25, and once finding it, he lowered the chopper to the ground in front of the main hangar doors. A lone figure emerged from the door at the side entrance and waved to the two men in the helicopter. A second figure emerged. Beardsley leaned over his seat and opened the door for the two men dressed in trench coats as they approached the chopper.

"Good evening gentlemen." Beardsley addressed the two men as they entered the helicopter taking seats and strapping themselves in. "I hope you had a pleasant flight from Washington. I am Major Robert Beardsley and this is Captain Tom Becci."

The four men exchanged handshakes. "I am Mitch Kaminsky and this is FBI Director Everett Weaver."

"I was told you would brief us on the nature of this mission." Beardsley stated. "I'm assuming this is something big."

"You bet it is, Major," Weaver said. "It's big enough for me to have given up my tickets to a Raul Di Blasio concert at the Kennedy Center, a concert I've been planning on attending for over six months."

"Sorry about that, sir."

"No need to be, Major," Kaminsky cut in, half laughing. "Old Ev, here, gets to attend enough concerts and parties all year long. I'm sure he'll have another opportunity to hear Di Blasio real soon. Can we get underway now and I'll fill you and the captain in on what this operation is about."

"Yes sir, but we'll need to refuel before departing," Becci commented, as he watched the fuel truck approach the craft.

During the ten minutes it took for refueling the four men made small talk. As the fuel truck backed away, Beardsley motioned to Becci to contact ground control.

"Ground control, this is November Charlie 987."

"This is Albuquerque, November Charley 987. Are you ready to depart?"

"Affirmative."

"November Charlie 987, there is a Continental heavy on final, runway three left. Touchdown in 12 seconds." Becci turned to the two men in the back seat and motioned them to place the headsets on. "Can you hear me okay, gentlemen?" They nodded their heads at the same time. "Because of the noise in here this will help us communicate better. And, please don't worry, our conversation will be only heard by the four of us. No one else."

"November Charley 987, you are cleared to runway three left. Tune to frequency 632."

"Roger. Switching to frequency 632. This is November Charley 987. Do you read me, control?"

"Affirmative. November Charley 987, climb to an altitude of 9,000 feet after take-off, then take a heading of 180 degrees. November Charley 987, you are cleared for take-off."

"Thank you, Albuquerque." Becci, climbing out, eventually turned the chopper to the southwest, heading for the rendezvous point southeast of Alegros Mountain.

As the lights of Albuquerque dimmed and faded behind them, the military helicopter with no markings headed into the darkness of the night sky ahead. Mitch Kaminsky began to brief the two military men.

CHAPTER TWENTY SIX

Davis estimated he had been walking for about fifteen minutes. He shined his flashlight on his watch. "Goddammit!" he exclaimed loudly. "It's doing it again! This time my watch has stopped altogether." At this point, whether through fear or his concern for Susan, Little River and Running Horse, Davis thought it best to return to where he had left them. His private expedition was getting nowhere and he suddenly had a sense of danger. He stopped, shining the beam of his flashlight in a complete circle. Nothing! The silence was disting.disconcerting. Many times in the past, he had faced all sorts of dangers with careless abandon. This time, it was different. He had a feeling of being watched by someone or something in the darkness. All of a sudden he was aware of the humming sound he had experienced on his first trip to this area. But this time, the humming sound had a strange tone, a tone he couldn't identify. It was like nothing he had ever heard. A cold chill ran through his body. The hair on his head felt strange, like he was being zapped with a low dose of electricity. Was he close to the entrance? That was less important to him as he suddenly became extremely fatigued and had an overwhelming desire to sit down, close his eyes and rest. He knew the others were waiting for him and would be worried. His determination to keep moving back to where he left them was slowly being drained away, as if some mysterious force was taking control of his body. Reluctantly, in hopes of regaining his energy, Davis found a tree to rest against. Sitting down, he placed the flashlight on his lap, still spilling its narrow beam through the darkness of the forest. His eyes were transfixed on the woods at the end of the beam. As his eyes became less focused, Davis knew he was not going to be able to fight the urge to sleep. Beginning to drift off, he was suddenly aware that he was no longer alone. He placed his hand around the rattlesnake bracelet on his wrist hoping that if anything was happening he would be protected. As hard as he tried to keep his eyes open and focus on the figure approaching him through the beam of his flashlight, Davis fell into a deep sleep.

The time to close all the access roads leading to Pie Town was scheduled for 2330 hours with Operation Alegros to commence at exactly 2400 hours. A command center had been in place since 2100 hours in Horse Springs at the junction of Route 12 and the back road leading to Pie Town. According to plan, two roadblocks had been placed just west of Datil at the intersection of Routes 12 and 60. The contingent of 200 soldiers of the elite Alpha Force was in place by 2130 hours, one-half hour earlier than the 2200 hour rendezvous time. The plan was to assault Alegros Mountain with three helicopters, with

Major Beardsley's helicopter leading the assault. Access to and from Alegros Mountain would be cut off at exactly 2300 hours allowing any vehicle passing through the checkpoints to be completely clear of Alegros Mountain by the beginning of the operation. All three blockade points were manned by a combination of Alpha Force personnel, FBI and New Mexico State Police. Lieutenants Dugan and Conway, who had been left behind in Horse Springs by Beardsley and Becci, were joined by the remainder of the Alpha Force assigned to participate in this operation shortly after the helicopter departed for Albuquerque. Conway took charge of the command post at Horse Springs awaiting Major Beardsley's return with the federal government officials, while Dugan took the remaining force to Datil where they joined with the FBI and the state police. Since traffic was expected to be light from the west through Pie Town, a smaller force was placed at the blockade on the eastern side of Pie Town. All three posts were connected by walkie-talkies using a secure frequency. According to one member of the Alpha Force at the Datil intersection, only a few vehicles had passed the Datil and Pie Town checkpoints. Horse Springs had no traffic at all. In addition to the car being driven by J. B. Foster past the Datil checkpoint, there were only five trucks heading west and two heading east. Conway checked his watch and then the night sky towards the east, looking for Major Beardsley's helicopter.

The Bronco carrying Colonel Parker and Lieutenant. Nelson

passed the Datil intersection approximately ten minutes after J.B. Foster. Nelson was the first to speak. "What do you think, Colonel? Are we going to have trouble with this?"

Parker, lost in thought, didn't respond.

"Colonel! Did you hear me?"

"What?" The colonel responded, turning around to get a last look at the men gathered at the intersection they had just cleared. "Are we going to have trouble with this? Is that what you asked me?"

"Yes sir! Until now, I've been okay with this, but it looks like we've taken on the whole U.S. government."

"Nonsense!" Parker shot back belligerently. "They're only a small force and besides, once we're inside the compound we'll have all the armaments we need to blow up this whole mountain, maybe the state, and everybody in it."

"If we do that, we'll get killed too!"

Parker laughed. "I see you really don't know what goes on in that mountain. Believe me, nothing can happen to us. In fact, I have a feeling once we get control of this project, we will be very powerful and rich men. After all, you helped me get rid of all the obstacles: General Brantfield, Sheriff Frank Cooper, and Big Bird. Now, aren't you happy that you're part of my team?"

The illumination from the dashboard didn't provide enough light for Parker to see the frightened expression on Nelsons face. He had his doubts about the colonel from the beginning, but as an obedient military man, he blindly followed his superior officer's orders. At this point, he felt completely trapped and knew there was no turning back. Had he been following the orders of a madman, thinking the assignments he was carrying out were in the best interest of national security?

"Hey, I'm talking to you, Lieutenant. Did you hear what I said?"

"Oh, yes sir! I'm really glad I'm part of your team." Nelson said with enough conviction as not to raise the colonel's suspicions. "By the way, Colonel, what do we do if we run into the same greeting party we ran into the last time?"

"Do you forget the arsenal of weapons we have in the back of this vehicle, lieutenant? We will simply blow their freaking heads off. Capish?"

"Yes, sir." Nelson turned onto the dirt road leading up to the entrance of the compound. He remembered the last time he visited this place. It was in broad daylight and he wasn't initially frightened. As he drove the five miles to the entrance, this time in pitch blackness except for the light of the Bronco's high beams, Nelson was silently praying he wouldn't have to deal with these visitors face to face again.

"Stop the car, here!" Parker shouted out. The vehicle came to a sliding halt on the soft sandy road.

"What is it, colonel?"

"Look up ahead, there, about 50 yards on the right side, just off the road. See them?

Nelson, who suffered from nearsightedness, especially at night, squinted and strained until he too, caught a glimpse of two vehicles on the side of the road. "I see them now, sir. Looks like a dark blue or black car and a white van."

"Right! Let's pull up alongside and check them out." Parker patted the dashboard. *I wonder who else has business with our friends in the compound.*

Nelson lowered the high beams and slowly maneuvered the Bronco alongside the white Mitsubishi. Turning off the motor, he turned to the colonel. "Sir, shall I see if there's any identification in the vehicles?"

"Good idea," Parker responded, as he opened his door and quickly moved to scout the area around both vehicles.

Nelson, having completed his task, moved to where Parker was standing in the road. "Colonel, they're both rentals, one out of Socorro and the other out of Albuquerque. Whoever is driving the Mitsubishi left the keys in the ignition. Do you want them?"

Colonel Parker, who was bending down, shining his flashlight in the dirt road, responded, "Nah, no use to us. I sure would like to know who else is here. Come here, lieutenant and look at these footprints." Nelson crouched down alongside the colonel. "What does it look like to you, lieutenant?"

"Well," Nelson began, taking the flashlight from the colonel and shining the beam further down the road towards the compound entrance, "it looks like two separate sets of footprints. I would say that there were two men, each arriving at a different time."

"What makes you think they didn't arrive together?" the colonel queried.

Nelson smiled smugly. "If they had arrived together they would have been walking side by side. It's obvious one set of footprints is being walked on by the second set of footprints. That wouldn't have been the case if they arrived together."

"That's very good. It's the same conclusion I came to." Parker took the flashlight from Nelson and started back to the Bronco. "Come on lieutenant, let's get our weapons and grenades."

As both men filled their outside jacket pockets with several grenades and placed a 380 automatic in each of their oversized inside jacket pockets, Nelson asked, "How much firepower should we bring with us?"

Picking up an Uzi and several rounds of ammunition and handing it to Nelson, Colonel Parker sneered, saying, "This will be fine for our first assault. We don't need to load ourselves down. We can always come back and get the big stuff when we need it. The colonel picked up his Uzi and ammunition. Okay, we're ready for anything now."

The men began moving towards the compound entrance, another 50 yards beyond the parked cars. "Where's the opening, colonel?" Nelson was the first to speak. "All I see is a solid wall of sandstone. I don't remember this being here the last time! Everything's different."

"You're right, lieutenant! Everything is different. Our friends are quite clever." Parker felt the wall, looking for something to indicate that there was a secret entrance not visible to the naked eye. "Well, well! Clever indeed! Nelson, feel your sandstone wall."

Nelson reached out and touched the wall. What the hell is that? The lieutenant quickly pulled his hand away and shouted out. "It looks like sandstone, but feels as if it's some sort of plastic."

"Ah, yes." Parker sighed. "I'm sure it's one of our visitors' many inventions that we don't know about. I'll show them how they aren't fooling us." Parker gave Nelson the flashlight to shine against the wall, then raised his Uzi, taking the butt end of the gun and making a motion to bang it against the wall. Before he could slam the gun butt against the wall a figure stepped from the darkness and pulled the Uzi from his hands. At the same moment, another figure grabbed Lieutenant Nelson' hands, knocking the flashlight to the ground. Parker reeled around to fend off his attacker, but was quickly subdued and forced to his knees. Nelson was completely caught off guard and so paralyzed with fear at the sight of these two tall figures, that he just stood there, motionless.

In the darkness, both Parker and Nelson, on their knees, couldn't make out who their attackers were. The only thing they could make out was a glowing disk hanging from each man's neck. They were pulled to their feet, facing the wall, as one of the tall strangers made a motion with some sort of device that made the wall dissolve. Nelson and Parker tried to back away from the entrance, but were powerless against the strength of their captors. With great force they were pushed through the opening. As both men continued to resist entering, one stranger was heard to say, "You were warned!"

Major Beardsley's helicopter had just passed over Socorro en route to its final destination of Horse Springs when the chopper began experiencing the same wild gyrations it had experienced earlier that evening. Becci and Beardsley turned to each other. "Here we go again, sir." Becci said nervously. Beardsley merely shrugged his shoulders.

Mitch Kaminsky, a veteran of many helicopter flights, leaned forward and asked, "Is there something wrong?"

"No, sir!" Beardsley said, as he turned to address both men seated in the rear, trying to offer some reassurance that everything was okay. The chopper, with its instrument dials spinning wildly, continued to react violently, forcing the two government officials to grab hold of their seats to save them from being thrown against each other.

"I would dare to say," Everett Weaver offered in a tentative voice, "that we are experiencing a major malfunction of this helicopter."

"And," Mitch Kaminsky interrupted, "I would like to know what that pulsating blue glow is."

Becci, struggling to maintain control of the wildly gyrating chopper, tried to join everyone in looking toward the ground below them, which, indeed, was pulsating with a blue glow.

"Gentlemen," Beardsley called out, "Did you just see all those lights on the ground go out?"

"I've been trying to keep us flying, sir and too busy to pay any mind," Becci responded.

"Anyone else?" Beardsley wanted to know. Kaminsky and Weaver both shook their heads no. "Wait a minute!" Beardsley shouted out. "Everyone look around outside. What do you see?"

Everyone in unison answered, "Nothing! Why?"

"There are no lights on the ground, anywhere, in front of us, to the side of us, behind us. Nowhere!" Beardsley continued to scan the horizons. "No lights from Socorro, Albuquerque, Magdalena, Horse Springs, nowhere! No lights except that damn blue glow for as far as we can see."

"What do you think that means, major?" asked Kaminsky.

Before Beardsley could respond, Becci called out, "Hey, the instruments are acting normally again and we've stopped bouncing around. We seem to be over our problem. However, gentlemen, from the way it looks, I would say there's been a major power outage throughout this area, stretching back up to Albuquerque. I could check it, but I'm supposed to maintain radio silence."

"Continue to maintain radio silence, Captain," Beardsley said, "We'll figure this one out once we're on the ground."

"Major," Becci said excitedly. "Something spooky just happened."

"What's that?"

"Have you noticed how quiet it got all of a sudden."

All four occupants of the chopper removed their headsets. "Absolute quiet! How is that possible?" Kaminsky wanted to know.

"Well, that's not all!" Becci said nervously. "I don't know how to explain it, but were standing still! Not moving!"

All four men looked at each other, but said nothing. A brilliant light began to fill the interior of the helicopter, getting brighter and brighter by the second. The four occupants looked out their windows and were blinded by the intense brightness above them.

"Is this some kind of sick government demonstration for our benefit?" demanded FBI Director Everett Weaver.

"If it is, you can call it off now," Kaminsky shouted.

Beardsley, shielding his eyes and still looking up to see where the light was coming from, responded, "You can bet your ass we have nothing to do with this."

"My God!" Becci yelled, pointing to a giant saucer-like object hovering over them.

"Holy shit!" Kaminsky stammered. "We're having an encounter!"

By this time, the entire interior of the helicopter was bathed in a bluish-white glow. Everyone was transfixed and said nothing. The chopper was under the control of this space vehicle and there was nothing anyone could do about it. Suddenly, the helicopter began a silent descent to the floor of the Plains of Agustin, evidently being lowered by an unknown force from the space craft. As the chopper settled softly onto the ground, all four men jumped out, looking to the sky as a saucer shaped object, the size of three football fields and as tall as a 10 story building, slowly moved off in the direction of Alegros Mountain.

CHAPTER TWENTY SEVEN

Brad slowly opened his eyes, aware that he was no longer resting against a tree in the forest of Alegros Mountain. He rose from the modernistic reclining chair, surveying his surroundings. The room, devoid of any furniture except the futuristic looking Lazy Boy, was dimly lit. Many questions immediately came to mind. How did he get here? Who or what brought him here? Where were Susan and the others? Were they safe? Davis knew his first priority was to determine where he was and then to find the others. Was he a prisoner? He really didn't believe that for a moment. There was this sense of serenity and well-being. How long had he been sleeping? He looked at his watch, realizing the second hand wasn't moving, and further realizing it showed the exact time he last looked at his watch before dozing off. Was he in a place where time stands still? Davis suddenly realized the soft light filling the room was coming from all four walls, as if the outdoor sun was being filtered through window curtains. Looking towards the ceiling, Davis noticed the ceiling seemed to give off light. The only difference was that the ceiling light was dimmer, almost like the azure color of the last light in the evening sky. He walked towards the closest wall and reached out to see if he could determine where the light was coming from. As his hand touched the wall, the light emanating from all four walls slowly darkened. Davis withdrew his hand quickly. Not only was he mystified at the dimming of the lights when he touched the wall, but by the feeling of the strange rubber-like texture of the wall itself. Davis had trouble believing what he was seeing and feeling. The wall was solid! Yet, it gave off light! And, oddly enough, it had the feel of a substance he had never experienced before. Davis touched the wall again. The room darkened even more. This time he banged the wall with his fist. Immediately the room was very bright. As Davis turned to view the remaining walls, he found himself looking at two four-foot grey figures, standing a few feet away. Startled, he leaned back against the wall, causing the lights to dim. He couldn't believe his eyes. They looked exactly like the alien creatures that are depicted in all the encounter stories. Had he been abducted or was he having a nightmare? Davis didn't have time to pinch himself as the two creatures turned and gestured for Davis to follow them. But follow them where? There didn't seem to be an opening in the room. The creatures stopped at the most distant wall, turned to each other, waved their arm-like appendages. Suddenly the wall disappeared and the room darkened.

Davis followed the figures along a tunnel-like hallway where the lighted walls seemed to be similar to those in the room he had left. The arched ceiling gave off a blue glow. "Hey!" Davis called out in the eerily quiet hallway. "Can you people talk?" No response. "Can you hear me or don't you understand English?" Still no response as Davis continued to follow the figures. "Where are you taking me?" The figures stopped and turned to the wall on their right. Stepping aside, they motioned Davis to pass between them. "Are you kidding me? What am I supposed to do, walk through walls?" The figures raised their appendages, as they had done earlier, and the wall disappeared, revealing a large room where, seated at a long silver table were several familiar faces.

"Mr. Davis, so good to see you again." Big Bird stood and walked to greet Davis. They shook hands.

Brad, looking beyond Big Bird, saw Sheriff Cooper sitting at the table. He was speechless. Running Horse and Captain Gerard of the New Mexico State Police had said he was killed when he was driving Davis' vehicle back to Magdalena. How could he be alive? "Hello, Big Bird. Good to see you, too."

Sheriff Cooper rose from the table and joined Big Bird in welcoming Davis. "What's the matter Mr. Davis? You look like you've seen a ghost."

"I thought you were dead."

Before Davis could respond, another voice, seated at the table, called out. It was General Brantfield. "Mr. Davis, Big Bird, Sheriff Cooper and myself were all dead. You are seeing living proof that people can be brought back from the dead, under certain circumstances."

"That's impossible!" Davis responded incredulously.

"Please, Mr. Davis, sit at the table while we wait for the others to finish their business and join us." Big Bird said, offering Davis a chair. "We will tell you the whole story, including why Sheriff Cooper was trying to protect you, even against General Brantfield's wishes."

"Before I hear any of this," Davis said, "I want to know what happened to Susan, Running Horse and Little River."

"Ah, yes!" Big Bird smiled. "I assure you they are quite safe within the compound. In fact, they are being given a tour of our facilities and are meeting with the inhabitants. Your Susan is quite lovely. Little River is a bit feisty, but Running Horse seems to be handling her. She has more questions than your reporter girlfriend. Now, Mr. Davis, we would like to begin our story at the point of when you first showed up in this area."

"I want to know the whole story from the beginning," Davis said.

"In due time, in due time, you will be told everything." Big Bird responded. "Anjou will tell you everything you want to know."

Beardsley, Becci, Kaminsky and Weaver had been sitting in the darkened helicopter ever since the strange object that had forced them to the ground had disappeared in the direction of Alegros Mountain.

"It's no use major," said Becci, "The engine won't turn over, and I can't contact anyone by radio. Everything is dead. And, the ground, for as far as I can see, continues to pulsate with that blue glow. We don't know what time it is, either. All our watches stopped working the minute we encountered the UFO."

Beardsley checked his watch again, shaking his head. "I figure we've been sitting here for over an hour. Anyone else care to venture a guess?"

"Sounds about right to me," Kaminsky answered.

"I figure its somewhere after 2300 hours. Major, do you think these creatures, or whatever they are, up on Alegros Mountain, are responsible for this?"

"Can't say, Mr. Weaver, but from what we were told to prepare for, I would say yes. However, I don't want to jump to any conclusions just yet," Beardsley cautioned.

"Major," Kaminsky asked, "what the hell is going to happen to Operation Alegros if we can't launch the assault on the mountain at precisely 2400 hours that your orders called for?"

"Mr. Kaminsky," Beardsley replied, "we don't know for a fact that our three checkpoints are without power and communications. We may be an isolated incident. In any event, Alpha Force, if they have the capability, has orders to begin the assault at 2400 hours, with or without me. Since we are in the middle of nowhere and it's too far to walk, we'll have to sit and wait it out."

Lieutenant Dugan, in charge of the Datil roadblock, was nervously pacing back and forth across the road. There were no lights of any kind at this road block. It had been that way since the ground around them started pulsating with a blue glow, about the same time the lights in the town of Datil went out. Shortly after that, everyone at the post saw a huge unidentified object pass over them. Radios, cellular phones, watches, flashlights, helicopter and car engines all went dead at the same time. There had been no traffic since that time. Dugan, unable to contact Conway at the command post in Horse Springs, assumed he was having the same trouble since he hadn't heard from him. "Damn!" Dugan said out loud. "How are we supposed to launch an attack if we don't know the time and can't get our chopper up in the air?" In the darkness of the moonless night, Dugan couldn't see if anyone was close enough to have heard him.

All of a sudden there was light in the distance, approaching the roadblock. Everyone focused their attention on the lights coming closer and closer. It was obvious that they were the headlights of a vehicle coming from the east. "How could that be?" Dugan asked himself. "Was this strange phenomenon over?" He tried his flashlight. Nothing! "Sergeant," he yelled out in the darkness. "Try your radio and the chopper power supply."

"Nothing!" came the reply.

The ground continued to pulsate and glow. Dugan shouted out, "Everyone take their positions!" The wooden barrier across the road would surely bring the oncoming car to a halt. "No vehicles are permitted to pass!" Dugan shouted again.

All eyes were focused on the lights of an approaching car. Suddenly, the lights seemed to stop. "Lieutenant!" the sergeant called out. "It looks like the vehicle has stopped about 200 yards from here. Do you reckon they've seen our roadblock and don't want to come any closer?"

"Most likely, sergeant. Everyone maintain their positions!"

"Lieutenant, look! The lights have gone out. What do you think they're up to?"

"Don't know. Maybe they turned around and headed back to where they came from. Keep your eyes peeled, just in case."

It didn't take long for everyone to forget about the car lights, move away from the roadblock, and start conversations again about the blue glow and the huge object that had passed over their heads earlier. Lieutenant Dugan, feeling frustrated, leaned against the helicopter, still trying to get a response from his radio.

Two hundred yards from the roadblock, an old Chevy Caprice with its headlights turned off had come to a stop. The two occupants of the car were able to distinguish every detail of the roadblock through their infrared windshield. They waited for everyone to clear away from the roadblock. It was not their intention to harm anyone as they drove through the barrier. When the last individual moved to the side of the road, the driver activated a black box on the dashboard, placed the car in drive and proceeded to move toward the roadblock. The Caprice was doing 50 miles per hour as it crashed through the barrier, scaring the hell out of everyone at the roadblock.

Dugan dropped his radio and ran to where the barrier had been placed across the road. "What the hell was that?" He looked down at the broken pieces of the wooden barrier. "Did anyone see anything?" There was no answer from the group who had joined Dugan to look at what remained of their roadblock. "Did anyone hear anything?" Again, only silence. "What the hell are we dealing with here?"

Both men in the Caprice smiled as the car moved swiftly up the mountain road towards the cut-off for the entrance to the compound. They knew that time was growing short and that they needed to be ready to leave this place. They certainly didn't want to be left behind. Fifty-two years of living in a strange land was enough. They were more than ready to go home.

Parker and Nelson had been taken to a room where they were left without anyone watching them, or so they thought. Outside the room that served as a prison for them, there were many curious eyes looking at them. While the prisoners couldn't see beyond the lighted walls, the inhabitants of the mountain compound were curious to see these two individuals, who, they were told, represented all that is evil in the world today. One of the curious onlookers, speaking in his own language, told those that were gathered, that Anjou said it was because of men like these that we are no longer going to help America. He continued to tell his listeners that the evil deeds these men had done included the killing of General Brantfield, Sheriff Cooper, and our own brother, Big Bird. The speaker paused. Taking one last look at the men trapped beyond the wall, he told everyone to return to their homes, pack their belongings, and meet at the transport ship. "We're going home!" He concluded, as the onlookers moved away from the wall.

"Where are we?" Nelson asked, with a hint of dread in his voice.

"Damn you, Nelson! These bastards got the better of us, again!"

"There was no way to avoid it, sir. It was like they were waiting for us."

"No, they were just lucky again. But we outsmarted them this time. All they got were our Uzis. We still have our automatic weapons and the grenades. Let's give them a little more time to see if anyone shows up. While we're waiting for them, let's come up with some sort of game plan to overpower them and get out of here. We're going to have to kill them. Are you up to it, Lieutenant?"

"I'm always with you, sir."

"Good! Now here's how I figure we can take these characters out."

"General, I still don't see how you thought I was a big enough threat to get rid of me?"

"Nothing personal, Mr. Davis. I couldn't jeopardize Project Anasazi. The sheriff and I have been dedicated to this project for over fifty years. He was getting a little tired of the cover-ups that seemed to be becoming more and more frequent. I asked him to take care of you and he refused. Quite truthfully, I would have preferred you dead, but I would have been satisfied if you went away and forgot about studying your Anasazi Indians. As it turned out, the sheriff was right. It was time to bring Project Anasazi to conclusion. Big Bird had already told me the end was near. I don't know if I didn't believe him or if I really could stand to have a project I spent my whole life on come to a conclusion."

"There are two things I'm curious about," Davis said. "When I first arrived in Magdalena I met Jake, the old-timer at the gas station. Later, I learned he was always intoxicated because something frightened the living daylights out of him. Can you tell me what it was that frightened him so badly?"

"I can answer that one," the sheriff said. "It must have been about ten years ago when Jake's car broke down on the highway, right near the cut-off to the entrance to the compound. He had no idea about the compound. He still doesn't. While he was checking under the hood, a transport ship passed over his car on the way to the compound."

"What do you mean a transport ship?"

"Our visitors come and go quite frequently, bringing new residents and taking away those that wish to return home. The transport ship, a small disc shaped vehicle capable of transporting 25 people at a time, travels between the compound and the mother ship. It was on this one occasion that old Jake got a glimpse of one of these visits. Evidently, he had binoculars in the car and watched from a distance as the ship descended through the opening in the sun shield. Two of our inhabitants were coming back from Magdalena in their Caprice when they spied Jake observing the landing. In their best alien way, they put a scare into him so severe that he passed out. The two inhabitants transported Jake and his car back to the highway outside

Magdalena. Well, Jake has been drinking and babbling ever since. He tried to tell everyone about his experience, but no one believed him. Everyone laughed at him. That led him to drink more and more until he no longer talked about the incident. Quite sad, really."

"What about Sam Johnson, Mattie's husband?"

"I'll answer that one, Mr. Davis." Brantfield folded his arms in front of him. "Sam Johnson was out serving as a guide for a fellow named Steve Bryant, who was looking for Anasazi ruins. Did you know him?"

"He's the reason I came out here to explore the Anasazi mystery of where they came from and where they disappeared," Davis answered.

"Well, while Sam was out there, over Mangas Mountain that is, Bryant was trying to get Sam's help in finding an Anasazi ruin that Bryant had come across several weeks earlier. It seems Bryant couldn't find it again and needed Sam's help. Unfortunately, Sam slipped on an outcropping and fell, breaking his neck. Luckily, four of the compound's residents were over at Mangas retrieving materials from the ruins. They transported Bryant and Sam back here. These people, Mr. Davis, have the power to bring back the dead. Actually, their technology in the field of medicine is remarkable. Sam's body was placed in a machine for which there is no English word. The machine is able to heal bones, regenerate the heart, improve circulation and actually reverse or stabilize the aging process. The fountain of youth in an alien incubator."

"Where was Bryant during all this time?"

"He was being given a tour of the entire compound. He was fascinated, enough so that he wanted to remain here and learn everything he could about these people from another planet."

"How come Sam died?"

"Like our own medical care here in the United States, there are mistakes made. Sam was one such mistake. His broken neck healed so well that no one would ever detect that he had broken it."

"Mattie said Bryant came and told her that Sam had fallen off a cliff and broken his neck and died. I guess it was your compound Indians that brought Sam's body back two weeks later. But, why so long and why was his body gray?"

"Sam Johnson had many things wrong with him and they tried to fix them all, but it was just not to be. The process the body goes through when being treated causes it to turn gray. Usually, you survive and the gray color disappears. They actually tried for two weeks to fix everything. Sam needed a miracle. They came close, but as they say, no prize."

"What about Bryant? What happened to him?"

"He was offered a chance to travel to Dacon, which he accepted. After telling Mattie about Sam's accident, he went home, packed all his belongings, and returned to the compound. After spending a month doing his research, he, along with a number of compound residents, boarded a ship for our planet."

Davis sat quietly. While what he had heard was fascinating, it was also difficult to believe. All of a sudden, three figures were standing in the room, apparently entering from where, moments before, a wall had been. Davis immediately recognized Billy Stiles. As the new arrivals to the meeting moved away from the doorway, the opening in the wall disappeared.

Big Bird stood and introduced the three new guests to Davis. "Brad, Billy Stiles you already know. I would like to introduce JB Foster of Transunion Enterprises and Anjou, the Supreme Council Governor."

CHAPTER TWENTY EIGHT

The Supreme Council Governor was a tall, impressive looking man. Dark skin tone, high cheekbones, black hair; exactly what one would expect of an American Indian, except this individual was not of this planet. He was dressed in a one-piece, red metallic suit. He wore black plastic type boots that came to his mid calf. His English was perfect, with no trace of any accent as he greeted everyone by name. Foster and Stiles, following behind Anjou, also greeted everyone.

"Brad Davis," Anjou smiled, as he shook Davis' hand, "you have caused quite a stir around here in the last few days."

"No disrespect, sir," Davis answered, "but I hardly feel that I'm the one who has been causing a stir around here."

"You are quite right! However, you are now in the middle of a boiling pot." Anjou took a seat at the head of the table. "You see, Mr. Davis, your government is about to try and attack our compound."

"What are you talking about?"

"Let me fill you in, Brad." Billy Stiles interjected as he approached

Davis. "By the way, I hope there are no hard feelings about the way I left you all out there."

Davis would have liked to punch Stiles out but his facial expression and his voice didn't show his feelings on the matter. "You and I will discuss that later. Right now, I want to know what is going on here."

"I'll tell you what, Mr. Davis," Anjou responded. "We'll fill you in on everything after you've had time to visit our compound. Believe me, after you have had a tour, there will be many more questions you'll want answered. I promise, all questions will be answered. We have a number of matters to resolve among ourselves and we must excuse ourselves from your company. You're welcome to stay, of course, but being a researcher and writer I am sure you will be more fascinated with what you are about to see than the mundane items that will be discussed here. Big Bird will give you the grand tour."

Big Bird led Davis through the opening in the wall and out into the hallway. "What would you like to see first?"

"I have no idea what there is to see, but I am concerned about my friends."

"Not to worry. They are perfectly safe. They're being given a tour by Falu and Krin, the two compound residents who have been here since 1947. Their role in the compound is security and you can thank them for rescuing Susan before those government people got hold of her."

"What government people?" Davis wanted to know.

"I'll show them to you in a moment," Big Bird responded. "It was Falu and Krin who brought Susan to Running Horse and Little River's house. In fact, we'll probably catch up with them on this tour. With that worry out of the way, we can proceed to our workshop." Big Bird motioned Davis to follow him. As they walked along the hallway, Big Bird stopped and pointed to Parker and Nelson beyond the see-through wall. "There, Brad, are two earth specimens that I spoke of. We plan on taking them to our home to find what makes them what they are. They will be interesting subjects to study."

"I don't follow you, Big Bird. Who are they?"

"They are employed by your government to carry out evil deeds. Their names are not important. There have been many evil men like these on your planet since the beginning of time. But as time has passed the technology to build weapons of mass destruction has caused individual countries to rise against other countries in hopes of dominating their people and natural resources. World control is what they want. America was never like this. America has always been the world's policemen. It was the reason that the Daconians decided to come here in 1947 and work to ensure that America would always stay strong and continue to seek peace throughout the world. But now even America is changing, being manipulated by power hungry men. There is much corruption in the American government today. Each passing day, without our help, even more powerful weapons are being built. The ultimate question is, how dead is dead? I talk too much. Anjou will speak to you of these matters. But, let me say, that these men will harm no one any longer."

"Can they see or hear us?"

"No. Now, let us be on our way." Big Bird moved down the hallway, passing stairways cut into the wall that seemed to lead to a higher level.

"Hey, where do those stairs lead to?" Davis called out.

"To the residents' homes," Big Bird responded. "Well, at least to where their homes used to be."

As they continued walking, Davis asked, "What do you mean used to be?"

"Since we are leaving, all the homes and furnishings are being stored for some possible future time when we may need them again."

"Are we talking about the 200 homes I saw when I was first stumbled on this place?"

"It was 140 homes and I do remember the commotion you caused for all of us. Luckily, you didn't stay around too long."

"I was drawn by a humming sound," Davis said emphatically.

"The humming sound comes from the equipment that is powered by our transport craft. That equipment creates a climate similar to our own planet. Our lungs can function without adverse effects for about three days. Then it becomes necessary to spend 30 minutes in the de-aging room."

"What kind of room?" Davis interrupted.

"We call it a de-aging room. We don't know how to translate the scientific name we have for it into your language. I will show it to you when we arrive at the workshop. Everyone from Dacon must use the de-aging room 15 minutes a day. It not only stops the aging process, if you stay in too long, you will become younger. It also acts as a natural tranquilizer."

"That sounds like an interesting prospect."

The hallway ended and Big Bird stopped, raised his hand, and the wall, just like all the other walls in this place, disappeared. Beyond was a brightly lit, music filled, two-story cavernous room. Ringing the entire room, placed against the wall were what appeared to be computers, the likes of which Davis had never seen before. Scattered about the room were individual work tables where, until recently, someone had been working on a project. The room was empty of anyone now. Big Bird did not stop Davis from wandering among the work tables. Davis would pick up objects, look at them and shake his head in bewilderment. He had no idea what he was handling.

"What is that strange music? I don't recognize it."

"Ah, yes!" Big Bird smiled. "That, my friend, is the music of our land. We, too have our own composers and musicians. Of course, their names would not be familiar to you, but they are our Chopin and Mozart. We play the music to alleviate the stress of being so far from home. I believe one of your expressions is, music calms the savage beast, is that not true?"

"Where is everybody?" Davis wanted to know. "It seems as if everyone suddenly stopped working and left the room. Did they leave because I was coming?"

"No, my friend. It's just time. We all knew that one day our time on your planet would abruptly come to an end. Nothing lasts forever, as you earthlings like to say."

"You make it sound like you're not one of us."

"I'm not. What would you say if I told you I was 300 years old?"

"Sure, Big Bird, and I'm Moses." Davis laughed out loud, not believing him for a minute. "Give me a break! Now, tell me what this thing is here? Davis picked up a small chip from the closest table."

"That is a microchip that will make Doppler radar pin-point accurate in forecasting storms giving people up to a half hour notice before a tornado strikes. This long thin tube, when placed in the ground in earthquake-prone regions, will give seismologists 24 to 48 hours advance warning that an earthquake is imminent."

"Come on, you expect me to believe all this Star Trek baloney? Next, you're going to tell me you can cure cancer and Aids!"

"Would you believe me, if I told you?"

Davis shook his head. "Hey, what's over in that room in the corner? The room, bathed in a soft pink light that Davis was pointing to was in the far corner of the workshop. From a distance it was difficult to tell if it was an open room or one of those many rooms similar to where the two government men were being held. On closer inspection, it was one of those see-through walls where Davis could see what looked like a hospital type bed. Above the bed were pulsating lights that cast intermittent beams of multi-colored light on the bed's surface."

"That is the room I told you about. I, too, have been de-aging all my life. It is how I have lived to be so old in earth years while maintaining a youthful look. It is where I was brought back to life after being killed by those two men I showed you. It saved Sheriff Cooper and General Brantfield as well. I'm sure you noticed how youthful General Brantfield and JB Foster appear. They have been using the de-aging room for 50 years. Sheriff Cooper was offered an opportunity to use the room but, he refused on some sort of religious grounds. Little River has used our de-aging room, also. Of course, she is not aware that she did. We brought her here from the truck."

"That can't be!"

"Were you not driving in the tow truck with Running Horse, trying to get Little River help? She was beaten by those same two men I showed you. Do you remember the bright light over the truck and then nothing? Do you remember how young she looked when you all awoke from your sleep?"

"How did you know that?"

"It was us, Brad Davis. Our people who have stayed and worked here have not aged a day. They are as healthy and vigorous as they are on their own planet. We have no diseases on our planet. We have been trying to help you with our technology to eliminate all earthly diseases, but it is over. No more. The work you see on the tables here is finished. Your scientists are going to have to discover these things without our help."

Davis looked at Big Bird in astonishment. "You really are 300 years old!"

Big Bird grinned, "Amazing, isn't it. By the way, you had asked me where everyone is. Originally, there were 300 of us who came in 1947. Over the years, half of my people stayed here. The other half would leave and be replaced by others. It is difficult for some to stay long periods away from their families. So there have been a few times our space craft, or UFOs, as you like to call them, have visited to transport the people back and forth. Since early this evening, our commuter craft has been taking the last of the inhabitants to the mother ship. There are two more trips to be made. One is for the last 25 people and the other is for Anjou and myself. Would you like to see our commuter craft?"

"Definitely!" Davis' eyes lit up.

Big Bird led him up a stairway carved into the wall. The door at the top of the stairs opened into one of the homes, similar to one he had entered on his first visit to the compound. This time the house was empty of all furnishings. It was as if the moving van packed up everything and took the household belongings to the occupants' next house. Big Bird motioned Davis to follow him out the front door. Once outside, Big Bird said, "Everything has changed."

"I'll say!" he answered, looking around the vastness of the outside. Davis couldn't believe his eyes. "This is the same place I was at once before, isn't it, Big Bird?"

"Yes, Brad, it is. If you look around you will see we are surrounded by trees on all sides, except for the west wall, where you will see our ancestors' cliff dwellings."

About 500 feet above the floor of the canyon, numerous cliff dwellings could be seen rising to almost the top of the mesa. The dwellings seemed to be almost 200 yards wide. Davis couldn't contain his excitement. "Yes, I remember seeing these dwellings when I was here the first time. I thought I had imagined them."

"No, they are quite real."

"Let me ask you another question that has bothered me for some time. "When I first discovered this place, I passed through an imaginary wall that looked like trees, and then found myself looking down on where we are standing now. How does that work?"

"I'm sure you have seen holograms, which, by the way, we provided you with that technology. Well, we have a far more advanced imaging system in place here. It helps keep out the curious."

Davis, surveying his surrounding, was astonished at how different everything looked. "Tell me why there's no trace of all the homes I saw here." Only the house that he and Big Bird exited remained standing. A short distance away, he saw four Indians standing alongside what looked like the walls of a dismantled house, all carefully piled on top of each other. Two of the four men moved to the far side of the pile while two remained on the near side. "What are they doing?"

Big Bird answered, "They are going to store what's left of the house in the mountain."

"How are they going to transport it?"

"Let's watch and follow them."

The two men on the far side faced the men on the near side. Simultaneously, they stretched out their arms, palms upward. The remains of the house slowly lifted until they were about 12 inches off the ground. The men, in unison, hands still outstretched, turned and walked towards the mesa wall. As they walked, the remains of the house moved with them. As they neared the wall, the solid cliff wall in front of them slowly, and without sound, rolled to one side revealing a large opening where Davis could see a shiny metallic object sitting just inside the entranceway. He was speechless.

"Well, Brad, are you duly impressed with what you are seeing?"

It took a few seconds for him to answer. "How did they do that?"

"Not a magic trick, I assure you! Our people utilize the forces in their bodies to enable them to transfer that force into energy waves that allow them to lift objects of any size and weight. It is that power that helped to build the pyramids and other wonders of your world. Mankind has never been able to figure how large objects were placed together in a time when there were no machines. We do not need machines on our planet. We only need the power of our minds."

Davis was still trying to digest all of what he was seeing and hearing. He pointed to the shiny object in the entranceway where the four Indians had disappeared into the darkness, still transporting the remains of the house. "What is that thing?" Davis, finally recovering, was able to ask.

A slight chuckle could be heard as Big Bird responded to his question. "Before I answer that question, I want you to look up and tell me what you see."

"It seems to be some sort of dome. I noticed it the first time I was here. What is it, exactly?"

"It is a dome, a dome that retracts like the lens of a camera."

"What do you need a dome for?"

"Remember, I told you we needed to control our environment on earth. This dome controls our atmosphere helping us to simulate our planet's atmosphere. At the same time, it blocks out the sun's rays. On Dacon, we are further from our sun than earth is from your sun. We would be severely burned if we were exposed to the ultraviolet rays for any prolonged period. This way we are protected. The equipment powering this system makes a humming sound that can be heard as far away as Taos."

"While we're on the subject of strange sounds and other phenomena, can you explain why my watch always seems to lose time here?" Davis asked.

"Sorry, but this equipment causes anyone in close proximity to the equipment to have their watch stop. The further away from the equipment you get the watch will begin to return to its normal time function. Any more questions before I take you aboard our ship?" Davis shook his head no. "Good. We are now ready to board. Follow me!"

Both men stepped in front of a silver, saucer shaped object. A set of stairs rose from the ground up into the center of the space vehicle.

Davis, with all his years of research, had never experienced anything like this. His heart was beating a mile a minute from the excitement of what he was experiencing. They slowly moved up the stairs onto the main deck of the ship, where they were greeted by Falu.

"I'm still here, Big Bird," Falu said. "They are so interested by the ship and everything about it they won't leave until they learn everything they can. Krin is with them, still showing them everything."

"That's alright, Falu." Big Bird patted Falu on the shoulder. "Mr. Davis will be going up to the top level when I finish showing him this deck." Falu stepped aside. "Brad, this is where the two control operators sit, pointing to two seats facing a panel of blinking lights. That small panel of lights you see is the brains of this ship. That's all we need. You will observe there are an additional 10 seats ringing the wall. There is a hidden screen in the wall that allows the people sitting in those chairs to view the sights as they travel to the mother ship. The screen is activated when the craft is in motion."

"Where are your engines?"

"There are none!"

"How does this thing fly, then?"

"A very efficient propulsion system powered by tonium."

"Tonium? Never heard of it."

"Of course not! It is one of Dacon's natural resources. Actually, we've only been using it for the last 600 earth years. Dacon's scientists came across it accidentally. It can power this small vehicle for a thousand earth years. The mother ship needs twenty of the 12 ounce pieces to power it for the same amount of time."

"Where is it on this ship?"

"Right here below the control panel." Big Bird showed Davis the receptacle where the tonium was stored. I should tell you that there are times when the earth's gravitational forces cause any uranium in the soil within a 200 mile radius of this site to pulsate with a bluish glow. Drives the natives nuts, I understand."

Davis looked into the receptacle and couldn't believe that a little piece of purple rock could actually make the saucer fly. "I still don't understand how this thing can fly."

"It allows the vehicle within the confines of gravity to reverse gravity and move the craft at any speed. Once beyond earth's gravity, the forces of the moon and the sun are used the same way to propel the mother ship. Now, remember, this craft does not travel vast distances into the universe. It is only a commuter craft which docks in the underside of the mother ship. Earlier this evening, the mother ship was directly over the compound, making the commute very short."

Davis laughed. "I'll bet that really scared the daylights out of some people!" Big Bird also laughed. "Okay, one final question. How do they fly this thing? I don't see any steering wheel!"

Directing his attention to the two control operators' seats, Big Bird pointed to a strange looking headset. "Here, put this on."

Davis picked up the headset and placed it on his head. "This is like one of those virtual reality headsets."

"Where do you think they came from?" Big Bird said smugly.

"How does this work?"

"Just like your earthly virtual reality."

"Wow! I see the floor of the canyon and straight ahead I see the forest at the other end. When I look up, I see the top of the dome." Davis removed the headset. "So, who uses them?"

"Normally, the androids pilot the commuter craft and they do not need to use the headsets. They are built to operate the craft with their built in robotics. But when they are not around, our people use the headsets to operate the craft. Would you like to see the top deck and rejoin your friends?"

"Sure, but tell me about the androids. What do they look like?"

"You've seen them. They were the life forms that brought you to the meeting room. I believe your people have referred to them as the grays. Very harmless really, but very efficient for our purposes. Anything else you would like to know before we proceed?"

Davis merely motioned for Big Bird to lead the way. At the rear of the main deck was a small elevator. Directing Davis to once again follow him they rode the lift to the top level. Stepping off the elevator, Davis was immediately greeted by Susan, who threw her arms around him and squeezed with all her might.

"Boy, am I glad to see you! You know, I thought they were giving us a story that you were okay and we'd be reunited soon, when, really, I thought they were going to whisk us off to another solar system." Davis was about to say something when Susan began talking again.

"Can you believe this place? What a great story this is going to make. Do you think anyone will believe this? Should we write a collaborative story?"

"Whoa! Slow down, Susan, and catch your breath. We need to sort out what's going on here and then get back to the real world. We can discuss all this when we leave this place and get back on familiar ground."

Running Horse turned around from one of the 25 seats ringing the interior wall of the top deck of the craft. "Hey, Brad, good to see you again!" he called out and then quickly turned around to listen to what Krin was explaining about the screen he and Little River were fixated on. Little River merely waved her hand in the air as a greeting to Davis.

Big Bird smiled as he watched Susan and Davis continue their long embrace. "Ahem! Can I have your attention? I hate to break up your reunion party, but we're on a schedule here and I'd like to show Brad the workings of this deck." Davis, hand-in-hand with Susan, followed Big Bird to where Running Horse and Little River sat engrossed in the screen in front of them.

"Brad, do you know what those glowing necklaces around the necks of the people who live here are for?" Susan asked.

"No, I haven't any idea."

"It's used for helping them talk in our language since they speak a different language on their planet."

"You don't say," Davis answered flatly while looking at Big Bird, who merely shrugged his shoulders.

CHAPTER TWENTY NINE

Big Bird, having given Davis a tour of the space craft, had returned to the meeting room. He asked Davis, Susan, Little River and Running Horse to wait outside until he received permission for everyone to enter. The wall closed behind Big Bird, leaving Davis to respond to questions from the others.

"I don't like this!" Little River was the first to speak.

"What's going on in that room?" Running Horse wanted to know.

"I think the real question is," Susan responded, "What's going on, period!"

"If you'll all please be quiet." Davis motioned for them to stop talking. "I think I can say without a doubt, that these people, who have lived here for over 50 years, are leaving."

"Brad, how could they have lived here all this time and we didn't know about it?" Running Horse asked.

"From what I gather not many people outside the general, Sheriff Cooper, Big Bird, Stiles, those two government men and Foster know about this place. You've all seen their workshop, I presume?" Davis looked at his three companions.

"Yes!" everyone responded.

"Something bad is going to happen, I can feel it'" Little River said.

"You want your rattlesnake bracelet?" Davis answered, trying to keep the sarcasm out of his voice. Little River was about to answer when the door opened and Big Bird waved the foursome into the room.

"Did you enjoy your tour, Mr. Davis?" Anjou asked.

"Yes, thank you," Davis replied. Big Bird introduced the members of the Davis party to the others in the room. Running Horse and Sheriff Cooper already knew each other, but this was the first time they were meeting Anjou, the general and Foster. Billy Stiles was already known, and not fondly, by Susan, Running Horse and Little River.

"Please have a seat everyone," Anjou said. "Big Bird, will you please have Falu and Krin escort our government guests to the transport craft and then return to this room."

Little River immediately jumped up. "You're not planning on taking us away in a flying saucer, are you?"

"No, you are quite safe and no harm will come to you," Anjou reassured Little River. "You have my word." Little River gave the Supreme Council Governor a disbelieving look. "Big Bird, has everyone else been accounted for?"

"Yes, governor. After we put the government men on the craft, only the people in this room are left. There is a craft ready for your departure."

"Good. You may shut down the power supply. That will end the blackout and cause our government raiding party to act swiftly. I think we have enough time to leave before we are visited." Big Bird left the room. "Mr. Davis, let me begin by telling you everything I think you want to ask me. If I fail in that task, please ask me anything I have not covered. This venture started before my reign as governor, so I must tell you that I have not had prior experience with General Brantfield until this time, my first visit. Many earth years ago, the people of our planet, came to this planet and mingled with the Incas, Mayas, and Aztec nations. We helped build their magnificent cities. We taught them astronomy and engineering. We tried to impart some of our advanced technologies and beliefs to them. Each of these nations thrived for a long period of time. They revered us as gods. However, each one of those civilizations became corrupt, thinking they were indestructible, all because we supported and taught them our ways. They made sacrifices to us, which was against everything we taught them. We eventually abandoned them, leaving them to their own devices. You know the rest of the story about their civilizations."

"What about the Anasazi?" Davis interrupted.

Anjou continued. "The Anasazi were comprised of the best of those three civilizations. We handpicked them and transported them to Chaco Canyon. There we helped them, just as we helped their ancestors. It is why the Anasazi have always been referred to as the ancient ones. They thrived for many years and spread across the land, which you call the states of New Mexico, Colorado, Utah and Arizona. Finally, we thought, we had found the right people to have our people join with and move among, teaching them our peaceful ways.

In the meantime, our planet was dying. It orbited a star in the universe that was about to come to a fiery end. We spent a hundred earth years exploring other planets that would be hospitable to us. Earth was still primitive and would not make a suitable environment for the majority of our inhabitants. A few thousand of our people, knowing the hardships of your planet, volunteered to come and live among the Anasazi. The rest of our people moved to another planet called Dacon, where we have been living since before the first millennium on earth. The entire universe could see the cataclysmic ending to our beloved planet. It took until the year 1054 for the light from that explosion to reach the skies of Earth."

"Daconians, as we now called ourselves, continued to visit Earth, making sure those of our former planet were getting along in their new home. They were true adventurers. Our leader, Sillius, had given a proclamation when those people journeyed off into the unknown of your planet. The proclamation read, IT HAS BEEN DULY RECORDED IN THE TIME OF SILLIUS 45793 THAT A BAND OF EXPLORERS HAS LEFT OUR LAND TO JOURNEY THROUGH THE CONTINUUM TO SETTLE AND CREATE

NEW EMPIRES. THEIR COURAGE AND RESOURCEFULNESS WILL BE REMEMBERED FOR ALL TIME."

"Hey!" Davis shouted. "That's the writing that was placed on my windshield last week."

"Evidently," Mr. Davis, "someone was trying to give you a clue to our existence. I would venture to say Big Bird had a hand in that. For your information, that very inscription, since that time, is inscribed on the outside covering of every Daconian space craft. To continue my story, unrest became the order of the day among the Anasazi from one city to another. Drought conditions didn't help matters in Chaco Canyon. We assisted in building forty-foot wide roads to accommodate vehicles we built to assist the people to move around finding more water and better crop growing regions. Eventually we withdrew our vehicles and let these people handle their own matters. When we returned after a 250 earth year absence, we found only a handful of people. The true Anasazi were gone and those survivors had been absorbed by other tribes like the Utes. The once great cities we helped build were no more. Except for a few cliff dwellings, every trace of their existence was gone."

"In 1699, we returned again. We learned of a woman who had given birth to a brave who seemed to be different from any other brave. When we arrived in our space craft, the people were frightened. The baby had yet to be named but these people felt it was a sign and as a result the young brave was called Big Bird. We later learned that she?? could trace her ancestry to the space people, as we were

465

called. Big Bird has made many trips to Dacon. Have I answered all your questions?"

Susan, Running Horse and Little River sat quietly. "Why did you come back in 1947?" Davis asked.

"We came back when we detected the first atomic test in 1945. After all, we had vested interests in New Mexico. Then, in July of 1947, two of our commuter crafts, on routine surveillance of the Roswell air base, were struck by lightning. One of the ships crashed near Roswell. There were three androids on the crashed ship, along with two of our explorers. The second ship, while severely damaged, was able to retrieve the two explorers. The androids were beyond repair. The second ship made it over to Alegros Mountain, where the crew hoped to make repairs and then return to retrieve the androids and the damaged craft. I believe you have heard the weather balloon story. It was too late to stop the Army, who had moved in and were picking up the pieces, so to speak. JB Foster can fill you in on the last 52 years."

"Anjou, you seem to travel great distances between our planets in a short period of time. How is that possible?" Davis leaned forward in his chair, anxiously waiting for an explanation.

"Einstein's theory of relativity comes as close to the answer as you possibly could in solving space travel. The right craft, hitting the edge of the universe at the right speed will enable you to skip across your universe into our universe. Your scientists will discover someday what we discovered over two thousand years ago. Some of your scientists already are discussing the skip theory, but they still don't know how to make it work. That is one of the things we are not going to share with you. JB, would you like to tell your story?"

"Thank you, Anjou. I'll be very brief. President Truman, learning of a possible alien space craft landing in New Mexico set up a task force to investigate the incident. General Brantfield, here, was in charge over at Roswell in those days. He's the one who named this Project Anasazi."

"Mainly," the general interjected, "because this incident occurred in the land of the Anasazis."

"Right, general! The President's task force was called the 'Majestic 12'. Milt Goldberg and I were supposed to be going out to Roswell to do an onsite inspection. The plane was sabotaged and everyone on it was killed. Goldberg had a nervous breakdown and was put away. I got together with General Brantfield and learned of the existence of Big Bird. We convinced our friends from Dacon to help America be better world policemen, while helping us to find cures for serious illnesses. We set up this compound here on Alegros to have their people help us. I set up Transunion Enterprises to take the inventions they created and make them into a reality. They didn't bring anything from their planet, other than the people, to develop a great many of the things that have made all our lives better. Everything my company has made comes from the workshop in this compound. They include microchips, integrated circuits, fiber optics, accelerated particle beam devices, navigational guidance systems, super tenacity fibers used in bulletproof vests, lasers, infrared vision technology, the stealth bomber, Doppler radar, star wars technology, microwave weapons, the polio vaccine, electromagnetic imaging equipment, and many, many more, too numerous to mention. It would have taken America another 25 to 50 years to successfully achieve space travel if it weren't for the Daconians providing the space age technology. I have become a very wealthy man because of Project Anasazi, but you should know I give a great deal of money to charity. I have also shared my wealth with the general, much to his dismay. To this day, he has refused to touch that money."

"I have never received a cent from this operation," Stiles said. "I have always been honest in my dealings as a member of the FBI."

"That's true," Foster answered. The general nodded his head in agreement.

The door to the room opened suddenly. Standing in the doorway was Big Bird, out of breath.

"What's the matter, Big Bird?" Anjou demanded.

"The two prisoners have escaped. They had guns hidden in their jackets and they overpowered Falu and Krin."

"Where are they?"

"They're in the commuter craft with the androids. And, another thing, I thought I heard helicopters overhead."

"That's probably the U.S. military. They don't know what they're looking for. The dome looks like treetops and any sensing devices they have can't penetrate the dome. Get Falu......."

Before Anjou could finish his order, Falu and Krin were at the meeting room door. "Your Excellency," Krin said in a shaky voice, "the craft with the two prisoners has passed through the dome. The dome is now open and vulnerable to attack."

"Alright," Anjou said calmly. "It is time for all of us to leave."

"Not me, brother!" Little River shouted.

"I told you not to worry," Anjou responded. "JB, the general, Sheriff Cooper, Billy Stiles and Big Bird are the only ones leaving on the last commuter craft. They have agreed to return to Dacon with us. General Brantfield and JB Foster have both donated all their wealth to charity. Mr. Davis, please see to it that these affidavits are mailed when you leave here. We must leave now, quickly. Falu and Krin will escort you back to your car which is parked outside the entrance. Your car has been equipped with a device so that the military will not be able to see you. One thing, though, your friends must forget this entire encounter."

Davis was standing out of hearing range from the others when he heard Anjou's words. "What do you mean, forget this encounter How can they?"

"When they reach the car Falu and Krin will make them forget everything about this place."

"They won't hurt them, right?"

"There's nothing to it."

"What about me?"

"You, Mr. Davis, and I are destined to meet again. It is important you remember. I trust you will not divulge what you know. Falu! Hurry and take our guests to their car and then you and Krin meet us at the craft as quickly as possible. Goodbye, Brad Davis."

"Goodbye, Anjou." Falu and Krin led Davis and the others down the hallway to their car while Anjou disappeared down the hallway in the opposite direction. Davis took one last look back. Anjou, General Brantfield, Sheriff Cooper, Big Bird and Billy Stiles were gone. "See ya!" Davis said softly as he turned to catch up with the others.

CHAPTER THIRTY

Within ten minutes of power being restored and all checkpoints affirming that all systems were back to normal, Major Beardsley's helicopter was circling over the top of Alegros Mountain. The three other helicopters notified Beardsley of their readiness and were on their way with members of Alpha Force on board to rendezvous at the mountain top.

"Major," Becci called out, "I don't see any clearing through the trees below. In fact, I'm not getting any life form reading on our heat sensors."

"There has to be something there," Beardsley responded. "The government wouldn't be sending us here unless they had verified the existence of an alien base. Get closer to the tree tops. Maybe we can see through the trees with our searchlight."

"Major," Kaminsky said, "I know you doubt there's something here, but let me and the FBI Director assure you that we are dealing with something very real. These people are so far beyond us with their technology, I'm sure they have some sort of cloaking device."

"Look, sir, I agree with you. I have a gut instinct that there is something down there. What it is, I don't know. But, you can be assured, if it's there, well find it! We'll continue to circle until the rest of Alpha Force joins us. At that time, we'll take action!"

No sooner had Beardsley finished talking when Becci shouted out. "Sir, I see movement below us."

"Pull back and let's get a better look." All eyes were on the small opening, like the lens of a camera, getting larger and larger. "Will you look at that! Its pretty dark down there, captain. Shine the spotlight down there. Do you see anything?"

"No, sir," Becci responded. "My infrared scope doesn't show anything either.

"Gentlemen, can you see anything down there?" Beardsley asked.

"Not a thing!" Kaminsky responded.

"Me neither!" came the response from Weaver.

Suddenly, Becci was having trouble with the controls of the chopper again. "What now!" he yelled.

"Look!" Beardsley shouted, pointing to something moving away from the face of the cliff wall.

"It's round and silver like a saucer." Becci exclaimed excitedly.

"A flying saucer! Is that what you're trying to describe?" Kaminsky said.

"My God!" Weaver yelled. "There really are flying saucers! Who do they belong to?"

"They're not ours!" Kaminsky answered.

"Definitely not ours!" echoed Beardsley.

"Hey, the saucer is moving towards the middle of the clearing and starting to rise," Becci said. "I'm backing off and giving that thing plenty of space."

"Good idea!" Beardsley agreed.

All four men watched as the craft rose slowly through the opening in the dome. Clearing the dome's roof the saucer seemed to tilt slightly. The craft rose another 1,000 feet, enabling the helicopter's occupants to see the pulsating lights on the bottom of the saucer. In the blink of an eye, the saucer took off on a horizontal plane towards the southeast.

"Shall I follow it, sir?" Becci asked.

"Lieutenant Conway, did you see that saucer pass your position?" Beardsley asked over the radio.

"You bet your ass I did!" Conway responded. "Sorry, sir, I didn't mean to be disrespectful."

"Understood! You try and follow that thing and contact the others to join me up on Alegros Mountain. They'll see a large opening. Tell them to join us there."

"Roger!"

Beardsley motioned for Becci to bring the helicopter down through the opening. "Can you see the ground well enough to land?"

"Yes, sir! Got it under control, sir." The chopper came to a soft landing. "Shall I turn the engines off?"

"No. Keep them running just in case we have to make a quick getaway." All four men slowly exited the chopper not knowing what to expect. ",Keep your guard up gentlemen. We don't know what were dealing with here."

Setting the beam of the chopper to shine on the cliff wall, Becci was the last to exit. Looking up to see how large the opening was that they had come through, Becci exclaimed, "Uh oh!"

"What's the matter, captain?"

"I don't want to alarm you and the others, but the dome is closing over us."

Lieutenant Dugan's helicopter and a second helicopter, responding to orders to rendezvous with Major Beardsley's helicopter, arrived within a few minutes of the order and found no other helicopter in the vicinity. Dugan called Conway on the radio to notify him that there was no sign of Beardsley.

"Look, I've got my hands full following this saucer. Keep searching. Maybe he's on the ground."

"Okay, came Dugan's response, I'll keep searching. I hope he hasn't crashed somewhere."

Aboard the saucer carrying Parker and Nelson, the grays stood up from their control seats. "I told you to fly this thing to a remote desert location," Parker screamed. Parker and Nelson had overpowered Falu and Krin at the stairway to the saucer. Parker, more than Nelson, had the urge to kill both men because of the way they had treated them on more than one occasion. Nelson had calmed Parker down promising they would get their revenge some other time. Boarding the craft, they instructed the grays to transport them away from the compound. Parker knew full well that guns couldn't harm the robots, so he displayed the grenades, which he had saved for just such a moment. Up to this point, the grays had responded as robots. Now, however, in the skies over the New Mexico desert, they no longer seemed to be afraid of their fate, if robots were capable of fear. Their thought waves, distracted by the actions of the two men, made the saucer rock violently. Parker and Nelson both withdrew grenades from their pockets, holding them in one hand while the other hand pulled the pin. The grays moved closer to the two men, appendages outstretched to take the grenades away. As they did, their thought processes no longer concentrated on the controls of the saucer, and the craft began a steep dive towards the desert floor. The grenades fell from the hands of Parker and Nelson as they desperately tried to steady themselves and retrieve the live grenades. Faster and faster the craft plunged to earth as the grays and the two government men fought to find the grenades. At this point, the grays were incapable of reordering their thought process to regain control of the craft. Moments before the collision of saucer and earth a large, blinding explosion lit up the night skies of New Mexico. Seconds later, came a second, more deadening explosion as the saucer became part of the desert floor.

"Damn!" Conway shouted out! "Did you all see that! It must have been that saucer we were trailing. I don't see it on radar anymore!"

Conway turned and asked his pilot, "Where do you think those explosions occurred?"

"According to my coordinates, it looks like it was just northwest of Roswell," The helicopter responded.

Beardsley, Becci, Kaminsky and Weaver scanned the entire area, staying close to the safety of the helicopter. There was a certain comfort knowing they didn't have to wait to start the chopper's engines, if a quick getaway was required. With the roof closed above them, they were worried they may never get out!. All anyone could see was the vastness of the area, certainly devoid of any life.

"Is that a cliff dwelling I see up there?" Kaminski asked. Everyone looked to where Kaminsky was pointing.

"Sure is," Weaver replied.

"Probably Anasazi ruins," Beardsley guessed.

"What makes you say that?" Kaminsky asked.

"New Mexico was their home when they lived here. This is probably another site that no one has discovered yet," Beardsley answered.

"Major!"

"What, captain?"

"I think that wall below the cliff dwellings is moving."

Everyone's attention focused on the moving wall. "Everyone back in the chopper!" Beardsley ordered. "We don't know what we're dealing with here. We'll have some protection in the chopper."

Everyone scrambled quickly into the helicopter, all the while keeping their eyes focused on the moving wall. Finally, the wall stopped moving and another saucer-shaped object slowly emerged from the darkness beyond the opening of the wall. Kaminsky and Weaver sat transfixed in the rear of the chopper, as both Beardsley and Becci leaned forward to get a better look. Slowly, the saucer moved closer to the helicopter, seemingly hovering about five feet off the ground. The men prepared for a crash as the saucer moved closer and closer to them. Suddenly, the saucer stopped its forward motion and began to lift off the floor towards the roof. All eyes were on the silvery object lifting slowly towards the dome. They watched in amazement as the roof once again retracted allowing the space craft to disappear into the darkness of the night. Without hesitation, Becci immediately began working the controls, lifting the chopper out through the opening, which already was beginning to close. Once outside, their attention was captured by a bright object directly above them. Suddenly, the object was gone. Everyone remained silent as Becci pointed the chopper in the direction of Horse Springs. The two helicopters which had been searching for Beardsley saw the chopper rise from the middle of the mountain.

"Major, are you alright? We've been searching for you. What about Operation Alegros?"

Beardsley picked up the radio. "Operation Alegros is over. Follow us home."

EPILOGUE

"Mr. President, I have some bad news," Kaminsky said apologetically over a secure phone line. "Operation Alegros was a dismal failure. All we have is an empty compound and two saucers that got away. Fortunately for us, one of the saucers crashed over near Roswell. Major Beardsley and his Alpha Force are over there securing the site. Reports are that there were two funny looking creatures like you've seen in the movies and two humanoids. Both humanoids are barely recognizable. Also, it seems like there's debris all over the place out here."

"Mitch," the President responded, "I don't want another 1947 Roswell incident! Do you understand?"

"Yes, sir, perfectly!"

"The last thing I want to hear is another weather balloon story. We need to keep this under wraps. Make sure anyone involved with this is sworn to secrecy. Anyone doesn't agree, deal with them. Let's keep this to ourselves for the time being. Any questions should be passed off as a meteor striking the area out there. Got it?"

"Meteor. Sure thing." Kaminsky hung up the phone. "I sure hope they buy this one." Kaminsky said underneath his breath.

Davis had watched as Falu and Krin gently touched Susan, Running Horse and Little River on the back of their necks. They were placed in the car, apparently put to sleep by Falu's touch. Falu had told Davis they would remember nothing. He told him how the device on the dashboard worked, making the car invisible, and about the uniqueness of the car's infrared windshield, especially installed for this trip. The trip out of the compound onto Route 60 west was uneventful until Davis came within sight of the road block. Activating the button, he moved the car through the roadblock, breaking the barriers, as the police scattered in all directions. In the rear view mirror he could see everyone standing around wondering what had just occurred. Davis smiled as he moved down the back road towards Running Horse's home. At the top of the ridge where Davis first had experienced his car battery going dead several days before, the engine died. The lights of the car dimmed and then darkened. "What now," he thought. Stepping from the car, he saw the saucer. It was hovering about 100 feet off the ground behind where he was standing. Davis tried to get everyone to view the saucer. They were sound asleep. Looking up, he saluted the saucer and swore the saucer motioned a return salute. Leaning against the car, his right hand touched the rattlesnake bracelet on his left wrist, Davis smiled and waved as the saucer disappeared into the heavens.

"Good morning, Albuquerque! Here we go again! Did you see that bright light and hear those loud explosions about midnight. Sonic boom? Or have we been visited, again? Come on, give us a call! The telephone lines are open!"

THE END